The
Forbidden Link

Jan Crocker

Pen Press

Copyright © Jan Crocker 2009

All rights reserved

No part of this publication may be reproduced,
stored in a retrieval system, or transmitted
in any form or by any means, without
the prior permission in writing of the publisher,
nor be otherwise circulated in any form of binding or cover
other than that in which it is published and without a similar
condition including this condition being imposed on the
subsequent purchaser.

First published in Great Britain by Pen Press
an imprint of Indepenpress Publishing Ltd
25 Eastern Place
Brighton
BN2 1GJ

ISBN 978-1-906710-30-9

Printed and bound in the UK by Cpod, Trowbridge, Wiltshire

A catalogue record of this book is available from
the British Library

Cover design Jacqueline Abromeit

I dedicate this book to my son Oliver Stopp
and my family,
with thanks for all their encouragement and support.

Best wishes
Jan Crocker

With love to Viv
thanks for being
a friend.

About the Author

Born in 1941 in Wallington, Surrey, Jan Crocker started working as a secretary for the John Lewis Partnership in Oxford Street in 1957. In 1970 she moved down to Plymouth with her son, Oliver, then age two. After training as a teacher at the College of SS Mark and John; got a B. Ed teaching degree and subsequently taught English up to A level. Prior to her retirement she was running a City & Guilds NVQ training centre, delivering training courses in various work-related disciplines and also training work supervisors in their Assessor qualifications. In 2002 Jan was diagnosed with ovarian cancer and has since taken a GCSE in German, and last year achieved an MA in Creative writing at Plymouth University. She is at present teaching herself Latin (very hard!), going to German conversation groups and writing a photographically illustrated biography of my life for my grandson, Samuel. Having had much poetry published nationally as well as articles and short stories, she belongs to a local group called the Waterfront Writers who have so far published three anthologies.

CONTENTS

Part One, Chapters 1-5 2
Cornwall, 1890s

Part Two, Chapters 6-9 64
London, 1950s

Part Three, Chapters 10-16 108
Yorkshire, Surrey and London, 1960-1962

Part Four, Chapters 17-21 186
London, 1890s

Part Five, Chapters 22-25 256
London and Surrey, 1960s

Part Six, Chapters 26-27 282
London and Cornwall, 1960s

Epilogue 300

Bibliography 304

When Father Tremayne Jago starts to experience the supernatural, it is both a challenge to his sanity and to his faith. A beautiful and alluring young girl from the past, with her baby, appears to him until his reality and hers seem inextricably mixed and he is no longer able to dismiss her silent pleas for his help. All his efforts to persuade himself and others that his experiences are real are for nothing, until another priest is called upon to help in ways which are both unexpected and impossible to ignore.

Part One

Cornwall, 1890s

Chapter 1

"I'm off, Mother," Tregony said. "Same as usual?"

Sarah was bent over the stone sink in the scullery, listlessly dragging a Reckitt's Bluebag through the white washing. She sighed and wiped the lank hair from her sweating face. "Don't be long, Tregony. My back's bad again and bending over this sink don't help! And Samuel and James'll need their teas when they gets in. There's bread and cheese on the dresser. We'd better have more eggs this week. And some milk."

She gave her daughter a piece of paper. Tregony took some time to read it. *"Six larg eggs nise brown ones speccald and milk."* She screwed the piece of paper up and put it in her pinafore pocket. "I'll get what they've got, Mother," she said, briefly, and went out through the back door to the lane. The errand was tedious, like everything else in her life, but she occupied the time by re-living her dream. The plan to run away had grown with every interminable day. London would be the place to go. That's where real ladies lived and everyone knew that ladies did nothing all day and had servants to attend to their every need. Real ladies had proper dresses down to the ground that didn't hang in rags round their ankles. They had little dogs to sit on their laps. She'd seen them in pictures on cards down at the shop and read about London folk in her school books. She told no-one of her plan, especially not Denzil Pascoe. They were expected to marry one day. Her mother expected it.

"He's not good enough for you," Sarah told her daughter, "but there's not much choice really. They Trefusis brothers is no good and we need a breadwinner. At least Denzil's got a trade."

Tregony accepted her mother's reasoning without argument. If her plan to run away was successful, she need never see Denzil again. She would have a choice of husbands and be free of this dull town forever.

Dorothea, Denzil's mother, considered the Welles family far beneath her socially and Tregony no better than she should be. The devil in Tregony almost made her want to marry Denzil to spite his mother. Almost, but not quite, for Denzil was a nasty bully. It added to the challenge and she never hesitated to fight back. She had seen him kick the feral cats away from the *Sea Hawk* when the catch was landed, aiming his great foot at them so that they soared into the air and fell in a mass of yowling and spitting. "Monster!" she would fly at him, while he held her flailing hands, roaring with laughter at her efforts to strike him. "Take a better maid'n you, Tregony Welles!"

And he had introduced her to the delights of love and a chance to flout her mother and Dorothea Pascoe, who would undoubtedly both be shocked that she had given herself before marriage, and, she had an unfulfilled ambition to achieve before she left Tamarleigh, which would shock her mother and the whole town if they ever found out. But Thomas Norsworthy was a challenge she couldn't resist. He was still a fine looking man and there was no mistaking the desire in his eyes every time they met. She knew she only had to give him a sign and he would be hers.

Many folk in the Cornish town beside the Tamar prophesied that she would come to no good. There was something about her that didn't fit in. She was wayward and cared little what people thought. Her mother had long since given up and, at 17, Tregony was insolent, artful and sharp-tongued. Her only saving grace was her extraordinary beauty. She was unlike the rest of the Welles clan. Her tiny face, creamy white with a sprinkling of freckles, was framed with an abundance of tawny-gold ringlets; her green eyes were wide and, seemingly, innocent. The heart of many a man had been melted by her wicked smile and there were few husbands in the little town who didn't go to church each Sunday especially to pray for her discretion.

But there were those who could look beneath the startling beauty and see a child who was her mother's drudge, foisted with too many duties, but Samuel and James, two years her junior, usually did what she told them.

"Don't forget they stone flags in the scullery has to be swept today," her mother constantly reminded her, "and get the vegetables pulled and washed. Bed sheets need soaking in the copper, then run down and collect my sewing for me. I'll need help tonight." Sarah mended garments from customers in the village and Tregony's own skills were put to use most evenings as she struggled to help her mother by the light of a weak gas mantle.

"Alright, Mother!" was Tregony's constant reply. She scorned her mother's dependent nature. Sarah had an innate subservience and her constant ill health stood her in good stead when it came to relying on her daughter. It was to Tregony the twins cried in the night when the bogeyman came, or ran with their scraped elbows and bloodied knees. And Aunt Admonition Pento, lifelong friend of Sarah's late mother, generally kept an eye on them, taking them to church on Sundays to hear the Reverend confirm their wickedness, and issuing advice whenever she felt it was necessary. Since their father's early death the three had run wild with Tregony the instigator of most of their pranks - invisible callers who knocked on doors and ran, or sneaked washing from lines and scattered it everywhere.

Occupied with her thoughts, she didn't even hear the dogcart turn into the lane. Suddenly, she felt herself flung against the hedge with such force that the eggs and milk hurtled from the basket and collided in a slimy mess on the grassy bank. She looked up into the frowning face of Dr Prowse.

"A fine thing to be run down by the doctor," she said in her irrepressible way. "You can mend me now!"

"You are very fortunate!" Walter Prowse replied, sharply, as he calmed the trembling horse. "Whatever were you doing, wandering over the lane like that? Get in. I'll take you home and no harm done, I hope!"

"No, 'cept I've lost me eggs and milk and Mother don't have money for more!" she said, with a winsome glance.

"I'll get you some more."

They drove to the farm where the doctor paid for replacements, then they bowled smartly back to the cottage in Chapel Row. Tregony enjoyed every minute of the ride. Closing her eyes, she imagined the little dogcart to be her own smart lady's carriage, with soft padded seats and perhaps a footman at the back, alert to her every command.

"Now what've you done!" Sarah exclaimed in her little girl's voice when she saw her daughter. "Got the doctor to bring you home! What's wrong with your legs?"

"There nearly *was* something wrong with them!" Dr Prowse said severely. "She's lucky not to be injured. Not looking where she was going, I'm afraid, but she'll live this time."

He looked closely at Sarah. It was clear the woman was dispirited. Since Jeremiah's death she had deteriorated. Nursing Jeremiah through his wasting disease could not have been easy, as well as losing the breadwinner, and Sarah was making ends meet as best she could. "How're you managing, Sarah?" he asked.

"Oh, fairly, Doctor," Sarah sighed. "But 'tis difficult with three youngsters. Tregony do help, though."

The doctor opened his bag and took out a bottle. "Take this tincture. It may give you some relief."

He glanced at Tregony. She had gone to sit by the fire, her body half turned towards him. Like others, he had much sympathy for her, but he sensed trouble. "Keep an eye on that little maid," he said as he turned to leave. He was unsure whether Sarah understood him or not.

Tregony got up from the fire. The spring night was drawing in and there was still tea to get. She went to the open front door. A penetrating mist was seeping up from the river, dismal and dank, the kind of mist that crept into every bone. She shivered. She would get the boys their tea then skip off. Anything was better than another dreary evening of her mother's self-pitying sighs and reproachful looks. Samuel and James, illuminated in the light from the mantle, were sitting on the front fence, oblivious of the mist. She called to them crossly.

"Jus 'cos I'm late, for once! Couldn't you get yourselves a bite o' tea?"

"S'pose we could," Samuel spoke in his slow drawl. "Didden loike ter. Didden know what there was." He spoke for his brother, as usual.

She looked at them as they trudged past her, and sighed. They couldn't help it. She'd made them dependent on her, but they had to look after themselves. After all, they were 15 now.

"Fetch the bread and cheese from the dresser!" she ordered Samuel. He brought the loaf and wedge to the table, and divided them between himself and James. She brewed the tea and put two steaming mugs in front of them. She didn't want anything. Bruises had begun to appear where the doctor's dogcart had caught her and she felt quite light-headed.

The boys finished their tea and went upstairs. Sarah looked after them and frowned. "Don't know what's wrong with they boys. Unsociable, that's what they are. To me, leastways. S'pose they tells *you* everything!"

"Not everything, Mother," Tregony answered, in a fidget to get away. "They're not bad boys. Just keeps theirselves to theirselves."

"No, not bad," Sarah sighed, "'cept when you eggs 'em on! Normally quiet as mice. They're not sharp, like you." The boys had neither the wit nor the intelligence to cause her worry on their own account. She wasn't sure whether that was a blessing or not.

Tregony went to the hook and took down her cloak. "I won't be back late," she promised, as her mother raised her eyebrows.

"Where you goin'? There's sewin' to be done," her mother called, but the door had slammed on her daughter's back.

Tregony turned into Fore Street. As she neared the Old King's Arms the side door crashed open and Denzil and the Trefusis brothers, Perran and Keverne, happily silly, spilled out into the night. Denzil was bearable when he was slightly drunk but not yet violent. Then she could pretend that she really did love him. He planted himself in front of her, his bulbous eyes red from drinking, his thick, fair wavy hair stuck to his head with sweat. He had the look of a rosy, pouting cherub and a nature quite the opposite. "Why, if it ain't my maid! Where you bin?"

"It's where *you* bin, Denzil, not me," she answered pertly in the way that he liked. "Can't take me on a fishin' smack!" He'd been away for a week. Now he was drinking his profits.

"Nor can I!" he leered. "But I'm back to make up fer lost time! Off agin termorrer. Hope you bin faithful, you're mine, remember?"

He slung a casual arm round her, staggered a little and planted a wet, beery kiss on her lips. The Trefusis brothers sniggered. They were both simple from having their heads knocked together so often by their father and were villains who weren't hampered by a conscience. Despite their lack of reason, or maybe because of it, they were universally despised by the community. Trust only existed between them and Denzil when they were within each other's sight.

They set off for Yonderberry Point, a place deserted at night and said to be haunted. Many people had testified to the strange sounds coming from the barn and it would have taken a brave soul or a drunken one to investigate. "Arter you, missus!" roared Perran, falling off the hayloft ladder and scrambling up again. Perran called all females 'missus'. Keverne hardly ever spoke, but stumbled up the ladder with an inane giggle. Tregony joined in the laughter, throwing herself down into the hay. She felt possessed by a kind of crazed madness, fuelled by her secret plans.

She drew up her skirts, waiting for Denzil to begin, while she adroitly avoided his breath. Keverne wandered away and stretched out, but Perran watched. Maybe his turn would come, maybe not.

Suddenly, there was a loud creak on the rickety ladder. A grizzled head emerged over the top rung, eyes popping, mouth agape. Old Silas Watkins, brave man that he was, had summoned up courage to investigate the noise he had heard from the nearby road. Tregony peeped over Denzil's shoulder and waved.

"Remember what 'twas like, old man?" she called out saucily.

Instinct made Silas Watkins start forward, until Denzil rose like a bull from the hay, balling his great hands into fists. "Just try it, ye old fool!" he roared. "I'll knock ye into the middle of next week!"

"I'm a-goin', young Pascoe!" Silas called in a great fright and descended the ladder as fast as his rheumaticky legs would allow. Jeers and whistles followed him as he stumbled across the field and out into the road. So much for the haunting. No ghost could have been as substantial as that great oaf Pascoe and no spirit could have uttered the passionate sighs that came from the Welles girl. He would be guaranteed free beer in the King's Arms for several days on the strength of this story.

Tregony left the barn at one in the morning, leaving Denzil and the Trefusis brothers snoring. She let herself in at the back door of the cottage and went upstairs. Lying in her bed, excitement once more possessed her, but not for Denzil.

She was awake at seven the next morning to wave a dutiful goodbye to Denzil. Still drunk, he lurched across the deck of the *Sea Hawk,* grabbing the boom as it swung over. "You be'ave mind, or it'll be the worse for ye! You'm mine, don' ee ferget!" She smiled sweetly up at him, but contempt burnt in her heart.

Chapter 2

Tregony lolled in the pew and watched Reverend Thomas Norsworthy through half closed eyes. She liked the way his voice rose and fell. His imposing 6 feet were added to by a shock of fair, wavy hair which sprang up from a widow's peak and flew around his head as he became increasingly fervent, giving him a curiously boyish appeal.

"And the good Lord gave Man an help meet," intoned Thomas. "And he made her out of Adam's rib and she was made to cleave unto her husband. It is woman's lot and she will be rewarded when the Great Time comes."

Thomas was always talking about the Great Time. Tregony didn't understand much of the sermon, but she did understand the looks that Thomas Norsworthy was casting her way.

Beside her, Sarah sat bolt upright, eyes wide and fixed on the Reverend's face as she drank in every syllable. She knew exactly what he was saying, except that she wasn't quite sure what 'cleave' meant. She had been a good wife to Jeremiah and given him twin boys. Now the reverend was saying that it was God's will that women should suffer, that they would be rewarded in heaven. Her place was certain, then. Tregony had caused her enough suffering to guarantee several people's places. She would not be able to rest until her daughter was respectably married and tied to her own home with little ones. She was vaguely aware that the reverend was paying too much attention to their pew.

Thomas was coming to the end of his sermon. The good folk of Tamarleigh listened in respectful silence. Ever since John Wesley had made his last triumphal appearance across the Tamar in 1789, an old man of 83, tiny in stature but great in message and magnetism, Tamarleigh had been a bastion of Methodism. The Reverend, who had been blessed with a gift of rhetoric which put even the great Gladstone to shame, preached in the time-honoured mould, with thundering emotion and much beating of his breast. It was very satisfying to repent, be saved, then burst heartily into song. The 'plentiful harvest' which John Wesley had hoped for had taken root and flourished in the little Cornish town and the Fore Street church was packed to capacity every Sunday.

Tregony was obsessed with Thomas Norsworthy. He had an older man's charm, his manners were impeccable and he was handsome. But she had to be careful, even though Denzil was still away fishing.

She glanced across at Dorothea Pascoe who was gazing raptly at Thomas, her mouth slightly agape. Tregony's eyes narrowed. She had seen that look of adoration before, and heard the town's gossips. There was no mistaking a likeness between Denzil and Thomas Norsworthy, the full, pouting lips and rosy, cherubic face, although it would have taken a fool to utter such a thing in Dorothea's hearing. Once, when she had been loitering at the side of the Pascoe cottage, she had heard Dorothea call her a trollop. It sounded bad, but she didn't care what Old Mother Pascoe thought and she'd got her revenge. One Sunday she sneaked into the Pascoe backyard when no-one was in and pulled the washing from the line. Running to the church, she left Dorothea's bloomers impaled on the church railings.

"Oh, my dear!" she heard Miss Whiddle exclaim to Mrs Tregantle when the congregation emerged at the end of the service.

"Look, Bertha! Whoever's those? Can't be mine, not that awful scarlet!"

"No, Elsie, true enough. And yours 'av' frills on 'em! Whatever next! Is nothing sacred?" It had been worth it to see Dorothea's face and see her struck dumb for once. Now Tregony watched, fascinated, as the reverend alternated his flashing glance between her and Dorothea. Then, as he turned to leave the pulpit, she sighed audibly, allowed a faint smile to hover on her lips and cast her trembling lashes downwards. She heard his intake of breath and exulted. Dorothea was rising to pass the collection. Tregony dropped a coin into the bag and smiled sweetly up at her.

After the service, Thomas waited by the porch, as was his custom. He took Sarah's hand and pressed it, murmuring, "God bless you, good woman!" Sarah was lost for words and Tregony nearly laughed. Thomas turned his attention to Dorothea, who clung to the proffered hand. Much too obvious. Young as she was, Tregony knew the bait which must go on the hook. Now it was her turn. She looked Thomas straight in the eyes, then dropped her beautiful glance, black lashes resting on the rosy cheeks. She offered her hand, then withdrew it slightly. Thomas took it, battling with a fierce desire to press it to his lips. Tregony withdrew her hand, at the same time lifting her wide green eyes to his face. She allowed her lips to part just a little, showing her perfect white teeth, and ran her tongue softly across her upper lip, smiling a gentle, innocent smile. At that moment a breeze lifted her tawny curls and played them across her cheeks, framing her face in vibrant colour. She had never looked more beautiful.

Thomas began to shake. He could hardly control himself. Tregony watched his efforts with amusement. "Thank you so much, Reverend," she murmured huskily, then lifted her hand to brush the errant curls away. The gesture completed the enslavement of Thomas Norsworthy.

Both Sarah and Dorothea had noticed the little by-play.

Sarah was horrified, Dorothea resentful. She would have given anything to be young again, desirable. To be that tall, proud figure who had come to Tamarleigh all those years ago and awakened the desire of any she chose. But she had never had the feigned innocence of the Welles girl. Simpering had never been in her nature.

Sarah knew the Reverend would call on her before many days had passed. He visited his parishioners as often as possible, making widows left on their own with children his priority. She hoped fervently that Tregony would not be in when he called, but her hopes were dashed. He came the very next day. Sarah's heart sank when she saw him proceeding majestically up the tiny path. Tregony was in the scullery, scrubbing potatoes. Sarah hoped that the apron and reddened hands would minimise her daughter's appeal.

"Good day, dear lady!" Thomas beamed, as she let him in. "For once God is smiling on us, is He not?" He nodded up at the sky. The winds and storms of the past few days had abated and a pale sun shone valiantly from between billowing clouds. But the weather was the last thing Sarah wanted to discuss. She ushered Thomas firmly into the front parlour. He stretched himself on the sofa and crossed his legs. It looked as if he were prepared to stay indefinitely.

"I was wondering whether your twins would consider assisting at the church fair in the summer?" Thomas began. "We need help with the trestles."

Sarah knew Samuel and James would object, but she would ask them in front of the Reverend when they could hardly refuse. She would be making some little cakes and fancies on the day and it would not hurt the boys to help.

"They're in the lane, Reverend," she answered. "I'll call them." She was soon back, but she was not in time to prevent

Tregony wandering in from the scullery, wiping her hands delicately on her white bib.

"Who is here, Mother?" she asked, innocently. "I thought I heard voices."

Her daughter's timed entrance did not fool Sarah for a second. "Tregony, the potatoes ..." she said, lamely, but Tregony was already removing her apron, a determined glint in her eye. Thomas rose hastily to greet her. He held out his hand, wishing that he could take her into his arms instead.

She dimpled prettily up at him. "Good day, Reverend," she said. "Has Mother offered you tea?"

"Not yet I haven't!" Sarah said. "The Reverend's only been here a minute. He wants to see the twins, not you!" She knew she sounded ungracious, but she didn't care. Then she saw that any effort on her part to forestall her daughter's intentions would be wasted. Thomas's gaze was locked with Tregony's and a shudder swept through him. Sarah felt sickened. "Come, Tregony!" she said, sharply. "The tea!" Tregony turned to leave the room, giving her mother a smile as she passed. Strangely, the smile calmed Sarah's nerves. Her daughter had been blessed with an iron will and a lukewarm heart and she somehow knew it would be the reverend who would suffer.

Thomas's business was soon accomplished. Samuel and James agreed diffidently to help at the church fair and Thomas went on his way in an ecstasy of longing. He had read Tregony's eyes and their message was as clear as day.

Tregony began to scheme. The next day she packed some of her mother's fancies into a little basket and took them to the parsonage. "The Reverend is out," the housekeeper informed her. "In any case, he don't eat none o' they fancy cakes."

Tregony ignored this. "Well, where is he?" she asked, impatiently. "Mother's sent these special and he must have them."

"Could leave 'em here, then," Mrs Knox suggested, peering suspiciously. She distrusted Tregony Welles.

"Is he at the church? Gone on visits?"

"Might be in the church," Mrs Knox replied. She watched as Tregony disappeared down the path. The maid wore her skirts far too short. You could see her ankles tripping beneath those patched frills.

Thomas was in the vestry sorting through church documents. He was absorbed in his task and didn't hear Tregony arrive. She stood watching him silently for some moments, but at last, sensing her there, he glanced up. She was cool, beautiful. He was entranced. She moved towards him, smiling.

"Here you are, Reverend," she said, holding out the basket. "Just a few things from Mother." He reached for it, trembling, trying to speak. She had appeared so suddenly, that for a moment he felt he must be dreaming.

"No need for thanks," she said. "Mother said it's a pleasure!" A little game. She was playing her part perfectly. He found his voice. His lips seemed to be numb. "I was not expecting you, Tregony," he managed, at last.

"Aye, I can see that!" She placed the basket on the vestry table, bent forward and began to lift the cloth covering the fancies. Her tawny curls tumbled around her face, her sweet scent filled his nostrils. Before he could stop himself, he reached forward and ran his hand softly down her back, slipping his arm around her waist. She feigned surprise. "Why, Reverend," she said, without looking up. "Whatever are you doing?" He groaned and pulled her closer. "I swear you're a witch or a devil sent to tempt me, Tregony Welles!" he muttered, burying his head in her curls.

"I'm just as God made me!" she said.

"Aye," he sighed. "That much is true. But sent to tempt me, nonetheless. And I must try to resist."

The conversation was boring her. She wanted none of his preaching now, or his pretended reluctance. She turned and slipped her arms round his neck. "The church says we got to give to one another, look at it like that," she said. His horrified rejoinder died on his tongue. Now she was moving her lips across his face until she found his, her little mouth soft and yielding.

With an urgency neither of them expected, he crushed her to him with a passion alien to her. A sweet fire began to burn through her veins, and she swayed against him, powerless, as he began to stroke her. Locked together, they sank to the floor, oblivious of the world. The basket of fancies toppled off the table, unnoticed. The church door opened and closed, unnoticed. They were blissfully unaware that Dorothea Pascoe, calling on some flimsy pretext, saw their shamelessness. She stood at the vestry door, staring at them, stupefied. She had known this would happen, but what perverse fate had led her to witness it. A desperate ache filled her, pushing away all other thought. She turned and stumbled from the church, her mind a turmoil of conflicting emotions.

The closing of the church door on her departure finally aroused Tregony. "I think someone came in," she whispered. Thomas scrambled to his feet and looked grimly down at her as she lay relaxed and flushed on the vestry carpet.

"Get up, Tregony Welles!" he said, sharply. "Get up and face me! Tell me this is a dream, a vision!" She arose languidly, patting her curls and smoothing her white pinafore.

"You in a sweat about nothin', Thomas," she replied. "Men and women are put here to do such things!" There was something unspeakably careless about her, a disregard which frightened yet fascinated him.

"But not this man, Tregony!" he cried, bitterly. "I'm an example to my flock. Or supposed to be!"

"And you are," she answered. "You do your best for folks. And you'm single, Thomas, no wife to fret about. Why've you never married?"

He had been asked that question before. He loved his church, but knew in his heart that he was really wedded to his own desires, shackled by them. And now, as his punishment, Tregony had happened to him and he knew she would break his heart.

"You see everything so simply, Tregony," he sighed. "If only it were so. I know I am not bound by vows of celibacy, as are our Catholic brothers, but even so, I should not be here with you. It is wrong."

Tregony was following this with difficulty. "What's selly something?" she asked.

"Catholic priests make a promise when they enter the church," Thomas replied. "It means they can never marry and have children."

She was thunderstruck. "You mean they don't never know a woman's love or have a wife and baby? You don't mean you want to be like them?"

"No, no!" Thomas said, hastily. "I have not made those vows. Even so, I should not be here with you like this …"

She'd never heard of all this nonsense he was coming out with. It was getting complicated. She picked up the fallen basket of fancies and replaced it on the table. "You should've said, I thought you wanted it as bad as me. I didn't notice no forcing of you!" She was cross now. "And as for all those priests! I never heard such riddles in me life! No woman, no child! How do they live like that?"

As she asked the question, a terrible blankness suddenly descended on her. Thomas and the vestry swayed through a mist and an unseen hand seemed to grip her heart. She struggled to bring Thomas into focus, but all she could see was a different face, a face with piercing black eyes, crowned with a shock of dishevelled black hair. The eyes looked right into hers with a flash of recognition and a great sadness crept into them. A corresponding well of grief rose suddenly within her, spilling over, and she reached out to touch the vision. She felt her hands grasped and looked up into Thomas's concerned gaze.

"My dearest one!" he whispered. "What is it? Have I hurt you so badly? It is not my wish. I love you, Tregony. Love you!"

Startled, she began to back away from him. "What's happening? You were ... different, it didn't look like you!"

He pulled her into his arms. "You're overwrought, darling. It's entirely my fault. This shouldn't have happened here when you deserve all the comfort in the world."

She rested against him, reassured. Yes, that was it, too much excitement. She smiled to herself. Thomas had come up to expectation and he'd get over all this rigmarole about priests. She left him then and walked back along Fore Street towards Chapel Row. She was no longer frightened, except that a chord she didn't know she possessed had been struck within her, heightening her senses so that she felt acutely aware of every movement, every sound around her.

As the days went by, other concerns took up her thoughts. Denzil had still not returned, but she had passed Dorothea Pascoe in Macey Street and Dorothea had stopped her. "When my Denzil comes back from fishing, Tregony Welles, make yourself scarce. I know what you're like. I've seen what you've done!"

Tregony looked at her, light dawning. So it was Old Mother Pascoe who had opened the church door, crept in and looked upon her and Thomas. She laughed outright, enraging Dorothea. "Jealous, then? I don't care what *you* think! Thomas loves me!"

"Loves *you!*" Dorothea spluttered. "A trollop! For that's what you are, make no mistake about it. Thomas is a man of taste, let me tell you!"

"*Your* taste I suppose! And, by the way, where's Denzil fishing this time? Round Treharne House? Plenty o' pickin's there. Pity his pa didn't teach him not to take things that don't belong to him!"

Dorothea stiffened. How much did the trollop know of her past? Nothing, she decided. The Welles girl was just guessing. Thomas would not be so foolhardy as to jeopardise his ministry and his reputation. But the truth of Tregony's words struck home, making her itch to slap that beautiful smug face.

"And don't worry 'bout me and him getting' wed," Tregony continued. "He's never been good enough for me. Me own mother told me so!" and she skipped away laughing as Dorothea stood looking after her, purple with rage.

To satisfy herself that Denzil was not in hiding, after reports of a recent robbery at Treharne House, she went there at twilight. There was a small, deserted cottage not far off. It would be just like Denzil to wait until the hue and cry had died down, then return and hide. She didn't want him back in Tamarleigh yet, she wanted to indulge her fancies.

Horses in the two loose boxes stirred at her approach and one of them whinnied, its ears pricked. She slid past like a shadow and crossed to the house. One of the downstairs windows was boarded up, but there was no other sign of the recent robbery. People were in the drawing room, laughing and talking, and the place was wreathed in smoke. She watched, fascinated, as they raised glasses and drank, braying at each other in an inane pantomime, the men smart in their velvet jackets, the women in elegant dresses. One day she would be dressed like that.

The cottage was deserted. She peeped in at the scullery

window and tried the door. It opened and she slipped inside. Moonlight poured through the curtainless windows. A quick search revealed nothing except the scurrying of mice. The washhouse was empty and the coalhouse contained only a few of last winter's logs. The tool shed and the apple store were empty and swept clean. There was no sign that anyone had disturbed the stillness of the cottage for a long time. Denzil must have got as far away as possible. No doubt he would pick up his fishing smack down the coast and return as if nothing had happened. Tregony made her way back to the house. Now a brougham stood before the door and a man and a woman emerged from the hallway, the man wrapping a shawl protectively around the woman's shoulders. The master and mistress of the house stood beneath a carriage lamp and waved. Tregony watched as the woman stepped daintily into the brougham. She could just see herself, tricked out in fine clothes, being escorted by a handsome gentleman. She pirouetted softly on the gravel, swishing an imaginary frill. Other people were emerging and she pressed herself back against the wall. More beautiful clothes, more gallant gentlemen. At last she roused herself and made her way home across the fields.

Her mother was not at home, but Samuel and James were lounging in their usual fashion against the front fence, illuminated by the gas mantle from the hallway. It was past ten o'clock. Tregony spoke sharply to them. "Get in, boys! Where's Mother? 'Bout time you was in bed!" They obeyed her, as they always had.

"Don't know where Ma is," said James, for once speaking first. "But we'se had our tea and yourn is in the pot."

"As if that matters!" cried Tregony. "Didn't she say where she was going? What time did she go?" Before the boys could answer, Tregony spied her mother, trudging up Chapel Row, a grim look on her face.

"Where've you been, Mother?" cried Tregony. "It's late!"

"Aye, I know it is," replied Sarah, shortly. "Too late, probably! Go on in, boys, I want to talk to your sister." She waited until the boys had disappeared to their bedroom then shut the parlour door on herself and Tregony. "I've been to see the reverend, daughter," she said. "Don't think to fool me what's been happening! I saw the looks which passed between you on Sunday. Blasphemous looks! You'll bring disgrace on us all yet! And Thomas Norsworthy isn't no better'n he should be! Well, I shall put a stop to it, if I can! Where've you been most of the evening, I should like to know?"

"Not at the parsonage!" Tregony retorted. "You should know that if you've been there!"

Sarah altered her tone. "When Denzil Pascoe comes back, you'd better marry him," she sighed. "It's time you were married with little ones. That'll keep you in one place. No time for philandering when you've a house to run."

Tregony laughed outright. "Aye, that's what folks expects. Him, too! And maybe me at one time. But I wouldn't marry him now if he paid me to, which ain't likely! I don't love him no more!"

Her eyes flashed. Her mother recognised the look. Tregony would do exactly as she pleased, as always. It was little comfort to Sarah to know that it would take a better man than either Thomas Norsworthy or Denzil Pascoe to tame her daughter. And she had some sympathy for her. Lately she'd seen some fading bruises which had alarmed her. Perhaps she ought to send her into service. Somewhere out of Tamarleigh where she could have a choice of young men, meet someone and settle down.

She was lost in her thoughts when Tregony's next words dropped into her startled ears like stones. "Any rate, Mother," Tregony said, casually, studying her nails and keeping her eyes lowered. "You did the same as me, didn't you? Oh, I'm not talking about the reverend, but about my own pa. My real pa!"

Sarah gaped at her, staggered, convinced she had misheard. At length she found her voice. "What do you mean? How did you know?" she whispered.

"I've known for years!" Tregony said, scornfully. "Or at least guessed. I ain't silly, Mother! I don't turn after you, do I? And no-one else in this family has my colour. You must think I'm a fool!"

There was silence. Sarah dropped into a chair and covered her face with her hands. At last she said, in a muffled voice, "You're right, I should've known you'd guess sometime. You're sharp." She paused. Tregony had found her out to be a hypocrite. It made her trip that afternoon to see Thomas Norsworthy a sham. The mother was no better than the daughter. "Your father was a sailor," she said. "Passing through."

Tregony made a strangled sound and Sarah looked at her shamefaced. "Oh, yes!" she cried. "I've no room to talk, I know! 'Cept that I've tried to make amends, bring you up respectable. Tried ... and failed, it seems!"

Tregony was suddenly sorry for her mother. "Were you in love with him?" she asked.

"I would have married him if he'd asked. If he'd stayed. Love at first sight, if you like." Sarah turned to her daughter, imploringly. "That's why I'm so a-feared for you, Tregony! Sometimes love can be mistook for ... well, other things. You deserve something better."

"Denzil ain't something better!" Tregony laughed. "And, besides, he don't love me like he should. He's cruel and spiteful."

Her mother nodded. "I suppose you're right. You'd be better off out of Tamarleigh altogether."

The Forbidden Link

Tregony smiled to herself. Her mother had never said a truer word. She went and sat at her mother's feet. "Tell me, what was my pa like? Am I like him, too?"

"Like him in colouring, like us both in nature, it seems! He had lovely auburn hair, like yours, and a wicked smile. Rennie, he was called. He was Scottish. I fell for him straight away. I went to the dock with Mary Pento."

Tregony gasped and cried, "What, Aunt Admonition's Mary? Her what went off up the line? Don't tell me she did it, too?"

Sarah frowned. "Don't talk that way, Tregony! Mary wasn't with me when it … it happened. If you want to hear the story, rest quiet and listen! We met some sailors and Rennie was one of them. He was a friend of Abraham's."

"Mary's brother?"

Sarah nodded. "'Cept he wasn't there, he was at sea. We'd never been to the dock before without our mothers. It was all new and exciting. The sailors bought us flowers and ribbons; we'd never been so treated! Rennie spent half a year's wages - twelve pounds!" She hesitated, remembering. There were some things that she couldn't tell Tregony - how Rennie had smuggled her past Agnes Weston, the formidable founder of the Royal Sailors' Rest, which was new in that year of 1876; how she'd wriggled with him under a blanket in the crowded hall amongst hundreds of sailors shaking down, then drowned in a sea of painful pleasure, for he'd been her first love. And afterwards, how they'd walked up Ker Street and Rennie had tried to climb the column dedicated to the re-naming of Plymouth Dock to Devonport, blowing her kisses over his shoulder. She remembered how cross Mary had been because she'd left her to stroll the dock with one of Rennie's friends who, she complained later, was "as dull as ditchwater!" Sarah couldn't help smiling at the memory. Dear Mary, she still missed her. Aunt Admonition had sent her away to be a maid in Bath and they hadn't seen each other for years. She had made Mary promise not to say anything about their hours apart and Mary had been true to her word.

As the memories came flooding back, she saw once again Rennie's handsome, laughing face, tawny hair and wicked green eyes. She would never forget those eyes, for he had bestowed them on his daughter. Her mother had found out the truth, of course. Aided by Admonition Pento she had foisted Sarah on to Jeremiah Welles, a youth of blank good nature and small intelligence. It had been an easy matter to convince him that the tiny red-haired girl had arrived early in the world. He had done his best for his family and, strangely, Tregony had been his darling right from the beginning. Sarah had often wondered whether his early death had accounted for her wild ways. And now here was her daughter at 17, the same age that she'd been then. No, she couldn't point the finger, she'd done it herself.

She gave herself a shake. Tregony was nudging her, eager to hear more. "And later, of course, you were on the way. Jeremiah never knew you weren't his. He was never sharp, not like you … and Rennie."

"Rennie!" Tregony savoured the name. "My pa! Didn't you hear from him again?"

Sarah shook her head. "Never! I didn't expect to. He's probably dead by now."

"Why, *you're* not!"

"No, but he was older than me. Anyway, it was all a long time ago. Jeremiah gave me a respectable name and he loved you dearly!" A tear slid out of Sarah's eyes and began to drip down her face. Then, to her surprise, Tregony reached up and put her arms round her. They had never shown each other affection. It was a strange feeling and Sarah liked it. She held her daughter tightly. "We should have done this years back," she whispered. "I've gone wrong with you, I know I have, Tregony!"

Tregony laughed softly and stood up. "I was meant to turn out like this, Mother!" It was said without rancour. She loved the story of her true father. It was romantic and it proved she was different and destined for something better. "As for that other thing," she continued. "I've always been wayward. I've heard folks say it; it's me they'll blame, not you!"

Sarah sighed resignedly. She'd had her say and now her objections must seem meaningless to her headstrong daughter. "Best look in on the boys," she said and left the room.

Tregony sat by the hearth and hugged her knees. She thought of Thomas and a delicious tingle began to creep through her. She was longing for him again. She thought of their passion, how he had held her in his strong arms, murmuring love words against her lips and stroking her hair. Yes, he was a fine man and she didn't doubt that many a woman had discovered so before her. Those practised arts did not come from a lifetime of devotion to duty, only devotion to love.

She heard her mother go up the stairs and called out goodnight to her. "Don't stay up too long," Sarah answered.

Tregony smiled gleefully. She had no intention of staying up long, not in this house, at least. She crept out through the scullery door, pulling it carefully behind her. A light spring shower did little to dampen her resolve. She made her way down Chapel Row and out on to Fore Street. There was a light in the parsonage. She tapped softly on the window and was rewarded by Thomas's face as he tweaked aside the curtain. For an instant he didn't realise that it was Tregony who stood there, covered as she was by her mother's linsey-wolsey cloak. Then recognition dawned and very soon she was slipping silently through the barely opened front door to find herself enveloped in a suffocating hug.

"My dear child, you are soaked!" Thomas whispered, crushing her. "I had no idea you were coming tonight." He led her into the front parlour where the remains of a fire struggled valiantly in the grate. He threw a large piece of coal on it and poked it into sparks. "Come here and take off that cloak, my angel!" he said, removing it and hanging it over a chair. He looked at her as she stood there, her hair clustering in damp ringlets round her beautiful face, her skin rosy and fresh from the rain. "Even bedraggled you look enchanting!" he said softly. "Come to me, Tregony, you are a gift from heaven!"

He held her gently, running his hands down her breasts and across her belly, while she stood passively, her face upturned to receive his ardent kisses. Commonsense had not deserted her. "You promised me comfort next time, Thomas," she told him. "Remember?"

"My darling, of course I remember! You shall have comfort." He tucked his arm around her and led her to the door. The passageway outside was lit by a single gas mantle and an open door at the far end revealed a curtained bed, billowing with pillows and a deep eiderdown.

"This is one of the guest rooms," Thomas explained, in a low voice. "You may know that I have many nieces and nephews who frequently come down from Taunton to stay?" Tregony nodded. She had seen some of them in church. "There is no need to worry about Mrs Knox," he went on. "She will not hear us from her end of the house."

Tregony couldn't have cared less about the housekeeper. The whole world could listen as far as she was concerned. "Oh, by the way, before I forget," she said. "Was Mother here today, Thomas?" He nodded and lowered his gaze. "I know I should feel shame, but I cannot! She told me she had plans for you. I think she hopes you will marry Denzil Pascoe."

"Not now!" Tregony exclaimed. "We've had a talk, Mother

and me. She won't force me. In any case, I've always done what I want!" She turned further into his arms and he closed the door behind them. He had a fleeting thought that his angel concealed a heart of iron beneath her desirable bosom. He was easily able to dismiss the thought.

The very nearness of her, her sweet fragrance, swept all caution away. If he heard the voice of his conscience at all, it called so faintly as to be understandably confused with her little cries of delight, like soft chirrups, which issued from her charmed lips like a mantra. Trance-like, he crept beneath the cloak of sensuality which she flung so carelessly round them and the feeble struggles of his conscience soon ceased in its enveloping folds. He sank with her in a bottomless sea of dark and dreadful waters, and he cared not one whit. For him, the world stopped entirely. For her, it faltered temporarily. He clutched her to him and smothered her with kisses which she ardently returned. His body was on fire. He felt he would die.

"Tregony, Tregony!" he burst out. "Never in my whole life have I felt like this!" She smiled, reaching up to pull his face down next to hers once again.

"Marry me!" he murmured at last, when the final fire had burnt out with the last quenching kiss. "Marry me, Tregony! I will die without you!"

She stared past his shoulder at the ceiling. A fitful moon peered between the clouds outside and intermittently streamed through a chink in the curtains to cover the bed with light. Marry Thomas? Now, that would be a fine thing! All the town would be agog with the news. Her mother would swoon from pride. And Dorothea Pascoe would be enraged. It was almost worth saying yes, just for that. But as she gazed at the patch of light she saw a vision of a beautiful girl, splendid in satin and lace, with her hair properly dressed and a handsome escort at her side. The girl was herself and the vision brought her back to reality. She could love Thomas for the time being, certainly, but marrying him would mean giving up the dream. She couldn't do that - not at any price. It would be denying her destiny.

Thomas propped himself on one elbow and looked down at her. "You are beautiful, Tregony," he whispered, gazing at her in awe. "This love is a gift."

"Does that mean you got no conscience now?" she asked. "'Cos if it do, Thomas, it's about time!"

He smiled. "Yes, it does mean that, my darling! How can this be wrong, this wonderful feeling?"

"Told you, Thomas. Said that was what we was all meant to do!" she yawned heartily.

He was only momentarily taken aback. "Once again, you have put it far better than I ever could, my angel!"

But she was no longer listening to him. Her thoughts had strayed back to the dream, a dream that didn't include Thomas. She nestled into his shoulder and, before he could say any more she had fallen asleep.

Thomas felt that a madness had possessed him. In her sleep she looked innocent, yet he knew that she was not. And there was something else about her. He sensed a foreboding, an evil, as if something unseen was whispering that she would move towards a sinister fate just as inexorably as waves return to the shore. He wanted to keep her with him, save her from it, but he knew in his heart that she would be his until she needed him no longer. After a long while, he slept.

Tregony stayed for several nights, returning home each day before dawn. He was as ardent as ever, but always after lovemaking reality returned for her. She noticed her patched clothes and work-roughened hands and her resolve hardened.

With the approach of autumn she was certain that she was pregnant. Carrying the minister's child out of wedlock would make her family outcasts. She could not do that to her mother. With the fulfilment of her body, her desire for Thomas waned. At last this was her chance to leave Tamarleigh. Life would be difficult with a child on the way, but as the weeks passed she grew excited about the idea. It was her secret and it would be something of her very own to love. And when she became a lady she wouldn't have to work anyway. She was beautiful, men couldn't resist her. It happened all the time in Tamarleigh, and it would happen in London. She had never yet been refused. She would miss her brothers, but they could take care of themselves now. At least she'd taught them that. She had an idea where she would go first, a kind of first stop to London, somewhere to have her baby. She was gone within the week, leaving her mother and the village to speculate.

Chapter 3

Sarah did all she could to trace Tregony, but her enquiries drew a blank. The driver of the St Austell carrier, which left the Old King's Arms three times a week, grinned when Sarah described her daughter.

"Er woulda bin welcome, but she in't bin on this 'un!" The watermen at the ferry, who knew Tregony well from the hours she had spent as a child watching them tar their boats, couldn't help either.

"Find 'er in The Dock, I'll be bound," one of them suggested helpfully, and Sarah felt a faint flicker of hope, thinking of herself and Rennie. Perhaps Tregony had gone to re-trace old footsteps. If so, she would be back soon. Her only hope was to go home and wait. Besides, she'd had a pain in her head lately. She felt a prickle of fear, remembering the typhoid outbreak of '83 when over a hundred people had died, her own mother among them. Perhaps *she* was dying, her punishment for being a bad mother. She didn't want to die, she wanted to live to make amends. She turned away from Ferry Street. The slipway was cold and deserted now. A ferry was mid-way between Tamarleigh and Devonport, half hidden in the perpetual December mist, its lights bobbing eerily. She must go home, find the boys and try to make an effort for their sakes.

On her way up Macey Street Sarah saw Dorothea Pascoe, just turning into her gate. Dorothea glanced up and waited reluctantly. Rumours were rife. She could only hope they were true. At last her Denzil was free from the clutches of that girl.

Harlot would be nearer the mark and everyone knew what the Bible said about harlots, but much as she despised the Welles family she felt obliged to be charitable to Sarah.

She gave Sarah a thin-lipped smile. "Daughter's gone then," she said in her compelling way. "She'll come back to Mother when she needs something. They all do!"

Sarah's face crumpled and for a moment Dorothea's armour was briefly pierced and she almost invited Sarah in. But before she had a chance to speak, Sarah said in that little-girl voice which so grated on Dorothea, "She's likely gone to Plymouth. Can't offer her much here, I s'pose!" and Dorothea felt her hackles rising at once at the tactlessness of Sarah's remark.

"Of course, marriage with my Denzil wouldn't have been exactly nothing, would it?" she said sweetly, allowing her gaze to travel to Sarah's feet. "But, all things considered, it's probably just as well. They weren't very well matched, were they?" She swept up her front path, leaving Sarah to stare at her departing back. She had never been equal to Dorothea Pascoe.

Dorothea went into her parlour and thumped her grocery bag purposefully on the table. She was already planning ahead. Now Denzil would be able to meet a suitable girl and settle down. Jane Chubb came of good farming stock, although she was somewhat unprepossessing. She had protruding teeth and what appeared to be a permanent cold, always sniffing into a handkerchief. But she would always know her place, would cling adoringly and never be disobedient. Many men preferred such females. There was wealth in the Chubb family and despite her inferior looks and adenoidal twang, Dorothea knew that monetary considerations would override any possible objections on Denzil's part.

Thomas Norsworthy was the last to know that Tregony

had gone. She hadn't visited him for a while, but he'd seen her walking with her mother in the town and she'd smiled - a cool, tight little smile. He had tried to ignore the growing fear that she was tiring of him, but there was no way of getting her alone. Besides, one of his Taunton sisters and her brood were visiting and the church fair had taken much of his time. He had paid his relatives scant attention and he was sure his sister thought his behaviour a trifle odd.

"Come back to Taunton with us," she said persuasively. "You need a change of air, a rest." He was tempted, but he was not fond of the train. It unnerved him, snorting and puffing like an irate bull. A silly, hysterical reaction, he knew, but he couldn't help it.

He sighed. "Very kind. But I have my parish duties to attend. Perhaps later in the year."

She glanced at him, troubled. He had always been strong, but there were areas of his life she knew were private. She must have faith that this air of detached reverie would resolve itself. She didn't mention the matter again.

Thomas decided a visit to Dorothea would help soothe his troubled soul. She saw him as he came up her garden path and her heart began beating unreasonably fast. Thomas was a fine sight, meticulously attired as always, displaying his clerical garb to perfection. It was no accident, Dorothea was certain, that he wore it just a little too tight. She wondered if he had heard the news. Probably not, if his swinging step was anything to go by. Well, it was her Christian duty to tell him. Honesty and openness had always been her creed, everyone knew that. And now that the Welles minx had gone, she, Dorothea, would be waiting to offer comfort and support to Thomas in his time of need. She had been longing for this day and now it had arrived like a Second Coming, a glorious chance to rekindle fires, which, for her, had never gone out. Excitement and triumph raged for supremacy in her breast and both were masters.

She could hear her husband Robert open the front door. She hesitated only a fraction of a second before emerging majestically from the parlour to greet Thomas, a gracious smile on her face. She held out her hand.

"Dear lady!" Thomas exclaimed. "My compliments to you! We could wish for better weather, eh?" He held her hand just a little overlong, squeezing her fingers. His blue protuberant eyes were penetrating and astute. She felt herself blushing and, mindful of Robert, withdrew her hand.

"Good evening, Thomas," she answered. "This is indeed a pleasure. What may Robert and I do for you?" Her voice was perfectly composed, her manner all-pleasing gentility.

"I come to crave your indulgence," Thomas beamed. Robert looked on woodenly. He just about tolerated the Reverend. Why couldn't the man speak plainly, like other folk?

"Please, Thomas, step into the parlour," Dorothea said. "Is it a little late for tea, do you think?" Robert started to follow his wife, but the Reverend swept past him and went to sit in one of Dorothea's comfortable armchairs. "Dear lady, how kind. Tea would be excellent. I promise I won't keep you longer than necessary!" He coughed deprecatingly and Dorothea cried at once, "Nonsense Thomas, our time is yours! We are at your disposal. Robert shall fetch the tea things!"

Robert groaned inwardly, went to the scullery and returned with a loaded tray. He settled himself opposite Thomas Norsworthy and prepared himself for a tedious interlude. Dorothea filled the teapot from the kettle and poured tea into delicate china cups. Thomas took one, exhibiting surprisingly dainty manners, crooking his little finger and taking tiny sips. He made no noise when he drank. It was as if the tea disappeared by magic.

"Do tell us what we may do for you, Thomas," Dorothea purred. "Is it the church flowers? I seem to remember it was Mrs Chubb's turn this week."

"It is not the church flowers, dear lady," Thomas said, "though how like you to think of such a thing. No, it is the union workhouse. It is our charitable collection next Sunday. My sister is visiting and I am afraid that I am unable to proceed with the delivery of any monies - should we be fortunate to collect enough," he added. He must think of himself, the collection for the minister. He felt confident in Dorothea, though. The hint would fall on fertile ears and they would get enough for the union workhouse and for his Sunday labours, too.

"Consider it no more!" Dorothea was saying. "Never let it be said that I cannot fulfil a need where I see one. I will take the money myself. We will," she added, looking at Robert. Taken off guard, Robert could only mumble assent.

"To be sure, Reverend," he said. "We'll go after the service. 'Twill do the horse good to have a run out."

Dorothea smiled at her husband. He'd said the right thing. She handed him another cup of tea, popping in an extra lump of sugar. His reward. Sugar lumps for being good, like the horse.

He looked up to find the Reverend staring at him with those peculiarly unblinking eyes. Strange eyes and disconcerting, at odd variance with the man's joviality. They made Robert uncomfortable and he could never prevent an uneasy feeling that there was more to the reverend than met the eye, a feeling that intensified when he looked at his son, though nothing would have dragged his suspicions from him.

Thomas relaxed in Dorothea's armchair. He regarded her warmly, watching with amusement the girlish blush staining her cheeks. He considered her to be a fine woman still. She sat straight in her chair, looking at him in open admiration. She reminded him of a ship's figurehead, breasts thrust out, riding life's storms. He felt a stab of conscience. He had not done the right thing by her and life with the colourless Robert could not have been very fulfilling. She had made the best of it, though, she ruled her little household and Robert was plainly fond of her.

Dorothea offered him one of her fancy cakes. He refused, of course. That was one area where he could confidently say he resisted temptation. The room was pleasantly warm. Opposite him, Robert Pascoe stared stolidly ahead, avoiding eye contact. Dorothea was busy with the cups and chatting. Or talking. Dorothea never chatted. Her vibrant tones were never wasted on trivia. Thomas could never imagine her gossiping with the town wives. He began to doze, eyelids drooping.

"...you expect from that Welles girl!" Dorothea suddenly said, a strange exultant note in her voice.

Thomas sat bolt upright, wide-awake now. His heart was banging against his ribs. He struggled to maintain his composure. "What, dear lady?" he enquired, faintly.

Dorothea glanced at him in feigned surprise, eyebrows raised. "Why, Thomas!" she said, softly. "Whatever is the matter? Surely you must have heard? There's been talk of nothing else! The Welles girl has left Tamarleigh. Even her mother doesn't know where she is. Which doesn't surprise me!" she added contemptuously. "Whenever did Sarah Welles know what time of day or night it was! Anyway, the little madam'll not be missed, unless I'm very much mistaken." She watched Thomas from under her lashes. "What do *you* say, Thomas?"

But for once Reverend Thomas Norsworthy was bereft of speech. He stared at Dorothea, mouth agape, eyes bulging.

This was wretched news indeed. He excused himself hurriedly and left, blind to Dorothea's cries of genuine disappointment and Robert's plainly bewildered expression.

His head spinning, he could hardly remember getting home. He was oblivious to the astonished stares of old Mrs Tregantle and Miss Whiddle as they stood talking at Miss Whiddle's gate. He heard a wisp of their conversation as he rushed on.

"Reverend looks upset 'bout somethin'," Mrs Tregantle said.

"Hmm! Mighta got a lot to be upset *about*!" sniffed Miss Whiddle.

"Oh, come now, dear, we must be charitable! There's always gossip in a small town."

Reaching the parsonage, Thomas wrenched the door open and stumbled blindly into his study. He sank into a chair, head in hands, and closed his eyes. Before his unwilling vision there flamed two wide green eyes and a mass of tawny curls, tumbling recklessly over creamy shoulders. The eyes were mocking him, taunting him. His premonition of disaster had come to pass, as he knew it would. Desperately, he tried to see Tregony as Eve to his innocent Adam, a theme he was so fond of. But all he could see was himself as the snake, the very embodiment of evil.

He dropped to the floor as the full realisation of his terrible sin at last struck him, but he was not to be spared. Behind his closed lids there paraded, in haunting caricature, his every sinful moment with Tregony. Her enchanting face and wicked smile, the wilful tilt of her head, the stubborn line of her mouth. He saw himself revelling in a forbidden love, in such flagrant disobedience to his calling that his voice rose in a great animal cry of pain. He had betrayed his flock, he had betrayed Tregony and, worst of all, he had betrayed his saviour. He knew himself to be surely lost, as damned as those he hypocritically preached about on Sundays. This was not an isolated mistake, but one of many. And Dorothea knew about Tregony, of that he was certain. There was no mistaking the triumph in her eyes, the spiteful edge to her seemingly innocent words. Her fury appalled him, but he stood condemned, for he had wronged her as much as any. His whole life had been a lie. He was filled with a vile self-loathing.

How long he lay on the floor, he didn't know. But when he arose, his mind was made up.

Chapter 4

"Where be off to, old mother?" enquired the ferryman as the stooped figure shuffled past him.

"Plymouth, if y'please," replied the crone, shifting a bundle from one arm to the other.

"We knows that!" guffawed a boatman. "But where after? 'Tis late to go a-junketing in this weather."

It was true. This was the last ferry across to Devonport and already the night mists from the Tamar were drawing in, obscuring the opposite bank and filling the air with dank mustiness. The moored barges in the Ballast Pound reared soundlessly in the fading light, like dumb tethered creatures, straining to be free.

The old woman smiled grimly and pulled her cloak round her and answered gruffly, "If me journey weren't partickler, I wooden be goin', if 'tis any o' your business!" The men didn't reply. She was one of half a dozen other passengers on board, so they fell to talking to more sociable sailors.

The old lady turned away and hid her face in her bundle. Her shoulders shook. So far, so good. No-one had recognised her, and both the ferryman and the boatmen knew her well. Tregony laughed to herself. This was an exciting adventure. The ferry pulled into the opposite bank and she shuffled off, limping and panting as she climbed up the hard and on to the road. A gentleman fellow passenger offered to carry her load and she mumbled a refusal. She knew the man and ducked her face further down into her cloak. It was Major Charles Penkilve, a partner in a Tamarleigh law firm. He was middle-aged, but still handsome in a florid kind of way and she had often considered casting her net in that direction. But soon she would be landing bigger fish than Major Penkilve. Her mouth set in a determined line and she made her way towards the Stoke Damerel road, climbing resolutely until she reached Millbridge. Another half mile or so brought her to Plymouth station. She had laid careful plans. She would go to her Aunt Josephine's in Exeter, Jeremiah's sister. She had been there once as a child, when Jeremiah had taken his family on a visit. She remembered her Aunt as a kindly person and it would be somewhere safe to have her baby before travelling on to London to fulfil her dream. It was late, nearly nine o'clock. She stopped a porter and asked about trains to Exeter.

"One left," he answered, without glancing at her. "Goin' through Tavi, be about hour an 'alf. Or you could go south about the moor, through Totnes. Only won't be till termorrer now."

She had no choice but to go through Tavistock. She climbed into a waiting carriage and lay full length on the seat. She wasn't aware that the train had arrived in Exeter until she heard a shout. "Exeter Central! Exeter Central!" She sat up and rubbed her eyes. Outside the grimy window a gas lamp swayed in the night wind. She gathered up her bundle and stepped gingerly down on to the platform. She remembered a little about her aunt's house, but not how to get there. The station clock said ten-thirty. She hoped her aunt didn't retire early. Her mother had told her that Aunt Josephine had been named for Bonaparte's empress, a circumstance which Sarah considered unpatriotic. She said Victoria would have been nicer, after their own dear Queen. Tregony knew all about her Grandfather Arthur Welles who had fought at Waterloo as a brigade major and won medals for bravery. Jeremiah had kept them in a box on the chiffonier and forbidden the children to touch them. The family was proud of its Waterloo hero and of the family name, so similar to the Iron Duke's, which Sarah said almost made them related.

A passer-by directed her to the police station. It was no more than a house with a lamp outside and an inscription over the door. A duty constable looked up disinterestedly from something he was writing.

"What is it, ma?" he asked. "Ain't you got no home to go to?"

"I bin travelling all day," Tregony lied, "to see Miss Welles, Miss Josephine Welles. She's expecting me," she added, hoping fervently her aunt hadn't died or moved. The constable knew Miss Josephine, but he was in no hurry to give her address away. "Forgot where she lives, then, eh?" he asked. "What's in yer bundle?"

"Me wordly goods," replied Tregony, in what she hoped was a feeble voice. "I've come all the way from ... Penzance!" She chose the remotest place she had heard of and opened the bundle to display the few meagre clothes she had brought with her. "I haven't seen me ... er, sister ... in years. It's took me a devil of a time!"

"Hmm!" the constable grunted. "It just 'appens that I knows Miss Josephine and you don't look like no kin to me. She's a proper lady."

Tregony gave a tremulous sigh. "Josephine's the rich side of the family. I comes from the poor side!"

"Well, she lives in Sylvan Road," he said at length, eyeing her with faint revulsion. Tregony saw the look and longed to fling off the disguise and see his look turn from disgust to desire, as she knew it would. No time for such games, though. Yes, Sylvan Road, that was it.

The constable seemed satisfied and let her go, even giving her a rough map, which Tregony found hard to follow in the poor light of the shabby room. It was a tidy step, taking her past the cathedral, along Sidwell Street and out towards the Tiverton Road.

All the houses in Sylvan Road were imposing, some quite new, and at first she couldn't distinguish her Aunt's. She peered at the gates and ventured up some of the paths until she found what she was looking for, a polished nameplate with "Sylvan House" engraved on it. She distinctly remembered tracing that elegant copperplate with childish fingers all those years ago and how overawed they had all been by the imposing Victorian house. She hung on the bell-pull beside the door and waited. A light flickered behind the leaded panes and an inner door opened. Bolts were pulled back and a key turned in the lock. The big door swung open and a face peered at her. With true presence of mind, Tregony pulled off her hood and let her tawny curls tumble about her shoulders. She smiled tremulously and said, "Is my old Aunt here? Tell her 'tis Tregony Welles come from Cornwall to see her." She allowed herself to sag wearily against the porch and a tentative tear began its way down her face.

The person holding the lamp swung it upwards and Tregony saw a middle-aged woman with a prim, tight-lipped mouth and startled round eyes. Tregony stared at her. "You're not my Aunt," she said, uncertainly. "Who are you?"

"More to the point, who are you?" the woman replied astonished, as she took in the dishevelled figure before her. "Is your aunt expecting you? She never said!"

"Not rightly expectin' me, no," Tregony answered. "But there's been some family trouble down home and I don't know where to go!" Whereupon she covered her face with her hands and burst into pitiful sobs. The woman leaned forward and grasped Tregony's arm. "I don't know who you are, but whoever, you'll not stand out there snivelling for all the world and his wife to see!" She yanked Tregony into the hall and pushed her into a chair. "Wait there!" she commanded. "I'll see what Miss Josephine has to say about this!"

Tregony gazed around her, vaguely recalling some of her childhood impressions. Everything spoke of tasteful gentility. The hall furniture was heavy, old and highly polished. A brass urn stood by the front door, containing an aspidistra that had reached the ceiling and was beginning its way across it. She went to the big mirror and looked at herself. The usual rose tint of her skin had paled with tiredness. She felt every inch the poor relation and was glad that her old cloak was respectable and the thin calico dress beneath was clean.

The woman returned. "Come this way. Miss Josephine wants to see you."

Tregony followed her through the fine old house. She was ushered into a small sitting room at the back of the house. There, in a chair with a tartan rug over her knees, sat a lady, not as old as Tregony had expected, but past middle-age. Her brown eyes were bright and alert. She was dressed in a blue velvet dressing gown and her thick, silvery hair waved girlishly about her ears. She had the rosy skin of someone half her age, and everything about her spoke of refinement and taste. She gazed at Tregony, a look of amazement on her face.

"Well, I'll be blessed if it isn't Jeremiah's little maid, after all! I could hardly believe Mrs Morrel when she told me, but I'd know that hair anywhere! What on earth are you doing here at this late hour, child? I haven't seen you in years - how many? It must be ten or more. Is it your mother taken poorly. Why didn't you write? Fancy coming this distance!"

The shock of seeing her aunt and the torrent of questions took Tregony off guard and she put her hands to her temples, swaying giddily. She felt sick and her stomach gnawed with hunger. "No," she said, faintly. "It ain't my mother. Please, ma'am may I sit? I'm so tired!"

It was only later, after hot tea and buttered toast that she began to rally. Fleetingly, she wondered whether she should lie about the reason for her visit, but instinct told her to speak the truth, as she would have to sooner or later. So she told her tale, omitting nothing except the true parentage of the baby, which she knew without doubt would shock her aunt into turning her out. The baby's father became someone whom her mother was forcing her to marry and her aunt did not question it.

However, she didn't take the news well. "Why should I pick up Sarah Welles' problems?" she demanded. "I never thought that woman good enough for Jeremiah and I said so from the start. Now I'm proved right or you wouldn't be in this mess. Well, the pigeons have come home to roost, except it seems they've come to the wrong loft!" She looked sternly at Tregony, her lips pursed. Tregony said nothing. "What will my neighbours say if they find out?" Aunt Josephine continued, indignantly. "I'm not a home for runaway girls in the family way! If it weren't for the fact that I was very fond of Jeremiah, I'd tell you to be off!"

Tregony hung her head and fiddled with one of the buttons on her calico dress. This was a small price to pay, but she could hardly blame her aunt, who sniffed, adjusted her shawl and continued. "And what will you do with the babe?" she asked, severely. "Babies don't go back once they're here. Have you thought of that?" Tregony gave her Aunt a meek look and sighed. "Yes, Aunt," she said, in a small voice. "I got three choices. I can go back home, carry on up the line or give it to the midwife for the orphanage. There must be someone who'll want a nice, healthy babe!"

"Don't you be too sure," replied her aunt. "Babies are a

nuisance, they need feeding. And, God forbid, it might not be healthy. You have to take what comes, my girl! Well, I can see you've thought about it, but you'll not take it up the line, that I can tell you! Better it died at birth than that!"

Despite the warmth of the room, a sudden chill struck through Tregony like a sharp icicle, and she found herself trembling.

"No," her Aunt was saying, more to herself than Tregony. "Much better to hand it over to the midwife. You're far too young to be tied down without a husband. Yes, that's the answer, then we can keep it all quiet, just between ourselves. I can arrange it for you. You'll have to stay here, of course. I can't very well turn out kith and kin!" She looked at Tregony again. The flaunting, bold colouring, the look which was both earthy and wistful. She had never been quite sure about the girl's parentage, but Jeremiah had loved his daughter, she knew, so who was she to quibble. And she had to grudgingly admit that she would quite enjoy caring for her niece. She rarely saw any of her relations these days, nobody bothered to keep in touch, and there was precious little else to do.

Over the next few days, Tregony settled in. Her aunt employed two staff - Mrs Mudge, the cook, and a housekeeper, Mrs Morrel. Both women were glad of a visitor in the house. They were disapproving about Tregony's pregnancy, but if their mistress had made up her mind it was not their place to question. And Tregony had an artful, coquettish charm which soon won them over.

The house was arranged on three floors. The top attic floor was the servants' quarters, although Mrs Morrel slept on the middle floor, next to Aunt Josephine's room. Tregony was given a truckle bed in the attic room for the time being, where she had to endure the loud nightly snores of Mrs Mudge in the next bed. She was allowed to use her aunt's dressing room, which had an enamelled bath in it, decorated with cream bunches of grapes and roses. The bath stood in gleaming isolation on four gold claw feet in the centre of the room. Round the edge of the bath ran a deep curled lip with indentations for soaps and sponges. To Tregony, used to an old tin bath beside the scullery fire on infrequent Friday nights, and even then sharing precious water, this was luxury indeed. On a nearby cabinet stood pots of witch hazel toilette cream and cream simon and smelling salts, next to tall bottles of rosewater. Tiny waxed fabric rosebuds floated in each bottle. No wonder her aunt's skin was so fine, thought Tregony. On a little frilled dresser beneath the window were ivory hairbrushes, inlaid with silver and a little duchesse pin cushion, made of pink lace over satin, and pierced with pearl headed pins, which Tregony saw pinning her aunt's black satin hat rosettes. Downstairs, there were two sitting rooms, a largish dining room and a small parlour at the back. A scullery led off this into a small kitchen, where Mrs Mudge spent most of her time. On the scullery wall was a row of room numbers and bells. It amused Tregony during her first few days at Sylvan House to ask Mrs Mudge to ring the bell pushes so she could dash and watch the little bells tinkling. Such childlike behaviour endeared her to the ladies.

They began to spoil her and she basked in such treatment. Here there was no pressure to look after recalcitrant brothers, or run endless errands for Sarah. Released from responsibility, she blossomed and became even more beautiful and the hard look in her eyes softened.

At the back of the house there was a court with a meat-safe built into the wall, and beyond that the gardens. First, a vegetable garden, with a row of cordoned apples trees forming a screen, then the flower gardens. It was still early in the season, but rhododendrons were beginning to bud and there was a little summerhouse that it was sometimes mild enough to sit in.

Tregony wrote to her mother - a hurriedly scrawled, undated note. *"...and don't set no-one after me,"* she wrote. *"I ain't coming home, not yet awhile anyway. I'm happy."* The postmark was smudged, there was no address and the writing was barely decipherable, but it set Sarah's mind at rest.

As Tregony's pregnancy advanced, Aunt Josephine insisted that her own doctor should examine her. "You want to come through this well," she reminded her niece, "even if this one is going to the orphanage. There'll be others some day, but not if you don't take care of yourself now."

Tregony had felt her child move, she felt at one with it. She spoke to it at night in the big new bed which she now had next to her aunt. She felt distinctly motherly and considered that her aunt had no right to tell her what to do.

"Just 'cos you'm an old maid what's never known the smell of a man!" she shouted, losing her temper. "This is my babe! It can hear things. I knows 'cos I talks to it! You'd feel the same if it was yours!"

Her aunt was shocked. She regarded Tregony with grave disappointment. "I shall forget you said that," she said, quietly. "Women in your condition are subject to instability, I believe. Just remember who took you in when you had nowhere to go. I think you should be grateful for that."

Tregony was at once contrite. She'd expected a boxed ear at the very least. She ran to her aunt and knelt down on the floor. "Forgive me, Aunt!" she cried. "I'm just a wicked maid! Mother's always saying it! I am grateful, I do love you!"

Aunt Josephine leaned forward and stroked the copper curls. At the mention of Sarah Welles she was reminded that this child had come to her in preference to her own mother, and her heart melted. "There, there!" she said, soothingly. "I'm only thinking of you, Tregony. I'll send Mrs Morrel round to Doctor Ferguson's tomorrow with a note. He can call in and examine you here. That will put our minds at rest, won't it?"

She fussed over Tregony for the rest of the day. Perhaps she had been a little hard. And of late she was starting to feel a tinge of regret that she had advised Tregony not to keep her baby. She had always been singularly unfond of children and a moment of guilt struck her when she thought of that drab little thing of a Sarah and her brood. She could have stayed in touch with them if she'd wanted to. Perhaps it was now her chance to show a little charity. Strange how the girl had turned up, after all these years. Well, she would do what she could and no-one would be able to accuse her of lack of care.

Tregony had learnt very early in life that meek agreement with others was the easiest method of getting her own way, so she let her aunt fuss over her, and settled back to await the arrival of the child she knew she would love.

One hot night in June, her own birth month, she felt a great surge of energy, so strong that she couldn't ignore it. She tiptoed downstairs to the kitchen where she found a great mountain of pressing to be done, laid out by Mrs Morrel on the nearby table. She put the little iron on its trivet on top of the range, which was always lit, and waited for it to heat up while she sorted out the clothes. Humming to herself, she had almost finished, when there was a rush like an open tap, and water streamed from her and down over the kitchen flags. She gasped and clapped her hands with delight. Doctor Ferguson had told her what to expect. Curiously, she bent down as far as she was able and peered between her legs. Where was the baby, then? Shouldn't it be coming out now? She gently pushed her distended belly, then waited hopefully.

Suddenly, a pain such as she had never known before shot through her loins and travelled agonisingly along each nerve in her body, bringing her to her knees. She was so shocked that she let out a great scream, which echoed through the silent house and penetrated the ears of the sleepers above. Soon, footsteps were hurrying overhead as her aunt rose from her bed, calling Mrs Morrel as she came.

They found Tregony on the kitchen floor, gasping and wailing at the same time. "Me babe's stuck! Doctor said it'd come when me waters broke, but it can't get out!"

Despite herself, Aunt Josephine smiled, while Mrs Morrel lifted Tregony up from the floor and sat her in the rocker. "Silly child!" she scolded fondly. "Don't you know more than that? 'Tis a pity Doctor didn't tell you, then! It usually takes a mite longer than a few pains!" She winced as Tregony crushed her hand in a vice-like grip.

"Go and fetch Mrs Phillips, the midwife," said Aunt Josephine. "Make haste!" Mrs Morrel hurried away while Aunt Josephine fetched water and a cloth and bathed Tregony's sweating forehead. She held the glass to the girl's shaking lips, then helped her up to the bedroom where she spread plenty of brown paper on the bed and made Tregony lie down. She knew she had to put water on to boil, but Tregony was gripping her hand so tightly she couldn't move. Drat Mrs Mudge and her snoring, she thought, then was relieved to see her standing in the doorway, rubbing her eyes. "Aye, water, madam, I know!" Mrs Mudge said and made for the kitchen, where all the big pans were soon put to use.

When Tregony's son appeared in the world, crying as lustily as his mother had been doing before him, she looked at the purple screwed up bundle next to her and a feeling such as she had never known stole over her. This ugly scrap of life was hers, the first thing she had ever had of her very own. A fierce, protective love flooded through her. She clasped the baby to her and closed her eyes, oblivious of the faces bending over her.

"Not too much of that!" said a voice. She opened her eyes and saw the midwife's tight-lipped disapproval. "Won't help when you have to give 'im up!" Mrs Phillips said, waving an admonishing finger. "You'll get fond of him and then where will we be!"

She returned the next day with a straw carrying cradle, prepared to take the baby with her, but Tregony set up such a howling and wailing that Aunt Josephine dismissed the woman. "I'll send if I need you," she told her. "It's probably best to leave it awhile."

"Then there'll be no point," Mrs Phillips shrugged. "Be too close to him by then." What did she care? She'd been paid - handsomely, too - although she did have a family in mind and there'd be some explaining to do. Still, girls had babies every day of the week. She could soon supply another one.

Tregony lay in blissful euphoria for ten days, strapped to the bed as the midwife had advised to shrink her stomach. She didn't care, she had her son and she didn't want to get up. She was quite happy to lie in bed and suckle him and have the administrations of the three women, who were happy to give them.

Her Aunt Josephine was realistic enough to know that Tregony would keep her child, and her heart faltered. She wondered whether she should offer the girl a permanent home. Things would have to change, her way of life would never be the same again. And Mrs Morrel and Mrs Mudge had to be considered. She could well afford to care for them both and much as she had always thought of herself as unmotherly, she was beginning to feel a bond with the tiny child. But Tregony seemed to be in a world of her own since her son's birth, pointing out yet some other wondrous thing about him and Aunt Josephine put the matter to the back of her mind.

"I think you should call him Arthur," said her aunt. "It was your grandfather's name, you know, my own dear father. He fought at the battle of Waterloo and shared the great Duke's name."

Tregony couldn't have cared less, but she was pleased to have made her aunt happy and agreed to the name. She crooned endlessly to Arthur and hugged him by the hour. Aunt Josephine had wanted to hire a wet nurse, reasoning that her niece needed to restore her strength, but Tregony insisted on feeding Arthur herself.

She knew that her aunt would like her to stay. The prospect was tempting. She would never want for anything again, but there had never been a moment when she'd lost sight of her dream. The vision that she had seen outside Treharne House and in Thomas's arms of herself, decked out in finery, the object of admiring stares, the toast of every drawing room soiree and party. Dreams like that could only be fulfilled in London, where the streets were paved with gold and everyone was rich. And she had an asset which was worth more than its weight in gold - her beauty. She would not be long in London, she knew, before a rich and handsome gentleman would fall in love with her. Besides, she had Arthur to think of now. To some he may have been a burden, but she was used to looking after her brothers. No, she would leave as soon as possible. She would tell her aunt a lie that she was going home. By the time the lie was found out, it would be too late.

Chapter 5

Then she made a startling discovery, which convinced her never to go back home. As Arthur's features changed from a screwed-up purple to a recognisable likeness and the blue, rather bulbous eyes gazed innocently into hers, she could see that the Tamarleigh gossips had been right. The pouting chiselled lips and the wisps of blonde hair spoke for themselves. From Arthur's face, Denzil Pascoe looked back at her. "You'm born unlucky," she told him. "An' so am I - born in Tamarleigh, that was my bad luck! But we'll not go back there. We're going to make our fortunes!"

No wonder Dorothea Pascoe had always been so coy and flirtatious with Thomas. No wonder the woman hated her! For all her mealy-mouthed pious pretence, Dorothea Pascoe was no better than Tregony Welles. A bubble of laughter rose within her and she rolled around the bed in mirth, while Arthur gazed placidly at his mama, blissfully unaware. Victory rose in her breast. She could have Old Mother Pascoe in her power at the snap of her fingers. Go back, make Thomas marry her, and lord it over the town for the rest of her life. What a sweet and dizzying prospect that was!

Then Denzil's face loomed before her and she knew that if he should ever find out, he would take his revenge. She must get away. If she stayed in Exeter her mother might eventually come looking for her and Sarah Welles had never been discreet. She would be sure to tell people and then Denzil would find her. And there was Thomas. He wouldn't be able to deny his sons' parentage. He would be finished, ostracised, forced to leave Tamarleigh. She cared little now and she doubted if Denzil knew that Thomas was his father, either. But if he discovered the truth, there would be murder done - he had always hated Thomas Norsworthy, calling him a canting loudmouth. The whole thing was a terrible muddle and she must leave as soon as possible.

Aunt Josephine was aghast. "Whatever'll your mother think?" she cried. "An illegitimate baby! You'll all have to leave Tamarleigh, mark my words! Stay here, child, let me look after you. When Arthur's weaned you can get a place in service. There are plenty of folk here who need a good maid."

"I can face a parcel of Tamarleigh nobodies!" Tregony declared. "I'm not letting Arthur go, whatever you say. The twins need me and so does Mother. She's always ill!"

Aunt Josephine knew she had lost. There was a determined glint in her neice's eye which set her wondering afresh. She had never seen such determination in either Sarah or Jeremiah, and her brother, certainly, had been a gentle, simple soul, easily led and malleable. With sadness, she helped Tregony prepare for the journey, secretly resolving to get in touch with Sarah Welles and try to make up for lost time. She bought Arthur new clothes and a travelling carrycot, and she insisted on buying Tregony a costume and two good dresses. Tregony had a twinge of conscience about this, but allowed herself to be taken to Gartner's new showroom in Queen Street, which discreetly advertised "English and French Novelties", where she tried a pretty costume of blue velvet, with cream lace Vandykes and a peplum with rounded ends. "A very stylish accessory!" the assistant told her, earnestly. The narrow standing collar was covered with crushed velvet with frill-finished ends, fastening at the back. Tregony had never seen such splendid clothes and was round-eyed with delight and, for once, speechless. Bouffant leg o' mutton sleeves completed the effect. Tregony twirled endlessly before the shop mirror, while her aunt smiled indulgently, wondering yet again how her brother had managed to father such a beauty.

"Oh, Aunt!" she cried. "How'm I supposed to choose?" fingering first the blue velvet, then the fluffy cream organdy with its double frill caps at the shoulders and wrinkled ribbon belt.

The assistant coughed genteelly and pointed out that the same dress could be had in dimity or India silk, if madam would care to see them. Madam did, and insisted on trying all three, swirling round the little easy chairs in great high spirits.

"Oh, Aunt!" she cried for the hundredth time. "Which one, which one? You choose for me!"

And so Aunt Josephine made the choice and they left with the blue velvet costume, the organdy tea gown and the same design in India silk. "And to finish off," said her aunt, "you may choose a hat."

A pleasant half-hour was spent at the milliners where Tregony chose a soft-crowned cream silk and ribbon bonnet, trimmed with apricot ostrich feathers. Outside in the street she hung round her aunt's neck, covering her with kisses. She felt real and deep gratitude for this woman who had taken her in and befriended her, and she was going to miss her sorely.

Aunt Josephine held her close for a moment, fumbling in her reticule for a handkerchief, tears in her eyes.

"I shall keep these for special, Aunt!" Tregony assured her. "For parties and such."

"Are there many in Tamarleigh?" enquired her aunt, as they proceeded to the cabstand.

"Well, er, no," Tregony answered, then added hurriedly, "But the folks at the Treharne House haves 'em sometimes and the church 'as a big 'un at Christmas!"

Her aunt smiled. Tregony looked like an exquisite china doll and spoke like a farm boy. What she could have made of her, had she been her own daughter! She sighed. Too late now to regret her childlessness. She had never had cause to before.

The day came for Tregony's departure. She insisted on packing the costume Aunt Josephine had bought her and wearing the old cloak she had arrived in, reasoning that travelling might stain the emerald velvet. The cloak had been cleaned and looked quite respectable. Tregony laid her clothes carefully in layers of tissue paper and put them gently in the portmanteau her aunt was lending her for the journey. She planned to leave it at Paddington, then send for it when she was settled.

The train ticket had been booked for Plymouth. Her aunt had wanted to write a note to Sarah, but Tregony had reminded her that her mother didn't yet know about Arthur. "And besides," she added, artfully, "Mother don't read good. 'Specially fancy writin'!"

She expressed some of her milk into a boat-shaped glass feeding bottle for Arthur and there was enough for two feeds. She ticked items off against her fingers. "Clean smalls for Arthur, food for me, bottle o' boiled water. I got everythin', Aunt. Journey won't be long. I'll be home afore I knows it!"

Tearful goodbyes were said to Mrs Morrel and Mrs Mudge. "You get into a carriage with ladies only!" they told her, anxiously. Tregony promised that she would, gave both ladies a hug and climbed into the waiting hackney with her aunt.

The charade continued as they arrived at Exeter Central. "Platform number one," said the porter, "stoppin' at Exeter St David's, Dawlish ..." His words were lost as Aunt Josephine hurried her onto the train. Tregony put Arthur carefully on the seat in his new travelling carrier. The portmanteau was stowed in the guard's van. Her aunt stood at the window, smiling

The Forbidden Link

tearfully as the guard waved a green flag and prepared to jump aboard.

"Goodbye, my dear!" said her aunt. "Come back and show us the little lad soon! Take good care of yourself, remember me to Sarah. Tell her I hope she fares better with her health."

"Oh, I will, Aunt!" cried Tregony. "She'll be that pleased you cared for me. We'll come back, I promise!" She looked so happy and excited that her aunt felt a startled foreboding as she stared at Tregony's sparkling eyes and rosy cheeks, now filled out and softened by motherhood. The sensation was instant and she dismissed it as morbid fancy at the thought of losing her beautiful niece and the companionship they had enjoyed over the past months.

They kissed each other tenderly as the train began to inch forward, then gather speed. Tregony's last view of her aunt was of her sniffing into a wisp of lace and waving forlornly. Then she was hidden in a swirl of smoke from the engine and Tregony pulled up the window and flopped into her seat. Her own eyes were brimming with unshed tears, which she dashed determinedly away with the back of her hand. She had no time for regrets. A new chapter of her life was beginning and the only alteration to the old one would be when she returned to show off her success.

Luckily she had the carriage to herself. She would get out at Exeter St David's, cross the line for the next up train to London, and say she'd got on the wrong train. It wouldn't be difficult to plead poverty when the train arrived in London. Her beauty had always opened doors. It went as she hoped. No-one was particularly interested in her, the station was busy, and there was a train just drawing in. Thankfully, she climbed into it, sorrowful that she had misled her aunt, but promising herself that one day, when she was rich and successful, she would come back to Sylvan House and her aunt would be proud of her. It wouldn't be long.

* * * * *

Everyone in Tamarleigh agreed that Thomas Norsworthy looked ill. Gone was the confident stride, the flamboyant manner. He seemed to have grown old in the space of a couple of weeks. There were two who could mark the actual beginning of his demise - Sarah Welles and Dorothea Pascoe. For both women sympathy was tinged with bitterness. Soon most people were remarking on the change in their parson, and Mrs Knox daily received little gifts from kind parishioners who thought Thomas's ailment was physical. Even Walter Prowse, relying on many years of friendship, took it upon himself to visit Thomas unasked. He found him preparing his Sunday address. He didn't bother with any preamble, but said bluntly, "Ye know ye're ill, man! Why, look at ye, all skin and bone! For heaven's sake, why haven't ye been to see me?"

Thomas pushed back his chair and motioned the doctor to sit down. "I don't know, Walter!" he replied, wearily. "Probably because I don't think there's anything you can do to help. No-one can!"

Walter Prowse gave an exasperated snort. "How d'y know if ye don't ask?" he said. "I can tell ye what I'd recommend, for a start! Ye need to get away. Been burning the candle at both ends, eh?"

"More than you'll ever know, Walter," Thomas said in a low voice. "I've been a fool. I'm ashamed to tell you how foolish, but heaven help me, I'd do it all again!"

Light was beginning to glimmer in Dr Prowse's mind. This was either to do with money, or a woman, or both. "Don't tell me ye're hard up, Thomas?" he asked, surprised. "Can that be it? No?" As Thomas shook his head, he continued, "Well, if it's not money, it must be a woman. Ye shoulda got married, Thomas Norsworthy, and put paid to all these philanderings of yours over the years. Oh, yes, I know! It's as plain as a pikestaff, a man like you, and all the women fluttering round ye. Been jealous m'self on more than one occasion!"

He smiled, but Thomas didn't respond and Walter Prowse began to feel alarmed. He leant forward and grasped his friend's wrist. He took out his fob and watched the second hand go round for a minute. Thomas didn't resist.

"Hmm, heart's fine," the doctor said, putting his fob away.

"No, it's not!" Thomas suddenly said in a stronger voice. "That's just it! I don't mind telling you, Walter, if it sounds alright, it shouldn't! Here am I, a man of middle age and gone all to pieces over a wanton slip of a girl! Worse, she's run off - I don't know where!"

Now Walter Prowse understood. "You don't mean the Welles girl?" he cried aghast. "Thomas Norsworthy, ye should be ashamed of y'self! To get mixed up with *her*, of all people! Why, ye're old enough to be her father, man! It's a good thing she has run off. Not before time!"

Thomas looked at him despairingly. "Don't, Walter!" he pleaded. "Don't you think I feel badly enough already? I came here for the cure of souls." He smiled grimly. "Far from curing them, I've contaminated them! There's only one thing I can do to make amends."

"What's that?" enquired the doctor sharply, beginning already to regret his hasty remarks. "I can give ye a tonic, if ye'd like. Ye're exaggerating all this. It's because ye're not well."

Thomas shook his head impatiently. "That'll do no good. No, I've only got one choice. I must confess my sin before God and my congregation!"

Walter Prowse was horrified. "Good Lord, man!" he cried. "How can ye be so foolish? Isn't enough damage done? The fewer people who know, the better. Let me give ye a tonic, we'll tell them ye're ill, then go to ye're sister's in Taunton. She'll have ye. Go on, man, get away while ye can!"

"No!" said Thomas, decisively, rising from his chair. A little of his old demeanour returned. He crossed to the window and stood looking down at the Tamar below and the barges tied in the Ballast Pound. He loved this place. He owed it to the people of Tamarleigh to confess his sins. After that, he would complete his plan.

Dr Prowse left, his mind in a turmoil. Try as he might, he couldn't persuade Thomas otherwise. He resolved not to attend church next Sunday. He could not bear to witness his friend's humiliation.

Thomas prepared his sermon carefully, crossing out any references to the downfall of man and replacing them with the trials of temptation and his own fleshly weakness. He would tell his flock that he was living proof of how far man had strayed from God's purpose and how he had wilfully gone his own wicked way. He would tell them that although he preached God's forgiveness, he didn't deserve to be forgiven. He would tell them all this, then walk for the last time from his church and his congregation and disappear from their lives.

When Sunday dawned, his resolve had deepened, but the intervening days had done nothing to lessen his misery. The day was cold with the interminable Cornish drizzle obscuring the surrounding hills. The muffled clang of the warning bells on the Tamar craft lent the day an eerie unreality. He was at the church at daybreak. He had been on his knees praying for most of the night and now, as day dawned, he felt a slight return of vigour.

The first parishioners began to straggle in at nine-thirty.

Mr Pole, the organist, arrived and soon a tentative breathy rumble announced the beginnings of an anthem. The organ was as wheezy as Mr Pole. It took much persuading and several false starts before any semblance of chords could be got from it.

Thomas took up his Bible and walked out of the vestry and up to the pulpit. There was a large congregation today. He looked at the faces below him, all waiting expectantly, and a great sadness gnawed inside him. His sin would never be forgotten by them, nor should it be, but he still owed them the truth.

He usually announced the first hymn now. He cleared his throat. "Good people of Tamarleigh," he began. There were one or two rustles and whispers, then a silence descended over the church as people began to sense something amiss.

"This morning's service will be somewhat ... different," Thomas went on hesitantly. "That is ..." He glanced at his sermon notes. Why bother with all that? There was only one thing that he wanted to say and better to get it over with. "I have something to say ... something which cannot be hidden any longer."

As if in a strange dream he saw Denzil Pascoe sitting at the back of the church beside Dorothea and Robert. His mind registered vague surprise. It wasn't often that Denzil was dragged to Sunday morning service by his mother. How ironic that he should be here on this of all mornings. He would hear more than he bargained for, but Thomas didn't relish the thought. He had wronged Denzil Pascoe just as surely as he had wronged everyone else. Denzil was part of his penance.

Thomas's hands gripped the edge of the pulpit and his heart felt as if it would fail him. "I have committed a terrible sin," he began in a faint voice. "I have ..."

"Speak up, Reverend!" shouted a voice from the back. "Us can't 'ear back 'ere!"

He looked up with a face of agony. Denzil Pascoe was sprawled in his pew, grinning.

Thomas closed his eyes and breathed deeply. Suddenly, as if the Lord took pity, a new strength flowed into him and he raised himself up and fixed the people with a burning eye.

"I, Thomas Norsworthy, have failed in my duty to you and Almighty God. I have succumbed to the wicked sins of the flesh, and ... *listen!*" he cried, as gasps went up and someone screamed. "Good folk! Listen, I beg you! I must confess before God and hope that you may find it in your hearts to ... not forgive me, I cannot hope for that. But, at least, to understand!"

He looked across the sea of faces until he found Dorothea's. Her eyes were glassy, her face waxen, while she waited, frozen, for his next words. She was breathing as if she had been running. Beside her, Denzil still sprawled, grinning, while Robert sat as if turned to stone, staring straight ahead.

"My sin has been with someone who has left this town and with someone who is still here," Thomas went on. "And, to my shame, I confess that Denzil Pascoe is my son, and ..."

He was interrupted by an unearthly howl from the back of the church, a sound hardly human. He quailed before it.

"*You!* My *pa!*" screamed Denzil, rising from his seat. "Nothin' to *my* shame bein' your son! You go to hell where ye belong, you dirty ole bastard! An' could on'y be one who's left Tamarleigh, that's Tregony Welles! You bin 'avin' my woman be'ind my back! What, she left 'cos she's in the fam'ly way, too, then?"

Uproar broke out. Sarah Welles slipped sideways in her pew and swooned dead away. Dorothea Pascoe stormed up the aisle and advanced on Thomas with such menace that he drew back, frightened, but Robert Pascoe jumped and pinned her arms behind her, forcing her back into the pew. His suspicions were correct, but Dorothea was his wife and it was his duty to stand by her. He had lived with the humiliating suspicion for as long as he could remember. Now it was common knowledge, she would need him all the more.

The church was filled with a cacophony of shocked screams and shouts, as Thomas's words sunk in. Several men turned on Denzil Pascoe before he could follow his mother and get to Thomas and he found himself heaved bodily out of the door and flung to the ground. He arose, snarling like an animal. "You wait! I'll get even wi' the lot o' you! Him in partickler! And her, the whore, wherever she is! They better watch out, that's all I'm a-sayin'!"

"Clear off, Pascoe!" they shouted. "We'm not frightened o' you, whoever's yer pa!"

An evil rage spread through Denzil. There were people in Tamarleigh who would be sorry for today's work. And there was a certain female who needed a lesson she wouldn't forget. He'd bide his time, he could wait. She'd wish she'd never been born.

Thomas swayed in the pulpit and looked at the terrible sight before him. Neighbour shouted at neighbour, children screamed, and all was utter chaos. He turned. The pulpit steps were blocked by two furiously arguing women. He pushed past them and fled to the vestry, struggling out of his clerical robes as he ran. He left them piled in a heap on the vestry floor and escaped out of a side door of the church, dressed only in his shirt and gaiters. He knew what he must do to complete his plan. He veered off to the left and ran until he came to Yonderberry Point and the little creek which ran into the hills. A small boat was moored at the jetty and he stepped into it. The place was deserted, the air silent and still. Panting, he rowed himself across the creek and pulled the boat up onto the little shore. He climbed up the bank and stumbled, half running, through fields and undergrowth until he came to St Germans where he was able to get onto the Saltash road.

Another half-hour brought him into Saltash town. He passed down Fore Street as one in a trance, his limbs seemed hardly to move. He didn't feel the pavement beneath his feet, he was deaf to the few carts which rolled past him, blind to the Sunday morning worshippers leaving St Stephen's on the corner. He noticed only the glint of water as he reached Lower Fore Street and saw the Tamar below him. He contemplated the glistening water. How easy it would be to feel the river closing in above him, to breathe deeply in its embrace and float out of the world. But atonement meant sacrifice and sacrifice meant suffering. It was the ultimate message of the church. His perverse and wayward nature had led him to this moment and now his only chance of redemption lay in his own suffering.

He turned off into the deserted station and along the platform towards Brunel's last great masterpiece, the Royal Albert railway bridge, which spanned the Tamar River. Slipping behind one of the great stanchions, he soon heard what he had been waiting for. The bridge shuddered and the rails seemed to come alive with the approach of a train. He watched as a massive black engine, hauling its load of carriages, began its inexorable crawl towards him. The sight filled him with dread - a great, snorting beast, belching smoke and fire, confirming his lifelong terror of trains. His heart lurched as the black monster filled his vision, roared through his brain and burst his ears with noise. It drew level with him and, as it did so, he closed his eyes and fell beneath its wheels.

Part Two

London, 1950s

Chapter 6

Tremayne Jago lounged on the divan in Claire Braithwaite's sitting room, listening to Claire in the kitchen and the soothing sounds of the Chico Hamilton Quintet on the radiogram. She came in with two steaming cups of coffee and put one down beside him. "Just time for this before the concert," she said. She took the tickets out of her handbag. "Chris Barber, Saturday, 30th October, front row stalls."

"How could I forget," he grinned. "You haven't stopped talking about it for weeks." He took her in his arms, softly stroking her breasts. She began to sigh and raised her mouth to his, kissing him hungrily before pushing him away.

"Oh, you!" she groaned. "It's always the same, I can't say no!"

"Don't, then!" he said, pushing her down on the divan.

She was silenced by his caresses and clung to him greedily, wrapping herself around him so that their bodies merged and they lay oblivious of everything but their need of each other. Somehow, she always felt that sex didn't mean the same for Tremayne, but tried to convince herself she was exclusive to him. He filled her world and held her spellbound, with his dark good looks, and black, expressive eyes. Lingering and intimate eyes, yet possessing a haunted quality. She knew that there was a part of him that was intensely private, but mostly he was happy-go-lucky, with an eager anticipation, which endeared him to others.

He stirred from her, kissed her affectionately and arose with the lithe grace which she adored. A delicious languor spread through her body. He grinned at her. "What about the concert now?" he joked. "Forgotten that, or shall we just be late?"

As always after lovemaking he was friendly, affectionate, but never lover-like, tender.

"Give me a minute," she replied, trying to hide her disappointment. She stood in the bathroom and looked at herself critically in the full-length mirror. She was shapely and firm and, at 19, only a year older than Tremayne.

He was waiting by the front door as she came out. The sight of him sent a renewed thrill through her, but he was already opening the door to usher her through.

They were late, of course, and hurried to their seats. Bertie King and the Chris Barber band were playing "Skokian" and people were stomping and clapping all around them. She snuggled close to Tremayne, savouring his closeness and the memory of their lovemaking. He gave her a brief, happy smile, already engrossed in the music, the lovemaking put away in another compartment. That was his gift, she reflected, and her tragedy.

The next day Tremayne caught a train from Victoria down to Surrey without Claire. He felt guilty leaving her, but he hadn't been home for weeks. It was like the return of the Prodigal Son whenever he went home - a huge meal in his honour, the best china, everything just right.

He let his thoughts drift as the train rattled on, past Battersea Power Station and through the maze of Clapham Junction. He was looking forward to seeing his sister, Sally, too. She was 18 months older and inclined to boss him. She said he was "bohemian" and that he looked like a refugee from an art school, but everyone wanted to look "dead bo" or you weren't in and black was everyone's colour.

He didn't know why, but he had been feeling odd lately,

disturbed by strange fantasies. When he was away from Claire he longed for her. Or for sex. The two were inextricable and he felt some shame. She had enslaved him and gratified him for weeks. Perversely, he felt she made herself too available and it tainted the relationship. He knew he was being hypocritical, but there was a part of him, a deep well, which longed for a different fulfilment. The feeling remained on the edge of consciousness, like a movement on the periphery of vision, tantalisingly close, but never tangible. The yearning for it occupied him more and more, and the elusiveness of it filled him with despair.

The train slowed down and drew into the station. The place was quiet, immersed in the usual Sunday inertia. Windows were open to the mild April air and the sounds of "Family Favourites" mingled with the smell of Sunday roasts. The leafy London suburb of Wallington was conventional, but for Tremayne the place was the catharsis he needed. His parents' house was on the bend of a typical street, rows of Edwardian houses, bordered by lines of elegant old plane trees and fronted by neat gardens.

His mother, red-faced from flying round her hot little kitchen, was dishing up as Tremayne walked through the back door. She looked up and smiled fondly. "Just in time," she observed, placing a dish of roast potatoes on the table before giving him a hug. She held him away from her, noticing the slightly drawn mouth and the tired look around his eyes.

"More late nights?" she asked, lightly. She guessed the kind of life Tremayne led in London, but she was realistic enough to know that times changed. It was little wonder his life was so aimless when he had nothing to aim for. She wished he would get a job instead of living on National Assistance, but he always said there was nothing at the Labour Exchange. She sighed inwardly and for the umpteenth time wondered if she should interfere.

"Late nights? Not many!" Tremayne kissed her cheek then turned away, unwilling to explain his absences. He was tired, but the reason was not wholly Claire, more, his own restless spirit.

"Here, make yourself useful, and take the plates in," his mother said, handing him the oven cloth. Margherita Jago was still a handsome woman, dark like her son, a large expansive woman by nature as well as aspect. She was a woman of elegant tastes and this was reflected in her home - clean, unfussy lines, and solid oak dining furniture, a present given to her and Edward for their wedding in 1933. On the walls hung several of her oil paintings, scenes of wild Cornish moorland and distant purple hills, shaggy moorland ponies and tiny stone cottages surrounded by brilliant gardens. She was proud of her Cornish heritage and had named Tremayne after a village near Launceston. She had longed to bring up her children in the freedom of the Cornish countryside, but Edward had been offered a job in London after the war, and they had moved to the pleasant suburb of Wallington. After the children were settled in school, she had worked part-time as a typist in London for an Oxford Street store, travelling the short distance every day by train.

"Where's Sal?" Tremayne asked, laying plates on the cork mats.

His mother followed him with the vegetables. "Gone to post a letter. She'll be back any minute." She put fresh linen serviettes at each place, then stood back to survey the table. Tremayne sighed contentedly. This was what he had come home for, to see the old familiar things, become immersed in the ordinary, everyday domestic pattern. This was a balm to his spirit.

His father came in, followed by Sally, who gave her brother an affectionate hug. "Hi, good to see you! Hmm! This looks good. How's Claire?"

"Claire's fine," answered Tremayne shortly, and helped himself to potatoes.

Sally looked at him. "Things getting too serious?"

He smiled. "Maybe it's time to move on, I don't know."

"You're too young to go steady. You shouldn't miss your chances."

"Don't worry!" Tremayne assured her. "I don't!"

His father looked across the table with raised eyebrows, mildly amused by his offspring. "I'm sure Tremayne knows what he's doing," he said. He was very much like Tremayne in build, smallish, with fine features. But there the resemblance ended, for he was fair with blue eyes and a fresh complexion, like his daughter.

His parents wanted him to stay. He agreed straight away, dismissing the thought of Claire waiting for him. He knew the uneasiness would return later, but for now he could sit with his family, play cards and listen to the glorious strains of the Jupiter symphony, pouring from the radiogram. Even his father, normally fanatical about listening to Mozart in silence, was relaxed, and humming along with the record. His family had missed him, they accepted him without question or censure, and he needed them.

He fell into a comfortingly familiar bed that night, and for once he was at peace. He stayed a week, telephoning Claire to explain his absence and listening, unmoved to her pleas for his return. He was unwilling to go back until he had done everything he wanted to do - visited relations, listened to his mother and Sally playing Marche Militaire in duet until the piano thundered and rocked, taken the two golden retrievers for walks in the park and accompanied his father to the cricket match.

He caught the late Friday evening train to Town, his mother's exhortations ringing in his ears. "Take care and keep warm, nights are still chilly! And don't forget to ring! Come back soon!"

Claire was cool, but tension was forgotten in the heat of seeing her.

They didn't go out for two days. He awoke on the third feeling jaded and despairing. He knew in that moment that he would have to end the relationship and that, in some inexplicable way, she made him feel worse about himself, not better. He found her sitting at her dressing table, plaiting her thick fair hair and winding the plait on top of her head. He stood behind her, putting his hands on her shoulders and looking into her eyes in the mirror. She smiled at him, unsuspecting.

"You're beautiful, Claire," he said, softly, and meant it. She put her head on one side, squeezing his hand against her cheek. "You're only saying that because it's true!" she joked, then faltered as she saw his face. He seemed to be gazing right through her with a look of deep sadness. She turned at once, alarmed. "Why the long face?"

He shifted his eyes and went to sit on the end of the bed. She came and knelt in front of him. "Look," she said, gently. "If you're unhappy, tell me." She waited while he struggled with himself.

"That's the trouble, I just don't know," he burst out at last. "There's a part of me that seems, well ... wrong." He dropped his head onto his hands.

"The part I can't reach?" she asked, suddenly very still.

He didn't answer.

"So I'm beautiful one minute and make you unhappy the next, is that it?" she said and he could hear her voice thickening with tears.

He looked at her wretchedly. "It's not your fault, Claire, it's mine. I seem to be chasing something and I don't know what it is. And you are beautiful, I meant that!"

Claire sat back on her heels, but continued to clasp his hands. Her own were shaking and a terrible fear was sweeping through her. She was losing him, and her mind shrieked with bitter words, but she said nothing.

Tremayne got up from the bed and went to stand by the open window, looking down into the street. Moments passed and neither of them spoke. Then he said in a low voice, "It's as if there's something just out of my reach and the faster I try to catch it, the more elusive it becomes."

She waited, still saying nothing, and the silence seemed to encourage him. "All I know is that it isn't just sexual fulfilment that I need."

Despite herself, she smiled ruefully. "Most people need more than just sex, Tremayne! They usually find mutual satisfaction in other areas of their lives, too. And I do love you."

He gestured faintly. "I know. That's part of the trouble. For a while I thought that was what I wanted too. I should get a job, but I can't seem to settle. Or maybe I just need to grow up." He smiled faintly, hoping she would understand, but he couldn't explain to her what he didn't really understand himself.

She wasn't sure how to comfort him. She tried again. "Perhaps we could have a break from each other. It might help you to sort things out."

He wanted her to rail at him, tell him to go to hell. Anything to let him off the hook. He was a coward and he despised himself for it.

As if she read his thoughts she got up from the floor and came to stand beside him. "I'm not going to make this easy for you, Tremayne. I can't. You've just broken my heart! I thought things were perfect between us. I'm trying to understand, but I can't even imagine life without you now. We're a couple in everyone's eyes, too!"

"Then people shouldn't jump to conclusions!" he cried, stiffly. "We've only known each other a few months! It would take longer than that for me to be sure!"

He was immediately sorry. She drew in her breath as if he had slapped her. She knew now that it was over. Better that they part friends. He was contrite in an instant and would have swept her back into his arms, but she stood away from him. "Let's stay friends, Tremayne," she said gently. "I couldn't bear to part anything else."

He nodded, relief flooding through him, and sorrow too, but he could no more deny his innermost feelings than he could cease breathing.

"I suppose I'd better leave … go now, then?" He looked at her hesitantly, part of him still unwilling to make the final break. She nodded and turned away. He collected his few things from the bedroom. She was waiting by the front door and held up her face. They kissed, not as lovers, but as two people who have come to a sad understanding. "Keep in touch," she said, and he nodded eagerly, grateful that she was making this easy. "You bet!" he answered, but they both knew it was only words.

That night Tremayne stayed at Bill Porter's studio off the King's Road, where he knew he would be welcome and where he could take his own time to reflect. Bill listened then observed. "Got off lightly, old boy. Nice girl. Every reason to feel blighted."

"I know!" Tremayne was shamefaced. "But it was getting too serious. I'm too young to be tied down. I need my freedom!"

Bill quirked an eyebrow. "Freedom? What's that? Let me know when you've worked it out. I'll have some!"

Tremayne sighed. Bill was right. To be totally free would mean to be rootless, drifting. He didn't want that, either. To Bill the subject was closed. He was usually too immersed in his painting to concern himself with the problems of others, which he couldn't solve anyway.

Tremayne did nothing but sleep and eat, watch Bill painting and listen to his tuneless whistle which accompanied the endless jazz records. He envied Bill's uncomplicated view of life. Bill was a born bachelor and lived only for his art. He was preparing for an exhibition and nothing took precedence over that. Nothing except his pint. After the natural light had faded he would fling his brushes down, put on his threadbare duffel coat and walk to the Six Bells to listen to the jazz.

Tremayne loved its unconventional atmosphere. It was crowded and they had some difficulty seeing across the bar. A group of CND supporters, with their banners resting against the bar, were arguing with some of the regulars. "We march from Aldermaston to London because we believe in disarmament," one of them said. "It's worth standing up for your principles when the world's at stake."

Tremayne found himself agreeing, but Bill was scanning the females. He never involved himself in intellectual argument, thinking it all a waste of energy. Tremayne went to get himself and Bill another pint. A group of people at the bar parted at his approach and he caught sight of a small blonde, with a cigarette in a long holder, trickling smoke from her mouth in a deliberately provocative fashion. He winked at her. "Drink?" he asked, delighted at her boldness.

"Why not!" she answered casually.

She was lightweight, he knew it. No fulfilment here, but

live for the moment, no strings. He'd had his fill of strings. She snuggled up to him. It was getting late, did he fancy a coffee?

Bill shrugged amiably, but felt it expedient to offer mild advice. "Careful, old boy. Thought you were retiring from the fray?"

Tremayne grinned. "Did I say that? That'll be the day! Don't worry, this is strictly a one-nighter!"

He left the pub with his arm round the little blonde. "What's your name?" she giggled, rosy lips parted. He liked her and the one night grew into several. She was good company, always ready for sex and fun. There was no side to her, and he never heard her say an unkind word about anyone in the short time he knew her. She called herself by the unlikely name of Free. "Because that's what I am," she told him. He never discovered her real name, but it didn't matter. She shared rooms with a friend called Pat, an attractive, willowy blonde. Free said that Pat was involved with someone, but it wasn't going well.

"Let's make up a foursome," she suggested one evening while they were making toast in her boxlike kitchen.

"Later!" Tremayne mumbled, stuffing down the last mouthful.

She giggled. "I didn't mean tonight!"

"Good," he said, "because I've got something else planned for tonight!" He picked her up and carried her across the hallway to the bedroom. She put up a mock battle, kicking and squealing, but she was practically undressed before they reached the bed, flinging her underwear to the left and right and smothering his face with buttery kisses.

Her ever-present eagerness inflamed him, so that his fire consumed them both and their passion became like a competition, each vying for supremacy and there was nothing but the rush of the oncoming torrent. But when the waves crashed he became separated from her, as always, and the reason for his need was not her at all, but a dark compunction which overwhelmed him. He was alone and the darkness swooped and clung, draining him, sucking the very essence from him. He had fed so often at her temple, worshipped at her shrine, yet just as the tide bore down, all thought of her fled his mind and the culminating flood carried him away and cast him, like flotsam, on an alien shore. Fire and water. A consummate deluge which doused his very spirit.

In the receding ebb, while he struggled with the aftermath of dissatisfaction, she began the inconsequential chatter which guaranteed the intrusion of the world, again suggesting a foursome. Only half aware, he agreed to it.

They arranged it for the following weekend. Tremayne and Free arrived early at the pub. Pat had gone to meet her boyfriend. "He's rather shy," Free explained. "At least," she paused, frowning, "I think he is. He doesn't say much."

"How did they meet?" he asked.

"They didn't really meet," Free explained. "She sucked up to him in the pub. I don't think he's that interested. He's devastating to look at. I wouldn't mind a shot myself!"

"Hey, wait till I've finished, if you don't mind!" Tremayne protested in mock annoyance.

"Okay!" Free giggled. She was nestling into him, nibbling his ear, when Pat and her boyfriend walked into the bar.

Free introduced them and Tremayne knew in an instant that he had met someone with whom he was linked, and that this moment had been inevitable. Here was a man of such brooding intensity and with a glance so piercing, that it felt to Tremayne that he looked right in his soul. It was a glance he came to know well and a moment he never forgot.

Chapter 7

"Tremayne, this is Benedict and Pat," said Free and clasped her friend in a hug. Tremayne felt his hand taken in a strong clasp, saw black eyes raking him and felt at once weakened and exhilarated by Benedict's powerful magnetism.

Benedict was not a voluble man, but when he spoke his words were tinged with an irony which puzzled Tremayne. He began to wonder why Benedict had come, then reasoned that small talk was probably not high on the list of his priorities, although he was polite at all times.

To Tremayne's surprise, Benedict readily agreed to another foursome and they met several evenings running until Free complained that she was getting too involved and she felt tied. Tremayne felt rejected. It was not a nice feeling. No more tumblings in bed, no more drinking at that blissful well or feeling those practised hands arouse him to fever pitch. He thought of Claire, so different from Free, so adoring. His words came back to haunt him. Still, there was no going back now.

"I did warn you," Free said. "I've got to have my freedom!"

"Have it, then!" he responded, crossly.

"Come on!" she chided. "You and I were never forever were we?" She went over to him and kissed him, her soft mouth parted, tongue searching for a pardon. He was sullen. His pride demanded this moment even if he did agree with her. He made a last grab, but she dodged out of the way and he gave up. They parted on good terms. "Just put me down to experience!" she said, airily.

From then on it was just a threesome. The tone of the evenings was light, but even so it was clear that Benedict was restrained and uncomfortable with Pat. It was equally clear that she wanted things to develop. Tremayne wondered if they were lovers. Pat flirted with Benedict, not in the way of intimate people, but with a kind of coy naivety, giving Benedict little squeezes, to which he responded with startled surprise. She grew possessive while Benedict grew increasingly remote.

One evening Tremayne arrived at the Six Bells to find Benedict on his own. The two drank in silence for a while, then Tremayne said, "Where's Pat?"

"Who?" Benedict asked, so innocently that Tremayne burst out laughing. "For heaven's sake! Who do you think I mean?"

Benedict had the grace to look sheepish. "Sorry, I'm afraid I was miles away. We just decided that we don't have that much in common, that's all!"

You decided, Tremayne thought, but he said nothing. Benedict seemed much more relaxed, cordial even, with no hint of that brooding intensity of their first meeting. Tremayne realised that he knew little or nothing about him and took advantage of the moment to say, "Tell me about yourself, Benedict. We've been meeting here night after night and I hardly know you."

Benedict seemed caught off guard, but after only a slight hesitation said, with a tinge of sarcasm, "I'm not that interesting. I'm 20, adopted, but I traced my real mother, Rose Truman, and that's the name I use. She died a few months after I traced her, but we became quite close in that time. She told me I was born at the London Hospital, which I knew from my birth certificate, and I was her only child. She never married and in 1934 that was a terrible stigma. I don't know anything about my father, she never spoke of him or her family. I don't think they knew I existed, she was still too ashamed."

"She must have been a very strong person," Tremayne said.

"She needed to be. I know that she was educated in Sussex and came to London to work afterwards. I didn't press her for information, it made no difference to me. But I was glad to meet her, if only to get rid of my adoptive parents' name."

He caught Tremayne's surprised look and smiled faintly. "There's little love lost between us. Besides adopting myself and two others, Jack and Angela, they fostered regularly, too, probably for the money. My childhood was filled with a strange assortment of bedfellows - literally! Beds were short in our house! However, we did go to Mass each Sunday, the perfect Catholic family!"

"And that's put you right off religion?" Tremayne smiled.

"Not at all! It's been a comfort, the family I never had and I'm a helper at the church. God is good to me." Benedict ran his fingers through his black hair. "It's better buried. Resurrections aren't always a good thing!" He smiled thinly. "My parents went out, to the pub mostly. They left us locked in cupboards. We spent hours in the dark waiting for them to come home …" His voice trailed off. Tremayne waited and after a moment Benedict continued, "I found it easy to withdraw from them. I read a lot, anything I could get my hands on, I trained my mind, cut myself off from all the unpleasantness of life. Eventually, I could switch off at will."

He stopped abruptly and looked at Tremayne, but the younger man didn't speak. At last Benedict sighed deeply and drained his glass. "There's not much else. I came down from Cambridge with a double first, don't ask me how. Despite my parents, not because of them. They didn't think education important. I didn't go back home. Perhaps I should be more understanding, but we're all hypocrites when it comes down to it."

Benedict seemed to protect himself with a veneer of aloofness, yet there seemed little of the escapee about him.

He appeared to face the world supported by a core of inner strength.

Tremayne watched the chiselled face, the veiled eyes, and wondered about the real man underneath. Something of the man's inner turbulence communicated itself to him, something disturbing and quite exceptional. To have turned such negativity around demonstrated a strength of purpose unusual in a man so young.

"I bet you're a Piscean!" he said suddenly, breaking the spell.

Benedict turned a searching gaze upon him. "You think so?" he asked, sardonically. "Are you a psychic or something?"

"No, but I find people fit into their star signs quite well."

"Star signs!" Benedict was scathing. "You'll be saying the moon's in my seventh heaven next! As far as I'm concerned I'm a product of my upbringing, that's all there is to it!"

"That, and a bit more," said Tremayne. "Are we a product of our genes or are we a product of our experience? What about nature versus nurture?"

"I can hardly answer that, since I'm only familiar with the nurture side."

"But that doesn't make sense," objected Tremayne. "After all, look at your adoptive parents. Not interested in education, yet you come down with a double first, just like that!"

"I concede the point," Benedict smiled. "But, of course, I could only be convinced if I met my biological family, which is hardly likely to happen! Now tell me about yourself. Where did you get that outlandish name, for a start!"

"I have my mother to thank for that," grinned Tremayne. "I'm named after a Cornish village. My parents are from Cornwall and I was born there. We lived there until I was nine. I loved it. It's beautiful, remote and mysterious, especially the north coast, like another land. In fact, in some ways I used to feel more at home in Cornwall than I do here."

Their discussion continued into the night and was the first of many. Tremayne found himself spilling his heart out to Benedict, in whom he found the fulfilment of a spiritual dimension previously unsatisfied. Benedict lived in rooms in the Edgeware Road, over a small shop. Tremayne found himself spending more and more time there, yet he hesitated in sharing his inner turmoil. There was still a private side to Benedict's nature which brooked no intrusion.

After a short respite in Wallington, he returned to London, as restless as ever. He met up with Benedict in the Six Bells. The sight of the tall, brooding figure at the bar, dark head bent politely towards the man at his side, gave Tremayne a comforting feeling of security and consistency.

Benedict turned and Tremayne's greeting died on his lips, his eyes drawn to what Benedict was wearing. Above his casual clothes Benedict wore a clerical collar and as his eyes met Tremayne's a grave smiled passed over the thin face.

Tremayne felt rooted to the spot. He stared, unable to take his eyes off it.

"Sorry," said Benedict, "I didn't realise it would be such a shock to you."

"Well, you told me you helped at the church, but I didn't know in what way." Tremayne said. "Look, can we talk? Not here, back at the flat. I just don't know where I am at the moment. I need to sort things out."

Once at the flat, Benedict pushed a coffee into Tremayne's hands and he sipped the dark liquid gratefully. He told Benedict everything - the restless dissatisfaction with life, his promiscuity and the rootlessness.

Benedict listened soberly, only moving to refill Tremayne's cup. Then he said, "Look, at the moment you're aimless and drifting. You need to have a goal of some sort."

Tremayne sighed. "I'm a bit of a drifter, I suppose, but I don't want to be."

"I can't offer any instant career solutions," Benedict said. "But there could be some help for your dissatisfaction. Why not come along to church with me next Sunday? Do you have any objection? You might find some peace there, then we could think this out rationally. You could stay here in the meantime."

Tremayne gave him a grateful glance. "Thanks, but I'm not sure about church. I think that's just a need to have a Big Parent tell us what to do. Someone we can run to if we've done something wrong, say sorry and feel better. It's more of a psychological need than a reality."

Benedict smiled. "Perhaps the problem lies in our human interpretation of what that Big Parent actually *is*. God is not just a controlling parent and we are not just naughty children. We all have free will. I see God as an inspiration who helps us come to our own conclusions. No amount of forcing can make anybody truly believe. We're all responsible for our own actions, whether we have a theology or not."

"But what about you?" Tremayne asked. "Why are you wearing that collar?"

"I'm a licensed reader at the church, a kind of novitiate, if you like. I've been catching up on my church duties while you've been away, that's all. In fact, it's my hope to become fully ordained one day, God willing. But I must test my vocation first."

"Was Pat one of the tests?" Tremayne asked.

"I would never say Pat was a test," Benedict smiled. "It was always platonic on my part. She knew that. There are others reasons, but I won't bore you with them now. In the meantime, you shall stay here."

Tremayne smiled, gratefully. "Thanks, Benedict, and yes, I'll come to church with you." He was rewarded by a smile of rare brilliance.

Sunday Mass was a blur of strange incantations and gestures, but as soon as he entered the church he experienced a feeling of oneness with the mystical beauty of the icons, the heady smell of incense and the spiritual fulfilment of a great need. Several times he glanced at the tall, remote figure at the altar - a Benedict he hardly recognised - but he quickly became immersed again and hardly noticed when Benedict appeared at last at his side. The experience affected him deeply. It struck his conscience. Impulsively, he embraced the Catholic philosophy with arms eager to seize redemption. Self-reproach led to an overwhelming guilt and hours studying the Bible. He knew he had so much to learn, so much time to make up.

In his feverish quest for the truth, he abandoned regular meals and found he couldn't sleep at night. Frequently, in the early hours, he was troubled by inexplicable visions and ceaselessly paced his bedroom floor, hoping for answers.

On his infrequent visits home, Margherita Jago became increasingly worried about his haggard appearance and weight loss. He seemed fanatical and she wished for a return to his old self.

When reasoning didn't get through, she became irritated, but he merely smiled and said, "I thought you'd be happy for me. Let me handle this my own way, Mother. There are many things I feel sorry about now and this is my way of making reparation."

"No-one's blaming you for anything!" she expostulated. "It's this man you've met. He's giving you these weird ideas! And you're not supposed to punish yourself in the process of redemption!"

He hugged her. "Oh, Mother, I'm not punishing myself, just clearing my head. Don't worry!" and he tweaked her cheek, reminding her so much of his father that she caught his hand and kissed it fearfully before turning away, unmollified.

Benedict worried about him, too, and in vain tried to explain that forgiveness first lay in self-forgiving. This was exactly what Benedict had feared - the over-zealous convert. Tremayne was so susceptible, so impressionable. "Forgive the cliché," Benedict said, drily. "But you would try the patience of a saint! This isn't what God wants of you. You haven't eaten properly for nearly a week now!"

Tremayne flashed him a look of scorn, before turning his face to the wall and saying, in a voice so quiet that Benedict could hardly hear it, "I hate myself!"

Benedict longed to comfort him, but forced his voice to be non-committal. "And you are doing everything to prove that by killing yourself?" he answered lightly. He got up and began to look through his collection of LPs, his hands shaking. Tremayne walked silently from the room. Benedict let the record fall and lowered his head into his hands. He was aware that they needed help. Perhaps one of the lay brothers, or Father O'Casey would counsel them if Tremayne agreed. He glanced at Tremayne's closed door, his dark eyes troubled. Ahead lay a challenge which would take every ounce of his strength and self-control. Tomorrow he would telephone Margherita Jago, although they had never met. Perhaps she could offer some help. Sighing, he retrieved the record and placed it on the turntable. The sounds of the Trout Quintet filled the room and he stretched himself on the floor to ponder the problem afresh.

When she heard Benedict's voice on the phone the next day, Margherita was sharp. "Is Tremayne ill?" she asked at once.

Benedict reassured her. "Not exactly. But he could be better, that's why I'm phoning you. I need some help."

Her voice was bitter. "And who better to ask than his mother!"

He was silent for a second, disconcerted by her anger. "I suppose you blame me for all this?" he said. "It might seem that way to you, but Tremayne was heading for something. This might have come at the right time."

"It seems odd, though, doesn't it," she said, a challenging note in her voice, "that Tremayne's trouble only started when he began dabbling in all this Maryology?" She was immediately aware of how rude that sounded and fell silent, now angry with herself. But to her, worship was plain and straightforward and she was a plain spoken woman.

"He needs an anchor," Benedict said, after a slight pause. "Something to hold on to. I only want what's best for him."

She clung to her defences. "We're his anchor," she replied, frostily. "What are families for? And I don't need you to tell me Tremayne isn't settled. If you really want my advice, leave him to snap out of it. He's always been impulsive and he'll get over it. He's only 18, he's got plenty of time ahead of him."

Benedict sensed that she was more worried than she cared to admit. He had no wish to offend. "Of course!" he agreed, "and Tremayne knows his family will always support him. But families can't always satisfy a spiritual search or an intellectual realisation."

She knew everyone had to find their own path in life, but she resented being told so by Benedict. "I'm sure if Tremayne comes home for a while he'll recover," she said, less certainly.

Benedict stepped into the gap of her wavering resolution and applied all his considerable will to the situation. "He needs us both," he said gently. "As to the church, surely it can't harm him?"

There was a pause, then Margherita said, "I'll come up straight away. Perhaps I can persuade him to come back with me for a while."

"Shall we wait awhile?" Benedict suggested. "Let me try

first, please. I've met similar problems before."

She declined to say that she wasn't surprised, but answered in a more relaxed tone, "You'll ring me, then?"

"Of course," he replied.

She replaced the receiver, feeling somewhat comforted. Her fears were aroused, but her son was young and strong. He would soon come to his senses, she was sure.

So she was dismayed to hear, less than a week later, Benedict's voice over the line. "Could you get up to Town? I'm afraid Tremayne's not at all well and I think you ought to be here."

In the Edgeware Road flat her son lay drenched in sweat and muttering to the phantoms that peopled his room, clutching Benedict's arm and gabbling hoarsely about dead babies. Benedict could only wipe the sweaty face and murmur, "There are no babies here, Tremayne, only me. You're quite safe."

Tremayne stared at him and said in a voice so strange that Benedict hardly knew him, "What about the babies, eh? What about them? Are *they* all dead, too?"

It took a moment for Benedict to notice the odd emphasis as he tried to force water between the parched lips. But as Tremayne fell back on the pillows, the inflexion penetrated and instinctively Benedict touched his crucifix and began to pray as he had never prayed before.

Chapter 8

The day was dry, dusty, little frissons of wind sending spirals of litter back and forth along the pavements.

From the window of his flat, Benedict watched Margherita Jago as she stood on the pavement below. She had an air of grace and dignity and he would have known her anywhere from her resemblance to Tremayne. She was well dressed, perhaps overdressed for London these days, and it was easy to see that she was an infrequent visitor to Town. It endeared her to him. He suddenly wanted to make a good impression. He turned from the window to anticipate her knock.

She was standing directly in front of the door as he opened it, and their eyes met immediately, hers never flinching from his face, his seeking the understanding and friendship he sensed were there. They summed each other up. She saw the tall, enigmatic figure she had expected to see from Tremayne's description and, unexpectedly, a naked vulnerability.

He reached forward, took her hand and drew her inside saying, "Hello, I'm Benedict. Thank you so much for coming up."

"Your telephone call frightened me," she replied. "Is this a sudden relapse? I thought there was no panic. At least, that's what you said a week ago." Her words came tumbling over each other, until she laughed a trifle nervously. "I'm sorry, you must think me very rude. All these questions!"

"Not at all," Benedict replied. "Naturally, you wish to know about Tremayne. And there was no panic ... then. Tremayne has actually eaten a little. That's partly why this is all a bit odd."

"What is?" she asked.

"I don't think it's physical anymore. I think it's spiritual."

This sounded like nonsense to her, but she merely said, "Yes, but is he having any treatment? You should have insisted he see a doctor!"

Benedict answered gently, "Look, let's go upstairs. We can talk up there and perhaps you would like some tea?"

She nodded and they began the long climb. "I'm afraid it's five flights up," Benedict apologised, but she only said, "I can manage it."

The flat was tiny, but furnished with only the necessary items, giving the impression of space. Margherita wanted to see her son straight away, but he was asleep and she needed to get the measure of this man first.

Benedict took her into the small lounge and showed her to an old, but comfortable, studio couch. She waited while he went into the kitchen to fill the kettle, then he came back and sat beside her.

"You were asking about treatment," he said. "Well, first of all Tremayne refused to see a doctor. Nothing I said made any difference. His idea of atonement. So far, all he's had is complete rest and some herbal remedies. He's been rootless, drifting, and people of his susceptible nature readily embrace a new theology. It isn't uncommon."

She answered, somewhat scornfully, "Hardly new! Tremayne had a perfectly sound theology and a fine example from us!" She resented the role Benedict had assumed, and the implied criticism of Tremayne's instability.

"Forgive me," he said, "but it might be an impulse, something that will burn itself out. I've no wish to influence Tremayne, but people change and in Tremayne's case he's overdone it and brought himself to the brink of exhaustion."

She felt quite disconcerted. It seemed that Benedict had wisdom beyond his years and now that she had met him, she understood how easily Tremayne had become bedazzled. There was a strange fascination about Benedict, something unfathomable, indefinable. And yet she was still certain that all Tremayne needed was some good, old-fashioned nursing.

"Why don't you go in and see him now?" Benedict suggested. "I'll bring you a cup of tea when it's ready." He rose and led her along a narrow hallway to a small room at the end and opened the door. "I think he's asleep again," he whispered.

She walked past him into the room. Tremayne lay sleeping, curled into the foetal position away from her. The bed was tidy, the bedspread pulled up underneath his arms. His hands were resting peacefully beneath his chin, fingers pointing upwards. They reminded her of Durer's picture of the Praying Hands which hung over the piano at home. At once, she wished she hadn't seen the similarity and she was uncomfortable. On the bedside table was a large flask.

Benedict appeared, carrying a tray on which was a pot of tea and a plate of plain biscuits. She waved the biscuits aside, but gratefully accepted the tea. He saw her glance resting on the flask and explained in a low voice, "I've been giving Tremayne some herbal drinks. They are very restorative. That is camomile, especially good for calming."

She could see the good in this man. "You've been kind to him," she said, "although I'm not sure I would have resorted to herbal concoctions. However, if you think it's working ..."

He glanced at the sleeping Tremayne. "I'm sure it helps. But, of course, it's not the complete answer. That lies within Tremayne himself. It will be a realisation and when it comes he will start to recover." He spoke unequivocally and she was compelled to believe him.

He left her alone with Tremayne. She was loathe to disturb

her son. She moved quietly to the window and looked out over the London skyline. To the right lay Hyde Park with Marble Arch, then the Bayswater Road beginning its journey out to Queensway. Her gaze swept back towards the West End, where she had worked at 32 Cavendish Square, the studio once owned by George Romney, where he painted his famous picture of Lady Hamilton. Looking left towards the City, she could see the great gleaming dome of St Paul's, which was visible from the High Street at Wallington. It was like seeing an old friend from a different angle. She realised, with a start, that she felt completely at home here.

The sleeping figure on the bed stirred and Tremayne rolled onto his back and opened his eyes. For an instant he stared unbelievingly, then he whispered, strangely, "Is that you? Are you real?"

She flew to the bed and gathered him close, holding him as she had not done since he was a child. He returned her embrace fiercely. "Couldn't you have contacted me, Tremayne?" she asked, gently. "And why haven't you seen a doctor? Perhaps there is some treatment you should be having, something to help you!"

He sank back against the headboard while she propped his pillows behind him. Although pale and drawn, he had clearly been well cared for. Benedict had been a meticulous nurse, the sheets were fresh, the room pristine. She thought of Benedict, his concern and his involvement with Tremayne. There were unanswered questions, but she now knew that the shoulder he offered her son was unequivocal and unerring and that it would be offered, come what may.

As if he read her thoughts, Tremayne sighed and spoke. "Benedict phoned you, I suppose? I knew he would. And I didn't want a doctor. Please don't ask any questions, Mum. It's all so complicated and I feel so mixed up that I couldn't give you any answers if I tried!"

"Well, I'm here now," she replied. "You'll soon be better. And Sally will be able to come up and see you next week. She's in Paris at the moment, she flew from Lyd yesterday, cheap flight, but long train journey to Paris."

His eyes were closed and he made no comment about Sally. Instead he said, childlike, "You'll stay, Mum, won't you? I'd like you to." The hand in hers gave a faint squeeze and she bent and kissed him. "I'm hoping to," she answered. "Perhaps there's a hotel nearby."

"That'd be great," he said and seemed to drop into a doze. She pulled up the bedspread then smoothed his hair away from his flushed face, before tiptoeing from the room.

She found Benedict in his tiny kitchenette, preparing food, measuring and mixing precise amounts of ingredients, sweet smelling herbs and spices and fresh vegetables.

"I was wondering if there was somewhere I could stay, anywhere you could recommend," she ventured, hardly daring to interrupt the punctilious operation going on before her.

"Of course," he replied, without looking up. "It's all arranged. I have already made up my bed. You shall stay here for as long as you wish."

"Oh, but what about you!" she exclaimed. "I really don't want to take your bed."

"Nevertheless, you will have it," he answered, matter-of-factly. "And you're welcome. I've slept on plenty of settees in my time, and I have a bedroll. It will do me very well. You are not to worry about me, so please don't be concerned."

She saw that he spoke without ambiguity and that he had simply made a decision that was best for them all. He washed his hands at the sink, then motioned her to follow him down the tiny passage to a room which overlooked the back of the house. The room was spotless, and the freshly made up bed was covered by a red candlewick quilt. Other than that small touch of colour, it was a spartan room. Two rows of bookcases stood under the window. To the right was a washstand with a pitcher and next to it a wardrobe. On the opposite wall was a chest of drawers with a kneehole opening, which doubled as a desk. She could imagine this serious and intense man reading and studying in this room.

"The bathroom is the next floor down," Benedict explained. "There's plenty of hot water in the geyser and you can use the pitcher if you need to." He left her to unpack. It didn't take her long. She had purposely travelled light.

She stayed ten days. During that time Sally returned from France and her bright and breezy optimism did them all good. Even Benedict unbent. She could see that he fascinated her daughter and she wondered afresh that someone so young could incorporate such maturity and mystery.

Sally called Benedict The Monk. "It's what you should be!" she told him in her forthright way. "Either that, or a priest!" They were spending an evening playing cards. Tremayne, now looking much better for his mother's loving attention, glanced quickly at Benedict. But he was smiling, unoffended.

"It's what I intend to be, God willing."

"And all things being equal!" Sally laughed.

"All things are rarely equal," Benedict replied, "for if they were, there would be no challenge!"

Sally looked up quickly. "You're a challenge!" she said, bluntly.

There was an awkward pause, but Benedict's black eyes shone. "Am I?" he said, keeping his voice steady.

"Yes," Sally continued, "you've got 'Hands Off' notices hanging all round you. That's the challenge!"

Benedict rose lithely to his feet and threw his cards on the coffee table. "There you are! Now you see my full hand, no tricks!" he proclaimed, dramatically.

"No, but I've still got some trumps, so beware!" Sally said darkly and nudged Tremayne in the ribs.

His mother glanced at him. "Tremayne's looking tired," she said. "I'll make some cocoa, then you'd better get to the station, Sal."

Sally was immediately contrite. "Sorry Trem! Didn't mean to wear you out! You should've said."

Within half an hour she had caught a cab to Victoria and Tremayne was asleep.

Every day he improved, although there was a curiously poised look about him, and sometimes he turned his head sharply as if he heard something the others did not. Margherita found that he would eat soup, and little else at first. She thickened it with potatoes and onions and she was rewarded by ever increasing amounts. When Sally next visited she brought her brother bananas and chocolate biscuits. Margherita was doubtful about them, feeling they were too rich and a whispered argument took place in the kitchenette, until Sally convinced her mother that Tremayne's favourite foods might be his catalyst. He ate some of the biscuits immediately, followed by banana custard, a combination which made Margherita cross her fingers and hope. It was a small victory.

Sally loved her brother dearly. For his sake she hid her feelings, but the sight of his emaciated face had horrified her. She spent as much time with him as she could, reading to him, talking, sometimes just sitting by him whilst he slept. She was thankful to see him grow daily more strong. His colour was returning to normal, the hectic flush subsiding.

There were many books in the flat, a wide variety from biographies to anthologies. Tremayne's favourite poet was Louis McNeice. Poetry was not Sally's idea of relaxation, but she read good naturedly to Tremayne until she began to feel heartily sick of poetry. His favourite, the strong and beautiful "Prayer Before Birth" she thought unnecessarily macabre. But she was never to know how exactly those words described Tremayne's sudden fear of the world and his instinct to hide in the womb-like sanctuary of the flat. His was not a fear *"that the human race may with tall walls wall me"* but a need. And when she read the lines, *"...forgive me, for the sins that in me the world shall commit..."* he understood entirely his part in the downfall of a perfect world.

Benedict's library reflected the man, ranging from medieval mysticism to the modern philosophers. Tremayne became absorbed in reading, especially in the Bertrand Russell's "Mysticism and Logic" essays, which Benedict had recommended, with their conflicting arguments between science and metaphysics, fulfilling in great measure his own inner questioning. Benedict was relieved to see the nervous hands stilled over the pages of a book, and the beginnings of Tremayne's peculiarly intense and charming smile enhancing his expressive eyes. Yet he knew that there was still something not quite right. Tremayne still looked up sharply now and then, as if someone had spoken, or as if he had heard or glimpsed something. At these times he seemed disorientated and Benedict had had to repeat himself several times. Benedict knew that fasting sometimes produced hallucinations, but Tremayne was eating almost normally now and had put on some weight.

Catechism had been put to one side, but the day came when Tremayne mentioned it himself. "I'm well enough now," he told Benedict one evening when they were relaxing over cards. They were on their own. Margherita had gone back to Wallington the day before, but not before persuading Tremayne to take some sedatives the doctor had prescribed.

"I feel ready to tackle it again. What do you think?" Benedict returned evenly, "That you must decide for yourself. My only concern is that you don't go at everything like a fat man at a party. I shouldn't think continuing catechism will harm you, only bouts of unexpiated conscience!"

Tremayne bit his lip. He knew he was impulsive, but he needed to continue. Part of him would starve without spiritual sustenance. Benedict was watching him closely. "Something on your mind?" he asked.

Tremayne hesitated, looking away. After a moment he said, "Of course I've got an unexpiated conscience. 'Man is born to trouble as surely as sparks fly upward.' "

"There's no sin that is unforgivable, providing you show true repentance," Benedict replied. "And the last thing you need is a Job's comforter. You're using religion as a stick to beat yourself with. Flagellation is out of date now, you know!"

Tremayne paused, biting his lip again. "There's something else, actually. I don't think I'm quite well yet. Nothing to stop me taking catechism, I'm sure, but it's just that …" he stopped, afraid of voicing his thoughts.

"Well, go on," Benedict prompted.

"I seem to be… well, seeing things!" Tremayne blurted. "Oh, I know it sounds strange, but it's true! I sometimes think I catch a glimpse of something… someone… I don't know …" he tailed off.

Benedict said slowly, "Could this be anything to do with a child?" he asked. "A baby, perhaps?"

Tremayne flashed him a surprised look, got up out of his chair and went to the window, hugging his folded arms and staring out at the London traffic. The day had been sultry and oppressive, one of those days, common in late June after a burst of unusually hot weather. Yellowish clouds were gathering on the horizon, casting an unnatural light over the city. A responding dullness suddenly echoed in Tremayne's heart and he wondered if the weather had been making him sensitive.

"How did you know?" he asked at last. "Yes, there is a baby. Or, rather, a woman with a baby. You frightened me for a minute, like the Oracle! Have I been talking in my sleep, then?"

Benedict went into the kitchenette. He filled the kettle at the sink and put it on the gas ring. They both needed some strong coffee. "Something like that," he called back. "But you were delirious, you know, and you did make rather an odd remark on one occasion about a baby. A dead baby, as I recall."

Tremayne came to stand in the doorway and when he spoke his voice was weary, resigned. "Well, this one isn't dead. It seems alive." He ran his fingers through his hair. "And so does the mother. At least, I assume it's the mother, and she has a terrible look on her face, a look of pain and anguish."

Benedict carried two cups into the living room and they sat down to drink. He thought for a while before answering. Tremayne still wasn't fully recovered. He needed reassurance, a prosaic explanation, and he would get one. "Do you recognise them?" he asked.

"No," Tremayne answered. "At least, I don't think so. There's something familiar about the girl, but I can't be sure. She's dressed in period costume, very elaborate, frills and bows, that sort of thing. She has a mass of auburn hair, very long and curly. She's young and pretty."

Benedict was startled. Tremayne had clearly had time to study the woman.

"She wears a bonnet," Tremayne was saying, gazing into the middle distance, as if he saw the woman. "The bonnet's a peach colour. Sometimes the child is looking at her and the woman smiles at it. But usually the baby is looking away, and then her face is full of sorrow."

Now Benedict was more than startled. He felt a prickle of fear. Tremayne was describing someone he had undoubtedly become familiar with, and yet he had said nothing until now. "How long has this been happening?" he asked. "Since you came here, or before?"

"Just since I've been here," Tremayne replied. "At first I put it down to my illness, but it's happened too often for comfort now. Is this house haunted, by the way?"

Benedict smiled faintly. "Not that I'm aware of. No unquiet spirits. In any case, it's no good thinking along those lines - poltergeists and the like."

Tremayne turned away. "Poltergeists!" he said impatiently. "I may have been ill, but I know what I saw and I tell you, it *is* haunting me!" His voice suddenly broke. "Tell me I'm not going mad! Maybe I should stop the sedatives?"

"You must finish the medication, that's the dosage," Benedict answered. He refused to accept any other explanation than the effect of illness on a volatile mind. Tremayne needed the help and comfort of prayer. That was the simple explanation and thus it was easy to soothe him. "I very much doubt that you're going mad. When you've stopped taking medication these things … visions … will disappear, you'll see."

But he was left with a faint stab of discomfort. How easy it was to get carried away and yet … the colours, the detail, the child, all so vivid to Tremayne. His thoughts dwelt on the vagaries of the human mind. For a minute he, too, had been willing to believe. Perhaps he needed Father O'Casey's advice just as much as Tremayne. He had neglected his spiritual nature lately in the pursuit of Tremayne's health.

He broke from his reverie to find Tremayne's eyes fixed on him with a look of such hopefulness and trust that he was struck to the heart and filled, as always, with an overwhelming tenderness. More than ever he knew that Tremayne had been sent to him and that his life would never be the same again.

Chapter 9

Father O'Casey was only too pleased to offer his counsel. A lost soul for the church. Besides, he recognised some of the devils in Tremayne. Many years ago there had been women sent to tempt him. He had succumbed. He was only human and the women had needed love to heal them. The sins were easily confessed, the good Lord had understood and forgiven him and the demons consigned to where they belonged. "I had to resist the temptations of Eve, believe me! It was me savin' grace that the Lord sent his saints to help me, and the sins of the flesh were banished," he told Tremayne comfortably, as they sat in his pleasant drawing room, drinking tea. In truth, he had almost forgotten those days, such a long time ago, all done with now.

"The good Lord'll guide ye. Ye've only to ask!" He let his contented gaze wander out through the open french doors to the charming rectory garden, colourful with pinks and scented lavender. Mysterious little paths disappeared round corners and led teasingly to nowhere. Huge ornate urns overflowed with syringa. A thick, high hedge surrounded the whole, creating an oasis in the heart of London.

Tremayne relaxed in the deep armchair and regarded Father O'Casey, truly a "wantowne and a merye", after a time-honoured tradition, his former sins of the flesh now substituted by the sin of gluttony, judging by his comfortable bulk. He had clearly achieved his own particular state of grace and now lived in obvious comfort, administered to by a devoted housekeeper and, in turn, administering to the souls in his care.

"Ye can start catechism anytime," the priest was saying. "Let's just see if Father Donnell's got a space this week." He crossed to a big, leather-topped desk and rummaged in one of the drawers, drawing out a parish diary. He riffled through the pages. "This coming Wednesday ...?" Benedict had told him something of the way of things. Ghosts and apparitions, indeed! The boy needed the Lord, and he, Father Seamus O'Casey, would see that he got Him! This was a challenge, to bring a lost soul into the church, round it up so to speak. He took his breviary from another drawer and put it on the desk. He would need it for Benediction. He had been forgetful of late, even once turning up in church without vestments. Ah well, he wasn't getting any younger, that much was certain.

He settled his bulk back into his chair and absentmindedly bit into another piece of Mrs Duncan's delicious chocolate cake. He sighed pleasurably and regarded Tremayne. If the lad was his challenge, then he would rise to it. "Y'see, young lad, it's like this. Ye've had the Lord call ye and ye must follow. Benedict has told me something of the nature of your case. Ye've been having your doubts and fears, I daresay, and they can have a powerful effect on the mind, so they can. But the Lord never said we wouldn't be travailed, only that we wouldn't be overcome."

Tremayne started. He knew those words from somewhere and they struck through him like the cry of a child in the dark. "All will be well," he murmured, half remembering.

"To be sure!" cried Father O'Casey. "And ye've read the blessed Lady Julian, too, have ye? She'll help ye, and so will our own Blessed Queen of Heaven!"

Tremayne remembered reading one of Benedict's many books, the 16 *Revelations of Divine Love*, shown to the anchoress Julian of Norwich 600 years before. He had been deeply affected by the beauty and simplicity of the words and had longed for a similar assurance. To be shown God's tender concern as Julian had been, so that he would have to search no further. He wasn't looking for an easy Road to Damascus, just a sense of God's reassuring presence to comfort him.

"I can see," Father O'Casey was beaming, "that ye're nearly one of us. Ye've had the signs, the temptations and now ye need the guidance." He turned thoughtfully to Benedict. "I'm not so sure a little rest wouldn't come amiss first, y'know, seeing as the lad's been ill. One of our brother houses, perhaps?" He lifted his eyebrows at Benedict, who nodded.

"Good idea. I might go with Tremayne myself, I have some catching up to do." Turning to Tremayne, he said, "It's a good idea. You need a period of complete rest before continuing. How do you feel about it?"

Tremayne sighed. "I do feel the need to sort out some questions in my mind."

"Now, then, let's see," Father O'Casey was musing. "There's the Franciscan Friars, or Capuchins, at Pantasaph in Wales and at de Lorris Hall in Lincolnshire, I believe. Fine order. They don't run retreats as such, but I know Brother Dominic. We'll get you settled in somewhere. There's the Sisters of Charity in East Anglia, but I'd say the Franciscans would be better. How soon can you be ready?"

Tremayne felt dazed. Benedict noticed his confusion and smiled. "You need time to think, don't you?" he said, gently. "You don't have to go, you know."

"No, it's alright," Tremayne answered. "It's just that, well … Capuchins? I thought they were monkeys!"

Father O'Casey roared with merriment, his red face beaming. "Monkeys!" he chortled. "I'm sure some of the brothers would agree with you! No, the monkey was named after the monks, as you might say, because of its head hair, like a little cowl! But very famous are the Capuchins, both for their eccentricity and the number of saints they produce."

They travelled to de Lorris Hall by train a little over a week later. It was early evening when a taxi drove them into the grounds of a priory. The house had once been a Franciscan priory, but had suffered under the Dissolution. The distinguished Catholic de Lorris family had bought it from the Crown at a high price. King Henry exacted a crippling revenge on those unwilling to conform to the new religion, but the de Lorris's were strongly united and not without influence, so he had contented himself with the addition to the Treasury of several thousand pounds. Thus, de Lorris Hall became the ancestral home of the ancient family, whose last member had died without issue in the late 1890s. Subsequently, the house had passed back into the hands of the church after 300 years and was now occupied by a brotherhood of Franciscan Greyfriars, dedicated to silence and the love of contemplative prayer.

The house itself had been well looked after. A grey and white variegated ivy clambered up the south side, reaching the ornate chimneys, but it had been carefully pruned away from the windows. A late sun still warmed the mellowed red brick and slanted off the mullioned lattice. A circulating hose flung a thin ribbon of water over the cropped lawn, which was bordered by beds full of dwarf rhododendrons and orange pelargoniums.

Benedict glanced at Tremayne's surprised face and laughed. "It looks almost too good to be true, doesn't it? But it'll be more spartan inside.

"I suppose you know a lot about these places," Tremayne remarked.

"I've been to a few," Benedict answered. "They differ in

some respects, but all observe long periods of silence, and you'll be expected to do the same. However, nothing will be forced upon you."

They were greeted courteously and shown to separate rooms. From Tremayne's window the flat Lincolnshire landscape stretched to the horizon, broken only by a clump of trees beyond a nearby field, but he didn't mind. The house and gardens were so delightful that he felt he had all he needed here. As he looked out a slight movement caught his eye. Half hidden by huge stone urn, Tremayne recognised Benedict talking to a tall figure, and as he watched, Benedict leaned forward and clasped the other's shoulders in a familiar gesture.

Tremayne was puzzled. Benedict hadn't mentioned being here before. He waited until he saw the two come towards the house, then slipped from the room. Resolutely ignoring his conscience, he concealed himself in an anteroom by the front door just as they entered.

"Are all your particular devils laid to rest?" the man was asking. There was a pause.

The two had reached a door on the far side of the hallway, which led to the refectory. Then Benedict answered, with a tinge of despair in his voice, "Will they ever be? When I think they are, a new one springs up."

Tremayne felt like an interloper. He didn't want to hear any more. He moved to the window and the murmured rejoinder of the other man was lost. When Benedict sought him out some time later, Tremayne thought he looked weary, but he gave Tremayne such a warm smile that he was caught unawares and, before he knew it, had blurted out, "Who was that chap in the garden? Have you been here before?"

Benedict's smile vanished and a closed look stole over his face. "No," he said, "I haven't been here before, but I do know Brother Dominic. We met in London. He's an old friend." He hesitated as if he would say more, but instead looked at his watch and said, "Come on, there'll be something to eat in the refectory at half-past seven."

The meal was surprisingly good, plain but cooked well. Fish, as it was Friday, but deliciously poached in milk and butter, and sweet tasting. "From our own pond," one of the serving Friars told them. Tremayne looked surreptitiously at the other guests. There were about 15 in all, ranging in age from a young and serious looking man to a grizzle-haired, wizened scrap of a woman who looked about her with the bright-eyed interest of a bird.

After the meal, they were to meet the Brother director of the Hall. To Tremayne's surprise the tall figure he had seen talking to Benedict entered the room and introduced himself as Brother Dominic. He begged them to avail themselves of the peace and spirituality of de Lorris Hall. He explained that there was no strict regime. "But we would ask you to observe our silence after evening prayer until next morning. We follow a strict regime ourselves, which you are welcome to join, if you wish. In all the bedrooms you will find ground plans of the Hall, together with the times of our offices. I very much hope that you will find here what you have come to seek." He turned to bow to the cross, then bid them goodnight in God's keeping.

"Brother Dominic will counsel you," Benedict said as they walked towards their rooms that night. "He has been a mentor and friend to me. You can tell him anything. Anything," he added, cryptically, with a little smile.

Tremayne awoke next morning to the silvery note of the acolyte's bell. Five-thirty and light outside. He opened his window. The air was crisp and fresh with a pale sun slanting across the gardens. As he watched, a file of figures wound along the cloister garth towards the chapel in the opposite wing. He dressed hurriedly and entered the chapel as the friars began their chant, seating himself, as a lay person, behind the rood screen. As the jubilant Benedicte rang out it seemed to Tremayne that it was the voice of God which rose to fill the vaulted chapel. He sat spellbound as Brother Dominic began to recite the ancient litany. The words seemed to strike a chord of memory within him, so that in his fancy it seemed as if he had sat on such a morning as this long ago, and had been at peace, his life fulfilled.

The office ended and a figure rose from a front pew. Tremayne recognised Benedict, but he wanted nothing to break the spell, so he slipped quietly from the chapel. Later, he sought out Brother Dominic and discovered what Benedict had before him. The friar had a strength which flowed round him and encompassed all who encountered it. By some blessed channel, he was able to open up the hearts of all those who came to him. Before he realised it, Tremayne had told him everything, his dreams and doubts, the strange visions and his hopes of becoming a convert.

The friar smiled. "It will happen if God wishes it," he said. Tremayne felt suddenly awkward. "Perhaps even later I may take orders ..." he ventured, then stopped, embarrassed.

Brother Dominic was aware that the influence of de Lorris Hall sometimes led people into unrealistic expectations. He asked gently, "What do you see for yourself, at this moment?"

Tremayne sighed and hesitated. "Well, I can't think too far ahead because it's not practical, and if I do I'm liable to be disappointed."

Brother Dominic smiled. "Take one step at a time and don't make a decision based on your experience here. And remember, there are three things a Christian must do, it is required of us. We must read the word of God, pray and seek the fellowship of other Christians. This last is a sign of the true believer. But God will be with you, whatever you decide. You may not be gifted for the celibate life. He doesn't ask what we cannot give and as to the other things you tell me about, sometimes we unwittingly open ourselves to psychic phenomena. Pray and He will take that burden from you. Our greatest need is that we should live in the right relationship with God."

He sounded so unequivocal that Tremayne felt vaguely let down. Was it really that easy? Perhaps Brother Dominic was right - he wasn't made for celibacy. Once he had loved sex - adored it, even. He sighed. Everything had altered since his illness. Now he felt differently, but would that last? To people like Brother Dominic and Benedict the answers were simple. Pray. Ask God. You will be shown the way. But maybe they had never had so much to forgive.

He thanked Brother Dominic and returned to his room, meeting Benedict on the way. He looked squarely at him. "Is life really simple?" he demanded. "Can any sin really be forgiven? Doesn't that mean we could do anything and get away with it? Just ask for forgiveness each time?"

Benedict quirked an eyebrow at him. "Of course not! You've had too much soul-searching. Don't complicate things for yourself.

Tremayne sighed. "I've got no patience, that's my trouble!"

He visited Brother Dominic several times and, with his help, began to see a clearer path. He knew he could never go back to what he once had been. He wanted to close that part of his life forever, shake off the past and renew himself to avoid temptation. "That's naive," Benedict said, when Tremayne told him. "You're never without temptation. It comes in all different forms," he added, and a dark look crossed his face. Tremayne, wrapped up in his own thoughts, did not see it.

Benedict recognised the signs. Always impetuous,

Tremayne must have the answers the minute he asked the questions. He had much to learn.

Tremayne was gazing morosely over the garden. The day had begun brightly, but now a sickly sun wavered, hesitating, above the firs that bordered the west wall of the Hall. Benedict struggled to control the flood of protectiveness which Tremayne always stirred in him. He breathed deeply, then said with only a hint of tremor, "You should realise that your search for answers is as nothing, compared to some. Many never have complete answers and have to make decisions based on faith alone, not proof. In fact," he laughed, shortly, "you have been shown things which you haven't recognised. The first time you came with me to church, remember what you told me? That you experienced a feeling of oneness, of empathy? How you forgot everything around you?"

Tremayne nodded, slowly.

"You were privileged," Benedict went on. "And I know you've been at Matins here every morning. It was obvious to anyone that nothing else seemed real to you!"

Tremayne started to smile. "If I could only believe you!"

Suddenly, Benedict crossed to him and gripped his shoulders. "If it has taken me to show you, then God be thanked!" And he held Tremayne fiercely before letting him go and turning away.

Tremayne saw the bent head and a great gratitude rushed through him. "I'll never know as much as you, or be as good!"

His words struck Benedict to the heart and filled him with a piercing isolation. How thankful he should be that it was so easy to lift Tremayne's spirits, yet it left him more alone than ever.

"I'm not good, Tremayne," he said. "But I will be here when you need me. That's a promise!"

Tremayne smiled, his spirits completely restored. "This is

an answer to prayer, Benedict. You're like the sower in the parable. You sow the seed and it falls on my ground."

"Wrong. God sows the seed," Benedict said, in a low voice. "I just provided the water, if you like."

"Well, whatever, it's grown and flowered," Tremayne answered. "It's all so perfect!"

Benedict said, in a voice so faint that Tremayne could not catch it, "The flower has to die before it is reborn."

Tremayne, suddenly serious, took his friend's arm. "I'm not much good at this kind of thing," he said, awkwardly. "But, for what it's worth, you're the best person I've ever met and I hope we're friends for life."

"Yes," Benedict echoed, hollowly. "Friends for life!"

Part Three

Yorkshire, Surrey and London, 1960-1962

Chapter 10

The conversion to Catholicism was an easy decision after the healing atmosphere of de Lorris Hall. With the fervour of a convert, Tremayne basked in his new faith and he approached the idea of the priesthood with the certainty of Divine intervention. Benedict, whilst not doubting his friend's sincerity, wanted proof of the integrity of Tremayne's decision. But as the days passed, he questioned his right for proof. He began to see that Tremayne's conversion and the support of a loving family had helped so much more than the years of familial isolation that had dogged his own path. Tremayne's faith was as it should be; he was blessed by a simple acceptance of what seemed entirely natural to him.

The baptismal ceremony was emotional. Tremayne's family shared his warmth of spirit and accepted his decision with cheerfulness. He had chosen Benedict as his saint's name, a heartfelt compliment to his friend. He knew Benedict's was Jude. "More apt than you would understand," was Benedict's cryptic comment.

Now they were both in Hawkesworth House seminary on the Yorkshire coast, and as Benedict lay in bed and listened to the swish and suck of the waves on the shore below, he felt a dreamy contentment, a sensation so alien to him that he thought he must be light-headed. A new hope surged through him that at last his demons would be laid to rest. He turned in his bed and let his mind drift on.

Tremayne lay in the room next to Benedict's, which he shared with four others, and listened to the same rhythmic sounds of the sea far below. A deep peace pervaded his whole being. He knew with quiet certainty that this was the way his life was meant to go. He had recovered well from his illness and now looked on it as a test of his spiritual stamina. He felt fulfilled, or as fulfilled as he could be until his ordination. The dark shadow that still sometimes flitted across his spirit was a bruising which would soon heal. The seminary was all he could have wished for. It overlooked the sea and was surrounded on three sides by wooded parkland. Majestic oaks and stately elms dominated the landscape, creating a feeling of strength and protection. The sumach trees which crowded each side of the drive, their foliage just turning to brilliant golds and reds, reminded him of his mother's garden, filled at this time of year with the warm colours of autumn.

A sudden snore from the bed in the corner reminded him of his roommates. He'd met them at tea in the large dining hall. They had all been assigned a "mother" to introduce them to the seminary and to their roommates. Tremayne's "mother" was in the final year of his six years' training. He was an enormously tall, gawky man, whose clothes looked far too small for him. He extended a thin, bony hand, which darted from his sleeve as if it had been lurking, and offered it to Tremayne in a limp handshake. For all his unprepossessing appearance, Tremayne soon discovered that Richard Peake was an intensely sincere individual who had a genuine interest in all those about him. He did his "mothering" thoroughly, taking his group all over the campus and earnestly assuring them that he was there to help at all times.

The bed was hard. Not what he was used to, but he had slept on worse. For some unknown reason a picture of Claire suddenly flashed into his mind. Her soft, supple body, the comfort of lying close to her, then her pleading face.

Shaken, he sat upright and fumbled for his watch. One-thirty. The seminary was asleep. As he should be. Why had he suddenly thought of Claire? He had atoned for that, and she had forgiven him, too. He had seen her with a man quite recently, in London. The man was gazing at her with all the ardour of a new lover and Tremayne had felt relieved. She'd seen him, called out and waved, forever closing that episode of his life.

The moon slid into view and flooded the room with silvery light. Tremayne turned to put his watch on the bedside table and as he did so a shadow by the window caught his eye. He froze, heart thumping. The shadow half turned towards the silver light and he saw, with a sickening lurch of his heart, that it was the same girl who had haunted him in Benedict's flat. He sat paralysed, his mind in a turmoil. The girl was intensely still, waiting, yet he could feel a palpable force of energy emanating from her. Then, suddenly, he felt an overwhelming pity. Summoning his courage, he wet his parched lips and spoke in a low voice, "What do you want from me?"

She turned, and he could see her face, the same beautiful face that he remembered. A look of terror passed over her and the spell was broken. Suddenly she was gone and it was just the curtain moving gently to and fro in the breeze from the open window. Tremayne remained motionless, his gaze straining towards where she had been standing. Or had she? Now he was no longer sure. He slid quietly from his bed and crossed to the window. The moon had sailed further across the sky and bathed the seminary garden in light. He stood where she had stood and, as he did so, a power rushed through him, an explosive charge which seemed to open up a communication in him, and he experienced a great sensation of anger and bereavement. Clinging to the window frame he turned to look down across the park and there, still and shining between the great oaks, stood the girl, looking back up at him.

Now he knew he hadn't been mistaken. He had been called upon to help in some way, he didn't yet know how. Somewhere ahead of him lay a path which would test him to the limit, a path he was not supposed to tread, yet had to.

The next day he approached Benedict with some trepidation. The unearthly experience of the night seemed fanciful in the light of day, yet he must confide in someone and he didn't yet know any of the teaching priests. They breakfasted together, two groups with their "mothers". Richard Peake was as solicitous as ever, enquiring gently if Tremayne had slept soundly and expressing concern to hear that he hadn't.

"Oh dear!" he said. "Perhaps our beds are not quite what most people are used to. The pillows do tend to resemble concrete!"

"No, the bed was fine," he replied. "It was just … being in a strange place, I suppose."

"Ah, yes," Richard reminisced. "My first evening here was fraught, I remember. My "mother" had been taken suddenly ill and my group were left more or less to ourselves. Not the best thing for a lot of rowdy youngsters!"

A less rowdy person than Richard was hard to imagine and Tremayne couldn't prevent a chuckle.

"You may laugh," Richard said, earnestly, "but, believe me, I was not the person six years ago that you see now. We all mature and grow in faith. You must make sure you get enough rest tonight. We will be having the tonsure ceremony tomorrow. It's a symbolic cutting of hair. Don't forget," he added, "you have your own spiritual director who will advise you on any matters of theology, or counsel you if you wish."

Tremayne turned to Benedict, who was listening nearby. "I need to talk to you," he said, in a low voice. "Where could we go to be quiet?"

Benedict looked at him quickly. "Meet me here at lunchtime

and we'll go into one of the recreation rooms, or the garden." There was no time for more. They were plunged immediately into the way their lives would run for the next six years. Seminars in dogmatic theology, which aimed to cover all the principles of the Catholic church, began that day and Tremayne was soon immersed in the breakdown of theological facts and how they operated in practice.

When at last he was able to meet with Benedict his experience seemed far-fetched and exaggerated. Benedict listened, then said, "I expect it was just a vivid dream. Everyone dreams like that now and then. A dream that seems so real it colours the rest of your day."

Tremayne resented being fobbed off. "But I've seen that girl before!" he insisted. "I saw her several times in your flat, remember, and you believed me!"

"I did believe you … then," Benedict answered, "because, of course, you'd been ill. A trick of the imagination. And that's what it was last night, too."

Tremayne fell silent. It was obvious that Benedict wasn't going to take him seriously and in a way he couldn't blame him.

"Look," Benedict said, gently. "I'm not trying to belittle your experience, dream, call it what you will. But everything you're telling me goes against all reason, therefore there has to be a reasonable explanation." He felt inadequate, but he wasn't sure what Tremayne wanted him to say, or what he could do. It seemed that Tremayne was developing an unhealthy interested in the supernatural. The prickle of fear stirred again and he found he couldn't dismiss this as easily as he wanted to.

"Why don't you see your spiritual director?" he suggested. "I'm afraid I'm not being much help, am I? This is outside my experience. All I do know is that notions which question the doctrine of the church should be discussed with someone far better than I to deal with it."

Tremayne smiled and rose to his feet. "Sorry, Benedict. I shouldn't have burdened you with this. But I think I'll wait, carry on with my reading or something. Heaven knows we've been given enough already! Come on, let's get back. Moral theology this afternoon."

His tone was light and Benedict was painfully aware that he had let Tremayne down. Together they walked back under the cloister which led from the priests' garden and entered the seminary to go to their studies.

The days passed into weeks and neither man mentioned the conversation again. The regime of the seminary was rigorous and left little time for fanciful imaginings. Tremayne soon came to think of his experience as another vivid dream. It was not surprising. The speed with which his life had changed irrevocably had been breathtaking. Occasionally, though, there were doubts - not about his decision, but about something unfulfilled. Vague, intangible doubts, too elusive to name, but they were there.

His theologians were impressed with him. If he was an unexceptional novitiate in some ways, he more than made up for that in his eagerness to please.

Benedict, however, seemed remote and unreadable, his participation in discussions minimal. But it was a strange novitiate who entered the seminary without so much as a stain on his soul. Mostly, those stains were easily rubbed away with a willingness to overcome them. They had encountered before that intense melancholy which he exuded. With the quiet certainty of those who believe in Divine Providence, they left the problem, if there was one, in the hands of the Almighty.

Tremayne breezed through his days with cheery optimism, failing to notice Benedict's morose withdrawal, which had brought his nerves to snapping point. After the day's instruction, they frequently walked through the park, although it was now winter and often freezing, with biting, snow-laden winds sweeping in off the North Sea. There were times when Tremayne would have preferred to be in the warmth and comfort of the common room, but it seemed to suit Benedict to walk, unspeaking, through the grey twilights. Reaching the cliff top they would stand, looking silently out at the heaving ocean as great waves swelled and hurled themselves on the rocks beneath, reflecting Benedict's dark moods. Then, for the first time since they started at the seminary, he discovered that Benedict was seeking counselling.

"Things not going too well?" he ventured one evening on their walk. "Anything I can do? Is it the philosophy sessions?" They had been covering some particularly difficult doctrinal points and this had resulted in some heated discussions amongst the novitiates.

Benedict paused before answering and turned his gaze on the grey seas. "It isn't the philosophy," he said eventually. "God is my comfort, my rock to cling to. And you, of course," he smiled briefly. "Your friendship means everything to me. You shine, as the great Bard said, like a good deed in a naughty world!" He drew his heavy coat round him and blew on his hands to warm them.

"Why don't we go back?" suggested Tremayne, wondering yet again why he accompanied Benedict in this freezing weather. But Benedict seemed not to notice the wintry skies or the flurries of snow in the air. He stood, strong and tall, staring out to sea, his breath wreathing from his nostrils in white plumes. He reminded Tremayne of an impatient animal, straining for release, but about to spring forward into nothing.

"Is it news from home, then," Tremayne tried again. "Are Jack and Angela OK?" He knew Benedict was in touch with his adoptive brother and sister.

"No," Benedict said, after a moment. "It's not that. Everything's fine with them. It's just that ... well, part of my trouble is that I can't forgive. What sort of priest will I make if I can't forgive?" He laughed and the sound fell like a stone on the wintry air.

"Who can't you forgive?" asked Tremayne, surprised.

"My parents, for one," Benedict answered, harshly.

Tremayne's heart sank. He thought Benedict had come to terms with that part of his life.

"You can't go through life bearing grudges," he ventured. It sounded a paltry thing to say. He half expected Benedict to be angry, but instead he seemed deflated. "You're right, I can't," he said. "But, more than that, I can't forgive myself. Things I can't tell you about now. But soon I will, I promise!" He swung round and started to walk quickly away, so that Tremayne had to run to keep up, and arrived back at the seminary puffing and red in the face.

Later, he reflected on their conversation, trying to make sense of the complicated nature of his friend. Benedict was forever throwing up question marks and there was an odd incident which had occurred, when he had come across Benedict and Charles Devereaux closeted together at a corner table in a coffee bar in the nearby town. Tremayne was just about to join them when he realised something was wrong. Charles was staring angrily at Benedict. They were clearly in the middle of an argument, but Charles looked more than angry. He looked upset, even tearful. Benedict's face held its usual closed remoteness, but as Tremayne watched he saw him lay his hand on the other's arm in a gesture of compassion. To Tremayne's horror, Charles Devereaux grabbed the hand and pressed it frantically to his lips.

He drew back, feeling like a voyeur. This was surely more than an ordinary disagreement. It looked very much as though Benedict was being propositioned. What a damnable thing to happen! When he looked again, Benedict was shrugging on his overcoat, while Charles still sat at the table, his head bowed, coughing and blowing his nose into a large handkerchief. Benedict waited politely until the little pretence was over, then he turned quietly to leave. Tremayne ducked back out of sight. He was filled with admiration. Benedict had such dignity. He wondered whether to mention it to him, then decided against it. It was such a private matter.

That night at supper Benedict behaved as usual, but Tremayne noticed that Charles Devereaux was not in the refectory. It was the least the man could do, he thought. Thank heaven he had *some* sensitivity!

Chapter 11

Their wintry walks became less frequent. Great gales roared nightly round Hawkesworth House, interspersed with heavy downfalls of snow. But Tremayne knew that if Benedict had wanted to continue the walks, he would have gone with him, come what may. It sometimes seemed to Tremayne that he was Benedict's only friend. He was still morose, however, and it was all Tremayne could do to get him to respond to the most elementary conversation. He tried probing again. "You've been moody and strange for weeks, Ben. Is it still the same thing? If you don't tell me what's wrong I can't help you, can I?"

"You think I need help?" Benedict asked, abruptly.

"Well, something's wrong. Just tell me what it is!" Tremayne went across to the percolator and unplugged it. They were the only people in the lounge. Usually it was crowded, but there was a final return rugby match for Hawkesworth and most people were out on the field.

Tremayne poured two cups and handed one to Benedict. As he did so their hands touched and Benedict was seized with a spasm so violent that his cup flew out of his hand and crashed to the floor, sending a stream of coffee over both of them. Tremayne jumped back, startled. The coffee was hot and he pulled his stained shirt away from his chest. He looked up, grinning ruefully, then froze. Benedict was reaching out for him like a blind man, a look of intense pain and longing on his face.

"Hey, what's up?" Tremayne spluttered, backing off. "What

are you doing?" for Benedict was pulling him roughly into his arms, crushing the breath out of him in a fierce embrace and muttering thickly, his hands pressing Tremayne's body against his own.

Tremayne was weak with shock. He crumpled against Benedict, powerless to fight him off, his gorge rising in his throat so that he was sure he would vomit. Disgusted, he fought feebly to restrain Benedict, all the while feeling the other's desperate manhood thrusting against him in sickening proof of his intent. Then, suddenly, a blazing anger ripped through him and his strength returned.

"For pity's sake man, get off!" he managed at last, shoving Benedict away from him as hard as he could. They faced each other, panting. Benedict flung his head back, his black eyes glittering. He glared savagely at Tremayne, his whole body shaking uncontrollably.

"Now you know what my problem is!" he cried, bitterly. "Go on, say you despise me, that this is against God and nature! That's what you're thinking, isn't it? How disgusting I am, how perverted?"

Tremayne felt frightened as well as angry. He thought that Benedict must be ill, that he was feverish, perhaps even delirious. Then he remembered the crushing arms, the searching lips and his heart revolted. Resentful tears sprang to his eyes. "How could you!" he choked. Suppose someone came in? How could we explain this? They might think I encouraged you!"

Benedict made a sound of pain and turned away. "Is that all this means to you?" he said harshly. "What other people will say? Do you think that I haven't fought against this every step of the way? Didn't you guess? I thought you, of all people, would have known!" His voice broke suddenly and his shoulders sagged. "Now you know why my saint's name is so appropriate. I'm a lost cause."

Then Tremayne remembered the conversations, the hints, the times when Benedict had promised to tell him more one day. He could hardly believe it. "Damn you!" he cried. "Why couldn't you leave well alone? Are you telling me you love me, or something?"

Benedict didn't answer. The crudity of the question struck him to the heart. He turned his livid gaze on Tremayne and in it lay all the longing and all the anguish he had ever felt from the day they had first met.

Tremayne's anger and revulsion were pierced by the look. Now the pattern was complete, but to know the truth broke his heart. He stumbled to a chair and fell into it, covering his face with his hands. "How could you do this? You've spoilt our lives together! How can we be friends after this? You were like a god to me!"

Benedict laughed bitterly. "And now I have feet of clay, is that it? And you wish someone would rid you of this meddlesome priest? I admit you'll have to ask yourself whether friendship with the tainted one is worth it. You could be shunned by all your friends, family even!"

Through his grief and shock Tremayne faintly heard the desperation behind the words. A feeling of pity began to steal through him. "We've been friends for a long time. I thought that could go on forever," he said bleakly.

"Nothing's forever," Benedict replied, in a voice now filled more with sadness than with anger. "Except what I am. That's forever. I've known it for a long time. Just as I knew about you … how I felt … as soon as I saw you. You felt it, too, I know you did. I was hoping … always hoping …" His voice broke again.

Tremayne couldn't deny it. He'd felt the magnetism when

they'd shaken hands. But for him it had been charisma that attracted him, a meeting of minds, a knowledge that here at last was a man who could see beyond the trivial and penetrate his innermost thoughts. He had never wanted to be anything more than Benedict's spiritual brother and he was bewildered that Benedict had failed to see it.

"I'm sorry, but I can't seem to take it in," he said at last. "You knew all about my affairs, my girlfriends. You knew I wasn't ... well, like that. And I didn't guess, although ..." he stopped and looked down.

"Go on," said Benedict. "Although what?"

"Well, I did see something once," Tremayne replied. "In the coffee bar in town. You didn't notice me. You were there with Charles Devereaux." He looked up, questioningly.

"Ah, so you saw that little scene, did you?" Benedict said, with a return of his customary irony. "And you thought Charles was making a complete idiot of himself, no doubt! Anything else occur to you? That he recognised me for what I am because that was his inclination, too?"

Tremayne winced. "What about Father Dominic at the retreat?" he blurted. "You seemed to know him pretty well!"

Benedict made a sound of disgust. "If you're thinking that, forget it!" he said, scornfully. "Father Dominic has known me for years! He knows how I've suffered, the persecution. It isn't easy, you know, being cursed with an illegal inclination!" He paused, then continued in a low voice. "I told him about you ... how I felt. I needed his counsel." He turned to the wall to hide sudden emotion. "And you still didn't guess, did you?" he continued in a muffled voice, "when you came to me and I looked after you, when I encouraged you to take catechism, then Holy Orders? Didn't it ever cross your mind that I loved you?"

It was out. Tremayne must either accept him for what he was, or spurn him.

There was a long silence. Benedict stood with bowed head,

unmoving. He was drained, a pitiful sight to Tremayne who had honoured and revered him for so long.

After an age, Benedict moved towards the door. He stood on the threshold, his back still turned.

"I've shocked you, I know," he said. "But I had to tell you. I can assure you I'll never embarrass you in such a way again!"

Tremayne suddenly sprang forward, his feelings overflowing. "Benedict!" he cried. "Please forgive me! I'm so muddled, I can't tell you … the shock … Oh, damn, don't go!"

Benedict turned instantly, his face illuminated. "You are not to be blamed," he said. "I should never have let you know, but we can't choose whom we love. For me, it was you. It could no more be prevented than our meeting. That, too, was meant to happen." He reached for Tremayne's hand. He would be true to his word. His love would find compensation in the church, but he would be faithful to his heart. He would love no other but Tremayne. He saw Tremayne's consternation and smiled faintly. "If you can find it in your heart to remain friends, that's all I ask."

"I said that we'd be friends for life, didn't I?" Tremayne reminded him. Benedict nodded. "Well, I meant it then and I mean it now. You're still a special friend and, yes, I did know that when we met. It's just that I can't be what you want me to be. Especially now, when it would be so wrong for both of us."

Benedict tightened his clasp. "What I want you to be," he replied, "is what you are."

With that, he was gone and Tremayne was left to reflect on all the implications, and the future that Benedict would have to face. He saw, perhaps for the first time, what an exceptional person Benedict was, and that he had probably broken his heart. His own ached unbearably. Shock had made him condemn. He knew he must try to support Benedict, yet dreaded seeing him again. We're all sinners in so many different ways, he thought, then remembered something that Benedict had once said. "The church *is* for sinners, and liars and cheats." Feeling somewhat comforted, he went to his room to think.

Another, more serious incident prevented their meeting for a while. Late that night he was called to the phone and he picked it up with trepidation. His mother was on the line, her voice anxious. "Your father's had a small heart attack. We thought you ought to know, although there's no immediate danger, the doctor says."

"How did it happen, where is Father?"

"He's in hospital now," she replied, "but it happened in the garden this evening. I tried to tell him not to tackle that tree by himself!"

"You can't mean that great elm at the end?" His father had been saying for a long time that he must get the tree pollarded. Successive winter gales had undermined it and Edward Jago had several times contemplated trying to do the job himself, but Margherita had always dissuaded him.

On the other end of the line his mother sighed. "The very one! And, yes, whatever you're going to say, you're right! I wouldn't have let him if I'd been there, but you know what your father's like! I always thought the risk would be falling out of it, not this!

"I'll come down right away," Tremayne said. "I'll leave in the morning."

"I wouldn't ask," his mother said, "only it would be a comfort if you could. Just for a few days, till your father comes home. Sally's on her way down from Sheffield. The baby's due very soon now, but she insisted on coming down." His sister had been living in the North for a year now. He knew his mother missed her, but she was settled and happy.

He hung up worriedly. By noon next day he was in London, making his way to Victoria Station to catch the train to Surrey.

"Sorry to have dragged you back," Margherita said, meeting him from the train, "but it is good to see you! Things have been hectic. We've not had much sleep, but that's the least of our worries. How's Benedict?"

"Fine," he replied, shortly. She looked at him quickly. His face was unreadable. Something had happened, then, and she had a good idea what, having long ago resolved all the imponderables she had felt on first meeting Benedict and his manner towards Tremayne. She squeezed her son's arm. "These things happen," she said, gently. "Don't take it too hard."

He looked down at her, thunderstruck. "So you knew! Who told you?"

She smiled. "No-one told me. One doesn't have to be told everything. I think I always knew it about Benedict." Whatever had taken place between the two, she knew there would have to be much understanding on both their parts, but now more pressing matters were on her mind.

They collected Sally from the house and went to the hospital. When Tremayne saw his father he was shaken at his ashen appearance. Edward's skin had a sickly pallor and there was a bluish tinge around his mouth. He knew now that his mother had underplayed the situation, there were tubes and monitors everywhere. On the drive home, he glanced in the driving mirror and saw that his mother was crying quietly in the back seat.

"Oh, Mum!" Sally said. "He'll be okay, just you wait and see. I think he looks better, compared to yesterday. Let's go to Zita's in the High Street for a cuppa and a cream bun. That'll cheer us up!"

Despite herself, Margherita smiled. For Sally, food was the answer to all ills.

They heard the shrill bell of the telephone on the hall table before they got out of the car. Margherita answered it, and as they watched her face, they knew.

"We'd better get back to the hospital immediately," she told them, faintly. "Your father's had another unexpected attack. We must prepare ourselves, the nurse said."

They were there in 15 minutes, and as she gently stroked his forehead, Edward Jago closed his eyes on the world and his beloved wife at the same moment. Margherita turned into her children's arms and wept.

Tremayne stayed for six weeks after the funeral. His mother was inconsolable. She had been married to Edward for 23 years and was as much in love with him when he died as on their wedding day. Tremayne and Sally took care of all the arrangements. Their mother was financially secure. Edward had worked for a printer at Puddle Dock, Blackfriars. A meticulous saver, he had made sure his financial affairs were in order long before his heart attack.

Margherita was full of self-recrimination. She was sure she could have done more for Edward if she'd stayed at the hospital with him, "Instead of gallivanting!" as she put it.

"Mother, we weren't gallivanting!" Sally protested. "No-one could've done more for Dad! Who can tell when these things are going to happen?"

"That's true, Mother," Tremayne agreed. "If the doctors can't do anything, how should we be able to?"

Easter came and went. In all the time Tremayne spent at home he tried hard not to think of Benedict. He continued his reading and had been in contact with his theologian. Benedict had rung and expressed his condolences, having heard the news from Sally, but Tremayne was out when the call came through. He was trying hard to come to terms with Benedict's sexuality, but try as he might, he couldn't help feeling betrayed. The mystery and remoteness that was Benedict had dimmed. He had shown himself to have an Achilles heel, and it didn't help Tremayne to know that he was the one who had pierced it.

Finally, however, he had to return to Yorkshire. A new term had started and he had a lot of catching up to do. There was no opportunity to see Benedict on the night of his return as it was late, and after a hurried supper he went to bed.

He awoke late next morning and was almost the last into the refectory. He stood in the queue for breakfast, making his choice, his heart thumping. Now he would have to face Benedict and try to pretend that all was well. Suddenly, the beautiful words of Julian's Revelations came to him:

"All shall be well, and all shall be well, and all manner of thing shall be well.

"I am the ground of thy beseeching. First it is my will that you should have it, then I make you want it, and then I make you pray for it, and if you pray for it, how should it be that you should not have your prayers answered?"

It was true. He had no doubt that prayers were answered.

All he need do was give the problem up to the Almighty and just wait. Benedict was still essentially the same person, after all, and would still be a source of unending strength.

Benedict was sitting on his own. Looking up at Tremayne, he smiled a slow, questioning smile. In it was a plea for forgiveness and understanding, which shot straight to Tremayne's heart. He went over. As they met, Benedict's black eyes searched Tremayne's face and found there what he was looking for. "I was sorry to hear the news," Benedict said, quietly. "These things are never easy, but I hope everything went off okay. And Margherita, how is she?"

Tremayne sighed. "She's okay, but it's been a difficult time, the more so because we thought it was only a mild attack at first. We weren't prepared at all. Sally's still at Mother's"

"When did you get back?" Benedict asked.

"Fairly late last night. How're you? Have I missed much?"

"Nothing you can't catch up on. You can borrow my notes."

There was an awkward pause, then with the perception of close friends, they both started talking at once, stopped, stared at each other, and grinned. "After you!" said Benedict.

"I've had time to think while I've been at home," Tremayne began. "And I can't pretend I wasn't … well … dazed, when you … when you … you know!" he stopped, embarrassed.

"Dazed?" Benedict murmured. "How kind! Some might have put it more strongly than that!" A sardonic smile played on his lips. It was the old Benedict back. Heartened, Tremayne rushed on. "I can't tell you how awful I feel about it. How bad my reaction was! Can you forgive me?"

This time Benedict was genuinely surprised. "Me? Forgive you? And all this time I've been wondering how you'll forgive me! What different perceptions we've both had!" He paused, then went on. "I've been having some confidential help and I can now learn to live with what I am. I felt the need to confess, too."

"What was your penance? Were you absolved?" Tremayne asked, anxiously.

"Of course!" answered Benedict. "Who isn't? The priest was lenient. They've heard it all before, no doubt! I repeat ten rosaries a day. I've done it gladly."

"No so bad!" Tremayne changed the subject. "I'm so relieved to be back. It's been hell at home and I hardly liked to leave Mother, but Sally'll cope. She's been a wonder."

"As, no doubt, you have, too!" Benedict said, quietly.

Tremayne smiled at him. "I'll go to confession, too. Tonight. I have plenty to be sorry about."

Benedict quirked an eyebrow. "Don't take too much guilt on yourself. The fault was mine, not yours. Your reaction was natural."

Across the other side of the refectory, Charles Devereaux saw the two dark heads bent together and felt a stab of jealousy. No use running up that street again. It was plain where Benedict Truman's affections lay. But Tremayne Jago? Surely not! He would never have guessed it. Envy and pique churned in Charles's breast. Why couldn't life be simple? Instead, he was caught in an uncompromising triangle.

Tremayne and Benedict got up to leave and passed right by Charles. He looked up eagerly ready to speak, but the two men went by without noticing him. He stared after them, nettled. There had been no mistaking the look in Benedict Truman's eyes. At that moment, Charles Devereaux would have given anything to change places with Tremayne Jago.

Chapter 12

There were so many to be ordained that the ceremony was held in the cathedral and not in the college chapel, which couldn't cope with the number of relatives and friends who were expected.

The weather was perfect; an auspicious sign, Tremayne thought. Sunshine flooded into the ancient building through stained glass windows, casting myriad patterns of coloured light on to priestly robes and reflecting off the bishop's mitre and crozier. Tremayne looked with pride at his own robes and adjusted the cincture slightly. Soon each candidate would be invested with his stole and chasuble by the assisting priests, in keeping with the solemnity of the service.

Above the pulpit a statue of the Madonna cast her eyes forever heavenwards, a saintly smile on her rosy lips. She held the infant Jesus on one arm, in her hand was a Bible. Jesus gazed up at her, one chubby arm extended to her in silent supplication. Both had been freshly painted. The Virgin's blue robe spun around her in rigid, gleaming folds and her golden hair cascaded over herself and the Holy Child, mingling with his own blonde curls.

Tremayne thought the statue beautiful. In all his six years at the seminary, he had never ceased to thrill at the ornately carved images in the chapel and the Virgin had become real to him. He sent her a silent prayer, begging her intercession at the start of his chosen path. As he looked he thought he saw the corners of the painted mouth curve upwards and the blue eyes, which before had been fixed in space, seemed to glow with a special warmth for him. He felt an overwhelming love for the Queen of Heaven as she stretched out her pale hand and he felt her blessing on him. He was at once filled with the mystical union of his spirit with God. He bowed his head in humility and worship as the line of candidates carried him along towards their seats, and the moment was broken. But nothing could take away Mary's most definite confirmation that he was God's priest on earth, and thanksgiving filled his heart.

Heartened, he stole a surreptitious glance at his fellow novitiates, Benedict among them, gravely dignified. Charles Devereaux had left the seminary a short while after Tremayne's return from his father's funeral and neither man had mentioned him again. But that was all a long time ago and the theologians who had once had their doubts were forced to admit that Benedict Truman had confounded them all.

Benedict sat next to Tremayne, waiting for the ceremony to begin, and looking out over the congregation for familiar faces. Tremayne could see Jack, and Angela with her family, sitting in a front pew. They were smiling proudly up at Benedict, and next to them was a man Tremayne didn't recognise, talking animatedly to Angela.

"Who's that?" he whispered to Benedict.

"Nathaniel Grant," Benedict whispered back. "Haven't seen him in ages. He's a jazz musician. We lost touch, but I think he kept in touch with Angela. Nice chap."

There was no time for more as the Calling to Orders began, followed by the presentation of the candidates. The concelebrating priests in their snowy white surplices flocked slowly down the aisle, like sleek white birds. Tremayne's eyes were filled with light and the whole cathedral flowed with shining brilliance. Music and words poured through him, as if he were the vessel discharging them, and he became lost in the mystical union of his spirit with the will of God, the fulfilment of six years' longing for this day. He heard the joyful words "Christus Vincit, Christus Regnus, Christus Imperator" ringing down the aisles of the cathedral and beside him he felt Benedict shudder. The congregation were called to voice any objections to those being ordained. Then came the Promise of Obedience, followed by the Invitation to Prayer and the Litany of the Saints. At the Prayer of Consecration Tremayne prostrated himself before the bishop with awe. All the newly ordained priests were then invested with their stoles and chasubles by the assisting priests.

When the time came for the Anointing of Hands, to prepare them for the sacred offering of the Mass, Tremayne looked at his own and rejoiced that they were to be dedicated. He felt the bishop's firm clasp and smiled up into the kindly, but austere, face. The bishop didn't speak, but a faint smile hovered on his face for an instant as he saw the earnest one before him. Such a one he had been many years before, and he prayed that those being ordained today would find the joy that service to God had brought to him. The choir continued with an antiphon, based on Psalm 110, solemn and beautiful. "The Lord hath sworn and will not repent, thou art a priest for ever after the order of Melchizedek."

But for Tremayne, nothing in the ceremony could surpass the moment of the symbolic transference of power through the silent laying on of hands, as Jesus had laid his hands on the apostles. At that moment, a steady burning began within him, spreading through his body until he felt filled with fire. The silence of the cathedral was palpable, crystallising into tiny pinpoints of sound, which rang and resounded in his head until it felt as though it would burst. Giddily, he swayed with the rhythmic flow of pattern and colour swirling round him, and the past and present seemed to merge into one.

At that moment, there flashed into his head the memory of

that night, long ago at the seminary, when he had seen the ghostly vision and stood in its shadow and felt the strangeness. The girl had ceased to frighten him, although he had felt that strangeness many times, the grappling to synchronise the past and present. But nothing could detract from the glory of this moment, and when he felt the bishop's hands on his head, hands charged with the transference of the Holy Spirit into him, his joy was complete. He glanced towards Benedict who had stepped to the other side of the bishop, and as their eyes met, Benedict smiled his grave smile, then lowered his eyes. In that look Tremayne saw a steadfast and unambiguous love. Benedict had never swerved in his loyalty or in his feelings, and it was his ultimate joy that Tremayne should be happy. Now here they were, sharing in what they had worked and prayed for.

Finally, came the Presentation of Gifts and the Kiss of Peace and the ordination was over. Tremayne and Benedict joined the throng moving towards the coaches waiting to take them back to the seminary and the ordination breakfast.

Tremayne caught sight of Nathaniel Grant, and said, "Oh, look, here's your friend. Introduce me."

Nathaniel, followed by Jack and Angela, was elbowing his way through the queues. Angela rushed forward and threw her arms around Benedict. "I was so proud of you!" she cried. "It was so moving!" She turned and gave Tremayne a smile.

Jack held out his hand and warmly shook Benedict's. "Well done, Ben, made it at last, eh?"

Benedict said nothing, but gripped their hands. Tremayne felt unaccountably embarrassed and started to move away, but Benedict said, "No, don't go. This is a special day for all of us. In any case, I'd like you to meet everyone."

He turned to Nathaniel. "It's good to see you after all this time. When was the last time? Wasn't it at the Barber concert?"

"Must've been!" Nathaniel grinned.

"Fifty-four."

With a shock, Tremayne realised that they were talking about the same concert that he had taken Claire to. How strange to think that Benedict had been there, too. Their lives seem to have been linked from before they met, in the odd way of coincidence.

"Hey!" Benedict nudged. "I've been trying to introduce you to Nathaniel for the last five minutes!"

"Sorry," Tremayne smiled. "I was miles away. At the Festival Hall, in fact. That was the concert you were talking about, wasn't it?"

"That's the one," Nathaniel replied. "And hi! I'm Nathaniel. You like jazz?"

Tremayne shook the proffered hand. "Sure, I'm a jazz fan, sadly behind the times now, I'm afraid."

Benedict and Nathaniel fell to chatting about old times. Tremayne felt a wave of nostalgia for his jazz days as he listened. Looking at Nathaniel it was obvious he was a dedicated jazzman who lived for his music. A bit like Bill Porter and his painting, he thought. He hadn't heard of Bill for years, but he knew the time apart would make no difference if they were to meet again.

The queue was beginning to thin out and he soon saw his mother and Sally, calling and waving. No-one could miss Sally for long. Then he was enveloped in their arms, savouring the love which came from them and feeling a bitter disappointment that his father hadn't lived to share his triumph.

As if she read his thoughts, his mother said, "Dad would've been proud of you today, darling! He knew you'd make it! It was me who had the doubts, wasn't it?" He hugged her closely, thinking for the hundredth time how lucky he was in his family.

The rest of the day passed in a haze of celebration, so that by the time Tremayne tumbled into bed he was full of charity for the whole world. He lay quietly and a delicious sleepiness began to steal over him. Strangely, just before he dropped off, he thought he heard a baby cry.

* * * * *

The newly-ordained priests had to wait three weeks before their fates were announced. Benedict was to go to Ireland and Tremayne back to Surrey to be a curate at St Elpheges in Wallington. He went searching for Benedict. He found him in the porter's lodge, alone, booking a taxi for the following day.

"You'll keep in touch, won't you?" Tremayne asked, unnecessarily.

Benedict smiled. "What a question!"

There was no going back on what had passed. There had never been any allusion since that dramatic day, only an occasional unguarded look. Now Tremayne struggled to find words to express himself, and couldn't.

Benedict was looking out over the park. "Remember all our walks?" he said. "I never really thanked you for coming with me. It meant a lot to me, and I did know what a sacrifice you were making."

Tremayne started to speak, but Benedict went on as though he hadn't noticed. "And everything else we've been through together. How understanding you've been. Always willing to forgive and forget."

"Really, Ben!" Tremayne was embarrassed. "There isn't anything to forgive! In fact, I should be asking your forgiveness. All that agonised soul-searching, how patient you've been!"

Benedict looked at him at last. "That may be the way you see it," he said, "but I remember every little thing, and to me it was all good." He paused. "You know I wish you God-speed.

I'll write, and send you my phone number. And ..." he hesitated once more, turning away again to look out over the park. He was silent for so long that Tremayne wondered whether he should go. When Benedict spoke his voice was little more than a whisper and Tremayne had to strain to catch the words.

"I can't get you out of my heart! It seems that you are too much a part of me. Pray for me, Tremayne!" And with that, he turned abruptly and left the lodge.

He was not alone with Benedict again, but just before they said their final goodbyes, Benedict pressed an envelope into Tremayne's hand, saying quietly, "Read this when you've a spare moment, and think of me."

Tremayne was travelling to London with several others, so there was no opportunity to open Benedict's letter until he stopped at the station buffet at Victoria to wait for his connection. He pulled the envelope from his pocket and turned it over in his hands. He was almost afraid to open it. Slowly, he tore open the flap and withdrew a slip of paper. On the paper Benedict had written, *"We are always in someone's thoughts, and the more we are loved, the more we are remembered. You will be in mine. Be assured that the link between us will never be broken."*

There was no signature. Tremayne covered his face with his hands. Benedict said he wasn't alone, but he felt it. In fact, he couldn't have felt more miserable. He was missing Benedict already, but also the life of the seminary and the friendships of the past six years. He sat for a long time until the lady at the counter called across, "Everything alright, luv? Oh, sorry, Father, didn't see the collar!"

Father! That sounded nice. He got up. "Yes, thanks. Everything's fine." He left the buffet. To his surprise he'd been there for over an hour and missed two trains.

He stayed with his mother for a few days while he settled his things in the presbytery of St Elpheges. The church was very near her house, but he would not be living there. The presbytery housed two novice priests, a bursar and Father Daley, a man in his late fifties, gentle and compassionate. Tremayne was one of two newly ordained priests. The other was Laurence Burgon, who, Tremayne discovered, was as nervous as he was. Father Daley took High Mass, but Tremayne and Laurence were both expected to officiate at other services. Their first was a time of anxious joy for them both. Laurence kept dashing in and out of the sacristy, hissing, "Is the altar prepared? Did you fill the ewer? Have you got the Host?"

"The altar's always prepared," said Tremayne. "And you've got the ewer in your hand!"

Laurence gulped, then grinned. "Oh, dear! They didn't tell us it would be like this!"

"They did where I was," smiled Tremayne. "But look, let's have one more check, just to set our minds at rest."

The novices had prepared the altar meticulously, as always. A crisp, white corporal lay in place under the chalice, which was veiled with silk. The spoons and cruet were set out and the paten to hold the Host was nearby. The altar lamp burned as constantly as ever, the Missal lay ready.

When the moment for Asperges came, before the principal Mass, Tremayne sprinkled the altar three times, intoning, "Thou, Lord, wilt sprinkle me with hyssop and I shall be clean," and marvelling anew at the miracle of transubstantiation about to take place. The acolyte rang the bell three times as Tremayne bent over the altar, praying silently, lips moving slightly, "... and so, through Jesus Christ ... pray and beseech thee ... accept these offerings." He consecrated the Host and carried it to the altar rail in the ciborium and blessed those waiting there with true humility of heart. When all had communicated, he returned to the altar and replaced the ciborium in the tabernacle. His eyes met Laurence's. They smiled at each other.

There were inevitably one or two tense moments. Tremayne was sure Laurence had forgotten the prayers for Russia, until he heard his resonant tones, "To thee do we cry, poor banished children of Eve." Then, suddenly, the day's Collect went entirely out of his head, but they helped each other and the Mass concluded smoothly. Tremayne poured the wine and water over his fingers and dried them with the purificator. He lifted the chalice and drank the contents, purified and veiled it. Then Laurence gave the dismissal.

Several people were waiting for them as they came out of the sacristy, having deposited their stoles and chasubles. "Very nice, young man!" an elderly woman said. "You could do with being a bit louder, but never mind, that'll come!" The parishioners were kindly people and hastened to put new priests at their ease.

"It's your turn for Confession next Saturday," Laurence reminded Tremayne. "I heard some odd things last night, I can tell you! Or, rather, I can't!"

"Everyone needs someone to talk to," replied Tremayne. "And everyone needs God. We can pass on absolution into the bargain. What could be better?"

His training had prepared him for all eventualities, but he had to give himself time to think the following week when a nervous young girl confessed to something he could remember only too well.

"Forgive me, Father, for I have sinned," she began hesitantly. "It's me boyfriend, you see. He comes round every night."

Tremayne knew what was coming. "I can't say no," the girl went on, warming to her confession.

"Yes, yes!" Tremayne said, hurriedly. "But where are your parents?"

"At bingo," the girl replied. "They get back about ten, but by then it's too late!"

Of course, he couldn't condone it, she must learn self-control. And there was the risk of an unwanted pregnancy. For some reason, he shuddered at the thought.

"You must say three Our Fathers and three Hail Marys," he told her. "That may help you to focus yourself under temptation." He had given her a responsibility, but it was all too late and her good intentions wouldn't last.

"Thank you, Father!" she gasped. She'd expected a harsh lecture and she left the Confessional hurriedly before he changed his mind.

Tremayne settled in quickly. The parishioners liked his smiling, eager manner and he soon became popular. Leaving church one Sunday, the week before Easter, he was eagerly accosted by a knot of earnest looking youngsters. "Are you joining the march next weekend?" they asked.

"What march?"

"CND. Ban the Bomb. From Aldermaston to Trafalgar Square. It's in a good cause!"

"I'll try, but it's Easter, you know. A busy time for us." He frowned thoughtfully. Laurence could hear Confession. He could take the Sunday Mass himself and join the march on Monday. Suddenly, he recalled his first visit to the Six Bells with Bill, the CND discussions all those years ago and, later, his first meeting with Benedict. Little had he dreamed then how his life would be changed forever.

"Yes, I'll come," he said. "But I can't start from Aldermaston. Where's a convenient pick-up point?"

"Turnham Green," said a youth. "There are some others going from there and leaving here by car. You could go with them next Monday."

So it was arranged. Two parishioners, Joan and Peter Wilkinson, called for him early on the Bank Holiday, the 18th of April, in their station wagon. "Mind the banners, Father!" laughed Joan, indicating two long poles arranged across the back seat.

"This is a good one," said Tremayne.

"Who did it?"

"I did," answered Peter. "Yes, it is pretty good, isn't it? I don't suffer from false modesty, as you can see!"

A long piece of canvas, nailed to a pole at each end, bore a gruesome picture of an exploding H-bomb, raining fire on to a nearby town. People were running away from the inferno, their mouths stretched into screams.

"It looks like something out of the last minutes of Pompeii!" Joan shuddered. "Either that or "The Scream.""

"A cross between the two!" Tremayne laughed. "You can't deny it's noticeable, though!"

Turnham Green was packed with marchers, most of whom had started from Aldermaston on Good Friday. All were looking footsore, but the atmosphere was united and cheerful. Several jazz bands were entertaining the crowds and, to his surprise, Tremayne recognised Nathaniel Grant. He hurried across to him. "Hi! Good to see you!"

Nathaniel looked up, then grinned. "Hallo to you! Things going well? Heard from Benedict? Come up to the Flamingo some time. Or the Marquee."

"Yes, I might just do that," Tremayne replied. "And, no, I haven't heard from Benedict. Have you?"

"Had a postcard from Dublin the other day," answered Nathaniel. "Didn't say much, but it appears he's getting on okay."

So, Benedict had contacted Nathaniel, but not him. Tremayne felt a stab of disappointment, then shook himself.

Benedict would write when he was ready and would surely be thinking of him.

Soon the marchers were stirring again, ready to complete the last leg of their journey through West London and on to Trafalgar Square. Peter and Joan Wilkinson picked up their startling banner and prepared to unfurl it.

"It's heavier than I thought!" panted Joan, struggling with her pole. "I don't know how far I can carry this!"

"Here, let me," offered Tremayne. He made to cross to her, reaching out his hands for the pole.

Suddenly, the air was filled with a mighty rushing wind, then a great and terrible stillness descended. Bewildered, he shook his head, thinking that he would faint. He certainly felt cold, and when he tried to walk it was like wading through syrup. Horrified, he looked at the scene around him. Joan and Peter, in the act of grappling with their banner, were frozen in time. Joan was laughing up at Peter. Her smile didn't waver. The banner, bellying out in the breeze, was unmoving, etched against a sky where clouds hung motionless. The emblem, showing half fire, half town, was folded across itself, defying gravity. All around him silent people were cemented like statues on the landscape, some half risen from sitting positions, others shaking out groundsheets which flew out, unmoving, in front of them. Some were still eating or drinking, sandwiches halfway to their mouths, pouring tea from flasks, the liquid hanging motionless. Traffic on the nearby road was still and silent, like toys stuck on a child's board game. Everything had been captured in time, like a photograph where only he was living. A terrible foreboding gripped him as he struggled to make sense of what was happening.

Then he saw her. She stood under a tree at the edge of the Green, the baby in her arms, a breeze ruffling the hem of her blue gown. Her tawny curls were blowing across her face and she was staring straight at him, the only moveable thing in a grotesque, silent parody. Even from a distance he could see her startlingly green eyes and see the soft parted lips.

They were the only real people, caught in a frightening distortion of time. Their eyes met. As when he had seen her at the seminary, the fear suddenly left him. He smiled at her and her eyes widened with understanding, as if she read his thoughts. Her mouth lifted just slightly. Then she turned her face to her child and, before Tremayne realised it, she had vanished.

Suddenly, the scene around him sprang to life. Movement began first, then an enormous roaring filled his ears as the sounds of modern life burst through once again. Joan Wilkinson was handing him her pole. "Here you are, Father. I say, are you alright? You look a bit white."

"I'm fine," he answered. "I expect it was the journey. I get carsick sometimes."

Joan was concerned. "Look, I can manage this for a while. You can take over later if you like." He was grateful for the suggestion. It gave him time to gather his wits. As they passed Queen Charlotte's hospital at Hammersmith nurses and patients alike hung out of the windows, cheering and shouting their encouragement. Peter Wilkinson called up to them. "Brothers and sisters, join the march!" And all around them the marchers started their chant. "Ashes to ashes, dust to dust. If the H-bomb don't getcha, the fall-out must!"

The march turned right from Oxford Circus and wound its way along Regent Street to Piccadilly Circus, barracked all the way down by the fiercely right-wing Empire Loyalists, and watched by some of London's most colourful street characters. Prince Monolulu, the well-known racing tipster, resplendent in his gaudy finery, ostrich feathers waving jauntily from his toque, and the Happy Wanderers, the West End's own Dixieland jazz band, who accompanied them to Trafalgar Square, shuffling along the kerb in single file in their usual fashion.

As they crossed the Haymarket, Tremayne felt an unaccountable chill. He was exhausted. He had carried the banner with Peter since Kensington, and he hadn't yet recovered from his ghostly experience. They entered Trafalgar Square, already crowded with 60,000 people. Still more poured in behind them. They managed to inch their way forward to get a reasonable view of the platform and speakers, Canon Collins and prominent politicians.

The great philosopher, Bertrand Russell, one of the founders of the CND movement, was speaking over the tannoy. Small and frail, with a mass of white hair, his querulous tones gave away his age. But he could still command his audience. The tannoy was crackly, but Russell's diction was perfect, his words carefully meted out, each one skimming across the waves of people and rippling to the far corners of the packed square.

"War does not determine who is right - only who is left. The idea of weapons of mass extermination is utterly horrible and is something which no-one with one spark of humanity can tolerate."

Tremayne gazed at him in awe, remembering the "Mysticism and Logic" essays, and now he was hearing the great man in person. Russell's theories of time fascinated him.

"It is poetic imagination, not science, which presents time as a despotic lord of the world, with all the irresponsible frivolity of a child."

To see time as a "despotic lord of the world" made sense to Tremayne, but he knew that his experiences were not just poetic imagination. He wished that there was a scientific explanation, a proof that time did exist on different levels, each level running parallel and each parallel hidden by veils which were occasionally pierced. Time had certainly got him in its grip, behaving "with all the irresponsible frivolity of a child." He was at time's beck and call, being whisked in and out of a continuum as a child might either favour or discard a loved toy on a whim. It was true, he reflected, that a despot was certainly both tyrannical and whimsical. And it was almost as if Russell had anticipated the day's unearthly experience when he wrote of the past having such "magical power" going on to say:

"The beauty of its motionless and silent pictures is like the enchanted purity of late autumn, when the leaves, though one breath would make them fall, still glow against the sky in golden glory."

He slipped away from the general crowd and made his way to stand shoulder to shoulder with those on the steps of the National Gallery. From there he could look out across the square to the raised dais at the far end, and see the speakers better. He thought how odd it was that Benedict had given him that particular book. Was it a premonition, or just a happy coincidence? He sighed. Things didn't just happen, they were part of a plan, a life plan, and if one accepted this, all coincidences made sense. He had to feel that God was guiding his life and that he was in safe hands.

He could see Joan and Peter making their way towards the steps. Together they walked down Whitehall, through Victoria Street to the station to catch the tube back to Turnham Green to fetch the station wagon.

Chapter 13

London, 1962

As if confirming coincidence, the next day brought a letter from Benedict at long last. He was well, enjoying his parish and working hard. *"There is much poverty here,"* he wrote, *"and the daily lives of most people are depressing. Too many mouths to feed and not much money to do it. But I know it is the Holy Father's will that no-one be denied a seat at the banquet of life, though all too often it's more like a meagre meal. I'm sorry it's taken so long for me to send you my address, but things have been hectic here."*

Tremayne thought that there couldn't possibly be more difference between his parish and Benedict's. He felt almost embarrassed to reply. He reached the last page. *"You know that I am thinking of you,"* Benedict concluded. *"There's always a place for you in my heart. I trust to God that you are settled."*

He sat down to answer the letter immediately. *"You're obviously worked off your feet, but I seem to have fallen on mine. The people are friendly, the parish prosperous. The only thing of great moment which has happened lately is the Ban the Bomb march, which we went on yesterday. We saw Bertrand Russell, and it was great seeing the man in person."* He wrote for nearly an hour. By the time he had finished, numerous sheets lay scattered on the bureau in front of him. He sorted them out and re-read the whole thing, then finished *"Your Brother in Christ and in spirit"* which he truly felt.

As the weeks passed, Tremayne found himself becoming used to the familiar, easy routine, but as if to guard against his becoming too complacent, he was called to Father Daley's study early in November. "We have to say goodbye to you, Tremayne," the priest said, smiling. "You've been sent a challenge! You're to be transferred to Our Lady of Mount Carmel in Inner London."

Tremayne gazed at him, dumbfounded.

"Close your mouth, Tremayne," Father Daley chuckled. "It's not unusual to be moved around quite a lot. You'll find a difference there. You've been spoilt with us, but no matter. You'll soon get into the swing of things."

Tremayne was filled with mixed emotions. He wasn't ready to move on, he'd made good friends.

The priest was eyeing him understandingly, and as if reading his mind, said, "Our service is to God, Tremayne. The making of close friends interferes with that. Just as you fitted in with us, you'll fit in with them. You've the kind of personality and warmth which will endear you to anyone." A compliment from Father Daley was about as rare as a visit from the Archangel Gabriel, and Tremayne modestly muttered a disclaimer, but there was a method in Father Daley's madness. The young priest showed promise. He had a mixture of tenderness and practicality, which were just the right ingredients to make a good priest and a good communicator. Better that he should go forward with positive encouragement.

Tremayne went to seek out Laurence. "I'm leaving!" he announced, baldly. "Soon, in fact. Wish me luck!"

"You already carry your own good measure of that."

Tremayne laughed, surprised. "What do you mean?"

The Forbidden Link

"It's part of your personality," Laurence said. "You're such a positive person. I think you walk with the Lord."

Tremayne was overwhelmed. It was clear that Laurence and Father Daley saw qualities in him which he didn't dream he had. He held out his hand. "Just in case I don't get the opportunity to say this before I go, it's been good to know you, Laurence."

Laurence shook his hand warmly. "Same here! You never know, our paths might cross again some day. Don't forget to leave me your address and phone number."

Joan and Peter Wilkinson held a farewell party for him in the church hall. Joan had made a cake with the words *"To Father Jago. Love from us all"* inscribed in pink icing. On the goodbye card Joan had written, *"We'll miss your special qualities."* He had been so lucky to know these people, his church family and a step on his theological path.

He travelled to London on a wet and windy day in December. The journey had been disheartening. First of all the goodbyes at the presbytery, then the train had been cancelled and Tremayne had been forced to wait over an hour for the next one, although a small fire struggled in the tiny grate in the station waiting room and he had managed to keep warm. Then he was unable to see anything from the train window. Early dusk was falling and incessant drizzle reflected lights from the train, which made looking out useless.

His new parish was welcoming, the church imposing. Set in a London square, it was surrounded by a busy commercial and shopping district and there was constant noise and bustle. The priest was Father Howell Jones, a Welshman, rotund and red-faced. Tremayne, missing Father Daley and Laurence, found him a trifle curt to begin with. But this impression soon passed and he realised that Father Jones was a retiring man, for all his bluff appearance. The redness of his skin was akin to a permanent blush and not, as some unkind people had suggested, a fondness for the bottle.

The church was near Shepherds Market, famous for its high-class prostitutes. Some of them earned hundreds of pounds a week and had famous names amongst their clientele. Not for these girls the beat of the Piccadilly pavements. Their clients arrived by limousine and were collected by chauffeurs. Paradoxically, many of the girls attended church every Sunday. When he reminded the congregation that true contrition rendered no sin unforgivable, it wasn't long before some took this to heart. A group of them waited in the church porch one Sunday.

"Were you referring to us, by any chance?" they asked, as he wished the last parishioner farewell.

He looked surprised. "Not especially," he commented, but he knew they wouldn't let him get away with that.

One of them, a tiny dark-haired girl, wrapped in an expensive coney fur, said in a velvety voice, "If there weren't any customers, we wouldn't be here. It's the downfall of man, not woman!" The others laughed.

Tremayne couldn't help smiling. "I'm sure you're right," he said, "and I'm also sure that you're accepted by God just as you are. Remember, 'Let he who is without sin cast the first stone.' "

"Some of us had no choice," one of the others said, "and we couldn't give up all this." She pointed to their good clothes and expensive jewellery.

"He forgives people if they want to change," Tremayne answered. "But you already know that. Go and read Matthew 6, 28-34! And give St Jude a challenge! Everyone sins, there'd be no need for church if there were no sinners and Christ would have died for nothing!"

An echo of Benedict's cryptic comment all those years ago flashed into his head. He had said his saint's name was appropriate, but Tremayne knew that no-one was a lost cause to God and he felt assured that his daily prayers for Benedict were heard. And renewed prayers for himself. Since his transfer he had experienced strong flashbacks. He had the distinct impression that he knew these streets intimately, except now there was a subtle difference. He had a feeling of knowing exactly what was round each corner, but the buildings looked shabbier, the streets cleaner. And there was one place in Brewer Street, an innocent enough place - Floris Chocolates - that he couldn't pass without feeling a suffocation so strong he felt he would choke. He decided it was his "poetic imagination" at work. He threw himself into the job.

Just up the road were the smart stores of the West End and the many jazz clubs and night clubs which littered the area. Life was never dull. Office workers rubbed shoulders with the rich and famous. The whole place was vibrant, alive, and a daily joy to Tremayne.

Laurence telephoned announcing his transfer to the cathedral church in Plymouth, which he welcomed wholeheartedly. He had relations in the southwest; he would enjoy being nearer to them. Tremayne wished him well and promised to keep in touch. Apart from his church duties he was free in his own time to do as he wished. While in Trafalgar Square on the CND march he had noticed the soup kitchen in the crypt at St Martin's-in-the-Fields, which was always crowded with dozens of the poor and needy. He decided to volunteer and went down to introduce himself to Rob Bucknell who ran it. Rob was a large, grey-haired man in his fifties, a Church Army captain who also ran a rehabilitation centre in Brixton, South London. He had a gentle, astute glance, which missed nothing. If there was ever a man who could replace his own father, Rob Bucknell was that man. They had been working flat out one day and at last there was a break in the seemingly endless queue. "Forgive me if I'm putting a foot wrong here," Rob began, "but it seems to me that there's something troubling you. Thought so since we met. Tell me to mind my own, if you like!"

Tremayne was astounded. "How could you tell?"

"Ah, so I'm right!" Rob said. "Like to talk about it?"

"It's true, I do have something on my mind, but I didn't think I was that easy to read!"

"Only to the older and wiser!" Rob replied. "I bet you anything you like, though, that Father Jones has noticed. Just hasn't asked you yet, that's all."

Tremayne thought he must be more transparent than he realised. Even now, he wasn't quite sure he wanted to say anything, but Rob had such a sympathetic nature, that before he could stop himself he had spilled out the whole confusing story.

Rob listened, wisely making no comment until Tremayne had finished. "You know what I think?" he said, at last. "Two things. Firstly, when you're new to the ministry you sometimes get doubts and temptations. It makes us vulnerable. Secondly, you never leave time for yourself. Overwork can often trigger stress. Take some time off, I can manage here, there are always plenty of volunteers who'll give a hand."

He turned away thoughtfully and began stacking the last of the bowls. It was clear that Tremayne needed more help than a break. He knew the young priest well enough to know that Tremayne had a suggestible nature, yet he was at a loss what to say next.

Before he could speak, however, Tremayne said abruptly, "What about a haunting? Oh, I know it sounds ridiculous," as Rob raised his eyebrows, "but, these things aren't unheard of, are they?"

"No, they're not," Rob answered. "You must be careful, though, Tremayne. This could be a matter for your bishop to deal with. Is it benign or malevolent, would you say?"

"Oh, definitely benign!" Tremayne said, quickly. "I always get an overwhelming feeling of pity, of pleading. The girl's face is so sad! She's really clear, too, right down to the type of clothes, colours, everything."

He described the girl as best he could and Rob said, "Sounds Edwardian or Victorian. You must tell Father Jones. I'm not sure how your church deals with these matters." He paused reflectively, before adding, "I think for your own peace of mind you should settle this once and for all. It's not good for you for it to continue."

Tremayne left the crypt and made his way back to Mount Carmel through the Haymarket. He was conscious of some disappointment, yet resigned to people's reactions. He thought of Father Jones and smiled wryly, imagining that good man's startled surprise. Well, perhaps he would mention it if the occasion arose, but he wouldn't pursue the matter with any vigour. He was glad he'd told Rob, though. Not since Benedict had he felt so at ease with someone.

The events of the next few days brought surprising news, however. Father Jones handed an envelope to him one morning at breakfast, addressed to the diocese. He was happy to tell Tremayne that they'd been left quite a large sum of money. "The Johnson's grandmother," Father Jones explained. "To thank you for your spiritual care, God rest her soul. She wanted you to decide how the money's to be spent. I've been in touch with the bishop and he's agreed. Of course," he hinted, gently. "the church roof needs repairing."

Tremayne listened with astonishment. He'd certainly helped old Mrs Johnson out of this life, but he'd done no more than his priestly duty. "How much is it?" he asked.

"Five thousand pounds!" answered Father Jones, and laughed when Tremayne's mouth dropped open. "Yes, it's a princely sum, isn't it? Well, it's yours to dispose of as you wish." He waited, expectantly.

Without hesitation, Tremayne found himself saying, "I'd like the money to go to the National Council for the Unmarried Mother and her Child." He was almost as amazed as Father Jones at what he'd said. Where had that idea come from?

Father Jones was looking at him a trifle oddly. "Well, if you're sure," he said. "Nothing else occur to you? Speak now or forever hold your peace!"

"No," Tremayne answered, now firmly resolved. That was exactly what he wanted and the conviction grew with every minute.

"Very good, then," Father Jones murmured, the church roof fading from his mind. "A deserving charity. Our Lord was born in those circumstances, of course. We must never forget that!"

The arrangements were made and Tremayne took the cheque to the North London headquarters. He was invited to one of the homes, where the mothers flocked round him, attracted by his charm and his dark good looks. He looked at their babies, wondering which were going home with their mothers and which were destined for adoption. It took a brave girl to choose either option.

Adoption brought his thoughts round to Benedict, and a cloud darkened the day. He hadn't heard from Benedict for quite some time and wondered if he was well. The fleeting association of ideas should have told him what to expect, but when he returned to the presbytery and saw a tall figure looking out over the square, he still didn't make any obvious connection. The figure turned and smiled. Tremayne stared in amazement "Is that you?" he gasped. "Blessed Mary, answer me!"

The figure answered in dry tones. "It seems that, one way or another, I am forever fated to startle you. I apologise. I shall try not to do so again!"

Tremayne hurried to grasp the outstretched hand. "I can't believe this!" he cried. "Benedict! It's great to see you! But what on earth are you doing here? Why didn't you write? I'd no idea you were coming!"

Benedict smiled. "There was no time. I was only told myself a couple of days ago. Apparently, this is my new parish!"

Chapter 14

There was no restraint or embarrassment. In Benedict guilt persisted, but Tremayne's exuberant nature had long since reasserted itself. The two were bound by a set of circumstances which brought them into continual contact with each other, and it was as if they had never been parted.

Father Jones soon discovered Benedict's strengths, his quiet reliability, his strong faith and unswerving loyalty to the church. In Tremayne he had his communicator, in Benedict his philosopher, the pourer of oil and also, as it turned out, an excellent administrator. He began to put more and more on those dependable shoulders and Benedict accepted the load with ease and, oddly, gratitude. Yet he sensed that Benedict was tossed on forbidden and troubled waters and that most of the tempest came from the lonely barque in which he sailed, although the young priest behaved at all times with solemn, even austere dignity. But in Tremayne's company, a transformation came over him, which no-one could fail to notice, and there was about the two a shared confidence. In each man Father Jones saw a spirituality and a godliness, although he sensed that Tremayne was uneasy about something. There was sometimes a haunted look about him, a drawn kind of stillness, as if he watched and listened. Perhaps he would broach the subject, get Tremayne to open up and talk. He wondered if Benedict had noticed. He made up his mind to ask him as soon as he got the chance. He needed some leads.

Tremayne settled in well at Mount Carmel. His particular

strengths were his compassion for children and his endearing, almost childlike eagerness. This stemmed from a true acceptance of his faith and gave him an air of maturity, a man who was both sensible to the vagaries of the world and able to understand them.

The opportunity Father Jones sought presented itself quite soon. He found Benedict alone in the sacristy one morning and said, "I need a quiet word with you, Benedict. Could you come to my study?"

Benedict looked up, surprised. "What is it, Father? Something wrong?"

"I hope not," Father Jones replied. "But I've something on my mind which I need to discuss with you."

The two men went to the study and Father Jones made some coffee. The study was his bolthole, cluttered and comfortable, with its open hearth, deep armchairs and book lined walls. Benedict longed to browse round those shelves and looked enquiringly at the titles. Father Jones noticed and said, "You're a bit of a bookworm, eh? Well, feel free to come and borrow anything you wish, provided you bring it back again, of course!"

Benedict smiled. "That's kind of you, Father. Yes, I am a bookworm."

"I'm glad you've settled in, Benedict," Father Jones said, pleased to see a smile. "You'll be an asset here, and to the church, if I'm not mistaken." He handed him his coffee. "Sit down. It's about Tremayne."

At once a shadow passed over Benedict's face. He looked at Father Jones warily.

"I'm not asking you to betray any confidences," Father Jones said, hastily.

Benedict relaxed a little. "Then what is it, Father?"

"I think that Tremayne's worried about something," the

priest said. "I've felt it from almost the first day he came. I was hoping you'd be able to throw some light on the subject. I don't like to think he's troubled, or that he can't talk to me."

"Perhaps you should ask him to," Benedict said, quietly.

Father Jones smiled. "I know. And you're right. I will ask Tremayne, except I wondered if you could throw some light."

Benedict was silent for a moment, then said reluctantly, "I know Tremayne is having spiritual experiences which conflict with the faith. Visions, dreams, call it what you will. I want to believe it's his imagination, but ..." he paused and frowned, "... he seems quite adamant it's real. He's convinced it's a lost soul, a girl, come to him for help. I think he could be under some strain and overtired." Father Jones felt some alarm. He finished his coffee and stood up. Benedict's eyes were now ranging round the shelves, so he considered the conversation closed. "Borrow anything you like. Take your time. I'll speak to Tremayne straight away. He'll be at the crèche."

He crossed the church yard to the hall where the nursery was in progress and found Tremayne, a youngster on each knee, his dark eyes glowing with that intense look that had their mothers fluttering, although he thought that his young priest looked tired and drawn. It crossed his mind as to why Tremayne had become a priest. It was plain that he could have married and had his own children, and maybe should have. Tremayne looked up and smiled. He put both children down and beckoned to Father Jones. "Come and join us? You're welcome, we could do with some fresh ideas!"

"No, no!" said Father Jones, hurriedly. "I'll leave that to you. I'd like a word with you, though, if you can spare yourself. Say if it's not convenient."

"No, it's okay, I can spare some time," Tremayne answered. The young mothers were visibly disappointed. The sex appeal was vanishing.

"Don't forget you promised to read the story!" they reminded Tremayne, giving Father Jones frosty looks. Their toddlers, sensing that they were about to miss something, took up the cry and grabbed Tremayne's legs, rooting him to the spot.

"I promise I won't keep Father Jago long, ladies," said Father Jones, fervently hoping that he wouldn't. He couldn't cope with the wrath of so many women.

Tremayne disentangled himself and followed Father Jones out of the church hall and across the paved yard to the presbytery.

"We'll go into the lounge," Father Jones said. "I believe Benedict might still be commandeering the study."

"Benedict?" Tremayne was surprised. "I thought he'd gone round the parish?"

"I needed to speak with him," replied Father Jones, "and now I need to speak to you. Look, I'll come straight to the point. I've been meaning to have a chat with you for a long time. You've found your niche here, I think, and certainly your work in the parish is exemplary. But I sense some kind of uneasiness in you, as if there's something on your mind, and today you look extraordinarily tired. If you're unhappy in any way, I need to know. I spoke with Benedict first because you two are good friends."

Tremayne's heart sank. He'd been hoping to avoid this moment. "What did Benedict say?" he asked.

"Not much. He's the soul of discretion, of course," replied Father Jones. "But I'm always here if you feel like talking. I know it's been difficult lately - like ships that pass, so to speak. Every time I'm in harbour, your tail lights are on the horizon. We never seem to drop anchor at the same time!"

Tremayne was silent. At any other time he would have appreciated the metaphor, but he hardly knew how to answer.

Events earlier that morning were pervading his whole being and he endeavoured to conceal his feelings with a superhuman effort. He had awoken at six, feeling unusually restless and tense. Rob Bucknell's advice suddenly came back to him and he resolved to take it. He needed to relax or his church duties would suffer. He would take some well-earned leave. He washed and dressed, feeling relieved that he had made a long overdue decision. He was adjusting his collar in the mirror when he began to feel a sensation of floating unreality and as he gazed at his reflection another face looked out at him. A shock like a lightning bolt rocked him on his feet as he desperately tried to bring his own image back into focus, but all he could see was the face of the girl, her green eyes penetrating his very being, until he felt he only had to lean forward to touch flesh and blood. He was filled once again with a great desolation that he still didn't know what to do for her. He turned sharply from the mirror, gripping the edge of the dressing table to steady himself. When he turned back again she was still there and it was as if he and the vision were one, seamlessly merging back and forth through time. Her consciousness became his consciousness, her will his will.

A sudden and stupefying thought rushed unbidden into his head. Perhaps he *was* the girl. Perhaps this was himself, reaching out from the past, warning him, giving him a chance for reparation for some great injustice he'd committed. The enormity of the revelation filled him with horror. No, it could not possibly be, *must* not be. Such heretical thoughts would threaten his work, his whole life. Yet through the deep stillness he was aware that the world had stopped and that he was a part of an inexplicable mystery, a mystery given to him to solve. *How*, he didn't know, yet he was filled suddenly with a great certainty that the time was drawing near.

He fixed an unwavering gaze on the girl until she gradually

faded and the sounds of other people moving in the presbytery once more intruded. He'd missed breakfast, but couldn't have eaten anyway. He went straight into the church to pray, to regain some composure to face the day ahead. Even now he still felt shaken and Father Jones's timing couldn't have been worse.

At long last he said, "Benedict knows that I've been worried about something, but we've discussed the usual explanations for it."

"For what?" Father Jones prompted.

Tremayne looked at him and took a deep breath. "For some time I've been having strange visions - or dreams maybe, I don't know which."

Father Jones leaned forward, his face serious. "What sort of visions? And what do you mean by 'the usual explanations'?"

"It's a woman," Tremayne replied, "and sometimes there's a child with her. We put it down to some kind of nervous exhaustion. It happens when I least expect it." It all sounded so silly and dramatic.

Father Jones frowned. "For heaven's sake, man!" he said, sharply. "You're not telling me it's our Lord and His Blessed Mother?"

Tremayne couldn't prevent himself smiling at the comparison. How convenient that would be. He wished with all his heart he could say yes.

"No," he said, "I wouldn't be in this dilemma if that were the case, and I would've told you."

Father Jones was thinking hard. These visions weren't unheard of, but they would need to be proved. Then he thought of all the publicity if it got out. Good revenue for the church, of course - a place of pilgrimage. No, it would be too much, he couldn't cope with all that. He was beginning to wish he'd never asked. Tremayne's next words, however, dispelled any fears he had of the world's press, and replaced them with fears for his young priest.

"She's very brightly dressed, almost overdressed with frills and ribbons, and she has an earthy look about her, tarnished really."

No, Father Jones decided. Definitely not our Blessed Lady. It must mean, then, that Tremayne was sickening for something, or had been duped by the enemy.

"Look," he said. "You'd better start from the beginning and tell me when this began."

Tremayne was reluctant. He didn't want to drag through the whole thing again, but it was clear he had to tell Father Jones something. He explained his illness and his stay with Benedict, and the conclusions they had reached about the visions being the result of a breakdown. "Before I became ordained my life was rather useless," he concluded. "I was drifting and couldn't make up my mind what I wanted to do. That's why I can never thank Benedict enough. I think he saved my sanity and gave me a purpose."

Father Jones nodded. The picture was becoming clearer. Tremayne owed Benedict a debt of gratitude. The dissolute saved by the crusader. "You were happy in your previous parish, weren't you? Made lots of friends?"

"Yes, I was happy there," answered Tremayne. "But I'm happier here. There's more to do, every day is different and it's more of a challenge!"

"Of course," Father Jones said. Converts were always the most zealous priests. "You may not experience any more phenomena now that you're settled. These are possibly nothing more than waking dreams. You have some leave owing. Perhaps you'd better take it. But if you sense anything evil we shall have to deal with it. The bishop will have to be told, for one thing. In fact, I'm not so sure he shouldn't be told, anyway!" he added.

Tremayne was anxious now to drop the subject, accept Father Jones's explanation and leave. "Yes, I'll take some leave. I do feel tired. I don't expect I'll see her again, but if I do perhaps we could hold a special Mass for her?"

"You mean an exorcism?" Father Jones asked, uneasily. He wasn't used to such things and had never performed one. He didn't relish the thought.

"No, just a Mass for her soul."

"I'll leave that to you," replied Father Jones, rising. He had settled the matter satisfactorily. It was a delicate subject, of course. "It may be that you have an open channel for these things. Be careful!"

Tremayne thought of Father Dominic at the Retreat who had a constantly open channel for all-comers. Even he had not ventured to guess the nature of the visions, or why the girl had appeared. Now he was back where he started, carrying the burden himself and not able to relinquish it. But it was his burden, he realised, and the girl had come to him for help. So far he hadn't been able to offer any, but perhaps he was an open vessel, attuned to the soul hovering just beyond his reach. He got up and went to the study door. "Thanks for listening, Father," he said, pausing with his hand on the doorknob. "And thanks for the help." He hoped he sounded sufficiently non-committal.

He hurried back to the nursery. The mothers and children were just leaving. "A story tomorrow," Tremayne promised, absently. The little crowd left, calling goodbye. He was conscious of disappointing them.

Benedict had already laid out the vessels and linens in the church for midday Mass by the time Tremayne joined him. "Thank you," said Tremayne, gratefully. "I'm sorry to leave it all to you."

"That's alright," Benedict replied. He smoothed the altar cloth, removing imaginary wrinkles. "Have you spoken with Father Jones?"

"Yes," Tremayne answered. "He said I looked tired and wanted to know if anything was wrong. I told him about the visions."

"What did you tell him about them?" Benedict asked.

"Not everything, just that they started before I came here. But I didn't tell him what I really feel now. I couldn't. Something happened this morning. And now I feel ..."

"What's happened? What do you feel?"

"Well, I feel it's ... it's a lot more complicated now," Tremayne answered hesitatingly. He wanted so desperately for Benedict to believe him, yet he knew that was almost impossible. "I saw the girl again this morning. Yes, I *did*," as Benedict made a sound of disbelief. "She looked back at me from the mirror. She was there! I tell you, she *was*! I could've touched her. She was as real as you are."

Benedict felt completely helpless and at the same time fearful, knowing how vulnerable Tremayne was and how this could well be some dreadful challenge that Tremayne must use all his will to surmount. After an immense effort and trying to keep his voice light, he said, "Tremayne, you must have a break. You need to relax more. You even work on your time off! Take a bus into the country, read, do anything. But forget church work once in a while, then you'll find that these strange sensations pass."

"Another thought has come to me," Tremayne went on, as if he hadn't heard. "And I know this sounds completely crazy. It could be a haunting, perhaps. But maybe it could also be a case of ..." He hesitated, knowing what was to come. "A case of ... reincarnation!" he finished with a rush. "What do you think?"

Benedict snapped his brows together. "What do I think about reincarnation? I don't think anything about it. Neither should you. You'll believe in metamorphosis next! What will you be, Kafka's Gregor or Woolf's Orlando?"

He turned his attention to the altar and began rearranging the vessels needlessly, moving them in and out of juxtaposition with each other, finally placing them where they had been. A desolate anger that Tremayne's theology should be so questionable swept through him and in that moment he wished with all his heart that he could walk away from all knowledge of it.

Tremayne had only ever seen Benedict angry once, at the Retreat. His anger usually manifested itself, as now, by aloof withdrawal, he watched while Benedict continued his absorption with the cruets and knew that he had angered him. "I'm sorry!" he blurted, at last. "I didn't mean to shock you."

Benedict straightened and turned to face him. "Yes, I am shocked," he said, coldly. "Not so much by the concept, which is pedestrian and most certainly false, but by the fact that you seem to have embraced it." He made a noise of disgust. "Reincarnation! It's a preposterous explanation and if you continue to entertain it, you could jeopardise your ministry. That I do care about!"

"What about a haunting, then?" Tremayne persisted.

Benedict's expression softened somewhat. "I think the same as I've always thought about all this. It happens when you're tired or overworked."

A niggle of irritation began to grow in Tremayne. "Everyone seems complacent about this but me!" he said crossly.

"Everyone?" Benedict queried. "You didn't mention reincarnation to Father Jones, I hope?"

"Of course I didn't!" Tremayne retorted. "I gave him the explanation other people usually give me - that I've been overtired lately!"

"I give you credit for some sense, then!" Benedict said. "Who else have you told?"

"Rob Bucknell at the soup kitchen. But I only suggested a possible haunting, never reincarnation!"

"And what did he say?"

"More or less the same as you. In fact, he suggested a break from St Martin's. Maybe I won't go down for a few weeks."

Benedict sighed, his anger evaporating. "There you are, then. He's got a point. Wouldn't it be worth thinking about a break?"

"I suppose so," Tremayne admitted, grudgingly. "Anyway, I'm tired of thinking about it now. Can you take Mass? I'm going out on the parish," and he swung on his heel and left abruptly. Benedict looked after him, his eyes troubled. As always, his protectiveness for Tremayne rose strongly within him, but there persisted the faint doubt that he was wrong and that Tremayne had, indeed, encountered something which defied explanation. He was in danger of judging and had certainly been angry. He left the church after Mass and made his way to his room to pray for tolerance.

Chapter 15

Much as he enjoyed working with the nursery group, Tremayne felt that he might be better used elsewhere in the parish and took his idea to Father Jones, who agreed. "I need another pastoral visitor," he said. "I know that you'd be absolutely right for that and it would help me enormously. And we can safely leave the toddlers with their mothers, I think, as long as someone's here if there's any kind of emergency. Now what about that leave?"

"I'll have it in a couple of weeks, if that's alright with you," Tremayne answered. "I'll see that the nursery's OK first, though. I thought I'd go to Mother's at Wallington for a few days, then on to visit Sally, perhaps, up North. She's married now, with a baby, it'll be nice to visit." He got on well with Paul, Sally's tolerant husband and he looked forward to getting out of London for a while.

He had no premonition of how enforced his leave would be or that it would be many weeks before he saw either his Mother or Sally.

Father Jones was aware of a coolness between Benedict and Tremayne, but thought it best not to interfere. Tremayne spent his spare time reading in his little room, which looked out over the square, trying to find a satisfactory answer to the belief in the transmigration of souls, which the great Eastern philosophies espoused. Emanuel Swedenborg's *Spiritual Diaries* made fascinating reading, especially his account of the death of his former teacher Christopher Polhem, who it was said, was present at his own funeral:

"Polhem died on Monday. He spoke with me on Thursday and when I attended his funeral he saw his coffin and thus who were there and the whole process, and how his body was laid in the grave. He conversed with me, asked why they buried him when yet he was alive. He afterward asked why the minister said that he should rise at the Last Judgement, when yet he had been resuscitated for some time."

Swedenborg's writings had all the hallmarks of someone who had the certainty of heaven. He had seen and spoken to angels and, after their deaths, three people he had known in life. He believed that existence never ends and made the interesting observation that when people become spirits they cannot tell that they are not in the body they had in the world.

"I have even talked with three people I had known in the world, telling them that their funeral rites were now being arranged for the burial of their body. When they heard this they were struck with astonishment, saying that they were alive; people were burying only the thing that had served them in the world."

This Tremayne could perfectly understand and it also made sense of the woman appearing in her body. The idea of a soul returning as a punishment for wrongs was not logical either, for human beings would never be perfect until they had received redemption. He recalled quoting the Book of Job to Benedict when he had first tried to explain the mystery, "Man is born to trouble as surely as sparks fly upward," and Benedict replying, "There is no sin that is unforgivable, providing you show true repentance." And he was right or what was the point of redemption?

Swedenborg had been urged by departed souls to tell people what he had seen, but he knew he wouldn't be believed, surmising that any such disclosures to those still living would be dismissed as *"among the visions which are illusions."*

Tremayne was able to take some comfort from that. Perhaps it had been a mistake to mention anything to Benedict.

He finished the last book and put them on his bureau to keep. It was a mild and starry night, yet his head felt heavy and his thinking had become clouded. Lights were on in the church hall. He crossed the paved yard and pushed open the door, just as someone on the other side pulled it the other way. A female voice uttered a muffled exclamation and a child joined in with a wailing protest.

Startled, Tremayne eased himself round the door. A young girl and a toddler were crowded behind it. He'd seen the girl once before. It was Betty Parker. She and her daughter had recently arrived in London. The child glowered up at him and clung to her mother's legs.

"I'm sorry!" he apologised. "My fault! I shouldn't always be in such a hurry!"

"No trouble, Father," she replied, in a broad Mancunian accent. "We was just talking to Father Benedict. We've been 'elpin' at the youth club, but it's time to be gettin' Rosie 'ome!"

More than time, he thought, glancing at his watch. It was nine-thirty and almost dark. It seemed likely that Betty Parker had no more idea of a regular routine for her child than Jack Idle had for his farm. Rosie was overtired and fretful. Tremayne had no idea what they'd been talking to Benedict about, but as Benedict had little or no interest in the concept of time, he could imagine the experience had been rather tedious.

"Father Benedict said he might be able to 'elp uz," Betty explained. "I need a job. I don't want no trouble livin' in London. Plenty o' that at 'ome, especially since she were on the way," she nodded at Rosie. "Dad threw me out. If I don't get work I might 'ave ter go back!"

Intrigued, Tremayne looked at her more closely. She was of smallish build, with a pert, rather foxy face, but pretty all the same. Her hair hung in two long blonde ropes across each shoulder. Her clothes were poor, but clean, and the child was clearly not neglected. Betty would be considered desirable by some, he thought, then instantly dismissed the idea.

She was eyeing him curiously. "What's up, Father?" she asked. " 'Ave I lost me label, or summat?"

Tremayne chuckled. "Sorry, I didn't mean to stare. What did Father Benedict say, then?"

"He said he'd talk to Father Jones."

"About what?"

"I told you. A job. I said I was looking for one."

"Look, you can't go rollicking around the streets at this hour with a child. I'll walk with you to the tube or bus," Tremayne suggested. "Where do you live?"

"Got a room along Tottenham Court Road, near Goodge Street," she replied. "And you don't 'ave ter walk wi' me. We're used to it, me and Rosie."

"Well, you can get unused to it tonight," he said, firmly. "I wouldn't dream of letting you go off by yourself!"

She considered for a moment, then nodded. "But I'd rather walk. It's a nice night."

"What about Rosie," he asked. "It's quite a way, you know."

"Oh, you can carry her when she gets tired," Betty answered casually.

Tremayne grinned and swung the child onto his shoulders. "I asked for that, didn't I?"

They began walking down Oxford Street towards Tottenham Court Road. Betty chatted inconsequentially for most of the way, but she was not boring. She had a fund of trivia at her disposal, mostly about her large and chaotic family in Manchester, and a talent for telling it amusingly, so that the walk passed quickly. They turned left at the junction of New Oxford Street. "'Spect you're busy all day," Betty remarked. "Church an' all."

"It's not all work," Tremayne replied, panting a little. Rosie had fallen asleep and was slumped across one shoulder. His right arm was numb and he was beginning to wish they'd taken the tube. "We get time off, if there's not a meeting or a club or something."

"Ever go to the pub?" Betty asked, casually.

"We go to The George or The Coach and Horses," Tremayne said. "There's jazz there. Sometimes The Blue Posts on the other side."

Betty pulled a face. "Coach is alright," she said, "but I don't like The George. Too full of toffy-nosed film people. Had a bar job there for a few days."

"I should've thought you'd like that," Tremayne smiled, glancing down at her.

"Don't you want to be discovered? You're pretty enough!"

She looked sideways up at him. "If I was gonna be discovered, I woulda been by now!" she said. "They 'ad their chance. No-one gets a second one wi' me!"

I bet they don't, thought Tremayne.

"So they better take the first one." She moved closer so that he felt her left hip bump against him. She moved away immediately. "Sorry Father. It's a bit crowded, In't it?"

It was true. Crowds were emerging from The Dominion and the late night theatregoers jostled the pavements. Even so, he knew her move was calculated. He was not annoyed, only amused. It was satisfying to see her admiring glance and enjoy her femininity. He was quite used to the admiring glances of women.

At the door to her first floor flat he handed over the sleeping Rosie, who lay like a lumpy parcel in her mother's arms. Betty kicked open the door with her foot and Tremayne held it while she passed into the hallway. He half expected to be invited in and began to wonder how he would make his excuses, but to his surprise Betty only said, "Ta, Father. See you at church. Pull the door shut for me, will ya?" Taken off guard, Tremayne could only nod and do as he was asked.

He caught a bus going back along New Oxford Street and arrived at the presbytery, surprised to find it was nearly eleven o'clock. There was no sign of Benedict or Father Jones, so he made some coffee and took it to his room. He thought of Betty Parker until he fell asleep. His sleep was restless and intermittent, punctuated alternatively by Betty and the mysterious girl of his visions, until the two became inextricably mixed, reaching out imploring arms to him. He awoke with a start at half-past four and didn't sleep again.

Benedict looked at him, eyebrows raised, when he stumbled into the kitchen heavy-eyed and yawning. "Bad night?"

"Yes, been awake for hours," Tremayne replied, pouring black coffee. "I met Betty Parker yesterday. She said she'd been helping at the youth club. She worries me a little."

"Why's that?"

"Well, doesn't she worry you? Tremayne asked. "Hiking that child around the streets at all hours. I had to walk her home last night, although she was quite prepared to go home alone. And she's ripe for the streets, if you ask me!"

"Surely not!" Benedict protested mildly. "In fact, I would say that Betty Parker has far more commonsense than that. I'd guess that would be her last option. Actually, we were speaking yesterday about a job."

"We must try and help her," mumbled Tremayne, his mouth full. "What about paying her to run the nursery? I'm giving that up now. Father Jones wants me to join the pastoral team."

Benedict collected the breakfast dishes and stacked them

in the sink. "Yes, he told me. And that is exactly what I had in mind for Betty. It would tie in nicely. I'll ask Father Jones. It might not be very well paid, though."

Tremayne watched him, half asleep still, as he methodically washed them, swishing the wire soap shaker with its little piece of washing soap through the water. Each item was systematically rinsed and placed in size order in the wooden rack, and Benedict was careful to mop up errant puddles around the sink. He remembered Benedict's punctiliousness in his little Edgware Road flat all those years ago. He had not changed, and somehow the whole fastidious operation was comforting.

"Hey, wake up!" Benedict's voice recalled him to reality. "Will you unlock the hall or shall I?" He was relieved when Tremayne nodded. He had things to do and needed some time alone before he faced the day. Lately, he had felt morose and depressed again.

Tremayne collected the big iron key from the hook and crossed the paved court to the hall. There was a little queue there already, calling out good morning as he approached. Betty was there with Rosie, smiling and looking unexpectedly smart. His step quickened. His tiredness vanished.

She walked past him into the little anteroom where the nursery equipment was kept, and began to drag things out into the main hall.

"I've spoken to Father Benedict this morning," Tremayne said. "We've got some ideas about work for you."

"Trouble is, Father, I en't got no qualifications," she replied, frowning. "We never done things like that where I come from. It was either leave school quick and get a job, or find a willing fella and get pregnant. Did it meself, didn't I? Only in the end, he wouldn't marry me."

It seemed to Tremayne that his life was somehow

inextricably linked with unmarried mothers. The desire to donate money to them and now Betty. Even the girl in the visions had a child. One thing was clear, however. He knew that life for all unmarried mothers was hard and it took a special person to face condemnation with courage.

"Father Jones might agree to your helping in the nursery, if you're interested," Tremayne said. "I mean paid help. I'm sure we could arrange it."

"That'd be great!" Betty said. "I like kids and they like me. As long as I earn enough to pay me rent and feed us!" He looked at her with renewed interest as she moved about the hall, setting up the doll's house and the little slide, the other mothers joining in and chatting together. She moved with a quick fluidity, energetic but never clumsy. Today her hair was tied up in a ribbon, its ends falling onto her shoulders, giving her an unexpectedly angelic look.

She caught sight of his gaze and stopped suddenly, motionless, returning his stare. Unsmiling, they looked at each other, their eyes burning the space between them while the busy activity melted away. He felt himself stirring and wrenched his gaze away, exhilarated, his heart thumping unevenly. What was happening to him? She was just an ordinary girl, like many others who came to the nursery with their children. There was nothing particularly special about her. She was pretty, but not outstandingly so, and she had a bold crudeness which repelled his sensitivity. Yet there was about Betty Parker an earthy sexuality which charged the air between them with chemistry, to which his own sensual nature responded without thought. When he looked back she was still watching him, waiting for him to turn as she knew he would. She lowered her eyes and a faintly provocative smile lingered for an instant on her lips. Then she moved away and the moment was broken.

Luckily, no-one seemed to have noticed. He slipped out of the hall and crossed to the presbytery, his mouth dry and his mind in a turmoil. He went to his room and flung himself on the bed. It was no use denying it, he wanted Betty Parker. Above all else, he was still a man, the longings always came back, no matter how long absent they had been, how much denied. He rolled over onto his stomach, cradling his head in his arms. After a while he fell into a fitful doze.

Thus Benedict found him two hours later. He looked at Tremayne with some concern, and knew that more than lack of sleep was troubling him. He hoped that Tremayne would confide in him, but he was still feeling out of sorts himself. He joined Father Jones in the Lady Chapel to prepare for Mass. The little chapel was not crowded, the usual devotees and some foreign visitors. The moment was solemn and beautiful for Benedict, as always, and lifted his spirits, so that when Father Jones said afterwards in the sacristy, "This old back is very broad, you know, if it helps to talk," he looked up with surprise, and some regret. He felt he had failed Father Jones. He had not settled in particularly well, despite Tremayne or, perhaps, because of him.

Father Jones was regarding him closely. "I am not as unworldly as you might think. No, you don't have to tell me what troubles you, it is quite plain to me," as Benedict started, "but you must come to terms with it. The church has had these problems ever since there's been a church ..." he paused, searching for words. Finally he said, "There's a possibility you might be transferred again soon. At least, one of you should go, either you or Tremayne."

Benedict nodded. He was silent for long minutes. His heart ached unbearably. To be constantly near Tremayne was to keep the wound open. It never seemed to heal. But away from him was torment itself. Strangely, for weeks he had felt no such pressure. It was simply a joy to be together and he had learnt how to deal with his guilt. An image of Betty Parker, sharp and clear, suddenly rose before him and beside it, his face fierce with longing, was Tremayne, just as he had seen them that morning as he passed the open doorway of the church hall. He'd glanced in unsuspectingly and had been the only one to see that burning look. It was the culmination of something he had sensed long before. He knew, in that instant, the real reason for his malaise. His depression and lethargy was jealousy.

"It's okay, Father," he said, at last, with a thin smile. "Perhaps it is time for me to move on. I think I need to."

"Nevertheless," answered Father Jones, carefully. "The weed needs to be tackled at the root or it will flower again and again."

"I've tried!" Benedict cried. "I think I've got it under control, then something happens, and I know I haven't. It's not so much a weed, more an insidious creeper, with so many hidden roots I'll never get rid of it!"

"Maybe not. You are how you are," replied Father Jones. "But creepers need not spread. They can be trained, kept within limits. Perhaps you need to stay and face it. But," he sighed, "St Mary and St Boniface in Plymouth is in need of another priest and either of you would be eminently suitable. It's a cathedral church, a good transfer."

"I'll go," said Benedict, resignedly. "It would be best. Although ..." he paused, thinking of Tremayne and Betty.

"What?"

"Perhaps Tremayne should be asked, at least. He might feel it's an appropriate time for him."

"He's on leave in a couple of weeks. We'll wait till he's back and talk again," Father Jones said and went thoughtfully on his way. He was glad he wasn't young any more. And glad he wasn't in Benedict's shoes. God had made people as varied and diverse as the world in which they lived, and there was no accounting for people's natures. He didn't want to lose either man, but before many days had passed the matter had been taken entirely out of his hands.

Benedict had no desire to be Tremayne's keeper, but drawn by a perverse compunction, watched him over the following days. No matter how determinedly he prayed for acceptance of what he was, it seemed that his path would be continually dogged by relentless reminders. Father Jones had given Betty an official job in the nursery and her new position gave her ample opportunity to flirt outrageously with Tremayne. Benedict saw the looks, felt the magnetism between them and knew that Tremayne was revelling in the attention, taking every chance to be near Betty.

Tremayne noticed nothing of Benedict's dilemma. He had taken to walking Betty home after her help at the youth club and she had started to ask him in. The first time he'd only stayed ten minutes, just enough time for a cup of tea. Then one evening Betty suggested he read Rosie a bedtime story. Taken off guard, he hesitated only a moment before agreeing. Rosie wanted Squirrel Nutkin. She'd heard the story at the nursery. Betty didn't have Squirrel Nutkin. "We got Timmy Tiptoes or Peter Rabbit," she said to Tremayne. "But the other belongs to the nursery. Give her Peter Rabbit. That'll do."

The request was swiftly accomplished and Rosie was asleep before the end of the story.

"She's overtired," said Tremayne, with concern. "Don't you think she goes to bed too late?"

"Prob'ly," Betty answered. "But it don't do her no harm. She always has a nap at the nursery."

Tremayne realised that Rosie would adapt herself round her mother and gave up. He settled himself on her old sofa and sipped the coffee she handed him, regarding him from under her lashes. She wanted him, she'd always wanted him. She vaguely understood the seriousness of the sin he would be committing, but she was a firm believer in fate and fate had put Father Tremayne Jago in her way. She was determined to get what she wanted, and she knew that he wanted her, too. She had seen his eyes light up when he saw her and felt how he trembled when he was near her.

Tremayne put down his cup and without a word they moved into each other's arms. He buried his head in her neck, savouring her sweetness, while she clung to him and sighed. "I've waited for this," she whispered against his hair. "And so have you." He nodded, wordlessly, feeling the world melt away, conscious only of her nearness and his wildly beating heart.

He lifted her across his lap. He could feel her breasts beneath the thin teeshirt and suddenly he was struck by a shyness which paralysed him. She took his hands and placed them against her soft skin and her warmth brought life back into him. An exquisite familiarity rushed through him. Nothing existed but this entranced moment of closeness and he began stroking her, a sweet fire burning through his veins. He revelled in the feel of a woman again and, emboldened, he began to kiss her hungrily. She was impatient for him, but she knew the race was not won until the final hurdle of his conscience had been cleared.

He was oblivious to her loosening his collar, didn't feel it slip from his neck. His urgent need blotted out all thought. She drew back from him. She was panting hard as if she had been running and her breath was punctuated by a grunt of triumph which penetrated his urgency. She was waving something in her hand. Something white and gleaming, which danced and shimmered in front of his stupefied gaze. He gazed at it, mesmerised, until at last he recognised it. His collar, symbol of his holy vows, dipped and swung before him, taunting him, flying to and fro like a thing possessed. As possessed as he was.

With a choking cry he pushed her from him, desire fleeing on the instant. His hands reached upward for the collar and for a brief instant they struggled for it, she sobbing with frustration and he desperate to feel its reassurance once more circling his neck.

With a stab of physical pain, he realised just how unforgivable his behaviour had been, and the strength ebbed out of him. He sagged back against the sofa and waited for her anger. It came quickly. Bitter and profane words began to tumble from her. He had so nearly been hers, but there was no mistaking that fixed look, the shock in his eyes and she knew for certain that she had lost him.

She leaned forward, deliberately raised her hand and aimed it at his face. He caught it and held it away from him. When he spoke his voice was toneless, mechanical. "Forgive me!" he said. "This is all my fault. God forgive me!"

That finished her. She sprang to her feet, tears running down her face. "Can't you forget you're a priest, for once!" she cried. "It wouldn't be such a sin, would it? Everybody knows priests do it! Or aren't you human, like the rest of us?"

He looked at her flushed face and saw the hurt pride and humiliation in it. She was a lonely girl, needing love. It was to his eternal shame that he had led her to believe he could give it to her.

"Yes, it would be a sin," he said, and stood up. "For you, but worse for me. I've made promises to God." His collar lay on the floor and he stooped to retrieve it.

She turned her head away as he put it on. "We wouldn't have said nothin'! No-one would've known!" she said, angrily.

He smiled faintly. "No, only us. And God."

Betty didn't live with God every day. If she thought about him at all, she saw him as a father she could deceive whenever she wished. She ran to the door and wrenched it open without another word. He passed her and she slammed it shut behind him.

He went quickly down the stairs and out into the street. His behaviour had been despicable. He'd led her on, then rejected her; he deserved more than her anger. *Lead us not into temptation.* He didn't need anyone else to lead him, he could do it very well for himself and, it seemed, lead others too.

Head down, he hurried on, past the late night crowds, enveloping himself in the noise and bustle of the streets. He could never face Betty again. He had spoilt a friendship and let a flirtation get entirely out of hand. He made up his mind to leave for Wallington the next day. He dodged between the traffic at the junction of New Oxford Street and Tottenham Court Road, pausing momentarily on the traffic island. Then, without thinking he stepped out into the road. A number 25 bus, bound for Victoria, swung around from his left. Tremayne heard the roar of the engine and looked over his shoulder as the bus bore down. He tried to jump back to safety, but it was too late. The bus caught him a glancing blow which spun him like a helpless leaf into the gutter. His head struck concrete and a million lights exploded behind his eyes, before darkness descended.

The bus screeched crazily to a halt and the driver leapt down from his cab. People began running from all directions. Tremayne lay motionless and a stream of bright red blood began to mingle in the gutter with the residue of water left by the street cleansing van. The knot of people grew and each person had the same thought: that the young and handsome priest, lying so white and still, was dead.

Chapter 16

Margherita sat in the dim hospital corridor, her head bowed in her hands. She had responded immediately to the urgent call from Father Jones, hurriedly boarding the dogs and taking a taxi to London. She had been led straight to Tremayne's bedside. His eyes were closed, his breathing so shallow that his chest hardly moved. The nurses were preparing him for emergency surgery to remove a blood clot and there had been nothing else she could do but slip from his room into the darkened corridor, where she sat feeling utterly helpless and alone, wishing that Edward was with her. A nurse passed by, pushing a rubber-wheeled trolley along the polished floor. The paraphernalia on the trolley jingled faintly to the rhythm of her stride, but Margherita didn't even look up and was oblivious to the nurse's friendly smile.

For the hundredth time she asked herself how this could have happened, but she would have to wait for answers. She wasn't aware of the time passing, but presently another nurse came and gently said, "We're taking your son down now. Would you like to come as far as the anteroom?"

Margherita nodded and followed the nurse. Tremayne was just being wheeled from the side ward. They had taken his pillows away and he lay, face turned heavenward, a deathly pallor on his lips. Margherita quickly took one of his hands in hers, holding it tightly as they descended in the lift. No-one spoke. One of the two burly porters glanced at her, then looked away, a frivolous comment dying on his lips. This was everyday business to him. Sometimes a joke or two helped take people's minds of things, but he thought better of it and began to whistle tunelessly through his teeth. The tiny rasping sound filled the moments until they reached the theatre and could hear the clattering of instruments in metal dishes. Margherita caught a glimpse of green-gowned figures as the porters wheeled Tremayne through the theatre doors, which flapped shut behind them.

The operation was long and complicated and when Tremayne emerged from theatre, Margherita was still there, waiting to take his hand once again. He was covered in a sterile sheet and only a small portion of his face showed beneath a swathe of dressings. As they neared the recovery ward, she saw Benedict waiting and a flood of warmth rushed through her. She hurried to him, her hands outstretched, but to her surprise he swept her into his arms instead. She needed only this one gesture of compassion to release the pent-up emotion that now overwhelmed her. She sagged against him, her strength failing. He supported her to a chair where she sat and sobbed until her tears dried. He waited, holding her. They didn't need to talk. She knew Benedict would be her strength and rock in the critical days ahead.

The lights in the ward grew fainter as daylight seeped through the drawn curtains. The still figure on the bed showed no signs of life, but beneath the dressings unknown voices and images sprang up and receded, unbidden. A voice which seemed terrifyingly familiar and which echoed and boomed round the whole world suddenly said, "Please enter my humble abode," then darkness descended once more and there was nothing for a while. Suddenly, it spoke again, high-pitched and wheedling. "Charges is five shillin' for the month," it said. The voice had an evil sound about it that sent a shudder through its unwilling listener. It went on, talking about a baby, feeding a baby, milk for a baby. Lost in his world of darkness,

Tremayne struggled to make sense of the voice as he slipped further back into unconsciousness. The people who stood with such loving and fearful anxiety beside his bed were not there to him at all. Only the images inside his head were real. Margherita and Benedict looked down at him and said nothing, though in each of their hearts silent prayers arose, Benedict's especially terrible in their pleading.

They left the hospital at six in the morning. "There's nothing you can do," the nurse had said. "The doctor'll be around later. You must get some sleep." Her practised eye took in the lines of exhaustion etched on Margherita's face. She glanced with curious interest at the tall, sombre priest, his black eyes burning with an intensity she had never seen before.

Margherita said, "We'll be back, both of us," looking up at Benedict, who nodded. The nurse smiled. She was rather looking forward to that.

When they returned Tremayne lay just as they had left him - white, immobile, attached to his life through drips and tubes. Late morning the surgeon made his rounds, stopping at Tremayne's bed and looking intently at him. He turned to Margherita and Benedict and smiled. "As you can see, he came through it. We removed a large clot, now it's up to time and Nature. Or God," he added, smiling briefly at Benedict. "The prognosis is a little better than we thought at first, but I expect a prayer wouldn't go amiss!" He passed on down the ward.

Suddenly, there was a convulsive movement from the bed and Margherita turned, startled. Tremayne's eyes had opened and he was staring sightlessly in front of him, his face such a mask of fear that Margherita cried out, "Darling! What is it? It's Mother, can you hear me?"

The surgeon turned at the sound of her voice and hurried back, drawing Tremayne's bed curtains with one swift movement. He took the limp wrist and shone a light into the sightless eyes. "Try not to worry," he murmured. "I'll get Sister to adjust his medication."

Margherita clung to her son's hand. "Can he see or hear us?" she asked, on a sob. "It's so terrible to see him like this!"

"No," the surgeon replied. "He'll be in a world of his own for a while yet." He patted her hand and slipped through the curtains. Margherita looked at Benedict. "I feel so helpless!" she said, despairingly. "What on earth can we do?"

"Do what the man says," Benedict replied. "Pray. Tremayne can't see us, but he may be able to hear something."

But beneath the still figure there was no respite for the troubled soul. Tremayne dwelt in another world, where he watched the scenes before him as one at a play, until the play became real and the little puppet figures swelled to life-size people, and he was one of them.

He saw a street, and a girl struggling along it in the rain and wind. There were some misty lights somewhere and a man standing across the street, watching the girl. Tremayne tried to shout to the girl to stay away from him, but he couldn't make a sound. He watched the man dodging splashing coaches until he reached the opposite pavement. Then, as if he had seen enough and could not contemplate what followed, his eyes at last closed and blackness claimed him.

Margherita returned to Wallington when Sally arrived from the North, leaving Paul with their baby. Her arrival brought comfort to her mother and helped dull the pain a little.

Sally shed dismayed tears at the sight of her brother, but she needed to be strong for her mother's sake. "He'll pull through," she said. "We love him enough, and that's got to count for something."

When Tremayne was well enough he was transferred to a

private Catholic nursing home in Surrey, and Benedict visited them as often as he could.

One night he said, "Look, I've been thinking and I've got an idea. It's quite usual to play tapes to people in comas - music, people talking, that sort of thing. What do you think?"

Margherita was interested at once, but she said, "I haven't got such a thing, only the radiogram. Where could we get one?"

"We've got one at Mount Carmel," he replied. "It's used for special services. It's a bit cumbersome, but it's worth a try. We'll record something from us all, including the children, and a piece of music perhaps. Tremayne's been listening to some Glenn Miller lately. I know he loves that. I'll bring it down the day after tomorrow. How's that?"

Margherita readily agreed. "That would be fine. In the meantime, we'll decide what we're going to say." The idea excited her. It was something positive to work on. Also, there was mail to sort and daily phone calls from well-wishers.

One night she received a phone call she didn't really understand. The girl on the other end said she was a friend of Tremayne's and that her child attended the nursery at the church. At first, Margherita thought her to be simply a member of the congregation, but from the tone of the girl's voice, which was low and almost despairing, Margherita knew there was more to it than that.

"Did they say how long he'll be at the nursing home?" the girl had asked.

"No," Margherita had replied. "They can't tell."

The girl was silent, then Margherita thought she heard the sounds of muffled crying. The girl said, "When he does wake up, tell him Betty phoned, will you? Give him my … regards." The girl rang off, but for Margherita some of the puzzle slotted into place. This had something to do with the accident. There had been desperation in the girl's voice. She decided she would risk mentioning her name to Tremayne, in the hope that it might trigger some reaction, but further than that she had no desire to know.

Benedict brought the reel-to-reel down from London and they made their recordings - herself and the family singing, messages from the children, the Glen Miller which Tremayne loved - normal homely things that might penetrate the darkness surrounding him. She took them to the nursing home and watched Tremayne closely for any reaction, but there seemed to be none, so after some minutes she switched off the machine and leant closer to him. She smoothed his forehead and kissed him. "Get well, my darling," she whispered. "We're all praying for you, we love you and can't do without you. Come out of that terrible black pit, or wherever you are."

Still no response.

"I had a phone call last night," she said. "Someone rang for you. I don't know who she was, but she left her name. She was called Betty."

This time the response was immediate. Tremayne's hand tightened within her own. Overjoyed, she pressed it. "What can this mean to you?" she wondered aloud. "Who is this girl? I know you can hear me."

She switched on the tape again, smiling faintly. A name which meant nothing to her, other than a voice on the phone, had provoked a reaction. Praise God for it.

Above the children's voices on the tape a relentless echo hammered in Tremayne's head - Betty ... Betty ... Betty. The blackness had been momentarily pierced, but the only thing that was clear to him now was a beautiful, tawny-haired, green-eyed girl. She wavered before him with her wistful smile and provocative tilt of her head, beckoning him on and up, out of his silent world, willing him through the waves of confusion that pounded at his mind.

And, suddenly, it seemed to him that he was awake, and he didn't know where he was or who he was. All he knew was that he was in a dark, wet and windy street, full of the noise of horses' hoofs and wheels surging through water, and that he was turning this way and that, not knowing where to run to - a lost soul alone on the streets of London.

"Hello, sweet maid!" said a voice.

At last Tregony had found a friend.

Part Four

London, 1890s

Chapter 17

Sometimes, when the luxurious living had been achieved, Tregony allowed her thoughts to go back to her arrival in London. How innocent she must have been to think that there would not be a price to be paid for such luxury. She had paid the price, even though the cost had been dear and the sacrifice great. If there was regret, she could do nothing about it now. She saw herself, all those months ago, struggling along a rain swept Marylebone Road, little dreaming that, in the eyes of one who watched from beneath a tavern light opposite, her fate was already sealed.

The continuous flow of carriage traffic had sprayed her with a deluge of filthy water and, although the hour was early, barely four o'clock, a wintry dusk had descended. The lamps on some street corners were already lit, rain slanting through the golden circles of light, illuminating hurrying people beneath. Absorbed in shielding Arthur from the rain, a man's sudden breathless arrival at her side startled her. She turned, frightened, and stared up at him. The lewd comment that rose to his lips froze there. He stepped back, startled. He had thought her an ordinary harlot. He saw that the bundle at her breast was a baby. That would not have deterred him, had she been what he thought. But she was not. The face she raised to his was the most enchanting he had ever seen, heart-shaped and framed by an abundance of tawny curls. Her green eyes were etched with the shadows of exhaustion, but still they shone like emeralds, fringed by lustrous black lashes. A faint rose, which deepened under scrutiny, stained her cheeks. He thought quickly. She was ripe for the pickings, he could see. The baby would be no problem. He dismissed that without a second thought. But she mustn't be scared away. Already she was glancing past him to the opposite pavement, where a group of people were beginning to mill about the lighted doorway of the tavern.

"Where've you come from, sweet maid?" he asked, hesitantly. Endearments were not commonplace with him. Instantly, her eyes flew back to his face. A tiny dimple appeared. "Are you …? Do you come from … Cornwall, too?" she asked, eagerly naive.

He relaxed. Now he had an opening. "Wish I did if they breed 'em like you down there!" he answered, smiling.

Something about him warned Tregony. His manner was unctuous, as though he were practising long forgotten arts. And he was rough. His jacket was strained tight across his chest, as if he had lived with it for a long time and his trousers were just short of his ankles. But she was desperate, Arthur needed to suckle. The bottle Aunt Josephine had given had gone nowhere. Besides, she was exhausted and hungry and she knew no-one.

"Going somewhere special?" the man asked, curiously.

"I'm visiting," Tregony answered, looking away.

Running away, he thought. So much the better. "You need rest," he said, trying for a gentle tone. "Come with me. I know a place where you and the baby can feed and sleep. My sister's." He saw her hesitate shyly. "Ain't far from here," he said, persuasively. "Walk it in five minutes." Then, brightly, "How old is the babe?"

That diverted her and made up her mind. Arthur must come before any other consideration. She nodded at the stranger. He was against the light, his features indistinct, and as she looked at him a strange sinking feeling possessed her. It seemed that she was not standing in a dreary London street. Nor, in that instant, could she have said who she was or where she had come from. I'm tired, she thought, alarmed, and the sensation vanished. The man took her arm and guided her along a few yards before turning left.

"How old is the babe?" he repeated, pleasantly, steering her round holes in the pavements.

Tregony clasped Arthur to her and snuggled her face into his neck. "Four months," she replied, a catch in her voice.

So, the brat could be a problem. She was clearly attached to it. No matter, he would cross that bridge later.

"Why did you call me sweet maid?" Tregony asked, suddenly.

"Because you are," he replied, glad of a change of tack. "One of the sweetest I've ever seen!"

She smiled to herself as if she had not heard him. "It's a Cornish saying," she said, softly, a longing for her home sweeping through her and, for the first time, doubts about her future.

"What's your name?" he asked.

"Tregony," she answered, adding hurriedly, "Cornish, Tregony Cornish."

"Cornish by name and by nature!" he exclaimed, now in high good humour. "Well, Tregony Cornish, lucky you chanced on me. This is a hard place. You need protection!"

Despite her fears, Tregony began to feel grateful. "I've walked from Paddington," she said, feeling some explanation was due.

"Sure you have!" he cried, "and a more sorry state I never saw! Look, we're here!"

A gas lamp enabled her to read the name Norton Street. The man preceded her down some iron area steps into a dank basement room. It was sparsely furnished with a chair and table, a bed and a chest of drawers. Clothes and crockery were strewn everywhere. The man pulled the chair forward. "M'sister'll be in the back, no doubt. Annie!" he roared into the nether regions of the house.

A worn looking woman appeared. "Alphonse?" she said on a question, after glancing at Tregony. She was raw-boned and dark, and looked as if she had spent a long time flying after her retreating youth and failing to catch up. Tregony knew instantly that this was not the man's sister and a prickle of fear went through her.

He was jovial, hearty. "C'mon, Annie!" he said. "We've got company! Clear some of this mess and make our visitor some food!" He nodded towards Tregony and gave the woman a sly wink. She understood her part perfectly. The girl wasn't the first he'd brought home and wouldn't be the last. She shifted her penetrating gaze to Tregony. A comely lass, promising, good for the trade she decided, and gave Tregony a fleeting smile. This time Alphonse had excelled himself.

"Ah, that's better!" Alphonse settled himself on the bed opposite Tregony, while the woman silently cleared up. Tregony began to feel warmth flood through her. Arthur was asleep, lashes curled against flushed cheeks. She must suckle him, even if it meant waking him up. She wondered where he would sleep, wishing now that she'd brought the carrying cradle with her instead of leaving it at Paddington with the portmanteau. But she'd needed to protect him from the rain and she couldn't carry everything.

"I must feed my baby," she said, looking up at the man.

"Don't worry me!" he shrugged, grinning. "Do it here!"

Shielding herself from his gaze, Tregony pulled her cloak around Arthur and released her left breast to his mouth. Automatically, he started sucking and Tregony began to relax with the familiar, rhythmical pull. The woman appeared with a plate of stew, placed it on the table and left the room.

The evening passed in a daze. Alphonse never left his position and his eyes never left Tregony. It was some time in the early hours of grey dawn when Tregony awoke and found herself lying on the bed, Arthur cradled in the crook of her arm and her back against a solid warmth.

Startled, she half rose, then realised it was the woman Annie who lay next to her. In the emerging light she discerned the man slumped in the chair and took him to be asleep.

"Awake, my pretty?" said a soft voice, and she realised, with a chill, that he had been watching all night - a giant vulture waiting to scavenge the remains of someone else's feast.

He arose and placed the sleeping baby in a drawer. He turned towards Tregony and with a shocking certainty she saw that she was lost. Crossing swiftly to her, he forced her back against the bed again and thrust his knee between hers. She gasped and tried to scream, but his hand was over her mouth, and her struggles were as nothing.

They rolled over onto Annie, who awoke with a start and took in the situation at a glance. "You be careful with 'er!" she said sharply, to Alphonse. "She ain't like the rest. Don't shit in yer own nest!"

"We all has ter pay for our vittles!" Alphonse growled triumphantly, as Tregony collapsed beneath him. "And this little maid has got more to pay with than some I could mention!"

Annie glared at him and got up. "Well, I don't 'ave ter watch, do I?" she sneered. "Seen it all too often! But you mark my words, take care of 'er. She could be yer goldmine, but she's young and she don't know the ways of London yet!"

"Soon will, though, won't she?" said Alphonse, roughly, as he crushed Tregony beneath him.

Annie snorted contemptuously and left the room as Alphonse crushed his mouth on Tregony's, forcing her lips apart and crunching her neck bones painfully. She whimpered once, then lay resigned, allowing herself to be washed away in a tide of loathing and disgust. She closed her mind to what was happening and tried to think of Tamarleigh and Thomas, even Denzil.

He finished quickly and got up from her. "That's just a taste!" he grinned. "So you'd better get used to it, pretty maid!" He reached down and scooped up her limp body, holding her away from him. "That's right, my pretty," he said, softly. "You and me's gonna have some grand times!" He drew her towards him and savagely bit her bruised breast.

She struggled free of him and ran to the back room door. "You'm just a beast!" she shouted. "No better'n the rams we got in our fields down home! Oh, I wish I was there!" and she ran through to the back room, followed by the sound of the man's mocking laughter.

The days blurred into one, until at some time, she didn't know when, they began to separate out again and were once more distinguished by feelings and events. Faceless people began to take on personalities, names, but mostly the endless stream of men were all as one to her. The advantages of having a roof over her head in London were quickly evident. She simply had no choice. She and Arthur had to eat. London had sounded so romantic and exciting, and she had naively supposed her beauty would make them their fortunes. In the dream, she had always seen herself as famous, an actress perhaps, but nothing like this - an object of men's desires and fetishes. No matter, the spark still burned inside her, and one day she would get away from the damp and dirt of Norton Street.

Alphonse was what he was, she accepted that now. Her feelings for him were ambivalent. He was not displeasing to look at, tall and muscular, and he was clean. He treated her almost deferentially and wouldn't allow her to do any of the skivvying. He hadn't forgotten his first glimpse of her as she stood under the lamplight in Marylebone Road and raised that wide, wistful gaze to his. He was fascinated, but he would stand no nonsense. She was a worker, like the rest, and she was already bringing in good money.

"Why's he got such a strange name?" Tregony asked Annie.

"Alphonse. Ponce. It's rhyming slang. Charley Alphonse, although he's never called Charley," Annie replied. "Might not even be his real name. Who cares?"

"What's a ponce?"

"It's a man like him, gets in customers for us. Be too dangerous for us to go out there. We need him. And he needs us. We brings in money."

"I don't see no money!"

"He gives us what he thinks and takes the rest to sluice the ivories."

Tregony was lost. "I don't know what you're talking about," she said crossly. "Speak plain to me!"

"He takes his money and drinks it, that's what I mean. Don't do it regular, though, got to keep an eye to business."

"And what about us? Suppose we get in the family way?"

Annie laughed. "He knows where to get quinine, had to take it meself lotsa times."

Tregony fell silent. She could hardly complain. She had what she wanted, for the time being anyway. She was sheltered, fed and clothed. It would have to do for now.

Arthur squalled daily, a thin sickly cry. Often he refused the breast and when he did feed he puked back part of it. Alphonse would have seen to Arthur long since had not Tregony so caught his fancy. He tolerated the child's perpetual whining, with bad grace.

"You'll have to get that brat looked after!" he muttered savagely to Tregony one afternoon. The day had been a particularly bad one. Cold, swirling fog, which had even penetrated the house, had kept customers off the streets and the women indoors. The man had brought in one or two carriage customers - men known to them who were prepared to travel for their delights. But, in general, trade was slow and both women were bored. Arthur was fretful, although Annie had dandled him for a while, which had made him chuckle briefly and delighted his mother. Alphonse regarded this scene with a surly eye and at his remark both women looked up sharply.

As always, Tregony's frank stare made him uncomfortable. He looked away. "Could be the reason custom's slow. A brat puts people off!" Both women were silent, watching him. He began to get angry. "Well, you want me to get customers, don't you?" he shouted, then winced as Arthur set up a responsive wail.

Tregony fixed him with a baleful glare. "Arthur ain't the reason for slow trade!" she hissed. "And if it wasn't for me, you wouldn't be as spruce as you are!" Annie shot her a quick look, but had the honesty to admit that Tregony's outstanding allure had increased their income enormously. Now all of them were well fed and dressed. Even Arthur had his good days.

Tregony drew herself up and fixed the man with glittering eyes. "I'm your best doxy, ain't I?" she taunted. "You can make more money on me in a night than a dozen of your other sluts put together! You daresn't lose me!"

He leapt across the room and would have struck her had she moved. But she didn't. She stood defiantly before him, so that he crumpled and began to paw her, stroking down over her hips, until his caresses became violent and he pulled her towards him, tearing at her dress. "You bitch!" he muttered thickly against her neck. "What spell have you put on me that I don't kill you right here with my bare hands?"

Tregony threw back her head and laughed gloatingly.

"Money, that's a good enough spell, ain't it?" Then, as he again began his violent stroking she allowed herself to feel a stirring passion, sagging against him, her eyes closed, until a thin wail broke the moment and she sprang from him, and ran to the drawer where Arthur lay.

"That's right!" he sneered. "See to him before I do!" He began to feel sorry he'd ever spoken. Damn her! Why did she fascinate him so? It was the money, he decided, and she still had her beauty, enough to make him the envy of other pimps. "Damn you and your brat!" he shouted, ashamed of his sentiment. He made to cross the room. "Get him out of here! Let someone else put up with his miserable puking! I've had enough!"

Annie glanced up and said laconically, "Another one for Mother Fry, eh? That woman has her uses!" She smiled at Tregony, satisfied that she had forestalled Alphonse for the moment.

"Who's Mother Fry? Nobody's having my baby! And, besides, I'm still feeding him," Tregony said fiercely, clasping Arthur even tighter.

"Don't fret so," Annie replied. "It'll be for the best. Mother Fry looks after babies whose mothers are ... well, not able to. She's looked after hundreds, I daresay. And Arthur can have a wet-nurse. Be better away from the damp here."

She was fond of Tregony and wanted to protect her. She'd seen women come and go, but Tregony possessed a rare quality in that bleak and dismal house - an unconquerable optimism and spirit. And she knew that Alphonse would not rest until Arthur had gone, no matter how that was achieved.

"Where does this Mother Fry live?" Tregony asked, apprehensively. She knew she had little choice. She dare not risk Alphonse's anger and put Arthur in danger, despite her bravado. And she trusted Annie.

"Just round in Euston Road," Annie replied. She crossed the room and put her arm round Tregony. "I'm fond of Arthur, too, you know. Much better to get him looked after. Mother Fry ain't perfect, but she's the best round here." She glanced at the man and lowered her voice. "Let's just say it'll be better for you and Arthur if someone looks after him and Mother Fry is as good as any."

The thought crossed Tregony's mind that she might do better to go back to Cornwall, face the disgrace and be done with it. But to go back would be a double dishonour now. She had Arthur and she had money. Cornish folk were canny. They would only have to take one look at her to see the fancy clothes, the new brashness, ways which could never have been learnt in a country backwater. They would know that the money to buy such things didn't come from running church tea parties or scrubbing floors for the gentry. And there was Thomas. She felt a tingle at the memory of that illicit love. She should have married him. Now it was too late, all of it. Her wilfulness and wildness had decided her life. She was reaping those carelessly sown seeds and she had no-one but herself to blame if the harvest was poor. Her throat felt choked and tears stung her eyes. "Alright," she said at last. "But I won't leave him unless I'm happy with this Mother Fry."

Annie said, soothingly, "Of course you won't," adding darkly, "no matter what he says!"

Tregony collected Arthur's things and, together with Alphonse, they went out into Norton Street. Despite the dismal day, prostitutes lounged half naked and enticing at every window, some running out in the gloomy mid-afternoon in their undergarments to drag in the few customers available. Alphonse came in for some good-natured raillery as they passed down the street. All the prostitutes knew him, he had supplied all of them at some time, beating off other pimps from the richer areas of the Haymarket and Lupus Street to bring back wealthy customers for his girls. Several times he had taken Tregony, his prize exhibit, to meet these well-to-do clients, some of them prominent public figures. She had enjoyed fine trinkets and expensive underclothes and had closed her eyes to the foetid breath, the old flesh and the laboured grunting that had come with the gifts. Those visits had been few, though. He didn't want to lose her.

Mother Fry's house stood at the junction of Euston Road and Bolsover Street. Her business had been built on the failed efforts of women to rid themselves of their unwanted burdens before birth, and those who didn't have the heart or courage to despatch a newly-born into a convenient bucket of water or a nearby ditch. Sometimes the women didn't come back after depositing their responsibilities with her and the deserted infants were handed over to the parish workhouse at St Pancras. Mother Fry had little pity for these poor unfortunates. She lived on the whims of women and she wasn't the world's conscience. Whether children lived or died depended largely on luck and being born into the right family. Money was her overriding motivation, but she was considered to be one of the more humane baby-farmers, a dying breed.

Groups of ragged children sprawled round the steps of the house, jostling and fighting. Tregony stared at them, frowning. Annie saw her look and smiled. "Don't take no notice of them," she said. "They're just neighbourhood children, I expect."

Tregony sighed, still looking doubtful. "This ain't like down home!"

Annie laughed. "Well, I ain't never been no further than the Mile End Road, and that was too far fer me, so I don't know about Cornwall. But in London there's lots of places like this!"

"C'mon!" Alphonse growled. "Forever yappin'! Let's get

this over with!" He pushed his way through the squabbling urchins and Tregony followed, clutching Arthur tightly. A birdlike woman answered his knock. She was dressed in a grimy uniform of sorts, with a once-white apron and bib, spotted with food. She was erect and thin, with red bony hands protruding from dirty white cuffs. She took in the situation at once and arranged her face into an ingratiating smile.

"Yes, sir?" she enquired, smiling coyly up at Alphonse.

"We wants Mother Fry," he said, curtly.

"I'm Mother Fry," the tiny woman answered. "No, don't tell me, you've brought this young man to me, if I'm not very much mistaken!" She grinned broadly, revealing gaps and blackened teeth. "And who do you belong to?" she cooed, tickling Arthur under his chin.

"He's mine!" Tregony declared. Arthur had never seemed so precious.

"Please enter my humble abode," said Mother Fry, and stepped aside to let them pass. The incongruity of her attempt at respectability suddenly struck Tregony as hilariously funny and she felt hysteria rise up in her. Choking it back, she followed the woman into the front room.

"This," said Mother Fry, with a grand sweep of her arm, "is the withdrawing room." Beside her, Tregony heard Annie give a muffled cough. About five or six babies of various ages sat or lay on the floor, and on a wooden settle another four were crammed head to tail. Most were asleep. Bowls of unfinished, colourless liquid had been left on the mantelpiece.

"You've got a lot of babies here," Tregony said. "Don't you have cots? Somewhere for them to sleep properly?"

Mother Fry smiled. "Bless you, dear, of course we have! Cots is upstairs, but these dear little things couldn't wait for that! Oh dear me, no! They was so full they dropped straight off after dinner, afore we could get 'em upstairs!" She patted

Tregony's arm familiarly. "Your babe will be alright, dear," she said. "We know how to look after 'em here." She took Arthur from Tregony and cradled him against her thin chest.

Tregony looked at the room. It was quite warm and a carpet, although threadbare in part, covered most of the floor. Heavy curtains, still retaining traces of their original floral pattern, hung in faded swags at the windows, looped back into ties. A handsome chiffonier stood along the opposite wall, with a large ornate mirror attached. On the chiffonier were arranged a great many small china ornaments - mementoes of important occasions, a tiny gun carriage from the Crimean War, a bust of Queen Victoria, a miniature watercolour of a young woman, smiling prettily, loops of shiny brown hair framing her face. Mother Fry followed Tregony's gaze. "They were my mother's from the Great Exhibition," she said, proudly. "Over 40 years old, some of 'em! And that's me." Tregony suddenly realised that the watercolour on the chiffonier was Mother Fry in her youth, and she glanced at it again, intrigued.

Mother Fry handed Arthur back to Tregony and tottered to a chair, lowering herself carefully into it, sitting ramrod straight and surveying the assembled company like an eccentric old duchess. Once Mother Fry must have been a handsome woman, Tregony decided, for there were still traces of gentility in the decay, as there was in the shabbiness of the room.

A young girl entered the room and stood looking at Mother Fry, awaiting instructions. She was about 14, plump and quite pretty, with dark hair that fell forward over her face. She had about her a wary look, almost as if she expected reprimand.

"Babies all fed?" Mother Fry asked her. The girl nodded without speaking. "This 'ere's me daughter," Mother Fry explained. "She's a good girl, but she do need the broom handle now and then. Gets a bit uppity!"

The girl looked sullen and shuffled her feet, casting a brief look at the visitors, then retiring to the settle, where she picked up one of the sleeping babies and held it to her.

"Now then!" said Mother Fry, briskly. "Down to business!" She patted her hair with a shaking hand. Tregony wondered if she was ill.

"I suppose it'll be you who's paying?" Mother Fry asked Alphonse. She didn't need to be told how it was. He wasn't the first pimp she'd had through her doors and he wouldn't be the last.

Alphonse nodded, impatient to get the business over and done with.

The young girl on the settle started crooning softly to the baby she was holding. The transaction going on before her hardly interested her. She herself had been part of a similar bargain a year or so before, deserted by a mother who couldn't be bothered with her and taken in by Mother Fry in return for her street earnings.

"Stop that row!" snapped Mother Fry, quelling her with a look. The girl fell silent instantly. "Charges is five pound for the month," Mother Fry continued, turning to the man. "More if you want milk. I can get you a nice wet-nurse, if you like."

The man handed her some coins. "See to the brat properly and there'll be more," he said.

Mother Fry looked more closely at him. Not that he cared much, she thought, but he must keep his best slut happy. Her gaze swivelled to the pretty girl before her. She focused her eyes with difficulty. Hmm, a handsome piece, she decided. Pity she hadn't found her first. She glanced at the girl nursing the baby. She was coming on nicely, though, already had several good customers and only 14 years old. No, she couldn't complain.

"… whenever you like," Alphonse was saying to the pretty mother. What had he said? She tried to concentrate. Something about visiting.

"Sh ... certainly," she said, politely. "I always encourage my mothers to visit. 'Sgood for the little one."

He turned to Mother Fry. "We'll have a wet-nurse. Who do you know?"

"Oh, several, sir," Mother Fry answered. "Your pretty mother here can have her pick. Always someone looking for that kind of work." She giggled, then pulled herself together instantly.

Much as she wanted to defy Alphonse, Tregony dared raise no protest. He was still her bread and butter and had the power to destroy her if he chose. It was only as they were leaving that Tregony realised that Mother Fry was rip-roaring drunk.

Chapter 18

Tregony found an old copy of the Mothers' Medical Adviser and insisted on some of the recommendations for a wet-nurse she read there, that *"the woman must be reasonably young, have an abundance of milk of a moderate consistency, "separating into curd over a slow fire"* she read to Annie, who had roared with laughter and cuffed her affectionately, crying "Lor! Think yerself lucky we've found someone who's got plenty. That'll do any babe! What next!"

Tregony remembered the wet-nurse her Aunt Josephine had wanted to arrange for Arthur and wondered what to expect. However, the woman was perfectly acceptable, but Arthur still seemed weak, causing Tregony much anguish and her fears to recede no less. She knew that in order to give him a chance she must find somewhere else for them to live, perhaps have Annie with them, too, when they could share in Arthur's welfare. Whilst she was under Alphonse's protection Arthur would always be an insurmountable problem.

She visited him as often as she could, delighting when his frail hand reached up to clutch her tawny curls. She began to hope that his sickly days were gone, that he would grow into a strapping, healthy lad, a son to be proud of.

Why, then, these strange blank moments which still came unbidden? And the voices that crowded in, accompanied by a rushing and whirring which she couldn't understand? Only one thing was clear in those moments – that Arthur was not part of her anymore, that he had gone far beyond her reach and she could not find him. And then terror gripped her heart and she would crush her boy to her so that he whimpered, puzzled at his mama's passion, reaching up with a tiny finger to dab at her tears, so that her heart overflowed with love for him. She and Annie took him special food, soft white bread, and mixed his gruel herself in Mother Fry's parlour. She encouraged his clumsy efforts to feed himself, endlessly mopping him up and changing the white tucker, one of her own, which covered him completely. He was beginning to speak. He could say "mama!" quite clearly in his high baby voice, and he knew Annie's name, too. Annie came as often as she could when Tregony visited her son. At each visit Mother Fry was as she had been at the first - erect, deliberate and sodden with drink.

Tregony had been able to retrieve Aunt Josephine's portmanteau from Paddington and, in gratitude to Annie's friendship, had given her the cream organdie dress. The others she had left in the portmanteau under the bed. They were special to her and she didn't want to associate them in her mind with the dreary rooms and Alphonse's protection. Arthur's cradle had been collected, too, and taken to Mother Fry's and used for the sleeping babies.

She was determined to start afresh by herself. She had good clients now and she could set up with Annie. She would bide her time. It was difficult to get Annie on her own, but sometimes if custom had been good, Alphonse made off with the money to the tavern in Euston Road and spent the afternoon and evening there. She found Annie one late afternoon cooking something in a caked pot, and confronted her.

"We must get away from here," she said. "From him. We can make do on our own, we have enough customers between us."

Annie's mouth tightened. She removed the food from the pot, poured water into it from a kettle and sat down. "And where'd we go to?" she asked, scornfully. "It's a hard life, we need protection. Besides," she added, without rancour, "he'd never miss me! You're the one who brings in the money!"

Tregony knew this was true, but she snapped, "Fiddlefaddle! Where's your spirit? We can do it together. I can't stand much more of it here!"

Annie didn't reply. She looked old and worn suddenly, and Tregony realised, with a start, how much Annie needed Alphonse, despite sharing him with others. Annie turned away from her gaze. "Don't pity me and don't ask me why," she said, defensively. "I don't know why. All I know is I can't leave." She blew her nose hard on a corner of her apron, then turned to face Tregony. The two women looked long and hard at each other, and in that naked look all Annie's vulnerability lay exposed, so that Tregony flew to her and clasped her tightly, her heart touched.

"I thought you felt as I do, that no-one could love such a man!"

"Or that love is only for pretty ladies, like you?"

Tregony laughed scornfully. "I'm not for love, I'm for money!"

"Yes, and that's the reason he mustn't never know where you've gone. If he knows, he'd have you in yer box before you knew what hit yer!"

"You mean …?"

"That's right. He'd beat you black and blue, if not worse. Stands to reason, you're his best earner. He'll have to take a cut in money. No doubt about it, though, you're destined for greater things than Norton Street. Knew it as soon as I saw yer." She held Tregony away from her, a spark of determination in her eyes. "Yes, we'll do it, we'll get you away - secretly, if we can, but if he finds out, I'll deal with him. I know a couple of girls in Baker Street, you can bide there, and have Arthur as well. They've got a pimp, he'll protect you from Alphonse if you pay him. And, anyway, wait till you see him! Alphonse wouldn't even attempt it!"

At her baby's name, Tregony's eyes grew misty and her lips trembled. "Oh, yes, Annie, let's arrange it soon!"

"Right, m'girl!" Annie gave her nose one more wipe, then became brisk. "Get some things together. He'll beat me for helpin', likely as not, but he won't do worse. In his own way he's fond of me, y'know!"

"I can't have you beaten for my sake!" Tregony cried.

"A beatin's nothin'. Had 'em before. Won't do worse though - he can still earn money on me. Don't worry, I'll deal with 'im!"

Tregony made as if to protest again, but Annie simply said, "There's lots of things you don't understand, nor ever likely will. He and me, we've been through some years together. Some good, some bad. And I know what you're thinking. How can I share him? I can because, you see, he always comes back to me!"

And so it was accomplished. They left one afternoon when Alphonse was at the tavern. Annie's friends had taken some persuading. Their pimp was a fearsome, pugnacious individual who got them some good business, but Tregony was young, beautiful and competition. One of them, a short fat girl called Sadie, had taken to Tregony straight away. Sadie had her own regular trade, men who liked her voluptuousness. Tregony posed no particular threat to her. But the other, Agnes, was slender and vivacious and instantly resented Tregony's beauty and nice clothes.

"Why should we put ourselves out for her?" she said angrily to Annie. "She'll take all our custom and leave us in the gutter!"

Annie replied soothingly, "You know Dr Merton wouldn't

look at anyone else but you! No, Tregony's bound for up West, or my name's not Annie Warran, and she's already got good clients, gents from the theatre even!"

Slightly mollified, Agnes smiled. Yes, her Harley Street doctor. He was coming along nicely and she always went to his rooms. He need never even see Tregony.

"Alright!" she conceded, grudgingly. "We'll give her a try. But she must stick to her own patch. We can't help her! And it won't be for long, neither!"

Annie sighed, inwardly relieved. She wanted the best for Tregony and was determined to fight for that. They had brought Tregony's belongings with them and she was in a fever to collect Arthur. "Slow down!" Annie laughed. "He'll still be there, he's not going to vanish into thin air!"

Later, her words were to haunt her unbearably. In all her thoughts of Tregony and Arthur in the years to come there remained the overpowering impression of transient personalities, as if they had been lifted out of a photograph and had left no clue behind them.

But now she was taken up in Tregony's longing to see her son and to have her man to herself for a while. Mother Fry's house was surrounded, not just by jostling urchins, but by an unfamiliarly large crowd, pushing and shoving each other to get a view of what was happening. Two enormous policemen directed operations in loud, booming voices, while clerks shuffled official papers and assorted Londoners proffered raucous advice and opinions. Mother Fry was not liked, but the policemen represented authority and the crowd was torn between moral outrage and natural suspicion of the law.

"Get her and her whore out!"

"Don't take a dozen of yer to get a few brats!"

"Serve her right, old drunk!"

Tregony and Annie looked at each other in alarm. The

hackney swayed to a halt and they fell from it, leaving the cabman to yell for his fare. With a sickening lurch of her heart, Tregony began to reel against Annie at what she saw, unable to support herself. Half lifting, half dragging her, Annie pushed through the crowd, arriving at the foot of Mother Fry's steps just as a policeman, his face flushed with importance, hastily ushered the team of clerks past him, their arms filled with covered bundles, their faces stiff with resentment at the abuse from the crowd.

Frantically, Tregony leapt forward, tearing at the bundles and crying in a voice of agony, "Arthur! Arthur! You shall not have my baby!"

"What's happened here?" Annie demanded of a second policeman, pulling his arm until he turned, irritated.

"Old whore's dead, that's what!" he announced, with satisfaction. "And good riddance! Drunk herself to death at last!" He began to laugh, then stopped at the grim look on Annie's face.

In the melee her voice rang like a bell. "What about the babies, eh? What about them? Are *they* all dead, too?" Beside her, Tregony groaned and slipped to the ground. Annie stooped to support her, looking up at the policeman. "Where are the babies, you bastards!" she cried desperately.

They stopped, momentarily diverted. "Dead, most of 'em," one of them said, grudgingly. For a moment an indefinable look crossed his face. The crowd had fallen silent, sensing trouble. The man glanced at them, then back to the two women. Both were well dressed, but probably whores. "And what d'you want to know for?" he grinned, recovering himself. "Plenty more where they came from, eh?" He winked at his neighbour, who roared his approval.

Some people started to laugh, and there were shouts of "Take the sluts along with you!" but not all were on his side.

Tregony's beauty and plight had stirred several hearts and there were several cries of "Give the girl her brat!" and "Let her have her baby!"

Tregony rose from the steps and, with desperate courage, began to peer into the faces of the dead infants. "Where are you?" she moaned. "Where are you, my baby?"

Annie pulled at the policeman's arm again. "Are there any alive?" she asked, angrily. "Tell us!"

He looked at her. Better tell her something. "Only two," he said, sullenly. "They was took on the parish. Find 'em in St Pancras, like as not!" And he turned away, shaking off Annie's restraining hand, his explanations done.

The crowd was appeased. The mother would no doubt find her baby in the workhouse, justice had been done to Mother Fry and life must go on.

"It's no good!" Tregony sobbed, despairingly. "He's gone! I know it! I've lost him!" She clung to the railings, almost senseless. Annie gripped her arm and forced her back onto the path.

"We'll find our little lad," said Annie. "We'll go to the workhouse, it's not far. They said two were taken there." She turned to hail a cab. One was spanking round the corner of Great Portland Street, and as it drew up she suddenly saw the young girl who had lived with Mother Fry slip furtively from the house and begin to walk down Bolsover Street.

"Wait!" she commanded the cabman and, lifting her skirts, ran swiftly after her. The girl looked round, startled, and would have run, but Annie was quicker, grabbing a corner of the girl's cloak and forcing her to stop. "What happened here today? Tell me!"

The girl began to back off, whimpering. "Don't 'urt me, missus!" she snivelled. "This is me best cloak!"

Annie yanked the girl's hair and pushed her face close. "Damn the cloak!" she shouted. "And damn you, too! Now tell us, or it'll be all up with you!"

The girl renewed her snivelling, coughing and dabbing at her eyes with a grubby piece of cotton, but gradually the story emerged. It seemed that Mother Fry had been ill and the girl had been too frightened to seek help. "I knows what them people thinks of us!" she cried.

Annie shook her. "Never mind that! Get on with it!"

"The babies died off," the girl said, "and someone told the Peelers. I hid in the loft and saw it all from a crack in the landing floorboards. Them Peelers didn't know half of it, they left because of the smell, 'cos old Mother Fry was stone dead in her chair."

Tregony seemed hardly able to take this in, but Annie could picture the scene only too well, imagining the upright, birdlike figure, as erect as ever and the essence of primness, even in death.

"The babies was all took, I think," the girl concluded, forcing more tears. "We 'ad so many I can't be sure. I know two was taken to the workhouse. I heard them Peelers say." She brightened, struck by a sudden idea. "Never mind! You could 'ave one o' them!" She beamed with the certainty of one who has found the ultimate solution.

Annie decided she had heard enough. She boxed the girl's ears soundly. "That's for sneaking off! And that's for the cloak! Won't be yer best now!" and she tilted the girl forward and rolled her expertly in the filth and muck of the gutter. "That'll teach yer! If I ever see the likes of you again round 'ere, I'll make sure yer customers don't recognise yer! 'Ere, them Peelers ought to know!" She turned to holler, but the girl slipped from her grasp and ran, roaring with fright, down Bolsover Street and into Clipstone Street, disappearing from view. Annie knew she would never find her again.

She turned her attention to Tregony, who was crouched against some railings, rocking and sobbing. For a moment her practical commonsense deserted her and tears coursed down her own face as she looked at her friend. Several people were gathering, attracted by Tregony's cries, curious to know the reason for such grief. A kindly woman stepped forward and thrust a bottle under Tregony's nose. "This'll 'elp, dear!" she said. "What's 'appened to the pour soul?"

Annie felt her throat constricting on the explanation. The woman listened and clucked sympathetically. "Most of 'em dead, eh?" she said. "Well, it 'appens, o'course, but you try St Pancras. He'll be there, I'll be bound!"

Annie nodded, not much cheered. Deep in her heart she already knew of Tregony's tragedy. Stooping, she gathered Tregony up and somehow got her back to Baker Street. Now was not the time to search. She had to face Alphonse when she got back to Norton Street and she felt drained already.

He knew immediately she opened the front door. "She's gone, ain't she?" he roared. "You thought to sneak her out behind my back!"

"You know you couldn't keep her forever, didn't you?" said Annie, wearily. "Come, Alphonse, admit it. She was made for better things than this and there'll be other ripe plums for the picking, you'll see."

To her surprise, he didn't argue, merely sinking down onto the bed, defeated, and covering his face with his hands. "You've always been faithful to me, but she was my jewel."

She crossed to him and held him to her till the silence of the night and her love took his pain away.

Agnes and Sadie did their best for Tregony, trying to calm her distraught nerves with laudanum. Their own 'mistakes' had always been speedily dealt with by copious amounts of gin or quinine supplied by a very willing chemist.

There followed days and weeks of fevered searching, always accompanied by the pugnacious pimp who rarely spoke, but kept himself alert for a fight, especially with Alphonse. A frenzied search of St Pancras very early on revealed nothing. The attendant, looking at Tregony's drawn, white face, had some sympathy, however. With a sweep of his arm he indicated a whole roomful of children and babies. "You're welcome to look, m'dear," he said. "But if your boy ain't 'ere, more'n likely he's dead. All the live ones was brought 'ere from that Fry woman's!" As Tregony stared at him in horror, he said in a gentler tone, "O' course, might not be dead, either. Babies gets sold sometimes, y'know. There's some ladies wot can't have nippers. They pays a good price for 'em!"

Tregony felt near to fainting, but willed herself to look at the wretched scene before her. Then, pressing her handkerchief to her mouth to stifle the sobs crowding her throat, she turned and stumbled from the workhouse and out into the cool of the street.

Parish registers were pored over, cemeteries visited, and the train, which carried the paupers to plots in faraway Woking, was accosted and searched before it had even left Waterloo. But no trace of Arthur could be found. Annie's heart ached for her friend, grown so pale and thin, her glossy brightness dimmed. Each time she saw Tregony's wild gaze, her throat ached with tears.

Gradually, though, Tregony began to accept that Arthur had gone forever. The patience of the authorities was wearing thin. A child not registered was difficult to trace and there were enough running loose in London to worry about. There was thinly veiled contempt for a whore who deserved all she got. All outward weeping ceased, but Tregony's heart was broken and daily her soul cried out for the child she had lost. She encased herself in a hard outer shell and lay within it, hidden away from the world.

But from a crack in the shell a metamorphosis emerged, as a chick from an egg, and a new Tregony stood before the world. Gone were the last vestiges of the Cornish homeland, no trace remained of the soft speech, the lanquid charm. The shining beauty was overlaid now with a tarnish which only those who knew her before could see. To all others she was sophisticated, utterly feminine and irresistible. Money was spent on refurbishing her wardrobe. She did not rest until she had cast out every stitch, renewed every patent boot and shoe. The chick had at last come of age, adorned in splendid shiny plumage, never to brood on the past.

The pugnacious pimp was more than happy to help his beautiful protégé and influential customers started to come her way, men from the world of politics and the theatre, who became her devoted slaves. She was their darling and they vied with each other as to who could most gain her favours. Tregony's female heart delighted in this rivalry and she was quick to exploit it, one minute coquettish, the next remote.

It drove Sir Nicholas Wassingborne to distraction. A distinguished Shakespearean actor, he was at the top of his profession, a position he maintained by a combination of haughty good looks and a compelling manner. He was every inch a successful knight of the theatre, thought to be about 45 years old, but admitting to 30.

Tregony was taken backstage after a performance of Romeo and Juliet. Doubly inspired by the tragic love story and her beauty, he had instantly seen Tregony as his own Juliet and himself as the definitive Romeo he had once been. He ordered everyone from the dressing room and, after the briefest of preliminaries, seduced her there and then, both of them revelling in the mutual attraction and the piquancy of the situation. It was her 19th birthday.

He wanted to set her up in a little town house. Annie and

the girls warned her. "What'll happen if he tires of you? What you need is a respectable house with a good Madame, some security. So far you've been lucky, only seen him backstage, but this place won't be good enough for the likes o' him!"

Tregony laughed, a high-pitched trill, certain of her charms. She smiled confidently. "He would rather die than share me."

Sadie regarded her, amused. "You know what keeps 'em interested? Competition, that's what! Give 'em a rival or two and they're yours forever!"

"Tell you what," Agnes said suddenly. "What about Deirdre le Bonne? She runs a good house. Plenty o' customers, well known ones, too. And Sir Nicholas'd follow you anywhere. We woulda gone, but our man's our protector and he gets us good business."

"Oh, Tregony, that's just the ticket," Annie cried. "Why didn't I think of that? You'll be alright there!" She gave Tregony a hug.

And so here she was, at Madame le Bonne's, supplier of only high class female flesh to a well-heeled clientele. The dream was fulfilled at last. Madame had interviewed her new protégé with an eye to business. It wasn't often such a prize came her way. Tregony was still worried about Alphonse, but Madame had dismissed him with a shrug. "We have men who deal with the Alphonses of this world," she said. "Now you are with us, he would be a very foolish man indeed to come anywhere near here."

So it was with relief that Tregony settled in and, true to Sadie's word, Sir Nicholas had resigned himself to competition, kissed her hand elaborately, murmuring, "I have full cause of weeping; this heart shall break into a hundred thousand flaws!" and become more devoted than ever.

She was spoilt and pampered. There were visits to the theatre and Sunday morning drives in Rotten Row. There were frequent trips to the Regent Street and Bond Street shops and Michael Marks's new penny bazaars where quality was synonymous with quantity. She enjoyed being flaunted and cared little for the moral censure she occasionally encountered, or the icy hauteur which greeted her entry into some of the drawing rooms of the rich. Experience had taught her to live for the moment and she had no conscience. If royalty could flaunt their mistresses, so could theatrical knights and she was equal in beauty to any of her rivals.

She was happy at last. She had a large room, furnished in elegant and expensive hangings, light, bright silks, covered in thin muslin, little gilt chairs and a canopied bed. Her dressing table was lined with pretty Cretonne curtains and a porcelain crystal shelf above her pitcher and bowl held her selection of tortoiseshell brushes and combs, all inlaid with ivory. Pots of Nadine Cream and Cream of Cucumber were neatly placed next to boxes of pearl powder and rouge. Dentrifices, the soap dish and bottles of orange flower water to remove makeup were on a lower shelf. The adjustable mirror was framed in silk and muslin. On each side of the dresser stood two large candles, forced into bobêches of coloured crystal to protect against dripping wax. These, together with an overhead chandelier, were lit for evening toilettes. Even the window glass was ornamented in pretty designs of flowers and nymphs, bordered with lace and draped in silk and muslin to match the hangings. It was luxury such as she had never dreamed of and it was easy now to forget the past, the hurt and heartbreak, the loathsome defilement, for now the dream had been achieved. This was what she had seen in her visions, this was the culmination of her life's ambition and if it had cost her dearly, so be it. But money counted for everything and was a most pleasant pacifier

She allowed herself to wonder what Tamarleigh folk would

say if they saw her now. What a joke that would be, to step off the ferry, saunter past Old Mother Pascoe's in Macey Street, thumb her nose at Denzil and casually hand over a full purse to her mother, saying airily, "Well, here I am, Mother, this is for you with my blessing! You always said I'd come to no good, and I'm glad to say you were right!" Yes, how funny that would be, how uproariously funny! And how envious they would all be! Her aunt was the only person she felt she had deceived. She sometimes thought of her and how she had promised to return, but whenever she did she felt shame, not triumph.

In the strange way of coincidence and almost as if her thoughts had brought about the event, she was shocked to see the Trefusis brothers leaving Madame's lounge one evening. "Roight, missus?" Perran leered. "Never thought to see us, eh?"

For a moment she couldn't speak. Her throat was dry, her heart thumping. "Why're *you* here?" she asked at last, an old fear gripping her heart. But they disappeared down the front steps and she was left wondering about their purpose in London. She was filled with an overwhelming foreboding.

She was Madame's most successful protégé ever - beautiful, hard and sensual. She refused to think of the future, but occasionally, if she allowed herself to ponder, that strange blankness would come, as if she walked towards a void, hardening her resolve to live life to the utmost.

March, 1897. Spring had nudged a reluctant winter aside and the days were warmer, the nights drawing out. But any weather was good enough for shopping and spending the hard-earned money that Madame allowed her girls. Tregony had a new dress - a vision of white lawn over pink and yellow glacé taffeta, with a close-fitting waist and a gored skirt. One of

Madame's girls, Maisie, watched Tregony flouncing in front of her long mirror and sighed tremulously. "Ooh, you're so lovely, Tregony," she said adoringly. "You've got all the looks. And the best customers," she added, without jealousy.

Tregony laughed indulgently and patted Maisie's blonde curls. "You're coming along," she smiled, immediately caught up again with her reflection. She turned this way and that, peeping over her shoulder, adjusting a ribbon here and there.

Maisie sighed again, her chin in her hands. "I'll never be like you," she said. "You're so ... so ... ladylike!" she ended in a rush.

Tregony burst out laughing, the dress forgotten for a moment. "Ladylike?" she cried. "Are any of us here ladylike? Can we be whores and ladies, too? I don't know!"

She patted Maisie's hand affectionately. "Here," she said, suddenly remembering. Stretching up, she pulled Aunt Josephine's portmanteau from the top of the wardrobe. Affection for her aunt had made her keep the blue costume and the India silk tea gown. She picked up the tea gown and held it against Maisie. "Keep it!" she laughed, as Maisie crowed with delight. "It could've been made for you!" Maisie was immature, still only 16, her figure unformed. Yet already she showed promise, roundly plump and smooth with pink and white doll-like prettiness. There would always be customers for Maisie and she would probably marry into money and settle down happily. Life would not hold any dark secrets or terrors for her, no drama or heartbreak.

Tregony sighed inwardly, then said briskly, "Anyway, look. Even some of the greatest ladies in the land haven't got this. So, yes, we must be ladies!"

Maisie rolled back onto the bed, squealing at the thought. "Me, a lady!" she gasped. "If I had a ma, she'd be proud of me!" This struck Tregony as so funny that she joined in, and both were lost in merriment to the tap on the door. A louder tap brought Maisie's finger to her lips. "Hush!" she spluttered. "Someone's at the door!"

Tregony crossed to it hastily, pulling her dress straight. "Probably Sir Nicholas for me," she said and opened the door.

For a moment she said nothing, staring unbelievingly. Maisie felt a little prickle of alarm. From the bed she could not see the newcomer. "Who is it?" she asked, anxiously.

Tregony held the door wide and the stranger stepped into the room. Maisie's eyes widened in surprise, and she looked quickly at Tregony. Before her stood a rough, unkempt figure, a man with a bold gaze and, belying his broad stature, a shock of wavy, womanish hair straggling to his shoulders.

The stranger turned to Tregony and looked her up and down arrogantly. Then he grinned. "So, m'dear. Who's a pretty maid, then?" His gaze travelled to Maisie. "Aren't you going to introduce me?"

Tregony regarded him coldly. She gestured towards Maisie, her eyes never leaving the stranger's face. "Maisie, may I present Mr Denzil Pascoe!"

Chapter 19

For a moment no-one in the room moved. Tregony was filled with a terrible inevitability. She had somehow known that this moment would come. The Trefusis brothers must have told him where she was. Perhaps he'd even asked Madame especially for her.

Maisie wasn't quite sure what to make of this hulking man, but Madame had taught her well. "How do you do?" she asked, politely. "I don't believe we've met." The banal formality broke the atmosphere.

"I'm doin' alright!" Denzil replied. "And so're you, by the looks!" He glanced appreciatively round the room. "Congratulations, madam! This is better'n Tamarleigh coulda done for ye!"

Tregony crossed to her dressing table and busied herself amongst the rouges and powders, trying to steady her nerves. She knew Denzil well. He would have come here for a purpose. He wouldn't have forgiven her for running away when his back was turned. But whatever he expected, he would find her changed. His old threatening tactics, his bullying, would not work now. She had protectors, and she was not the naïve country girl she had once been. And now, barging in without warning! Who did he think he was?

Anger rose in her, but a commotion in the hall below caught their attention. A vibrant masculine laugh echoed through the reception lounge, followed by bounding footsteps, taking the stairs two at a time. Tregony turned, relief flooding through her.

"Hola!" called a rich voice. "Where is my darling, my only

one?" and Sir Nicholas Wassingborne swept into the room, velvet cloak flying, tossing his top hat and cane onto the bed as he came.

His entrance was impeccable, his timing perfect. He halted in mid-stride and his glance raked the assembled company. Tregony didn't move, but her look and smile as she gazed at Sir Nicholas were not lost on Denzil. His heart filled with renewed anger.

He had spent weeks tracking her down. He had found a room in a cheap hotel at Paddington, combining his search with satisfying visits to London brothels and the expedient selling of booty. If it hadn't been for his hatred of the reverend, the devil take him, and his smarting pride, he would have given up. He was sitting at the bar in Paddington Station one night when the Trefusis brothers walked in.

"What you doin' 'ere!" he demanded, thunderstruck.

"We wants our money," Perran growled. "We 'elped get rid o' that Treharne stuff."

"How did you know where I was, then? You ain't got a brain between ya!"

"Knew you was up 'ere. 'Erd your ma tellin' Old Mother Tregantle outside 'er gate. Told Keverne, didn't I Kev?"

His brother nodded and grinned stupidly. "Yeah, told me. Told me to go to Lunnon wi' 'im, 'cos we wants our money. We 'int in Cornwall no more."

"And we seen your maid," Perran said casually.

Denzil was doubly shocked. "Tregony? Where? Tell me where!"

"Why you wanna know?"

Denzil thought quickly. "'Cos … 'er ma wants 'er back. She's poorly, and they twins is no good on their own." That much, at least, was true. Sarah Welles was always ill.

But Perran still had some wits about him. "First the money, then we'll tell."

"You'll 'ave it, you'll 'ave it," Denzil said. "First, we'll sup for old times, eh? Come on, boys! We 'ad good times, didden we?" They wouldn't get a penny from him.

Perran was suspicious, but Keverne immediately handed over his pint glass and Denzil got the drinks. He played them on a practised hook. He knew exactly how much ale it would take to stupefy them and he plied them relentlessly. It would be money well spent, and, too simple to comprehend, they soon told him all he needed to know. They had scores to settle, but Denzil had slipped away long before they realised he had gone.

He had a wife to keep now. His mother had at last prevailed upon him to marry Jane Chubb and he had discovered it was quite easy to ignore her permanent adenoidal whine. The money she brought to the marriage was a marvellous persuader. He'd fathered Jane, a daughter named for her Grandmother Pascoe, and would see to it that she had others to occupy her in the future. She was doting and clinging, but he had no conscience about leaving her so often.

But anger for Tregony still ate into him. She had made him a laughing stock and thanks to that dolt Thomas Norsworthy he had been forced to endure public ridicule and scorn. He'd never forgotten that morning in church. Folk in Tamarleigh hated him and that had given them just the opportunity they'd been waiting for. Not that he cared for them. He had ways of stopping people's mouths, and would have stopped Norsworthy's if he could have got to him in time.

All through the intervening months his anger grew. Nothing could banish it, except revenge. And now he'd found her at last. Still as shameless as ever and this time being paid for it. But she was changed, too. There was now something untouchable about her, almost secret. Her beauty was breathtaking, but in some strange way it angered him. It was artificial, gaudy. A brash veneer replaced the fresh sparkle of the maid he used to know.

And now her fancy fellow had arrived. Clearly the man was a fop, dressed like a painted dandy and lily-livered too, probably. Nevertheless, he hadn't expected this and his purpose faltered a little. But not for long. The wench was a whore and whores could be had by anyone. He had money and it was as good as the next man's. Once Madame le Bonne had seen that she'd let him in without demur. He'd get himself cleaned up and then lead Tregony Welles a merry dance. She had a greed for fine clothes and possessions, he could see that, and once she'd succumbed he'd make her sorry she'd ever left him. Let her try and turn his money down!

Tregony held up her cheek for Sir Nicholas's kiss. "Do I find you well, my sweeting?" he said. "I hope I am interrupting something!" He smiled at Denzil, taking in the rough clothes and the coarse look. He took out a lace-edged handkerchief and held it pointedly to his nose. "Such a close day," he remarked pleasantly. "A little air, perhaps?" He crossed to the sash and lifted it. A breeze blew in the sounds of the London street below, familiar sounds which comforted Tregony.

"Yes, it is close," she replied, avoiding Denzil's glare. "I think Mr Pascoe was just leaving."

"Not on my account, surely!" protested Sir Nicholas. "But I have come to take you out, my darling. First a drive in the park, then Covent Garden. I take it you haven't yet seen 'Aida'? Come, here's your cloak. We shall come back and change later. You look enchanting in that delightful dress, but not I think for the opera!" He swung her cloak around her and leaned close. "Screw your courage to the sticking place, sweetheart!" he murmured and gave her arm a squeeze.

His brougham stood before the door and a drive in Hyde Park, freely acknowledged as Sir Nicholas's favourite, did much to restore Tregony's spirits. Later, at the opera, she delighted in the stares and fawning courtesy shown her. She had chosen to wear one of Sir Nicholas's latest purchases for her - a gown of crushed figured brandy-gold silk. The low neckline, which exposed a tantalizing glimpse of soft white breast, was edged with silver tissue. She had added her own personal touch, of course, sending Maisie out to purchase some heavy gold rope silk which the two of them had embroidered on the back of the dress in a swathe of petal patterns swirling to the waist. She enjoyed passing on her needlewoman's skills. It felt comfortingly familiar to have a needle in her hand once again, and her mind went back to her mother, always bent over someone's work, straining her eyes, as she taught her daughter a skill for which the child had a natural aptitude. The task had been pleasantly absorbing and the hours with Maisie had fled by.

She thought the opera enchanting. The impressive Egyptian sets and the heavenly singing carried her to another world and she gazed, rapt, at every scene. Beside her, Sir Nicholas smiled tenderly as he watched the parted lips and the shining eyes. He accepted that he shared her, but he simply hoped that she would turn to him if she needed him. He loved her dearly, almost as much as his own wife. That lady had understood his penchant for a pretty face and figure and never a word of recrimination passed her lips. If Tregony Cornish had lasted longer than the other paramours, well, so be it. She hadn't borne his children, helped him through his career or entertained his theatrical friends, nor ever could, and it was these things that mattered to a man. Tregony Cornish was little more than a glorified prostitute and, therefore, "de trop" in acceptable society, even if Nicholas did flaunt her more than was desirable.

Tregony returned to Madame's late that night, hoping just to drop into bed. There were people in the reception lounge and she hoped fervently that Madame hadn't booked her any late clients. Activity continued through the night, of course, but Madame insisted on discretion. She might run an Establishment, but it was not a bawdy house and her girls were not drabs. The house was in a prime position in Chesterfield Street and had a high reputation to maintain. The lounge at night was most attractive. Huge, fringed lamps from Spain cast a soothing and enticing glow over deep cushioned chairs, sofas in pale pinks and magentas and large potted palms.

Tregony made her way across the lounge. The glittering evening had done much to relieve the shock of Denzil's visit, but now she was on guard and glanced warily at the gentlemen callers. Most of them she recognised, but there was one standing under a leafy palm by the stairs whom she didn't know. He had his back to her. He wore an imposing navy velvet-collared jacket and slim pinstriped trousers. His fair hair was short and oiled and he was glancing idly through a brochure advertising London events. As Tregony drew near the stairs, the stranger casually stepped backwards without looking round until he blocked her path. His eyes still fixed on the brochure, he murmured, "Not so fast, my pretty! I've not waited here these last two hours for naught!" and he turned slowly to face her.

She stared open-mouthed. It was Denzil, although she hardly recognised him. His pale face was red from shaving and bay rum lotion, his wavy hair cut short and tamed into submission, and his shirt points crisply white and gleaming with starch. He looked ludicrous. She felt a bubble of laughter rise up, but quelled it instantly. "It's late, Denzil, and I'm tired," she said. "Can't this wait till tomorrow?"

"Why should it?" he grinned. "This 'ere's a brothel, ain't it, and I'm as good as the next man." And taking her arm he propelled her firmly up the stairs. "I ain't spent good money on these clothes fer nothin'!"

On the landing she halted and faced him. "You couldn't afford me, Denzil Pascoe. I don't take just anybody, you know, not these days, especially not …" she paused, searching for the right words, "… well, my clients are high class gentlemen, not folks I'd rather forget!"

He itched to slap her there and then, but he kept his temper and reached casually into his jacket, bringing out a pigskin wallet. "Can't afford ye, eh? You don't know what I can afford, Tregony Welles, but you will!"

He stopped as she glanced hastily about her.

"I'm not called Welles anymore. My name's Cornish, I'll thank you to remember!" she hissed.

"Well, changed in more ways than one!" he sneered. "Too good for us down there now, are we? Not too good for this, though!" He withdrew a thick wad of banknotes from his wallet and waved them in front of her.

"What's that, stolen money?" she said, scornfully. "Is that why you and the Trefusis brothers are here? I saw them downstairs the other night. Are they after you, or with you?"

"Stolen money!" he scoffed. "When did you ever care where money come from? And I know they'm 'ere. I seen 'em t'other night. They might be arter me, but they'll need to get a brain between them to get any o' this!" He waved the banknotes again.

"Did you cheat them out of money?" she asked. "I thought there was honour amongst thieves!"

"Cheat! I allus did most of the work," he growled. "Any rate, I don't need them no more. I got lotsa little jobs goin', plus a little maid fixed up in a house in Plymouth. Gets lotsa trade, she do!"

She bit her lip furiously. He was unspeakable, but he was right. His private quarrels were no concern of hers and Madame must have agreed or he wouldn't have got this far.

As if he read her thoughts, he said, "I got permission, you needn't worry. My money's as good as anyone else's and besides, you and me's got to 'ave a talk, young lady. There's a few things what's got to be sorted out between us!"

She walked reluctantly to her door. "We can't discuss it for all the world to hear. You'd better come in." He followed her in. She lit her little dressing table candles and the overhead chandelier, then turned to face him. "Alright, I know you haven't come all this way for nothing, so what is it? Be quick, I'm tired!"

"Oh, I know you've had a busy day," he replied, sarcastically. "You forget I was here earlier. I saw the fop what took you out. Don't think I can't compete with the likes o' he! That's what I been a-doin' since I left 'ere this afternoon. Gettin' meself all spruced up to match, if that's what it takes. You was my woman, no-one else's, and that's what I'm 'ere for!"

"Denzil, it's been a long time," she answered, wearily. "I left Tamarleigh, to make a new life …"

"Oh, aye, you left!" he replied, his lip curling. "Left me an' all! Made me look a praper bliddy fool! I don't like folks laughin' at me. And they haven't forgot, neither! They still talks of nothin' else! Didden take long to find out why ye left, though, as the Reverend was only too willin' to tell everybody!"

"Tell them what?"

"Only what you an' him'd bin doin'. Told us in the middle of the Sunday service. *And* that I were 'is son. I woulda knifed him there and then, only I didden 'ave me guttin' knife wi' me. Praper uproar, there were, and folks knowin' you bin goin' wi' him be'ind me back! That's not somethin' I can forgive easy,

Tregony Welles, or whatever you calls yerself now. I got me pride!"

"He confessed to being your *father!*" She could only stare at him stupidly. She'd always known of his jealous obsession for her, but, more importantly, her suspicions about Denzil's parentage were right. She shuddered at the anger that had driven him to hunt her down. And what had possessed Thomas to confess everything in front of all those people? She hardly dared ask, but he saved her the trouble. He strolled over to her little Louis XVI chaise longue and stretched himself full length upon it.

"Oh, aye, dirty ol' bastard! I woulda got to him sooner or later. Only he got to hisself first, as you might say," he added, indifferently. "Threw hisself under a train at Saltash. And good riddance, too! Think I want *that* as a pa?"

At first she wasn't sure she'd heard him correctly, it was said so matter-of-factly. He could have been discussing the price of fish on the quay at Sutton Harbour in Plymouth. Her tongue seemed to stick in her mouth and she couldn't speak.

"That's right, I said a *train*," he repeated, watching her. She felt her head start to swim and the lighted candles began to dance crazily before her. She turned sharply away from him. Thomas dead? All that energy and vigour gone? The dreadful truth began to sink in. It was her fault. She'd done this to him. Why, oh why, hadn't she gone back and married him after Arthur was born? Then they might both still be alive. She could hardly bring herself to speak, but she had to know. "When ... when did he ... do it?" she whispered, through frozen lips, her face still averted.

"Oh, soon arter you went. Mother said you'd bin gone about two weeks, then I got back and he did it the next Sunday!"

So she would have been too late. She could only have saved him if she'd never left Tamarleigh in the first place, but she'd been determined to follow a dream, and for what? She had put a high price on her head and, in the process, sold off those who really cared for her. Worst of all, Thomas and Arthur had paid with their lives. And Denzil was right, he owned her as much as anyone did. She would never belong to herself, but always to any man rich enough to buy her. At the thought of her boy her heart seemed to break all over again. She deserved to be punished and Denzil was her Nemesis. He was the only person she had no regrets about leaving and, ironically, he was the survivor. He had come for his pound of flesh. Well, he could have the pound nearest her heart and her heart as well, for it was already broken. She struggled for control. She must pretend indifference to such terrible news, delivered in such a wanton manner, and not give him the chance to gloat at her suffering. And she must never tell him about Arthur. She turned to him. She would play her part to perfection. If he had come to teach her a lesson, she would teach him his place.

"So I am to pay the price for your hurt pride, am I?" she said, coldly. "Well, Denzil Pascoe, there are a few things you ought to know. I'm well thought of here and I've got influential friends. Yes, you might have money to pay for me, but if you think you'll be at the top of the list, you're fair and far off the mark. You'll take your place, just like any other customer."

Now it was his turn to stare. He'd not expected such icy calm, no tears. Why, the maid was a cold-hearted bitch and deserved anything she got. He'd half a mind to thrash her now, but something in her frozen face prevented him. Frustration rose within him. This was not going as he had planned. He thought she would be horrified, weep, do the things females were supposed to do, even fall at his feet and beg his forgiveness. Never mind, he would bide his time. He had something else up his sleeve, a trump card and at the right time he would play it.

She presented a daunting figure, flaunting her beauty and sensuality before him. He stared and felt his body begin to flame. He rose from the chaise longue and came close. "Doan 'ee forget why I've come 'ere ternight, Tregony Welles!" he said, belligerently. "I've paid me money, I wants the goods!"

She controlled the urge to throw him out. Yes, he certainly needed a lesson and the first was that not only was she the piper, she also called the tune. She forced herself to smile. Ah, yes, that was it. Show him the old Tregony, the roguish flirt. "Really, Denzil, do you mind?" she begged, persuasively. "I'm so tired. Remember, I wasn't expecting you. Can't this wait till morning?" She allowed a small sigh to escape her, and dropped her head so that a fringe of curls half hid her face.

Denzil dithered, caught between lust and a strange reluctance to violate her. He thought of the delicious scenes he had enacted in his head. He clenched his fists while he tried to fathom if she were serious or slyly laughing at him. He decided to play it safe. He returned to the chaise longue and regarded her sullenly. "This time!" he growled. "But I want me money's worth termorrer!"

"And you shall have it, Denzil," she smiled, opening the door for him. Thus dismissed he could do little but retire from the room ungracefully. She heard him descend the stairs, then voices rose from the reception lounge and she thought she heard Maisie's high-pitched giggle, then all was silent.

She went into her dressing room. Now she knew what to expect it would be easier to get the upper hand. She removed her rouge and pearl powder with witch hazel toilette cream and rubbed her slender body with perfumed rosewater. Crossing to her bed, she drew down the coverlet. She lay for many minutes, half propped against the lace pillows, from where she could see the moon peeping between the frilled muslin curtains. She had no choice in matters now. Denzil would have to be just like any other customer. But underneath her composure she was frightened and the news he brought had devastated her. She tried to think of her mother and the twins in Tamarleigh, her Aunt Josephine and all the people she had hurt, yet they all seemed unreal. The only reality had been Arthur and if she had to pay for her past she would not count the cost, for his sake. She had experienced great degradation and great luxury. What else was there to do? Find herself a rich husband, perhaps, one who didn't mind or care what she was. Several of Madame's girls had become successful actresses, and had won rich husbands for themselves.

She shifted her position in the bed and watched the moonlight stream across the carpet, almost as bright as day. The late night traffic still plied its way along Piccadilly, and she could hear the intermittent shouts of the cabbies and the rattle of wheels. She felt as if she would never sleep and tomorrow she must endure the rough embrace of that great country lump.

Still restless, she rose from the bed and crossed to the window, drawing aside the curtain and glancing down into the street. One or two late stragglers passed by the red glow of Madame's lamp. A small group of young men turned the opposite corner, skylarking and jostling. She watched as they stopped in front of the house, nudging each other and pointing. One held back, shaking his head and laughing nervously, but eventually he mounted the front steps and they all disappeared from view into the house. She could distantly hear their voices in the lounge.

Then, suddenly, all sounds ceased. An immense stillness entered her whole being and gripped her in a fist of iron. Frightened, she tried to hold onto the sill, but her muscles froze and ice ran in her veins. She seemed to stand in a great, dark womb from which all life was forbidden. She couldn't feel her heartbeat, her chest was still. A slant of moonlight fell across her, penetrating her very bones until her flesh seemed to melt within it. She was weightless, her whole being streaming out to become one with the universe. By an enormous effort of will she opened her mouth in a soundless scream and as she laboured to breathe, a great, sucking wind rushed in, filling her lungs.

Slowly, the world began to impinge. A footfall streets away fell like thunder into the room. The clop of hoofs and the rattle of a carriage passed on some highway. Her body was drenched in sweat and a vast trembling took hold of her. Now her heart was racing. It danced and leapt in her chest like a live thing trying to escape, and blood pounded through her head until every vessel threatened to explode. Terrified, she toiled to control her breathing. She turned to stumble from the window, and as she did so she was suddenly aware that someone was standing by the bed. A blurred and silent figure, formless, but with a pulsing energy flowing from it. Fearfully, she stared into the pool of blackness. Could it be Denzil? Could this be his revenge, creeping back to her room to do some foul work? She waited for him to make a move, crouching back against the window, gathering herself for flight.

The figure was motionless, then a low voice said, "What do you want from me?" It was not Denzil. It was no-one she had ever heard before and yet there was a gentle familiarity to it, a soft, tender anguish and a startling hope of eternal peace. A great sob rose within her. She started forward blindly, and as she did so, the energy ceased and the figure vanished.

She crawled to the bed and lay down, while sobs tore through her. She knew with a certainty that she had met with something known to her, something that held the key to eternal peace. Grief engulfed her and her tears were those of bereavement.

She was not conscious of sleeping, but when she opened her eyes bright sunlight was falling in patches through the curtains and warming her face. She lay for a few moments, remembering. Her pillow was still wet with tears, but she no longer felt grief. Her whole being seemed bathed in a rosy glow of relaxed contentment. She had slept more deeply than at any time she could recall. She convinced herself that she'd had a frightening dream, brought on by her distress at Denzil's news, and had cried in her sleep. She'd scared herself over a dream and let her fancy run away with her. She looked at her little gold carriage clock. Nine o'clock. Denzil would be here soon, and he would not be put off again. She felt refreshed now, ready to deal with him and as long as he didn't hurt her she would put up with him.

She creamed and scented her body, then dressed in a simple blue lawn day gown with a pretty lace vest insert. She let her hair fall naturally over her breast. A little rouge and pearl powder completed the picture of wistful innocence. Clients were fond of this image. It contrasted so deliciously with the amorous arts she used to arouse them. Nevertheless, such artlessness took an hour to achieve and she was surprised when there came a knock at the door and she realised Denzil had arrived.

She was glad at the slight gasp he gave when he saw her. They sipped coffee which Maisie brought them, tripping in with the silver tray and smiling coyly at Denzil as she left.

"I see you haven't wasted much time," Tregony observed, drily, pouring out the strong, sweet-smelling liquid into porcelain cups. "Be careful. Maisie's for someone better than you, Denzil. She'll marry well - and soon, if I'm not mistaken. She's attracting many of our better clients, and she's young enough to get out of this life, before it's too late."

"I don't need your opinion!" Denzil growled. "She's for sale, ain't she? Besides, I got a wife down 'ome. Jane Chubb."

Tregony hurriedly put down her cup and pealed with mirth. "You don't mean to tell me your mother got you married at last!" she choked. "I never did! Jane Chubb, too! Well, she's not so bad, quite suitable, in fact. She'll do as she's told and not ask questions. You could do worse!"

"Exactly what Ma said!" he retorted. "You, for instance!"

Tregony smiled. "I knew Dorothea never liked me. She was jealous of me because of … well, never mind, she always had ideas above her station, your mother!"

He started up, but she put her hand on his arm. She didn't want to begin any business with him in a foul mood. She would only suffer and her clients must not find her bruised. She stood up and crossed to the bed. "You can have half an hour for your money," she told him, matter-of-factly. "I do have other clients to see."

Her words stung. He grabbed her wrist and bent her arm back, forcing his mouth down on hers. Mindful of his unpredictability, she allowed him to push her hard down on the bed, enduring the hasty groping and the rough touch. Strange how she remembered the feel of him, of his weight on her, his hands gripping her. She could hardly believe she had once found him exciting.

He cursed her, crushing her lips and breasts, but he no longer had the same power to arouse her and he quickly sensed it. Bitter rage filled him and he wished he could make her suffer, as she had made him suffer. "You'm a demon, Tregony Welles!" he muttered through clenched teeth. "Don't think to bewitch me again!"

As he panted and strove above her, her fear of him suddenly receded. She gazed over his shoulder. How silly to be frightened of him. He might be coarse and rough, but what real harm could he do her? Smiling, she laced her hands across his back.

"If you're good, you can have an extra few minutes," she said. "And please try to remember, Denzil. It's Cornish, Tregony Cornish."

Chapter 20

It was good to have so many admirers. Recently there had been a young actor from Sir Nicholas's play. She'd not mentioned it, of course. She knew Sir Nicholas would be insanely jealous because the young actor was playing Romeo and Sir Nicholas was still proprietorial about the role. But she had mentioned Denzil and Sir Nicholas had been somewhat shocked.

"Of course, I cannot tell you what to do, but be careful, for my sake. The man looked a complete scoundrel!"

She smiled fondly at him. "Denzil will be going home soon," she reassured him. "He's from Cornwall. He's only renewing an old acquaintance." There was no need for Sir Nicholas to know more, but in truth, she had no idea when Denzil would return to Tamarleigh. He seemed to be making himself very comfortable in London and had moved from the cheap hotel and taken a lodging in Great Windmill Street, where he gambled at the casino and sampled the delights of the many prostitutes there. This hadn't prevented him from calling at Madame's nearly every day, however. Tregony wondered where he got his energy from, and he always had money. He paid Madame handsomely and there were presents to the girls, although he never gave her so much as a lace handkerchief. Not that she wanted anything except his money.

But she couldn't help noticing his continuously stuffed wallet and one day she said to him, "Fishing must be doing well these days, or are you fishing in a different pond now?" He was stretched out on the chaise longue, wreathed in cigar smoke, playing the gentleman. He regarded her through half-closed eyes.

"Always fished in different ponds," he said, diffidently. "Some o' the stuff's heavy to bring up, too! We 'as to get rid of it pretty damn quick, you know that. We 'ad lotsa plate from Treharne and there's been another big 'un since. Place you doan know. Big 'ouse in Somerset. Shouldn't be tellin' yer all this. Might blow me cover!"

He paused and looked at his nails reflectively. There was something else he'd been waiting to say and now was the time. Tregony noticed the gesture with scornful amusement. His nails were clean and pared. London had improved Denzil, but only in appearance, thanks to Maisie's eager ministrations.

"I got money comin' in from other places, too," he said, casually. "Not just what I told ye." He reached into his pocket and brought out a small bottle and a packet wrapped in a piece of flannel. He handed the bottle to her.

"Laudanum" she read. "Well, what's unusual about that? Anyone can get that. I have some here. I take it for headaches."

"I 'spect you do," he returned, "but I doan 'spect you knows what it does to ye!"

"Of course I do! It makes me feel better!"

He chuckled. "Oh, aye, it do that! Keeps ye goin' all night, too, doan doubt it. 'Tis a praper powerful drug an' lots folks can't do wi'out it once they take it."

She was intrigued. "So that's why you seem to have such energy! You must be taking a lot of it."

"I doan just take it, I sells it! I gets it cheaper'n ye can buy it, and more of it. Lotsa folk prefers it to drinkin'. Drink stops a man wenchin'."

"What's that other thing?" she asked, indicating the little packet. He unwrapped it and passed it to her. In her hand lay a little brown ball, hard and gum-like. "What's it supposed to do?"

He wrapped the little ball and pocketed it. "Do? It doos whatever you want it to! Or rather," he amended, "you can do whatever you want, when you've 'ad some! This 'ere's opium. Some o' they poets takes it. That's why they writes such folderol!"

She was fascinated. "You're a deep one," she said. "But at least that explains the money." A thought suddenly occurred to her. "Have you been doing any business here other than the usual?"

He grinned. "That'd be tellin', wouldn't it? There's some things that ain't good for little maids to know!"

She laughed rather excitedly. "I didn't know how strong laudanum was. I don't know much, do I?" He watched her narrowly, still playing the line. She wasn't quite hooked, but he was more than hopeful. The sprat had nearly landed the mackerel.

"Laudanum ain't dangerous," he replied. "Everyone takes it. Opium, now that's different. That's for folks a bit special, like they poets, or your Sir Nick. Lotsa actor fellas doos it. Stiffens 'em up for the performance!"

He got up from the chaise longue and strolled to the door. "I'm off gamblin'. Book me in fer Friday. All night, got some cash comin' in then," and he was gone.

She stared at the closed door. Sir Nicholas taking opium? She would ask him as soon as she saw him. She crossed to the window and watched as Denzil swung out of the house. Still the same familiar, swagger. He crossed the street and disappeared round the corner. He was beginning to be interesting. She was London's favourite at the moment, but she had to fight to keep that position. And now she could get something to help her and her clients, too. Just think what intoxicating pleasures she could bestow!

She went to the dressing table and sat down at the mirror. She took out her tortoiseshell combs and began to dress her hair. She had some satin ribbon somewhere. It would go well with her afternoon tea gown. She pulled open her ribbon drawer and began to rummage in it when something caught her eye. A little box tied with string lay on top of the ribbons. Curious, she untied it and out tumbled a little ball of brown waxy resin. She stared at it, realisation dawning. All that talk to whet her appetite, the casual sewing of the seed to whip up interest, then sneak the little package where it would be found, and leave it to reap the harvest. She'd underestimated Denzil. He was an opportunist, she should have known. Her hand trembled. She broke off a tiny piece, put it in her mouth and swallowed it. After some minutes, she took up her combs again and continued with her toilette.

She took tea later on that afternoon with Sir Nicholas. Maisie brought the tray up, but did not come in. Tregony resolved to speak to Maisie later, find out if Denzil had ever spoken to her about his wares. She didn't think so. Maisie looked just as soft and contented as she'd always been, happy to be near Tregony, and as pretty and compliant with the gentlemen as ever one could wish. There was no change in her manner or ways.

Sir Nicholas settled himself on the bed and sighed happily. He had brought with him a mountainous basket of delphiniums, daffodils and white, waxen lilies, their backs flushed with pink and great stamens dropping yellow pollen like gold dust. The basket was woven through artfully with vine leaves and decorated with peacock feathers. It was a vision of overwhelming colours that glowed and shimmered in a way she had never seen before, until the whole room seemed full of vibrancy. Tregony was quite overcome when he presented it to her. "It's beautiful, and so big! Where shall I put it?"

"My dear girl!" Sir Nicholas murmured. "Are we talking about the flowers? Modesty forbids!"

She smiled and put her arms round him, nestling her face into his waistcoat. He always smelt so satisfyingly of cologne and tobacco. "You are so good to me, so kind. The flowers are lovely. I know, I'll put them in the fireplace for the summer. We'll not have fires again this year, I think." It was late March and warm. "And lilies, where did you get lilies?"

"From Covent Garden early this morning, but they've come from Jersey, my love, especially for you. You are my own Jersey lily!"

Her vanity was touched. She had seen the great Mrs Langtry at the theatre once and been enchanted by her beauty and elegance. "If only I could capture hearts like her," she returned archly, then laughed as he swept her into his arms.

"Lily Langtry, who is she?" he cried, gallantly. "I would rather have my own Cornish rose!" Some minutes were spent while he proved this point. "On your birthday you shall have a whole roomful of flowers - roses and lilies!"

"My birthday is not yet awhile," she said. "June the 22nd. I believe I shall be 20."

"Three months away, my love. I have it in the diary," and he withdrew his little pocket book and thumbed through the days until he found it. "See, I have marked it in red. It is a Tuesday. It will be a red letter day, for do you know what else is on that day?"

She shook her head.

"Two things. The anniversary of our meeting and our own dear Queen Victoria's Jubilee procession, nothing less! The whole week will be given over to rejoicing. How auspicious that you should share your special day with her, Queen of my heart that you are!"

He was so amusing, so able to divert her. Yes, she remembered their first meeting. Was it only a year ago? She felt as if she had known him forever.

"I have an idea," he continued. "We shall watch our beloved Queen's procession and in the evening have our own special soiree!"

She glanced tentatively at his aristocratic profile and thought of Denzil and his opium. Should she mention it now, she wondered, then took the plunge. "Denzil was here earlier," she began. "He had a little ball of waxy stuff. He said it was opium. He said actors and poets take it. It makes them perform better. He says it's better than drink. Is that true?"

Sir Nicholas snapped his pocket book shut and turned to her in some alarm. "The great Bard said that drink promotes the desire, but takes away the performance. Admittedly, it was a reference to lechery, but to rely on drink or opium to enhance any performance is a tragedy, in my opinion! It has led to the ruin of many people!"

"I'm ruined already!" she replied, then as he vehemently protested, "Oh, yes I am, in some folks' eyes. But you need not worry. I don't need things like that!"

It was easy to lie. She had heard what she wanted to hear. Opium was bad, it was dangerous and it was exciting. As always, she was able to banish the outside world, so that soon he thought no more of the conversation.

An hour later he dressed and left. Tregony lay in the huge bed and rolled into the hollow he'd vacated, warm and scented with his odour. She was still dreaming when Maisie knocked at the door and slipped into the room.

"Ooh, it's a bit dark in here," she said, edging round the furniture. "Shall I take the tray down for you? There's a Mr Smith waiting, by the way."

Dusk was falling outside, Tregony was drowsy and had no wish for another client just yet. She roused herself with an effort and winced suddenly. A throbbing headache was gripping her head in an iron band and she felt oddly sick. She must take some laudanum. "Alright," she answered, climbing out of bed. "Be an angel, light the chandelier, will you?"

Maisie fumbled with the big box of matches and carefully lit each of the 20 candles in their crystal holders. The room blazed with golden light. She turned to lay the box down and her eye fell on Sir Nicholas's flowers, so magnificently adorning the fireplace.

She stared, horrified, then screamed. The sound tore through Tregony's aching head like broken glass. "What on earth ...?" she began, annoyed, then stopped at the look on Maisie's face. "What is it, sweetheart?" The girl looked terrible. "Don't you feel well? You look like a ghost!"

Maisie's face had turned a pinched grey colour and she turned pleading eyes up to Tregony and burst into tears. "You must get rid of them!" she sobbed. "You must! They're terrible bad luck! If you don't, there'll be a death! Oh, please!" she grabbed Tregony's hand and clung to it.

Tregony gently stroked her forehead and held her close. "Get rid of what?" she asked, bewildered. She followed Maisie's gaze to the flowers. Surely Maisie couldn't mean those?

"The peacock feathers!" Maisie wailed. "You mustn't have them in the house, especially not in your room! Peacock feathers mean death. A lady down our turning got hit by a hackney, and she had some in her hat!"

Tregony smiled and kissed Maisie's cheek. "For your sake I will, angel," she said, "though I don't believe it. How could they harm anyone, they're just from a bird and a beautiful one at that. Calm yourself! I'll call Alfred to take them out and burn them." She crossed to the feathers and removed them from the basket. Opening her door, she deposited them on the landing, then returned to Maisie. "There you are," she reassured her. "Don't worry, darling. Nothing is going to happen. We're quite safe!"

Maisie shuddered and dried her eyes. "I do hope so! Dear Tregony, what would I do if you was to take ill and die!"

"I'm not going to die!" Tregony said, firmly. "You mustn't believe such things, Maisie!"

She cuddled her friend, touched by her devotion. She had no premonition of danger.

Chapter 21

June, 1897

The Jubilee route was announced. Sir Nicholas and Tregony pored over a map after their lovemaking. She leaned against him and tried to focus on his finger as he traced where the procession would pass. He failed to see the glittering eyes and flushed cheeks. He only knew that she had excelled herself that day, and trying to keep pace with her, he had experienced a gripping pain in his chest that had left him breathless. It was not the first time it had struck without warning. Soon, he would no longer be able to ignore it. Even now his heart still raced painfully, drops of sweat beaded his brow and there was a bluish tinge around his mouth. Tregony didn't notice.

He forced himself to be calmer as they talked about her birthday, only three weeks off now, and where they would stand to watch the procession. "Piccadilly, or Trafalgar Square," he suggested. "Or we could wait until the return, through Horse Guards, Pall Mall. It will be a grand occasion!"

She agreed to everything, answering haphazardly. He dressed hurriedly and put the map in his pocket. He was late, or something about her behaviour would have warned him. She closed the door on him and, naked, stumbled to her dressing table and opened a drawer. From underneath her frilled petticoats she took a small packet, carefully shook out the opium powder into a glass of water and drank it. The powder was Denzil's suggestion, much quicker and neater, he said, than chewing waxy resin. In fact, he said, some ladies smoked the powder in little clay pipes, but she had baulked at that. Now she must get ready for the next client. Her reputation was spreading. She had lost count of the gentlemen who had come upon recommendation since Denzil had begun delivering his packets.

She peered at her face, touching it with shaking fingers. There were deep creases under her eyes and her mouth had begun a downward journey, giving her a sullen look. She must use more cream of cucumber. Or there was that recipe for plantain butter she'd found in a magazine. She had the orangeflower and rosewater, she would send Maisie out to purchase the other ingredients. And her hair! She pulled a bronze curl over her shoulder. She must change the soap, the green coal tar didn't suit it. For weeks now she had noticed handfuls in the basin after hair washing mornings. It looked faded somehow, dank and lifeless. She scooped it up for effect, but that was worse. Now she could see patches of scalp, shiny and pink. And when had that tooth started to turn black? She stared at her reflection. In the flickering light of the chandelier she looked old, but tingled unremittingly day and night with excited energy, interspersed with increasing bouts of lassitude. It hadn't taken long for the drug to have its destructive effect, but she had made her choice and this was a small price to pay for the extra custom, the increase in wealth, the enhanced reputation. Live for the moment and let the devil take the hindmost.

Sir Nicholas could talk of nothing else but her birthday and the procession. She was tired of hearing it. She was impatient with him, he was asking awkward questions, had become too possessive. He wanted a soiree, a dinner for two. She wanted a lavish party, to invite all her friends, and their friends. All welcome. Alarmed now at her changes of mood, the relentless energy, he protested. "I fear it may be too much for you, my angel, but you shall have whatever you want." He was certain now that she was drugged, and he watched her carefully.

The party was to be at Willis's Dancing Academy in Brewer Street, where the dancing was frequently wild and uninhibited. It would be just the place to work off excited energy. Thanks to Maisie, everyone knew about the party, even Denzil. She was so excited she had told nearly every visitor, but Tregony didn't mind.

And now her birthday was only a day away and she lay drowsily on the bed, her dim room lit only by dressing table candles. The preparations had weakened her, although Maisie had been invaluable, helping to arrange food and write invitations. What she would do without Maisie she didn't know. Tregony tried to muster her thoughts. Earlier, Maisie had brought up her new gown of emerald green shot silk with a shirred, lace-trimmed sash that tied in a huge bow at the back. The gown had been especially made. Where had she put it? Ah, yes, there it was, hanging on the wardrobe door. She narrowed her eyes, trying to focus on the shimmering material as it hung there. It was a beautiful gown, it fitted her perfectly now. She'd lost so much weight, it had been sent back twice for alterations because she was unable to face any needlework herself. She had enjoyed choosing it, but today everything seemed to be too much effort. She sighed. Soon she must get up and light the chandelier.

The door opened suddenly and Denzil strode in. He often did that now, barging in without knocking. She knew Madame would strongly disapprove if she knew. Clients were supposed to wait their turn, but Denzil was devious enough to slip past Madame.

"Not interruptin' nothin' am I?" he asked, casually. "Thought you'd be wantin' this!" He held out several packets and she started up from her bed, grabbing her robe. He grinned at her flushed face and shallow breathing, eyeing her narrowly. She was losing her looks and figure. She was gaunt and the roundness of her breasts and hips had all but disappeared, leaving her robe hanging. The corners of his mouth quirked, while his eyes held an implacable coldness. Soon she would be fit for nobody and would come crawling back to him, but he hadn't finished with her yet.

She jumped up, trying to reach the packets, while he danced them above her head tantalizingly. "Hold up, maid! What do I get fer me trouble?"

She flung herself at him, and they rolled together to the floor. A fierce triumph flooded through him at the sight of her protruding bones, the blue-veined hands as they clutched at him. Yet she still had a strength, which surprised him. Alright, double the dose or substitute the opium for something even stronger. He knew where to get it. Grimly, he pounded against her. Yes, Tregony Welles, it's been a hard lesson, but you've had a good teacher.

Deliberately, he bent down and bit her breast until she screamed. She tried to roll from under him, but he pulled her round again, cramming his fist against her mouth and crashing her head again and again onto the polished boards, until he saw that she had fainted. He got up and adjusted his clothing. He crossed to the dressing table and put the packets upon it, then he opened her hosiery and glove drawers and rifled through them for money. Nothing there. He turned his attention to her jewellery boxes. She had some very fine pieces. He was something of an expert, he'd seen rings this good before. He held up a large diamond and emerald ring, a present from Sir Nicholas, and watched the light from the candles flash from it, fascinated by the myriad colours. Jane would love this. He'd neglected her of late. This would make up for it.

He slipped the ring into his wallet. A cursory search produced a gold and sapphire bracelet, another good piece, and a paste necklace, pretty but of little value. Still, it might suit his little Plymouth doxy. It would have to do. He pocketed the bracelet and glanced casually at Tregony. She was motionless, but she was breathing. A steady trickle of blood ran from her left breast to the floor. He smiled cynically. He doubted whether she would even remember his visit when she woke up. He stepped over her and crossed to the door. He let himself out and went downstairs, whistling.

* * * * *

It was Tregony's birthday and nearly nine o'clock. Maisie entered Tregony's room with a jug of boiling water and a glass of coffee. The frilled curtains were drawn and she crossed to the window and flung them aside, letting in a bright stream of sunlight. She turned to wake Tregony, then stopped, horrified, gazing about her. It looked as if Tregony had been fighting, there were upturned drawers and scattered clothes everywhere.

Tregony was on her back on the floor, her eyes closed, breasts exposed to Maisie's shocked eyes, for she could see the ripped flesh and dried blood on the left nipple. Suddenly, as Maisie stared, it seemed as if she were seeing Tregony anew, the muddy skin and pinched mouth, the hollow cheeks and sunken eyes. It had been many weeks since she'd seen Tregony without her usual makeup of french chalk and rouge. Now she could see what really lay underneath, and she was shocked. She hesitated, wondering what to do. She must try to wake Tregony and ask her what had happened. She shook her friend. "Wake up, wake up Tregony! It's your birthday today. Madame wants to know where you are!"

Tregony flung her arms wide and groaned. "Shut the curtains, Maisie! I can't see! The light, it hurts!" Her head throbbed. Her eyes felt as if they had been shaken in their sockets, and every muscle of her neck and shoulders ached unbearably. Clutching the bed, she stood up with some difficulty and glanced at Maisie's shocked face.

"Maisie, don't mention this mess to anyone, do you hear? I don't want Madame knowing. I can deal with it. It won't happen again."

Maisie hesitated, then replied, "Well, if that's what you want. Who was it? We could all be done in in our beds! Madame ought to know if gents like that are coming in."

Tregony paused for a moment. Denzil was dangerous. She owed it to the other girls to tell the truth. "It was Denzil," she said. "And don't worry, I'll have him barred. He won't enter this house again."

Maisie suddenly gasped, "Oh, Lor! Denzil's already downstairs. And Sir Nicholas. Madame asked them to wait till I'd been up."

"Ah, he's here, is he? Go down and say I shall only see Sir Nicholas. And don't mention any of this."

A steady anger began to burn in her. She began taking great sips of the hot coffee Maisie had brought. She crossed to her dressing table stool and sat down. She looked at her bruised lips, her faded beauty and a hard core of anger started to grow within her. Through the murky depths of her opium haze she vaguely remembered Denzil Pascoe leering towards her, teeth bared, then the agony as they tore into her flesh. She remembered her head hitting the boards, each blow etching his evil face with terrible clarity on her memory. But he had done her a favour. Now she knew that he was mad, that he harboured a malice towards her so terrible that he was slowly killing her.

A chill crept through her. She had never encountered such remorselessness, such implacable malevolence. She would make him pay for this. His time had come. Madame's men would be at the party tonight. They would regard Denzil Pascoe as small fry, easily dealt with. And the Trefusis brothers, come to London to settle old scores. Both had little or no conscience. There must be nothing too drastic, just enough to frighten Denzil back to Tamarleigh with his tail between his legs. He had dogged her life for too long. He was like a blight, a creeping curse.

Maisie entered the lounge. "Tregony will see Sir Nicholas, not Denzil. She's resting for her birthday tonight at Willis's."

Denzil started up from the chair where he had been reading the paper and ignoring Sir Nicholas, and made as if to push past him. With characteristic aplomb, Sir Nicholas stood in his way. "Did you hear our little friend?" he murmured, with awful civility. "Miss Cornish doesn't want to see you. Miss Cornish is indisposed."

Denzil stopped short, his face dark red, bulbous eyes glaring. "So she will be, when I gets 'old of 'er!" he growled. "I pays me money, like the next man!"

"I think not!" Sir Nicholas replied coldly, turning Denzil round and pointing him firmly to the front door. "Miss Cornish is in the happy position of being able to choose whom she wishes to see, and this morning she doesn't wish to see you!"

Denzil shook off Sir Nicholas's hand. Something in the older man's face stopped him making a scene, an implacable contempt which warned him off.

"Alright!" he jeered. "You win this once, you prettied up dandy. You ain't a real man, you'll not keep her satisfied for long, not that one! I knows her of old and, besides, I got somethin' she needs, somethin' you can't give her! Calls 'erself Cornish, do she? Just shows what you know! She's a Welles, born and bred, and a Welles she'll allus be, call 'erself what she likes! Allus thought she were different, did Tregony Welles! Tell 'er I hopes she enjoys 'er party!"

He flung open the front door and backed off down the steps, much to the relief of Maisie, who was now very frightened. At the bottom he turned and fired a parting shot. "I can bide me time. I never forgets a slight!"

"I don't doubt it!" Sir Nicholas murmured and turned from the door to mount the stairs, his heart thumping painfully. Now he knew for certain where Tregony was getting her opium, and what had that lout called her - Welles? She was becoming like a stranger to him, he hadn't even known her real name. He felt hurt. He knocked on Tregony's door and waited until she called, "Come in."

The moment he saw her he knew that there was a change about her, a renewed glimmer, as if a wavering candle had suddenly spluttered into life. Her mouth, of late so drawn and pinched, was set in a determined line. She stood wrapped only in her robe, regarding him quietly. To keep him in ignorance had been a vain hope, and now an unnecessary one.

"Don't say anything. I know you guessed before this, and I know I've been a fool. Don't ask me how it came about, either. Greed, vanity, call it what you like, it comes to the same thing. But it's over now. Over for good. I've come to my senses, and not a mite too soon!"

As he saw the determined tilt of her head, heard the new strength in her voice, it was as if a chrysalis were breaking open before him and a new, tentative butterfly emerging. He longed for her to fly to him, fold her wings and be secure. He gazed at her, his eyes bright, filled with a deep gratitude that the agony was over.

She turned aside and continued with her toilette. "You knew it was Denzil, didn't you? I believe he's mad. He tried to kill me last night. Revenge. You might believe I've done something really terrible for such a punishment, but I only went with someone else, hardly a sin!"

"That may be enough for someone deeply in love," he answered, quietly. He reflected on the past weeks when he thought he had lost her for good. What would he have done in Denzil's place? Jealousy could make monsters out of mild mannered men. For an instant, he felt a stab of sympathy towards Denzil Pascoe, which vanished as swiftly as it had come.

She made an impatient noise. "Love! Denzil Pascoe knows nothing of love!"

"But I do!" he cried, striding forward and pulling Tregony fiercely into his arms. The tragedy of it all suddenly struck her. What strange destiny had shaped her life? This man who loved her could never be hers, yet Denzil Pascoe, who was obsessed beyond the bounds of sanity, could have been hers for the asking. Damn all men!

She dressed in a day gown of peach dimity with a little matching hat trimmed with jet. She carried only her silver guinea purse made of the finest chain mesh. The purse had a little finger ring, so that she could clutch it in her hand. When she had finished her toilette she felt ready to face the world. Sir Nicholas's brougham stood at the door, minded by a sullen Albert, whose expression miraculously changed at the sight of the guinea Sir Nicholas handed him.

"Should you like a rug, my angel?" Sir Nicholas enquired tenderly.

She smiled. "In this heat? No, don't fuss so!" but she was comforted by his concern.

The streets were already filled with jostling sightseers, all in festive mood on this happy June day. "We're too late to see

Her Majesty at Piccadilly," remarked Sir Nicholas, "but never fear, we will go down the back doubles and catch up with the procession at St Paul's."

The streets were jammed with merrymakers and countless hackneys and private carriages, but eventually, they arrived at Ludgate Hill, where Sir Nicholas left the brougham in the yard of King Lud's Tavern. They walked the short distance to St Paul's and managed to make their way to the front of the crowd around the steps.

A great cheer went up and the Jubilee procession came in sight, the Queen's coach flanked by her yeoman-warders. Tregony watched, fascinated, as the cavalcade passed. The Queen, a small black figure, looked out at her cheering subjects, a gracious smile on her pale face, her hand raised in acknowledgement.

They watched the procession as it moved out of sight towards Cheapside and the Mansion House, where the Queen would break her journey before continuing to London Bridge and through Borough High Street, before coming back to Westminster.

The atmosphere was jovial. London loved a pageant and it was in a mood to celebrate. Flags and bunting hung everywhere and people had begun to dance in the street after the last coach had passed. Tregony looked longingly at the laughing people. She would have loved to join in, but the short journey had tired her.

Sir Nicholas, glancing down at her happy face, noticed her fatigue. "Enough for one day, I think," he said, taking her arm. "Let's get you back now!" On the way back they detoured through Covent Garden and, true to his word, he loaded her lap with a mountain of June roses.

They spent a lazy afternoon. They drank tansy tea and ate muffins. He stroked her body with oil of frankincense and then made love to her, gently, tenderly. She lay smiling, passive, but looking on him fondly and tracing his laughter lines with her fingertips. They dozed, then woke after 20 minutes or so to continue their gentle lovemaking.

Afterwards, he was to remember this time with great love and sadness. He was to remember every bone that jutted from her thin frame, how he kissed the poor, frail fingers and held her carefully, fearful lest he should hurt her. He was to remember, with bitter anguish, her luminous green eyes as they gazed dreamily at him as if, unknowingly, she too was eager to memorise every contour of his face, every expression. He held those moments in his heart and forever after she was inviolate, perfect, the personification of woman.

At five they had a small dinner in her room. As the evening bore down upon her, she began to feel apprehensive. She began to wish they'd chosen somewhere other than Willis's. But the thought of Denzil Pascoe hardened her resolve. Whatever happened, he must learn to leave her alone.

She dressed in the new gown. When she was ready she looked beautiful, despite the thinness and the obvious lassitude. She had hidden her customary pallor with heavy rouge, which gave her a look of feverishness and, indeed, her head was spinning and she felt sick. She knew that this would be the first of many such symptoms and she must get used to it, hopeful in the knowledge that as the craving diminished, she would recover. She poured a tiny amount of laudanum into a glass and swallowed it. She needed something to help her over the worst moments.

Willis's was already crowded when they arrived at eight o'clock, the atmosphere hot with sweating bodies, nearly every table taken. There was a shout when Tregony entered and people began to crowd round them, pressing presents on her.

Someone pushed a drink into her hand, someone else tried to grab her arm and drag her onto the dance floor. Laughing, she protested. "Let me get in! What a crowd! And, Nicholas, look! What food!"

Against one wall was a table laden with all kinds of cold meats and savouries, salads and fruit. Mountainous jellies wobbled precariously on china dishes, next to crisp pastry tartlets and egg custards. There were floury rolls and tubs of yellow butter and great pitchers of beer and wine. And in the middle of the table, in a position of honour, stood a tiered cake, intricately iced with edible flowers and ribbons and decorated with glazed fruit. For a moment she was speechless. Her eyes moistened. She had friends; they wouldn't be everyone's choice, but they were loyal to her, and they loved her. It was no small compensation.

"Thank you! Thank you!" she said, her voice faltering.

Sir Nicholas was looking at her tenderly. "You see, my love. I'm not the only one who loves you."

She smiled and put her hand into his. She looked around, searching for familiar faces. Smoke wreathed the rooms, distorting the brilliance of the chandeliers and causing the shadows of the dancers to leap and writhe on the walls, like grotesque caricatures. She saw the Trefusis brothers over by the bar with a group of men who stood silently drinking and eyeing the company. Madame's men. They were well dressed for the most part, but hard faced and calculating.

"I won't be a minute," she said to Sir Nicholas and slipped from his side. He watched her gesturing and pointing as she spoke to the men at the bar and he was suddenly filled with deep misgivings. Something was plainly afoot and a flutter of fear swept through him. Tregony left the men and began to push her way back to him. He had to raise his voice to speak, the noise was so intense.

"Who are those men, my love?" he shouted. "What on earth were you saying to them?"

But she was saved the trouble of answering, for just at that moment Denzil Pascoe came through the door, and her reply died on her lips. He stood in the doorway, swaying and looking belligerently round him. His eyes were red-rimmed, unfocused, his mouth hung slackly open and spittle flecked his chin.

Perran Trefusis detached himself from the group and began to elbow his way round the side of the room, while Keverne set off in the opposite direction. Yet another man took out a large handkerchief, wiped his mouth carefully on it, replaced it in his pocket and started to elbow through the crowd, his eyes never leaving Denzil's face. The rest of the group fought their way through behind him, their lust for fighting heightened by drink and money.

At last Denzil saw what he was looking for. There she was, the bitch, still thinking she could do without him. Obviously she hadn't learnt her lesson well enough. He would teach her to turn him away. She had always thought she could better him. Tonight she would find out just how mistaken she was.

Tregony stood in the centre of the dance floor. Every line of her body was tense, but Denzil was in no condition to notice. Nor did he notice or recognise the men surrounding him. He lurched forward, grabbing at the dancers as he came. They pushed him roughly, and he stumbled from one to another, like a lumpy parcel being passed down the line. As he got nearer, Tregony moved out of his reach, making for Sir Nicholas, who steeled himself for action. Only a simpleton would try anything tonight, there were so many of Tregony's friends here. And those men, circling like lazy vultures. No-one stood a chance with them. The Pascoe lout would find he'd bitten off enough to choke him.

He leaned forward to seize Tregony's hand and pull her to him, but as he did so a paralysing pain, now all too familiar, shot through his chest and down his left arm, anchoring him to the spot. He staggered and clung to the wall. His arms were like lead and, try as he might to grasp her, his body felt as if it had been turned to stone. The whole thing was like an improbable drama, absurd, unreal, the people in the room like players on a stage and he a hapless spectator. He could only stand immobilised as the scene was enacted before his horrified gaze.

Denzil caught up with Tregony, shouting her name. Then he lunged at her, just as the men pounced. Her scream electrified the room. "Denzil! No!" Sir Nicholas saw something flash upward in Denzil's hand, saw the men grappling with him and knocking him to the floor, then a stream of bright crimson flew up and painted the icing on the birthday cake in obscene stripes.

No-one in the room moved. Then slowly, reluctantly, Tregony folded up like a wilting flower and drooped soundlessly to the floor. As she fell her arms reached out, coming to rest just inches from Sir Nicholas's feet. Across her throat was a fine red line and as her head fell lifelessly back, the line parted.

There was a moment of stunned silence, then the room erupted. Someone shouted, "Run for the Peelers!" The knife clattered from Denzil's hand and Keverne Trefusis bent to retrieve it. Then, grimly, the men lifted Denzil over the heads of the screaming crowd and towards the door. Their business was better done away from prying eyes. They disappeared into the night.

Frantic, Sir Nicholas twisted to look at Tregony. Several people were starting to lift her away from the trampling feet. He wanted to help, but he was powerless, held in the paralysis of pain that still coursed through him. He wanted to hold her just once more in his arms, but he couldn't reach her. He stared at the unseeing eyes, the tumbled curls, the great seeping red stain colouring the emerald dress. Then a merciful blackness descended and he slipped down the wall to the floor.

Part Five

London and Surrey, 1960s

Chapter 22

Tremayne opened his eyes. How long he'd been asleep he didn't know, but a pale sun streamed into the room and lit up a crucifix on the opposite wall. He put up his hands and felt his throat. It must have been a dream, then, a nightmare. There'd been crowds, noise, dancing and he was in the middle of it all. A voice had called his name, Tregony, then ... nothing. Only an incredible blackness, and gradual surfacing to full consciousness. The name hammered at his head, Tregony, Tregony ...

He turned his head slowly, puzzled. He didn't recognise the room he was in. It was all white. White walls, white paint, white sheets. I must be dead, he thought. This is heaven and soon I'll see God. That's why the crucifix is there.

From somewhere outside the room came the sound of muted traffic, and not far off he could hear the chink of crockery. Not heaven, then, but where? Quiet voices sounded outside the white door, then it was gently opened a crack and a head looked round. It was someone he recognised, but for the life of him he couldn't remember who. The door opened fully and a tall man walked into the room, bearing a tray with tea things on it. He was followed by a woman, wearing an anxious expression. When she saw the figure in the bed, her expression changed to one of happy delight.

"Oh, darling!" she exclaimed. "Benedict, look! He's awake! Quick, get the nurse!"

Benedict? Yes, that was the tall man's name. He vaguely recalled it, but he still couldn't place him. The tall man put the tray down and left the room, while the woman hurried towards the bed, hands outstretched. Love and warmth flowed from her and stirred a distant memory. Into his mind came a vivid picture. He saw himself as a child, a small girl near him. Between them a child's tricycle lay on the ground. He was crying and holding his knee. A woman was bending over him, kissing him and murmuring, "There now, let me kiss it better, then!" The woman had the same warm, flowery smell as this one. As she held his face to kiss him, a veil lifted from his mind and he began to remember other things. Playing with the little girl on a beach somewhere, riding in a steam train and watching the smoke stream past the window, opening birthday presents, a cake. There was a man, too, comfortable, familiar. He knew them all very well. He knew they were dear to him.

The woman sat down on the bed and clasped his hands. Her smile was brilliant. "Oh, it's so wonderful to have you back with us," she said. "You don't know how we've all prayed for this!"

Ah, prayer. Yes, that was it! That was his life, surely? He'd thought of God just a moment ago. And he knew God, there was no question about that, but why couldn't he place this woman?

He gave up struggling. He smiled at her. It was a friendly smile, pleasant, mildly curious. She knew at once that he didn't recognise her. Her heart sank. She must give no hint, treat him normally. These things happened. People were in accidents, they hit their heads, they lost their memories. Then they got them back again. Or sometimes they didn't. She refused to think about that.

Just then a nurse came in with the tall man. Tremayne looked at him again. Very tall, very dark, enigmatic. The man hardly smiled at all, but gazed hawk-like at him, an unreadable look in his black eyes.

"Would you like some tea, Tremayne?" the woman asked. She was looking straight at him. Tremayne, he thought. That's me, it must be. Unusual name. He was rather pleased. She poured out a cup and gave it to the tall man, then she came over to the bed and put her arm round his back, attempting to support him.

"I can do that," he said, suddenly. She stepped back, delighted. "There you are, you see," she said to the tall man. "He's stronger already."

She turned back to him. "We'll soon have you on your feet, darling! Oh, this is wonderful! Four weeks you've been away from us, you know! But it's over now."

So he'd been away. Yes, that must be it. He'd been away on holiday and had some kind of accident. That would account for the nurse who was approaching him with a thermometer in her hand.

"Just slip this under your tongue," she said. He allowed the nurse to plump up the pillows behind him, then he opened his mouth obediently for the thermometer. He sat with it under his tongue while they waited in silence for the minute to be up. He looked at them with friendly interest. The nurse took hold of his wrist and held it while she looked at a watch pinned to her pocket. She removed the thermometer from his mouth, examined it, then shook it.

"Temperature's nearly normal," she announced.

That's good, he thought. Something's normal then. The woman gave him a cup of tea. He noticed she had rings on, one of them a large solitaire diamond. He'd seen that ring before, many times. He remembered it lying on a dressing table somewhere. Another veil lifted.

And there was a house somewhere. The house was in a

tree-lined street. The house had a pretty front garden, with roses and chrysanthemums, where he played with the little girl.

He turned to the woman in the room. He held out his empty cup and she came and took it from him, putting it on the bedside cabinet. As she bent near him her face came close. He could see a mole by the side of her nose, almost unnoticeable, but familiar.

He looked across at the man sitting in the chair next to the door. The man's black gaze pierced him. A remembered feeling of fascination flowed over him. He was following the man called Benedict along a windswept cliff. The weather was atrocious; squalls of snow hit them as they walked, so that they had to bend their heads into the wind. Benedict walked fast, always ahead. He sensed that Benedict was special to him, a special person.

He looked at the woman. She was about to sit down again. He smiled up at her. He looked closer. The smile, the deft movements of her hands. Why, it was almost as if he were looking into a mirror.

Suddenly, the last veil lifted. A vast flood of remembrance rushed in on him. He didn't know whether to laugh or cry, for with lucidity there was also horror.

He leaned forward in the bed. He smiled with recognition this time and the smile was heartfelt and genuine. "Hello, Mother! Hello, Benedict!" he said.

Chapter 23

The memories haunted his dreams and crowded his waking moments; the cruelty and the degradation, the overwhelming malice, the last terrifying dream. And the baby. It had belonged to the girl, he'd seen them that day at Turnham Green, yet when he pursued the image it blurred strangely, and faded into a doubtful memory, names were indistinct, voices came and went. And yet, at other times, just before he dropped off to sleep, a cavalcade of crystal clear impressions would pass behind his closed lids, bringing him sharply awake. Diffraction patterns which shifted through the spectrum, faces which laughed or leered at him, all frighteningly real

They were sitting in Margherita's garden. He had not explained to his mother how the accident had happened, preferring merely to say, "I was in the wrong place at the wrong time," and she kept her conclusions to herself.

He made another effort to talk to Benedict about his visions. "I know who that girl is," he ventured. "I even know her name, or maybe it was *my* name. She was called Tregony and she needs help. My help, or why would this have happened to me? I get the feeling that something's reaching out to me."

Benedict answered wearily. "This isn't helping towards your recovery. And it's not Biblical. 'There shall not be found among you a consulter with familiar spirits, or a wizard, or a necromancer.' Deuteronomy 18: verses 10-11, remember?"

Tremayne didn't answer. He knew there was no way of convincing Benedict that the girl had been very real to him. Perhaps he *was* imagining it all, the after-effects of illness, perhaps. But he knew he must try and get some proof of her existence and he must get it on his own. The local reference library would have newspaper information about the time. Rob Bucknell had suggested Victorian or Edwardian England. Something so violent, if it were real, must have been reported in the newspapers of the day.

Somehow during his coma, he had relived and experienced the joys and woes of someone else. He had been abused, reviled, feted and adored. And poisoned. He had only to shut his eyes to feel once again the terrible sinking lassitude, the bursts of exhausting energy, the craving for something he couldn't name.

He said, "I remember everything about her. She was clear before, but now it's much more real to me."

Benedict yawned and stood up. He folded his deckchair and took it to the summerhouse where he stacked it neatly with the others. "I'd better be getting back to Mount Carmel," he said. "Now that you're better it looks as if one of us'll be moving on soon. Father Jones mentioned it last night again. You remember before your accident there was a possibility of one of us moving?"

It was the snub direct. Well, let Benedict think what he liked, he would not let it stand in the way of their friendship. "Yes, I remember. St Boniface in Plymouth, wasn't it? Laurence went there, a priest from my last church." Perhaps he should think about it, get away and make a clean break. Besides, it would be good to work with Laurence again.

He walked Benedict to the station and saw him on the London train. "I'll be down again on Monday," Benedict called out of the window. "Try and get some rest."

He watched Tremayne walk out of the station yard and was almost tempted to leap from the train, but he resisted the urge. He pulled the leather window strap out of its notch, hitched the window closed and settled down for the journey back to London. He knew he'd been short with Tremayne, but he'd thought all this nonsense about a girl and a baby was over. Now it seemed Tremayne was still obsessed. He would continue praying for Tremayne. His prayers had been answered so far. Tremayne had come out of his coma, with no physical ill effects and was getting stronger every day. All outward signs pointed to a full recovery. He tried to comfort himself, but he still felt uneasy. Tremayne had always brought out his protective love and now this was clouding his judgement of the whole affair. And who was to say what Tremayne had really encountered, if it were true. He believed it was an innocent girl, but who could say what it really was?

These thoughts occupied him until he reached Victoria. Soon he was walking through the square towards Mount Carmel. As he reached the church porch he was startled to see a figure huddled there. The figure stood up as he approached and he saw that it was Betty Parker. She was alone and clearly upset. She got up hesitantly and confronted him. "Sorry to trouble you, Father, but I gotta know, and this is the first time I could get here. Been up North to see me mam. Rosie's still there. How's ... how's ... Father Jago?" She rushed the name out as if it hurt her lips.

"He's improving greatly, Betty, thank you," Benedict replied. "He'll be away from the parish for quite a while, though. When he's fully recovered he'll probably be transferred somewhere else. As I will," he added, but she wasn't listening. Her face looked white and pinched and he felt unreasonable anger rising in him.

Suddenly, his mind went back to the day when he had seen Tremayne and Betty Parker together in the crèche, and a great realisation dawned. Fool that he was! He knew now, without a shadow of a doubt, that it was Betty Parker Tremayne was returning from that fateful night. He had only to look at her face, see the bitter love and anguish there, to know how much she suffered. Well, he had suffered too, and would continue to suffer. Daily, hourly, his forbidden love was brought home to him by a word, a gesture. Now she knew how it felt!

All the carefully hidden feelings, the repressed longings rose to the surface, but with a supreme effort of will he controlled himself and when he spoke there was no trace of emotion in his voice. "I will give your regards to Father Jago, Betty. I shall be seeing him next Monday. In the meantime, I'd get along home, if I were you. It will be dark soon and coming on to rain, if I'm not mistaken."

She knew of course. His voice was bland, detached, but she wasn't fooled for a second. As if she couldn't take care of herself on the streets of London, and as if he cared. She turned miserably away. It was plain she must forget Tremayne Jago, though it cost her bitter hurt to do it.

Benedict went inside the church and knelt in one of the pews, full of contrition in a moment. He had let Betty, and himself, down. She needed someone, she had come to the church and he had turned her away. But it was not that alone which he prayed for. He knew with a cruel certainty that his love for Tremayne was as deep as ever. The illness had proved it. All he wanted to do was hover about his friend looking after him, even forgetting his parish duties and just being there. What perverse fate had put this sophistry in him? Or, at least, not so much an absence of reasoning, as the wrong reasoning. He felt bereft, alone, as he had not done since his youth.

As he prayed a great sense of renewing and sustaining peace came to him, filling him with humble gratitude that, whatever his sins, he need only take them to the Lord. A line of scripture floated into his head. *"Do not fear, for I am with you ... I will strengthen you and help you; I will uphold you with my righteous right hand."* As always, his prayers had been answered. He was as he was. He had obeyed scriptural teaching. It had been hard, but for him the only choice. Now he must concentrate his efforts on helping Tremayne gain full health. And with a heart full of sadness, he silently begged Betty Parker's forgiveness.

The weekend passed with the usual church duties. Sunday proved to be a particularly busy day, with many tourists in London, but at nine in the evening he stretched himself on the old sofa in the lounge and dozed a little. The sounds of the novice priests in the kitchen making themselves a snack penetrated his drifting thoughts now and then. He felt relaxed, unwilling to make the final effort to go to his room.

One of the novice priests presently came in and sat with him. They talked in a desultory fashion about everything and nothing. Rarely had Benedict felt such peace, so untroubled by his usual tumultuous thoughts. The other novices came in and began a game of chess. Their intermittent low voices were soothing. He wondered what Tremayne was doing at this moment. He really ought to ring him, but he was too tired to talk. He got up from the sofa and said goodnight. On the way through the kitchen he poured himself a small whiskey and took it with him to his room. The night was clear and starry and he spent a few minutes before getting into bed just looking out at the night sky. The universe was full of order and balance, mathematically precise and the knowledge never failed to inspire wonder in him. He was reluctant to shut out such beauty, so left his curtains half open and switched on the little bedside lamp. He settled himself in bed and sipped his whiskey. The Sunday paper lay on his bedside table and he opened it casually and glanced over the news.

He didn't know at what time he dropped off to sleep, but

he awoke at about three o'clock with a bent and aching neck, the paper still spread across the bed. Mysteriously, the light was out, although he couldn't remember turning it off. As soon as he opened his eyes he was intensely aware that someone was in the room. His heart began to thump uncomfortably. "Who's there?" he asked in a low voice. There was no answer, but he felt a pulsing energy, so strong that it was like a physical force against him.

Then suddenly, a corner of the room began to glow, taking form and shape and across his mystified gaze a series of tiny but discernible scenes began to parade. He could make no sense of what he was seeing and would have leapt from his bed if he could, but his limbs were cold and immovable, as if he were spellbound.

Each picture had a different setting, but through every scene there drifted the stunning image of a young and beautiful girl. His heart leapt when he saw her. She had a dark, intense sensuality and his hand involuntarily strayed to his crucifix. The images were seemingly unconnected. First, a slipway somewhere, cold and deserted except for the girl, copper curls flaming, sitting against a wall. Then a city street, wet and dreary and a cloaked figure struggling against the rain. Yet another scene, filled with lamentation and anguish, with the copper-haired girl cradling a baby in her arms. Then a languishing, blurred outline and a distinct sense of erotic decadence, surely a demonic visitation sent to tempt him! The last vision was of a soundless supplicant in torment, a body flung out on a grimy floor somewhere, eyes open and fixed, bright hair spread around, noise, a sense of evil and injustice and a cry of despair which struck him to the heart.

Released at last from his invisible chains, he fumbled for the light switch. As light flooded the room, the tiny pictures vanished and the room resumed its everyday look. He got out of bed and went quickly downstairs and into the kitchen. He made himself some strong coffee then sat at the kitchen table, head in his hands. He was shaking, unable to come to terms with what he had just seen. Every part of his training had taught him to beware of such things, yet he was left with an overwhelming sense of pity and a need to put an injustice right. He closed his eyes. The red-haired girl's image had been so stunning that he could still see her against his closed lids, not voluptuous, not decadent, but tormented and lost, pleading to be sent into the light.

He groaned aloud in an agony of indecision. Was this a precursor of something more evil to follow? He knew he should be on his knees, but if this were indeed evil there would be no pity, only a ruthless need to rid the presbytery of such a thing. If he felt pity, there must be a desperate soul who needed him.

And then the full realisation of his vision struck him. Tremayne's description of the girl, repeated ad nauseam, fitted exactly. How many times had Tremayne asked for reassurance and comfort and been turned away! Now Benedict knew how heartless he must have seemed, how disparaging and dismissive. His sense of inadequacy and failure overpowered him. What a friend and mentor he had turned out to be! Worse, what a Christian! One who only believed what he could see himself. His name should have been Thomas, not Benedict.

He gulped back the rest of his coffee, and rose abruptly. It was five o'clock, already light and a golden sun was beginning to gild the windows of the square. There would be no trains at this early hour, but he needed to walk. He left the presbytery and walked along Piccadilly, through St James's Park to Victoria and Vauxhall Bridge. The walk gave him a chance to muster his thoughts and the more he walked the more convinced he became. The girl had come to him because of his arrogance and disbelief. He was determined that good should come from that.

He swung through Stockwell and Clapham Common. A newsagent outside the tube station was open. He bought some chocolate and continued walking on through Tooting and Mitcham, past the common and out along the London Road to Hackbridge.

He reached Wallington at eight and knocked on Margherita's front door. Her mouth dropped at the sight of him.

"Whatever …?" she began.

Benedict smiled apologetically, "Sorry to land myself on you like this. I couldn't sleep, needed some exercise. Besides, I promised Tremayne I'd call today."

If she was puzzled she didn't show it, but made him immediately welcome. Soon, Tremayne came downstairs, yawning. He stared in surprise when he saw Benedict. "Good grief! You're an early visitor! What's up?"

"Nothing," Benedict glanced at Margherita, but she was already making her way upstairs to change. "I have a WI meeting at nine. Benedict, I'm sure you'll excuse me. Don't tire him out, now!"

Tremayne immediately turned to Benedict. "What's happened? Quick, tell me! I know something has!"

"Wait until Margherita's gone out," Benedict answered. "Suffice it to say that I've had what you might call a revealing night and I've walked all the way here from Mount Carmel!"

Tremayne was astonished. "You must be done in! I expect you could do with some coffee."

They took their coffee into the lounge and talked of church matters until Margherita had left the house. Then Benedict recounted the night's events, while Tremayne listened, astounded, feeling as if a great burden was lifting from his shoulders. "Don't you realise what this means?" he cried. "You've seen Tregony, and she's come to you because you didn't believe. She's desperate!"

"She must be!" Benedict replied drily. "Now the question is, what do we do? And why has she come to us anyway? No, wait!" He suddenly jumped up, his eyes snapping. "How stupid of me! I should have realised. She's in purgatory, of course she is! A soul in torment. *That's* why she's come to us. Who better to ask to release her than priests!"

Tremayne stared at him. "Of course! You could be right. But …" he hesitated.

"But what?"

"Well, she could have gone to anyone in the church. Why us?"

"I don't know, but she's chosen us and I believe we need to do something about it. Maybe we'll find out why she's chosen us, but we have a duty as priests to respond to her call. Agreed?"

"Oh, of course," Tremayne answered quickly. "Tell me more about the visions."

"She was beautiful, even I could see that!" Benedict replied, smiling faintly. He described the pictures he had seen. "They were very small, like seeing down the wrong end of a telescope, but she stood out clearly, there would be no forgetting her."

"Did she have a baby with her?" Tremayne asked.

"No, she was alone," Benedict replied. "Quite significant, really."

"I saw it several times, but I don't know what happened to it," Tremayne said. "I seem to recall searching for it with someone. But the memory's blurred, just an overwhelming sense of loss."

Benedict smiled faintly. "It looks as though I owe you an

apology. I don't know how this has happened, but I know how frustrating it must have been for you to have me constantly disbelieving you! Now I've been roped in, so to speak, just to teach me!"

Tremayne looked embarrassed. "No need to apologise. It's enough to know you're on my side at last!"

Chapter 24

By the time Margherita came home at lunchtime, they were certain beyond all doubt that something extraordinary had happened. Somehow, two lives from two different ages had crossed and a lost soul was crying out to them. There were too many similarities for there to be any mistake.

"The point is, what do we do now?" Benedict asked. "We need to verify some of this. I suppose we should visit Somerset House, but we've only a first name to go on, albeit an unusual one. We'd need a surname to get anywhere."

"I've already thought of that," Tremayne answered. "I think our first step is to go to the reference library here and see what we can find in the newspapers of the day."

"All very well, but how will we narrow it down? It would take years to go through all those."

"Rob Bucknell thought it was either Victorian or Edwardian and something in my coma was very vivid. There was a procession, carriages, huge cheering crowds. And then there was some kind of attack, something very violent. It would have been reported if it really happened. We need to find out what important events took place then."

They left the house and walked to the library in town. Tremayne approached the counter. "We're looking for information from the Victorian or Edwardian era, some kind of procession which involved the whole of London."

The librarian was helpful. "We have newspapers on file and there would have been several large processions from both those eras." She leaned down and took a book from a shelf under the counter. She ran her finger down the index then flipped over several pages until she found what she was looking for. "The death of Edward VIII would have involved all London. That was in 1910. There may well have been a procession at the end of the Boer War, too, and also at the death of Queen Victoria in 1901. Before that there was the Diamond Jubilee in 1897. If you go across to the far room you'll find all the records you need on the right-hand side and if you need any further help, let me know."

The newspapers were bound into large volumes and referenced by year, each volume hanging on sliding runners. They quickly found what they wanted. "Twenty years' worth is a lot to look at," Tremayne said, "but the Queen's Diamond Jubilee seems to ring bells. I felt odd when she mentioned it." He slid out a volume and carried it to the table. "How long is a Diamond Jubilee - 60 years? It's not much to go on, is it?"

"We're not looking much further back than 1895, I shouldn't think. Let's try from there," suggested Benedict.

They quickly scanned down narrow columns, then Tremayne pointed to an advertisement at the bottom of the page. An elegant female, holding a pot of face cream in her hand, smiled out at them. "Look, plantain butter," he read. "Superior facial treatment for the discerning woman. I don't feel very pleasant looking at that. It seems almost sinister! I wonder why?"

"Forget that for a moment. It may come back later," Benedict said, "I think we ought to call it a day, don't you? I have to get back to Mount Carmel. I've only got one day off this week. And you're looking done in!"

He made to close the volume, but Tremayne was staring at a date on the page. "This is it! Look! Tuesday 22nd June, 1897, the Jubilee route. Buckingham Palace, Constitution Hill, National Gallery, Duncannon Street … right through London.

The Strand, St Paul's … yes, that's where I was! St Paul's! I was on the steps! The crowds, the noise, flags and bunting everywhere!" his voice faltered.

Benedict glanced at him. "You look awful. We've done enough for one day, you're overtired!"

"No, it's not that," Tremayne answered, faintly. "I feel more than tired. I feel as if I've been poisoned!"

Benedict shut the volume with a snap and took it back to the rack. "We've definitely done enough for today," he said, firmly. "And we've done well. It's confirmed a lot and proved we're on the right track. When you feel better we'll come and see if Tregony's death was reported. But I think you need to get some strength up first."

Tremayne agreed. He had no doubt at all that Tregony's hand, reaching out across the years, was now firmly clasped in his.

Benedict returned to Mount Carmel, but telephoned the following Thursday. "I can't get away until next week," he apologised. "How're things?"

"I haven't done anything since," Tremayne answered. "But I'm convinced we're on the right track, the memories are just as vivid."

"We don't even know if we've got her name right," Benedict mused. "It *is* an outlandish name, you have to admit!"

"What, Tregony? No more outlandish than Tremayne!"

Benedict promised to come down the following week and Tremayne hung up and went into the lounge. Margherita was bent over a tapestry frame, her needle plopping in and out of the canvas, trailing its load of coloured wool, making the only sound in the quiet room. She looked up as he came in. "Did I hear you say Tregony?" she asked.

"Yes, why? Do you know someone called Tregony?" Tremayne asked, surprised.

"Not someone, some*thing*. A place. It's a village in Cornwall!"

Tremayne stared at her and slowly sat down. "You're kidding! A village? Are you sure?"

"Of course I'm sure," she laughed. "And why should that be so unusual? You're named after a village yourself, don't forget!"

He continued to stare at her, dumbfounded. Then he leaned back in his chair and began to laugh. "Well, if that doesn't beat everything! Of course, it couldn't be anything else!"

His mother looked puzzled. "Would you please explain what's going on?" she said. "This isn't making any sense to me at all!"

"Sorry, Mother! It's just that … well, you'd better know the whole thing, I suppose. But don't interrupt and don't tell me I need a psychiatrist! I've been through all that and I know now for certain that … well, I'll start from the beginning!"

Margherita sat motionless while her son told her everything. She could hardly believe what she was hearing. The story was fantastic. Hauntings, Tremayne's self-doubt, the terrible climax to the story, Benedict's sympathetic experience and subsequent recant. The whole thing was almost too outrageous to believe, but there was no doubting Tremayne's earnestness.

"And now," he concluded, "you tell me that Tregony is a Cornish village, it's just too coincidental. There's no such thing as that kind of coincidence, it's got to mean something deeper."

Margerhita's head was spinning. "I'm trying to take it all in. But it's such a fantastic story. One of the hardest things to take in is Benedict's part in all this. I can imagine your coming to terms with it, somehow, but him! He's so orthodox!"

"Actually, I didn't really come to terms with it," Tremayne replied, slowly. "Not until Benedict did. Isn't that odd?"

She looked at her son and smiled. "No, not odd. That's

how it is with friends. And you should have known that Tregony was a Cornish word, you know. 'By tre, pol or pen ye may know Cornish men,' " she quoted. 'Tre' means 'house' in Cornish. This is all very interesting! I can't tell you what I make of it because I don't really know. But what do you intend to do now?"

"Follow our noses. Research some papers, probably go to Somerset House. Eventually, we need to find out why Tregony is so restless. But that's in the future."

"You mean Bell, Book and Candle?" asked Margherita.

"No, we need to pray for Tregony's soul. She's in purgatory, unshriven. But why I feel it all so personally is something I can't answer."

"And won't even try tonight," Margherita smiled, rising. "I'm off to bed now. Don't stay up too late. You look so tired!"

Tremayne stayed downstairs a little while, thinking over the night's events, then he went to his room. There was no fear now of a shift in time or the disorientation which heralded Tregony's appearance. Only a hope of redemption as she waited for the help which she knew he would send.

* * * * *

Benedict was able to travel to Wallington the following week and, once again in the reference library, in a daily for Thursday, 24th June, 1897, among the seven columns of print, were two unheaded paragraphs.

The account was both factual and pitiful. Tremayne read it in a low voice. *"At approximately ten o'clock on the night of Tuesday, 22nd June, the well-known London courtesan and legendary beauty, Miss Tregony Cornish, was fatally stabbed by one Denzil Pascoe, according to witnesses. Later, his body, identified by papers found in his wallet, was discovered in Green Park. He, too, had been stabbed. The killing of Tregony Cornish took place at Willis's Dancing Academy in Brewer Street, Piccadilly. She was 20 years old. Pascoe had been seen earlier in the evening at Willis's threatening Miss Cornish with a knife. According to a well-known source close to the deceased, Miss Cornish's real name was Welles, affirmed by a photograph of her, found in Pascoe's pocket with her name on it. She is known to have come to London from Cornwall, but this newspaper does not yet know from which part."*

They were both silent. At last Tremayne said, "Well, now we know that at least we got her name right. I never thought of her as being a prostitute. I'm not surprised she changed her name. She obviously didn't want her family tracing her. Now we know why she's in purgatory and why we have to give her rest. Pascoe must have loved her, in his way, if he carried a photo of her."

Benedict folded the newspaper and replaced it in the volume. "Yes, a strange kind of love. And someone traced her," he said. "Pascoe is a Cornish name. It looks as though he caught up with her and killed her, maybe out of jealousy. But, in that case, who killed him?"

"In the sort of world she moved, violence was an occupational hazard," replied Tremayne. "Whatever the true story, we know now she died violently. I wonder why she turned to prostitution?"

"Perhaps she had no choice," Benedict said. "She may have run away from home because of being pregnant. I wonder what happened to the baby. Maybe it died, not so unusual in those days. If so, that would account for her grief."

Tremayne nodded. "You're probably right, it must've died. Maybe she came to us because she needs the baby put to rest properly?"

"Maybe, but now I've read what really happened to her, I think it's more than the baby," Benedict said. "It's her as well. There was a lot of evil surrounding her and we're priests, who better to come to? You never know what circumstances led her to the streets of London. Perhaps she just wanted to leave Cornwall. She undoubtedly had courage. All sorts of vice and iniquity went on in Victorian London."

Tremayne nodded. "Perhaps she got pregnant and had to turn to the streets to live. You know, I always thought there was something odd about Brewer Street," Tremayne shivered. "Everything's fitting into place."

Benedict nodded. "I suspect we'll find more coincidences as we go along. He stood up. "We have to find out where Tregony came from and we also need to know where she's buried, so we can find her and arrange our own special service. And a visit to Somerset House would be a good idea, too."

Tremayne nodded. "The doctor's signing me off next week; it'll be easier in London. I'll be glad to be back at the presbytery."

Chapter 25

A week later Tremayne left for London with a clean bill of health and instructions from Margherita not to overdo things. She need not have worried. Father Jones was glad to see Tremayne back at Mount Carmel and he was willing for him to cover minimal parish duties.

He hadn't seen Betty Parker since his return. He'd missed Rosie at the crèche and asked Benedict where they were. He was quiet for a moment, then said, "She was here one night when I got back from visiting you. I'm afraid I was rather curt with her. She was asking after you." He gave Tremayne a shrewd look. "She was pretty upset about the accident, you know. I believe she's gone back to Manchester."

Tremayne said nothing. He was remembering the night he had walked them home and Betty had told him that she didn't give anyone a second chance. Now he knew that she did and what it must have cost her to do it. Because of his insensitivity he had put her through pain and humiliation. It was some relief to think that perhaps she wasn't angry anymore. Benedict made no further comment, but with the wisdom of bitter experience wished again that he had been more understanding of Betty Parker.

Benedict was able to get out one afternoon when Tremayne was dozing to research some burial records and he spent an interesting afternoon in the offices of a local historical society and Westminster City Council. He returned to the presbytery and when Tremayne came downstairs they were able to go through the notes he had made.

"It appears there were no burials in this parish in the 1890s," he said. "An Act of Parliament in 1853 prevented it. We have to assume Tregony wasn't a Christian so wouldn't be entitled to be buried in consecrated ground. There were three acres at Brookwood International Cemetery in Woking for non-conformists. Tregony would probably have been taken there. Coffins and mourners were transported to Brookwood Station in special trains, run by the London Necropolis Company from Waterloo Station."

"There was another station at Brookwood in those days," Tremayne said. "I read about it. It was used until fairly recently, 1945, I think. It was nearer the non-conformist area."

"The problem is, we don't know if she had enough money to pay for a funeral," said Benedict. "She may have come under the category of pauper, in which case she'd definitely be at Brookwood, but unmarked. If the funeral was paid for by someone else it may be marked, but if not …"

Tremayne wasn't daunted. "We're getting nearer and nearer all the time to finding her. It looks like Brookwood, here we come."

They travelled down by train from Waterloo on a warm June day, alighting at Brookwood Station. They walked along the platform, watching the train disappear down a track as straight as an arrow until it disappeared into the vanishing point.

"It's vast!" Tremayne said, looking round as they walked down the station steps into the cemetery. "It's going to take much longer than we thought."

Wide, tree-lined groves stretched as far as they could see, and everywhere poplars, larches and spruce trees shaded the burial areas. On the left was a small chapel, surrounded by tall evergreens. The sun cast deep shadows amongst the tall trees and blazed in patches of open ground, so that the whole cemetery seemed to be a tapestry of greens and golds, interwoven with splashes of colour from recently left flowers. A great sense of peace and stillness was all-pervasive. They looked about them as they began walking. All religions were represented, as well as Commonwealth nations.

"This is going to be like looking for a lawyer in heaven," said Benedict, as they arrived at the non-conformist acreage.

"Or a bone in an ossuary," Tremayne grinned. "Sorry, bad joke! It's going to take ages to look through all this!"

"Don't forget, Tregony might be in a marked grave," Benedict reminded him. "These are the unmarked ones and it doesn't look as if she's here. Let's walk back towards the station."

They searched for more than an hour when Tremayne, wandering ahead, suddenly let out a shout and pointed. Under a towering Scots pine stood a small, greystone tomb, with an elaborately carved gable roof and a cross at either end. On each side were four flying buttresses, extending to a small lower storey, which was surrounded by stone railings. Each buttress was topped by its own little cross. A tiny patch of garden straggled round the whole, neglected and bare. The tomb was modest by the standards of some, but it was beautifully carved and lettered. Tremayne pointed to the lettering. Benedict stared for a moment, unbelievingly, then gripped Tremayne's arm. "Yes, this is it! Almost under our noses! What does it say?" He leant closer and read aloud.

"In loving memory of Tregony Cornish, born 1877, tragically taken from us on 22nd June, 1897, aged 20 years. Forever loved and cherished. Also, in sacred memory of Sir Nicholas Wassingborne, noted Shakespearean thespian, died in the pursuit of his art, March 31st 1898, aged 46 years. 'Goodnight, sweet prince, and flights of angels sing thee to thy rest.'"

Both men stared in silence at the inscription. Tremayne

was the first to speak. "Well, we've found her at last! And not in the three acres! At least she was loved enough to spare her a pauper's grave. How strange it feels, to be actually here, where she has led us."

Benedict nodded. "And Sir Nicholas Wassingborne, just fancy! The actor of his day, choosing to be buried with her! He must have loved her very much, and paid for all this, too! And we've got her birth year here as well. The rest, as they say, will be plain sailing!"

Tremayne looked wordlessly at the names on the tomb. No, there was no such thing as coincidence, only a God-incidence. "He called her Cornish right up to the last," he said, softly, "but it must have been him who told the police her real name. Remember, 'a well-known source close to the deceased'?"

Benedict nodded. "And the photograph, which Pascoe carried with him. He loved her too, as we thought, and killed her in a jealous rage." He fell silent for a moment. Jealousy. He knew the scourge of that only too well.

"The next thing is to prepare for our little service." Tremayne was saying. "She deserves more than just a quick few words." They say it's better to travel hopefully than to arrive. but if I hadn't arrived at this moment, I think I might have gone mad!"

They turned and walked back up the steps to the station, both lost in silent thought. When they arrived back at Mount Carmel, they separated as if by unspoken mutual agreement, and went privately to their rooms to pray.

Part Six

London and Cornwall, 1960s

Chapter 26

Tremayne went to Somerset House by himself to research as much as possible while Benedict was busy with parish duties. There were several listings of Welleses in Cornwall for the period, all from a place called Tamarleigh and going back to beyond 1700. Reasoning that about 1850 would be a good place to start, since he would only need to trace Tregony's parentage, Tremayne began a thorough examination of the records from that date, beginning with the marriage of Samuel Jeremiah Welles to Eliza Duncan in 1851. A search for their offspring amongst the births produced the arrival in 1856 of a son, Jeremiah Welles, at Wilcove in the parish of Antony St Jacob. Apparently, Samuel and Eliza had not been particularly fertile, for Tremayne couldn't find any further issue. But Jeremiah had gone on to marry Sarah Trevelyn, born in 1860 and they had produced three children, one of whom, born in 1877, was Tregony Eliza Welles.

Tremayne stared at the name, his heart thumping. Here she was, in black and white, fully documented and proof, as if any were needed, that she had officially existed. He felt as if he could almost reach out and touch her across the years, as indeed he had in a spiritual sense on many occasions. Now she was not some nebulous figment of his imagination, but had lived and breathed, had friends and family, had laughed and cried, borne life's bitter woes and rejoiced in its pleasures, just like any other human being throughout history. She was real at last.

Tremayne left Somerset House and walked down The

Strand deep in thought. So many years seemed to have come together in the last few hours that he could hardly take it in. He returned to Mount Carmel weary, but anxious to recount his findings to Benedict. He found him sitting in the presbytery lounge, writing a sermon. "Well, I can see by your face that you've had some success. Come on, tell me!"

He listened while Tremayne told him what he had found, then nodded. "This is just what we needed! We'll hold our little service here at Mount Carmel, then how about a trip to Cornwall? We should be able to manage some leave together and we'll be able to tie up any loose ends."

"Yes, it'll be good to get a feel of where she came from," Tremayne agreed. "And perhaps we can visit Laurence in Plymouth. It would be great to see him again. I was a novice with him at St Elpheges in Wallington. I'll give him a ring."

"Which church is he at now?" Benedict asked.

"It's the cathedral church. St Mary and St Boniface," Tremayne replied. "Why do you ask?"

"Another coincidence, then," Benedict answered. "Father Jones suggested a transfer for one of us there. Then you had your accident and he hasn't mentioned it since."

"I'm quite used to coincidences now," Tremayne smiled. "It'll be good to see the church, in that case, and Laurence again."

Together they searched the Missal and devised a ceremony that they hoped contained the godliness they needed and the help that Tregony came for. They chose the day carefully, 1st November, All Saints' Day, when the souls of the departed were shriven and freed from their earthly sin. The day dawned blanket-grey and mist-laden. The intermittent drizzle which had dampened Londoners over the previous days had stopped and now and then a break appeared in the clouds and a pale sun shone through.

They decided to hold the ceremony after the daily Mass. When the church was quiet both priests approached the altar and genuflected, then Tremayne said in a low voice, "Our help is in the name of Lord who made heaven and earth." He held the Missal open and laid his heavy gold crucifix on its pages. He crossed to the credence, took up the small bell and rang it three times before cleansing his hands and wiping them with the purificator. Turning to Benedict, he gazed steadily at him, pledging with the look of love and loyalty which bound them together. After a moment, he nodded and Benedict began to speak in calm, measured tones.

"O Lord, teach us to do Thy will, teach us to converse worthily and humbly in Thy sight; for Thou art our wisdom; Thou knowest us in truth, and didst know us before the world was made, and before we were born in the world. In paradisum deducant te Angeli."

Yes, thought Tremayne, may angels indeed be waiting to lead her on. She had truly suffered for too long in purgatory.

"Requiem aeternam dona eis, Domine, et lux perpetua luceat eis, requiescat in pace," Benedict continued, while Tremayne murmured his own pleas for her rest in eternal light. He moved to the altar and lit the two big candles they had prepared. "The just shall be in everlasting remembrance. We beseech Thee, O Lord, of Thy goodness to have mercy upon the soul of Thine handmaiden and cleanse from every taint of sin, for no-one who has lived is altogether free from guilt; and, for the sake of these prayers of loving atonement, may she be admitted to have part in Thine everlasting mercy. Lord, let this our sister, Tregony, surrounded in life by so much that was evil and malevolent, be forever released from her bondage here on earth, soothe her anguished spirit with Your loving hand, dry her tears and bring her to peace eternal."

There was silence in the church, broken only by the muffled

sounds of traffic outside and the faint splutter of the candles. Both priests stood with bowed heads. As they did so, the air around them seemed to move, to be made thin, so that both felt a light-headedness that caused them to sway slightly. In that moment they were contained in a vacuum, from which something was plucked, leaving them free from a burden so long carried. They waited, unafraid, for the sensation to pass. A great relief and joy at once flooded through them and the church was instantly and wonderfully free of a great sadness.

Benedict turned and smiled and his eyes reflected a white light which suddenly blazed up from the candles. "Kyrie eleison, Christe eleison, Kyrie eleison," he said in a low voice, to which Tremayne immediately replied with the opening of the dearly familiar Lord's Prayer.

"Pater noster, qui es in caelis: sanctificetur nomen tuum: adveniat regnum tuum: fiat voluntas tua, sicut in caolo, et in terra ... sed libera nos a malo ..."

They finished the prayer, silently turned from the altar, leaving the candles burning, and left the church to emerge into the grey November day. Tremayne's thoughts slid back to the past. No need now to dwell on that. They had been brought to a full understanding and all was indeed well. He looked up at the sky. Through a break in the clouds, a beam of sunlight pierced the greyness and it seemed to him that the beam came straight from heaven and that it was dazzling in its brightness.

Christmas was busy and it was not until early spring that they were able to get time off for a short break together. They got a taxi from Plymouth Station to the slipway at Saltash Passage. As he gazed across the Tamar at the little town on the far shore, Tremayne felt he had come home.

They were to spend their short stay at the presbytery of St

Joan of Arc, where an old seminary friend of Father Clements was priest. They were welcomed warmly and shown to two plain but comfortable rooms. Dusk was falling on the little town. Tremayne stood at his bedroom window and watched the reflections of the last rays of the sun and the Tamarleigh street lamps as they danced and glimmered on the grey waters of the river Tamar. The bobbing craft sent out tiny gleams of light which pierced the fading day, and across the water he could see the golden dazzle of the great dockyard. He raised the sash and leant out, breathing in the cool, salty air. Everything seemed unfamiliar, yet known. Gone was the rattle of carts and the clopping of hoofs he almost expected. Gone, too, were the people who might have strolled the streets on a mild night like this, stopping to chat to neighbours, children laughing and playing, the friendly sound of voices, the rowdiness of the inn on the corner. Tamarleigh was civilised, different.

The next day was as fresh and sunny as its predecessor and both men set off after breakfast for Horson's cemetery that lay on the outskirts of town. It was a pretty little place, not large, with a little chapel at the top, from where they could see St John's Creek disappearing into a wooded valley. A great sense of peace and tranquillity pervaded it. There seemed to be an altered perspective to everything they saw, the light was brighter, the colours sharper, the air clearer. They were the only visitors there, except for an elderly man halfway down the hill, tidying up an old plot.

They began to walk away from the chapel along a neat path that led to the older part of the cemetery. "They look like the older graves," said Tremayne, pointing to a row next to a dividing hedge. "Look at the Celtic crosses."

Most of the graves had tall stone Celtic crosses, some of which had sunk sideways with the years, lending a haphazard charm to the whole row, with its listing stone angels and cracked cherubs.

They had soon wandered most of the cemetery, when Benedict suddenly exclaimed, "This is it!" and began to read the inscription on the grave in front of him. *"In memory of Jeremiah Welles, born 1856 at Wilcove in the parish of Antony St Jacob, died 1887, aged 31 years. And of his wife, Sarah, born 1860 at Tamarleigh, died 1901, aged 41 years."*

"Tregony's parents," said Tremayne, staring at the grave. "How tragic, all dying so young!" He sighed. "Well, now we can link them all up, her parents here and Tregony at Brookwood. The end of all her wanderings."

"They were at an end when we held our ceremony for her," Benedict said, quietly.

Tremayne nodded. "Yes, and perhaps now they're together."

"That's for the Lord to decide, in his graciousness," answered Benedict, "but we pray so."

Neither of them heard the elderly man come up behind them, so when he spoke, both men jumped. "Related to the Welles, are ye?" the man enquired, pleasantly. "Didden think there was any left." He stared at them curiously. "Can see ye're reverend gen'lemen, not from round 'ere, though?"

"No," Tremayne said. "We've come down from London. We're not related to the Welleses, just knew of them."

"Musta been from that there Tregony, then. She went off up the line. Left Tamarleigh the year I were born, and not a day too soon, 'cordin' to some folks! No-one 'eard nothin' more from 'er. The brothers never married, and both of 'em was killed backalong in the war. Twins, they was, so 'twas a good job they went together, so to speak."

"Killed in the war?" Benedict asked, amazed. "The First World War, you mean?"

The man laughed. "No, afore that! The South African war. Siege o' Ladysmith, 1899. Both of 'em gone at 20. Finished Sarah Welles off, it did. That and that maid o' hers, she was never the same. Only lasted 18 months arter the boys went. I were a little 'un then, mebbe five, six. Let's see, when were I born? Ninety-five? Any rate, I'm 70 now."

Here was a direct link to the past. Tremayne looked at the old man closely. "Forgive me, but you don't seem old enough to have known the Welleses," he said.

"Only remember them a bit," the old man replied, "but Ma knew 'em all. Still alive, she is! Grew up with Sarah Welles."

"Your mother grew up with Sarah Welles?" echoed Tremayne, astounded. "For heaven's sake, how old is she?"

"Ma's 103, born 1862," the old man said, proudly. "But as sharp as a pin. We're long-livers, all Ma's side, that is. Grandmother Admonition lasted till she were 100, so I've still got plenty o' good years in me yet, I reckon! Ma's in the home now, out along the Raleigh road.

Benedict said, "Would it be possible to speak with your mother? We don't want to intrude on her, but we'd like to find out more about the Welles family, if we could."

"Well …" the old man hesitated. "Seein' as ye're clerical gen'lemen, prob'ly be alright. Ma don't get many visitors now everyone's dead and gone. She never 'ad no other nippers and she do like a good old chin wag, does Ma. Me name's Joe Penberthy, by the way. Us can go termorrer if y'like. I'll tell her when I sees 'er terday."

"That's fine," said Tremayne. "How do we get there?"

"Oh, don't worry 'bout that. I'll pick 'ee up. Where you stayin'?"

"With Father Clements at the St Joan of Arc presbytery."

"Oh, aye, say near twelve, then?"

It was agreed and they began to walk down the little hill to the road where Joe's battered van was parked in the kerb. Tremayne and Benedict refused a lift, preferring to stroll around the little town to get their bearings.

"How odd that all Sarah's children died at 20. Another strange link in the story," Tremayne remarked, as they reached the end of the path leading to the creek and sat down on a stone wall. "Oh, it's so peaceful here, soothing for the spirit!"

Benedict turned to look at him. The afternoon sun struck sparks from Tremayne's eyes and Benedict saw that his black temples were beginning to be tinged with grey. He realised with a shock that the years were passing more quickly than he cared to think. A wave of nostalgia and tenderness swept over him and he knew, as he had always known, that Tremayne could still stir his heart.

Tremayne caught his eye and grinned. "Sorry to wax poetical. It's the magic of this place that does it!"

Benedict smiled and averted his gaze, thankful that Tremayne had misread his eyes. "Well, I was wondering," he murmured, watching the little boats skimming by on the water, "we can't have you turning into a poet, you know! A canting priest, what next! And, yes, it is odd. Another link, as you say."

He jumped up from the wall. "Come on! Let's make the most of the day. What say we take the ferry and visit Plymouth? Did you get in touch with Laurence?"

"Yes. He said just to drop in. He's usually in the church house in the afternoon."

They found Laurence in his study, preparing a sermon.

"Good to see you, Tremayne," he said, heartily shaking his friend's hand. "How long are you down for? Is it just a holiday?"

"We're only here for a few days," Tremayne replied. "We

wanted to see Cornwall, it's in the blood, remember? I was born there and I still have vague memories of it." No need for Laurence to know anything else. The story was too fantastical to explain.

Laurence turned to Benedict. "Hi, you must be Benedict. Come on through. I'm pleased to say you've interrupted me! I'll make some tea."

"If you can spare a bit more time later, come down into the town and show us round," suggested Tremayne.

"It looks fascinating," said Benedict, "what little we've seen of it, which was only from the station to the ferry. Very modern wide streets."

"Yes, Plymouth was heavily bombed during the war, which reduced most of the city to rubble, although the dockyard was the target," Laurence said. "It's been almost entirely rebuilt. And of course I can spare time. Not often old friends come to call. How about tea first, then I'll show you round the cathedral? We could do with more help, but I like it here very much. It's especially beautiful, and the reason why Plymouth is a city."

They spent the rest of the day walking Plymouth's wide thoroughfares, and up to the Hoe, where they leaned on the railings and looked out over the Sound, the headlands of Jennycliff on one side and Mount Edgecumbe on the other.

Later, after Laurence had returned to the cathedral and they had eaten, they went into the lounge and Father Clements poured coffee.

"We got chatting to an old chap this morning called Joe Penberthy," said Tremayne. "Interesting chap. Do you know him?"

Father Clements nodded. "Oh, yes, everyone knows Joe. He's the local odd-job man. Nothing Joe Penberthy can't turn his hand to. Tends the cemetery, too, and sometimes digs the graves if they need him, old though he is. Joe's quite a character and Mary Penberthy's even more of one. He tried to look after her until she was about 98-odd, but it was just too much for him in the end."

They didn't mention their plan to visit Mary Penberthy. As far as Father Clements was concerned, they were here on a short break, not a mission, the reasons for which were so intensely personal to them both.

They chatted with Father Clements about church matters for a while, then they excused themselves and went to their beds.

Chapter 27

Joe Penberthy called at the presbytery at 12.30 the next day, apologising for his lateness. "'Ad to 'elp with a bit o' farrowin'," he explained. "Old sow 'ad a good load this time. 'Ave to get 'em away, lest she lays on 'em, y'see!"

They squeezed along the bench seat in the front of Joe's big old van. He had a pile of old sacks and paint pots in the back, which neither Tremayne nor Benedict would have minded sitting amongst, but Joe wouldn't hear of it.

"Can' 'ave reverend gen'lemen scrabblin' round in that lot!" he said, horrified. "No, plenty of room in the front." And so they shunted along, managed to get the doors closed and set off.

The nursing home was set in pleasant grounds in an old manor just outside Tamarleigh. "This used to be a big, posh place once," said Joe, as they went up the drive. "Belonged to the Carew Poles I think. Treharne House. Been a nursing home for a while, though."

Tremayne gazed at the house, fascinated. Down the years there came an echo of laughter and the sound of wheels crunching over gravel. He could see a young girl peering out of the shadows, her eyes wide at the sight of haughty ladies and gentlemen. He saw the glow of a carriage lamp as elegant ladies passed beneath it, like gorgeous butterflies in their fluttering finery. There was a sudden lump in his throat and an ache in his heart as the scene flashed before him, some kind of unattainable longing which he couldn't fathom.

They passed a neat little cottage in the grounds, with crisp white nets at the windows and a riot of colourful spring flowers flooding the garden, daffodils and crocuses and grape hyacinths. In the old days there had been a coalhouse and an apple store just behind the cottage, Tremayne knew, but today both were gone, replaced by a cropped lawn and a tidy garden shed.

"Who lives here?" Benedict asked curiously, indicating the cottage. "It looks rather out of place, as if it should be in a little wood somewhere."

"Doan know 'bout that," Joe answered, phlegmatically. "Matron lives in it. Done it up praper good, 'er 'as. With my 'elp, o' course!" he added, proudly. "Were a ruin afore that. There were trees round it, or shrubs more like. We cut 'em right back."

They drove between neat privet hedges up to the big front door and parked the van. Their ring was answered by a young girl dressed in a nurse's uniform. She smiled at Joe.

"Hello, Mr Penberthy. You've brought some nice weather with you. Mrs Penberthy's just finished her lunch. You'll find her in the conservatory. You know the way."

Tremayne steeled himself to meet Mary Penberthy, but when he saw her he was pleasantly surprised.

She sat in a high-backed chair, overlooking the rear gardens which sloped down to cliffs above the sea. The room was elegant and peaceful, with double french doors leading out to a pleasant paved area, where spring flowers tumbled from stone urns and a pond bubbled with lively goldfish. Her head was turned towards the door. Her smile when she saw her son was immediate.

"Mother, this 'ere's the two reverend gen'lemen I told ye about," Joe said, bending to kiss her cheek. "Remember, when I come up yestiddy?"

Mary Penberthy nodded at Benedict and Tremayne. Her

glance was direct and alert. She waved a bony hand at some armchairs along the wall. "Pull those up," she said. "Joe'll get us some tea, won't you son, then we can be nice and comfy." She spoke without hesitation and her speech was almost devoid of dialect.

Joe went off to organise the tea, and Benedict and Tremayne drew the chairs round and sat down. "It's very kind of you to see us," Tremayne said. "We don't want to tire you out, you know. It's just that we're interested in Tamarleigh."

"I never mind visitors," Mary said. "Joe said you want to know something about the Welleses. Well, I'll tell you what I can. I knew Sarah Welles." She settled herself more comfortably and drew the rug around her knees. "We grew up together. Good friends, we were. She wasn't a Welles then, she was a Trevelyn and I was a Pento. My mother, Admonition, was like an aunt to Sarah's youngsters when they came along." She stopped as Joe came back into the room, carrying a tray with tea things on it. "That's right," she said, comfortably. "Joe, give me one of those little biscuits, would you?"

He settled her with a cup of tea and an iced biscuit, and sat down. "Remember what the doc do say, Ma. Not too much sugar." He turned to Tremayne. "Got diabetes, has Mother, but will she do as she's told? I tell 'ee, she's worse'n a child at times!"

"Fiddlesticks!" said Mary, placidly. "If the doctor knew what he was talking about, how is it I'm still alive? He won't be at my age!"

Tremayne grinned. "What do you attribute your long life to, Mrs Penberthy?" he asked. "Good Cornish air?"

"Only having one child," she replied. "Too many children wear women out. Didn't have Joe till I was nearly 33. Billy and I'd been married for almost three years then. And women knew their place in those days. Billy worked and I looked after the house and that's the way we liked it. None of this free love nonsense, like nowadays!"

"In that case, we should live to be ancient!" Benedict said drily, turning to Tremayne.

She recognised the joke and smiled a little. "Things're different now, I know," she said. "Better in lots of ways, but there was something to be said for the old days. We were a God-fearing community here, and it didn't do us any harm. Well, *most* of us were, anyway." She nodded significantly, lips pursed.

"Tell 'em about the Reverend Norsworthy, Ma," Joe said. "Cor, that were a helluva to-do. Folks still talks about it hereabouts!"

"What was that, then?" Benedict asked, curiously.

"To do with Tregony, that was," Mary said. "Sarah's girl. She was trouble right from a little maid, that one! All that copper coloured hair and a wicked smile, just like her pa. 'Twas plain to see who she belonged to the moment she was born and it wasn't Jeremiah Welles, for all that he thought otherwise. But Jeremiah was always slow. Too slow to catch a cold, we'd say. Though he did well by Sarah, give him his due!" she added, fairly.

"Who was Tregony's father, then?" Tremayne asked. "The reverend?"

"No, bless you!" Mary smiled. "He came into it much later. Me and Sarah sneaked off to the dock on the ferry when we were still young maids. She was a few months off 17 and I was 15, just over. It was the first time without our mothers, and we met up with some sailors on leave. No, Rennie was Tregony's father. Sarah fell for him at first sight. He was older than her, about five years. The two of them disappeared for hours. I was left strolling the dock, saddled with a friend of Rennie's who was as dull as ditchwater!" She sniffed. "Still, all a long time ago now. A few weeks after that, Sarah told me Tregony was on the way. I wasn't likely to tell folks, but Sarah still swore me to secrecy about Rennie. When her folks found out about the babe they soon got her married to Jeremiah. Sarah's mother went to pieces really, but my mother had her head screwed on alright. She helped Sarah's mother arrange it all, and she was a help to Sarah later, when Jeremiah died and the children needed churching. Sarah's own mother had long gone by then."

She paused and looked out over the garden to the shining sea beyond the cliff top. On the far horizon a tiny ship was sailing from right to left and she watched it absently, a smile of sad remembrance on her face.

"You must have wonderful memories of Tamarleigh, though," said Tremayne. "Remembering it as it used to be."

She sighed. "Mostly good, but the reverend was one of the bad ones, really. Him and Denzil Pascoe."

At Denzil's name, Tremayne and Benedict exchanged a quick glance and Tremayne said, "Denzil Pascoe? Was he a local lad?" That would explain their jealous lover theory. Another piece of the puzzle slotted into place.

"Yes, Denzil was walking out with Tregony," Mary went on. "I'd been gone some years then, but Mother wrote often, she was good at letters. She told me there was gossip about Tregony and the reverend, who didn't have the commonsense he was born with, it turned out! Proper taken in, he was. Just before me and Billy came back to Tamarleigh it all came out."

"You lived away from here, then?" Benedict asked. "You don't sound as Cornish as Joe here."

"Mother had me sent away to be a lady's maid in Bath soon after Jeremiah died. I was nearly 23. Tregony was about eight then, I think. Opportunities like that didn't come along often, I can tell you, and there was precious little choice of men in Tamarleigh! I worked for a lady and gentleman in Bath. That's where I met Billy. He was the master's coachman for a time, but he was a boilerman by trade. We came back down here in ... let's see ... 1895, I think it was. Joe was born that year. Billy got a job in the dock."

"Where did the reverend come in all this?" asked Tremayne. He was enthralled by what he was hearing.

"Ah, yes, the reverend. Tregony had run off up the line somewhere. Everyone thought she'd gone because she was in the family way by Denzil. She was expected to marry him, though he was a ruffian and the family weren't liked generally. Well, it turned out she'd been going behind his back with Norsworthy! Mother said there was an awful scene at church one Sunday. The silly man got up and said he'd succumbed to the sins of the flesh with someone who'd left Tamarleigh! Couldn't have been anyone else but Tregony. *And* - listen to this, mark you - that Denzil was his *son!* Not that *that* was a surprise to most people! Uproar there was! Sarah Welles never got over it, though it was her boys being killed that finished her in the end. By the time Rennie came looking for her, she was dead. That would have been about the same year the old Queen died, 'cos the boys were killed a couple of years before at Ladysmith."

"Rennie came looking for her?" echoed Tremayne, astonished. "After all those years?"

"Strange how things turn out, isn't it?" mused Mary. "He and my brother Abraham found themselves on the same ship and he brought him to Tamarleigh when they were on leave. I got to know Rennie quite well. He and Abraham had always kept in touch. Rennie was sad not to meet Sarah again, though he'd married and got a family in Scotland."

"Did he know that Tregony was his daughter?" asked Benedict.

"Well, I never said anything," Mary replied. "I was sworn

to secrecy, don't forget. And I don't think Abraham knew."

"And what happened to the Reverend? asked Tremayne.

"Oh him!" said Mary, scornfully. "Silly man! After causing all that uproar what did he do but throw himself under a train at Saltash!"

There was a stunned silence.

"Things like that are best kept to yourself," Mary said, decidedly. "Go opening your mouth and then everyone knows your business! Tregony never came back, so no-one would've been any the wiser! Denzil Pascoe disappeared after that, too. We never heard any more, but his mother knew. She changed something terrible after he'd gone, didn't last long after Sarah Welles. He left a wife behind him, and a baby, a girl called Dorothea, after his mother. Be about Joe's age, but she left here years ago."

The two men looked at each other and Benedict smiled faintly. Mary was clearly not given to agonising over the misdeeds of others.

"So Tregony's baby was probably the Reverend's then," Tremayne said slowly, and whistled. "What a scandal! Or could it have been Denzil's?"

Mary shook her head. "No, he was often away fishing. That was the trouble, left her on her own for too long. Anyway, the Reverend must've loved her, or he'd never have killed himself over her! We often wondered where she went."

Tremayne and Benedict exchanged glances. No need for shocking explanations.

The sun was beginning to cast long shadows across the lawn outside when they got up at last to leave. "It's been a pleasure to meet you, Mary," Benedict smiled. "We hope we haven't tired you."

"No, young man," she answered. "I like a trip down memory lane now and then, good exercise for the mind!"

They paused at the door and looked back at her. "Oh, by

the way," Tremayne said, suddenly. "What happened to Rennie?"

"Rennie? He left the Navy, so I believe, and went back to Scotland. He and Abraham have been dead these many years, of course, but I recall Rennie going before Abraham, because we had a letter from one of his sons, Wilfred, to say he'd died. That was sometime in the 20s, he would've been about 70-odd then. Just one letter, that was all. Wilfred never wrote again. I've still got it somewhere, I think."

"You don't happen to remember Rennie's surname, do you?" asked Tremayne. If they had that, they could possibly research Tregony's real paternal family.

"Well now, of course I did know it!" Mary bent her head on her hand, thinking. "After remembering all that, his name escapes me!"

"Never mind," Benedict smiled. "You've been a wonderful help and we've enjoyed meeting you so much."

They turned to go, and as they did so, Mary suddenly called out to them. "I've got it! Of course, fancy forgetting, silly woman that I am! Truman. His last name was Truman!"

Epilogue

Cornwall and London, 1965

Tremayne heard Benedict's faint intake of breath. A sudden stillness imprisoned the room. They were like painted figures, framed in time, afraid to move, afraid to break the moment. Slowly he turned his eyes fearfully towards Benedict's face. It was drained of colour, every line etched as if by hand, his body tense.

At last, Benedict turned and looked back at Mary Penberthy. His eyes were like black coals, his expression inscrutable. When he spoke his voice was polite, emotionless, and only Tremayne knew with what effort he said, "My name is Truman. Would you be kind enough to let me see the letter sometime? I've lost touch with some of my relatives. I would be interested to see if Rennie and I are connected."

His gaze travelled back to Tremayne. Their eyes met. In Benedict's there was a glimmer of a smile. His shoulders sketched a barely perceptible shrug. "Checkmate!" he said.

Joe brought the letter a day or so later and Benedict made a careful copy of it. It was dated 18th November, 1927, Inverness and simply said, *"To Mr Abraham Pento. I write to inform you of the death of my father, Rennie Truman, who passed away on November 1st after a short illness. Funeral already taken place. I remain, sir, your most obedient servant, Wilfred Truman."*

Benedict decided to make inquiries at Somerset House as soon as possible. His research turned up Rennie Truman's name without too much difficulty and a birthplace of Inverness in the year 1855. Following the Truman line had produced the names of Rennie's legitimate children, one of whom was Wilfred Truman. One of Wilfred's daughters was listed as Rose Truman, born in 1916, also at Inverness. Benedict felt that he had come home at last.

A tentative phone call to relatives in Scotland had produced a positive, if stunned, response, so he knew he would be welcomed.

"And to think," Tremayne said, "that all the time it was you who was nearer to Tregony, not me! She must have been your great aunt?"

Benedict nodded. "Yes, and Rennie was my great-grandfather. There was no mention of Tregony under the Trumans, of course, because none of the family knew about her, not even Rennie, from what Mary said. Luckily, I found out enough from her to be sure of what I was looking for. I knew my mother's age when she had me, and also my place of birth. Mother was Rennie's granddaughter. She was living in London when I knew her, no trace of a Scottish accent. I always assumed that she was English."

"Why did Tregony come to me then, do you think?" Tremayne asked, puzzled.

"You were more receptive, that's why. You were part of the link to me. And another strange link is that Rennie died on 1st November, the date of our special service for Tregony."

Unbidden, the comfort of Mother Julian's words floated into Tremayne's mind, "all shall be well and all shall be well and all manner of thing shall be well." Yes, that was the significance of it, that every part of their lives was, indeed, well.

* * * * *

It was the season for change. "St Mary and St Boniface in Plymouth still needs someone," Father Jones said. "But I've got that in mind for Benedict when he gets back. I mentioned it to him before, but then you had your accident, so we didn't come to a decision."

"Actually, we visited it when we went to Plymouth," Tremayne said. "An old friend of mine is there, Laurence. It's a beautiful church."

"Even better." Father Jones paused. "As for you," he smiled at Tremayne, "I've heard from Father Clements in Tamarleigh. Apparently, he was very impressed with both of you, but there is a vacancy coming up there. How would that suit you, do you think?"

Tremayne was stunned. "I think it would suit me very well indeed! What a coincidence! And just over the river from Benedict and Laurence. Thanks, Father. When do I leave?"

"Well, hold on a bit!" Father Jones laughed. "Don't be quite so keen to go! No, it'll be about three to four weeks to get two more priests here, but you should be there in about six weeks, if that's okay?"

"I shall miss Mount Carmel," Tremayne admitted. "But if I have to go, I couldn't have chosen a better place."

He imagined how surprised Laurence and Benedict would be. Father Jones nodded. "I'll let Bishop Cornish know. It's a large diocese which stretches from Cornwall to Dorset, but your parish will be in Plymouth."

Tremayne shot him a quick look. "Cornish, did you say?"

"Yes, he's a great spiritual leader, very popular, I hear. I was at seminary with Arthur many years ago."

Tremayne turned away. Cornish wasn't an unusual name. There must be hundreds of them. He wondered what Benedict would say. "Cornish? Just a coincidence!" Or would he? Was there any such thing as an ordinary coincidence? He shook his head. He was being fanciful. As far as they were both concerned, the links in the chain were complete.

He left Father Jones and went to his room. Tamarleigh beckoned and he would embrace the challenge with a thankful heart and an overwhelming sense of homecoming.

THE END

Bibliography

Bradfield, Nancy, 1981, *Historical Costumes of England, 1066-1968*, Harrap, London

Bradfield, Nancy, 1981, *Costume in Detail, 1730-1930*, Harrap, London.

Chaucer, Geoffrey, 1958 edition, A.C. Cawley, *The Canterbury Tales*, Everyman's Library.

Cook Jean, Kramer Ann, Rowland-Entwistle, 1981, *History Factfinder*, Ward Lock, London.

Corson, Richard, 2003, *Fashions in Make-up From Ancient to Modern Times*, Peter Owen, London.

Green, Jonathan, 2003, *Slang Down the Ages*, Kyle Cathie, London.

Greenwood, James, 1869, *The Seven Curses of London*, Rivers, London.

MacNiece, Louis, 1988, *Selected Poems*, Faber, London.

Sichel, Marian 1984, *History of Women's Costume*, B.T. Batsford Ltd., London.

Ulseth, Hazel, 1989 *Victorian Fashions, 1890-1905, Vol 2,* Hobby House Press Inc., Maryland, USA.

Barber, Chris, 1954, *Live at the Royal Festival Hall*, London, (Decca Records).

BBC Website, 2007 (www.bbc.co.uk/onthisday) accessed on 18.06.07 for information on Bertrand Russell.

Beer, Francis, 1992, *Women and Mystical Experience in the Middle Ages*, The Boydell Press, Woodbridge, Suffolk.

Biblical References: *Revised Standard Version*, 1952, *Matthew 6: vs 28-34, Job 5: v7*, Collins, London.

Hallam, Elizabeth, 1994, *Saints: Over 100 Patron Saints for Today*, Weidenfeld & Nicolson, London.

Jones, Steve, 1991, *London Through the Keyhole*, Wicked Publications, Nottingham.

Julian of Norwich, *Revelations of Divine Love,* Translation, 1998, Penguin Classics, London.

Kafka, Franz, 2007, *The Metamorphosis and Other Stories*, Penquin, London.

Publishers to the Holy See, 1959, *The Small Missal,* Burns & Oates, London.

Seton, Anya, 1954, *Katherine,* Hodder & Stoughton, London.

Swedenborg, Emanuel, 1993, *Awaken From Death*, Appleseed, San Francisco.

Swedenborg, Emanuel, 1875 *The Compendium*, Samuel L Warran, 10th Edition, Library of Congress, USA.

Swedenborg, Emanuel, 1875, *The Spiritual Diaries*, The Swedenborg Foundation, Bloomsbury, London.

Upjohn, Sheila, 1989, *In Search of Julian of Norwich*, Darton Longman and Todd, Wandsworth, London.

Russell, Bertrand, 1951, *Mysticism and Logic and Other Essays*, Allen & Unwin, London.

Van Roey, Archbishop of Mechlin, 1955, *The Sunday Missal*, Belgium.

Woolf, Virginia, 2004, *Orlando,* Dorling Kindersley, London.

Correspondence

Rev. Brother Gerard Hand, 1994, unpublished letter to the author, 14.05.94, Franciscan Friars of Atonement, 47 Francis Street, London, SW1P 1QR.

Stephen de Kerdrel, unpublished letter to the author 01.05.94, Franciscan Friary, Pantasaph, Holywell, Clwyd, CH8 8PE.

Brother Martin, unpublished letter to the author, 15.04.94, Society of St. Francis, Normanby Road, Scunthorpe, S. Humberside, DN15 6AR.

Collections, Archives and Websites

Chalfont Publication Company, Stroud, Gloucestershire, 1997, The Archive Photograph Series, Torpoint, photographs of Cornish Towns in the late nineteenth/early twentieth centuries.

Harris, Gladys and FL, 1976, *The Making of a Cornish Town,*

Torpoint and Neighbourhood Through 200 Years, Institute of Cornish Studies, Extra Mural Department of Exeter University.

Mail Newspapers, 1897, Circulation Department, front page of Daily Mail, information on Diamond Jubilee events, news items and advertisements.

Microfiche, 1996, Plymouth Central Library, information on Queen Victoria's Diamond Jubilee route through London.

Plymouth Central Library, 1936 Local History Room, *Trevol House, Torpoint* information on stately homes in Cornwall.

Plymouth Central Library, Local History Room *The Cornish Times,* 1989, information on towns in southeast Cornwall in the nineteenth century.

Plymouth Central Library, Local History Room, *The Cornwall Register*, 1847, information on towns in southeast Cornwall in the nineteenth century.

Site Visit, 1994, *Brookwood International Cemetery*, Woking, Surrey, search for a suitable sarcophagus for character in novel.

Site Visit, 1995, *Mother Julian's Cell,* St. Julian's Church, Norwich, Norfolk, information on Mother Julian Reckitt & Colman www.carbolicsoap.com/reckittsblue, www.fellpony.f9.co.uk/country/washday/dolly.htm and www.hullwebs.co.uk/reckitts accessed on 25.02.07 for information regarding laundry aids used in the nineteenth century.

The Soho Society, 1994, private correspondence to author, St. Anne's Tower, 55 Dean Street, London, W1, information on burial arrangements for Inner London in the nineteenth century.

Williams, J. Commercial Directory, 1847 *The Principal Market Towns in Cornwall*, Plymouth Central Library, Local History Room, information on market towns in southeast Cornwall.